CATEL & GRISSEAUX

BLUESY LUCY

THE EXISTENTIAL CHRONICLES
OF A THIRTYSOMETHING

HUMANOIDS

CATEL &
VERONIQUE GRISSEAUX
Writers

CATEL
Artist

ANNA PROVITOLA
Translator

ALEX DONOGHUE
U.S. Edition Editor

JERRY FRISSEN
Book Designer

•

FABRICE GIGER
Publisher

Rights & Licensing - licensing@humanoids.com
Press and Social Media - pr@humanoids.com

BLUESY LUCY. This title is a publication of Humanoids, Inc. 8033 Sunset Blvd. #628, Los Angeles, CA 90046.
Copyright © 2013 Humanoids, Inc., Los Angeles (USA). All rights reserved.
Humanoids and its logos are ® and © 2013 Humanoids, Inc.

Originally published in French by Les Humanoïdes Associés (Paris, France).

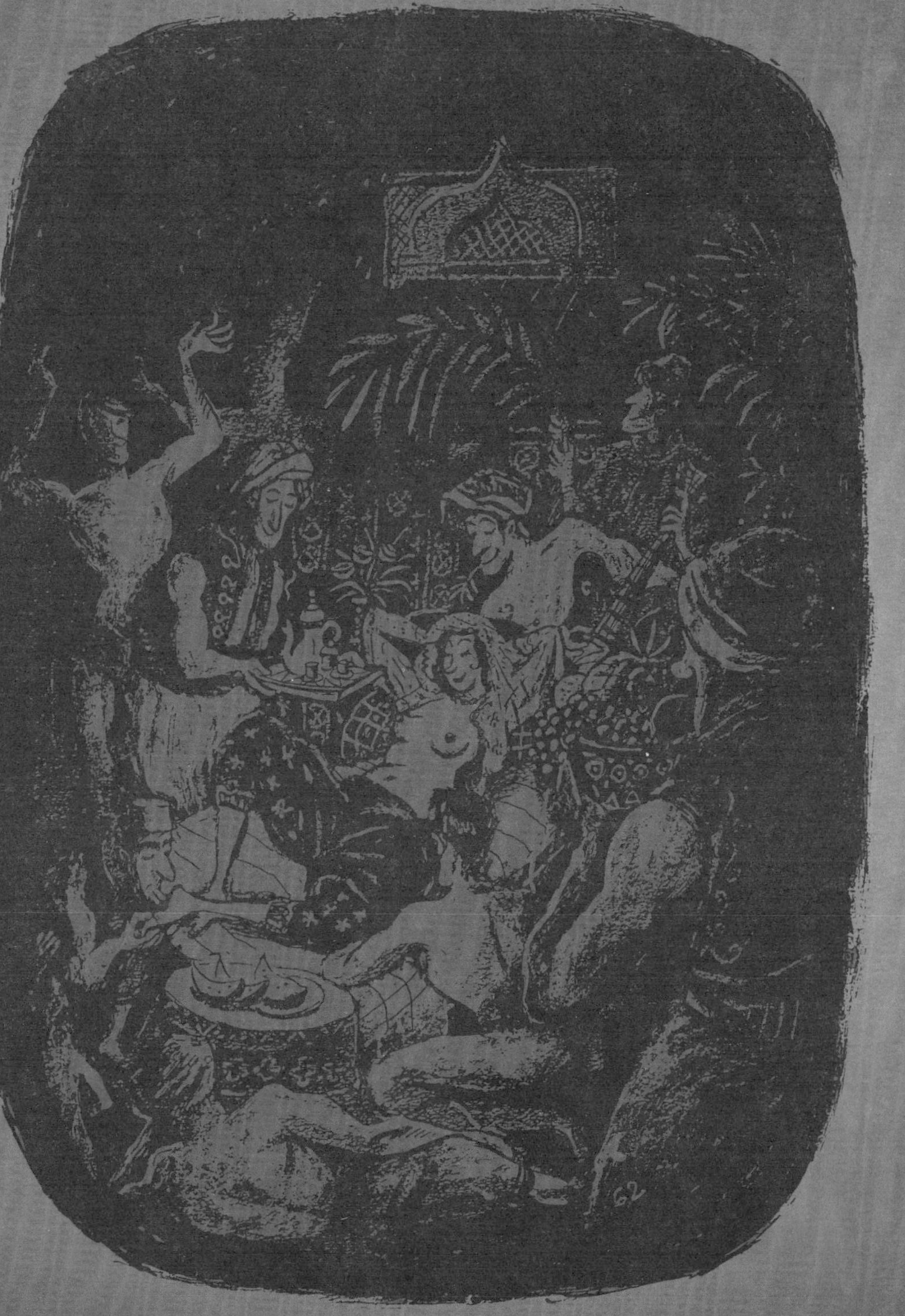
62

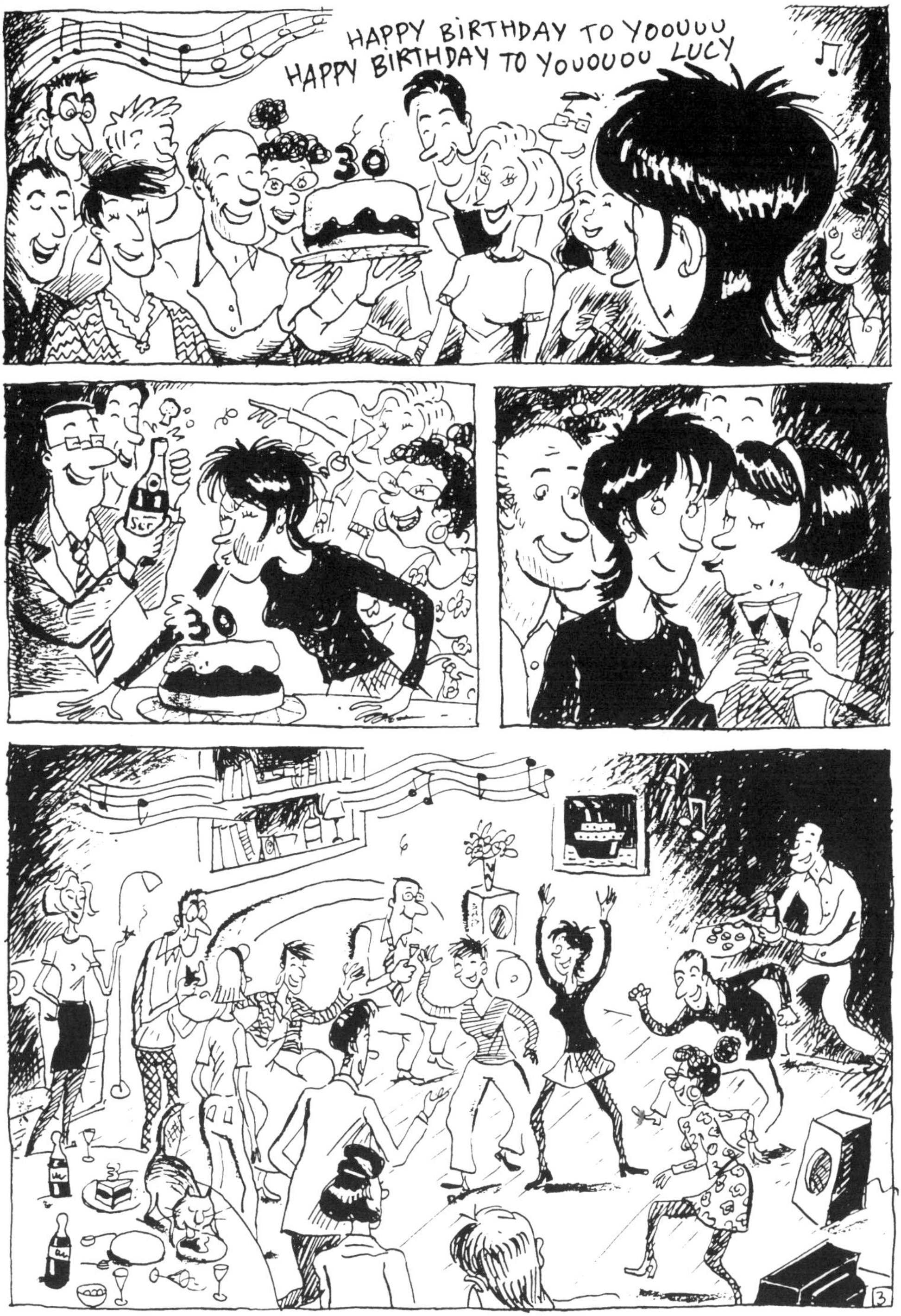
HAPPY BIRTHDAY TO YOOUUU
HAPPY BIRTHDAY TO YOUOUOU LUCY
30

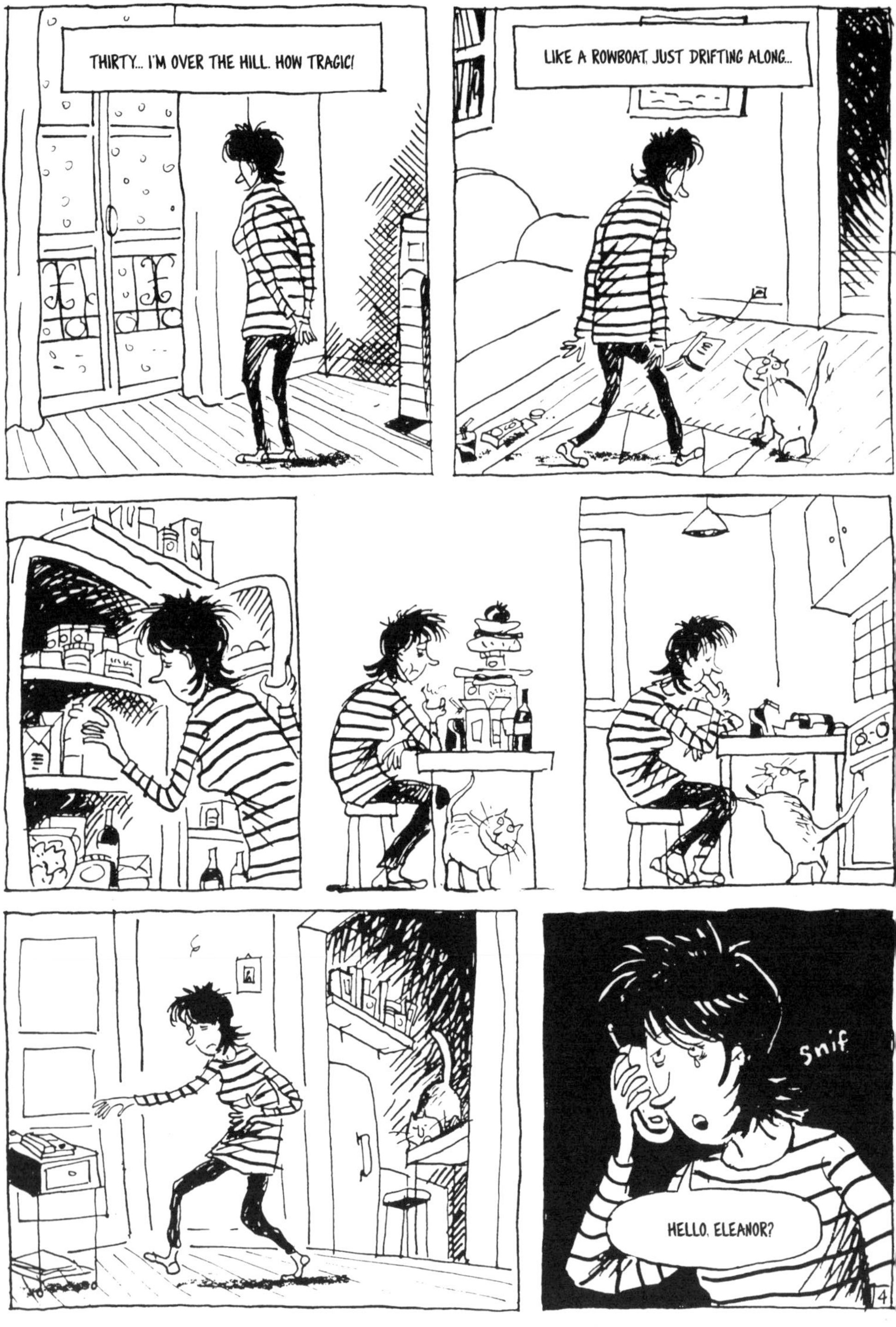
THIRTY... I'M OVER THE HILL. HOW TRAGIC!
LIKE A ROWBOAT, JUST DRIFTING ALONG...
SNIF
HELLO, ELEANOR?

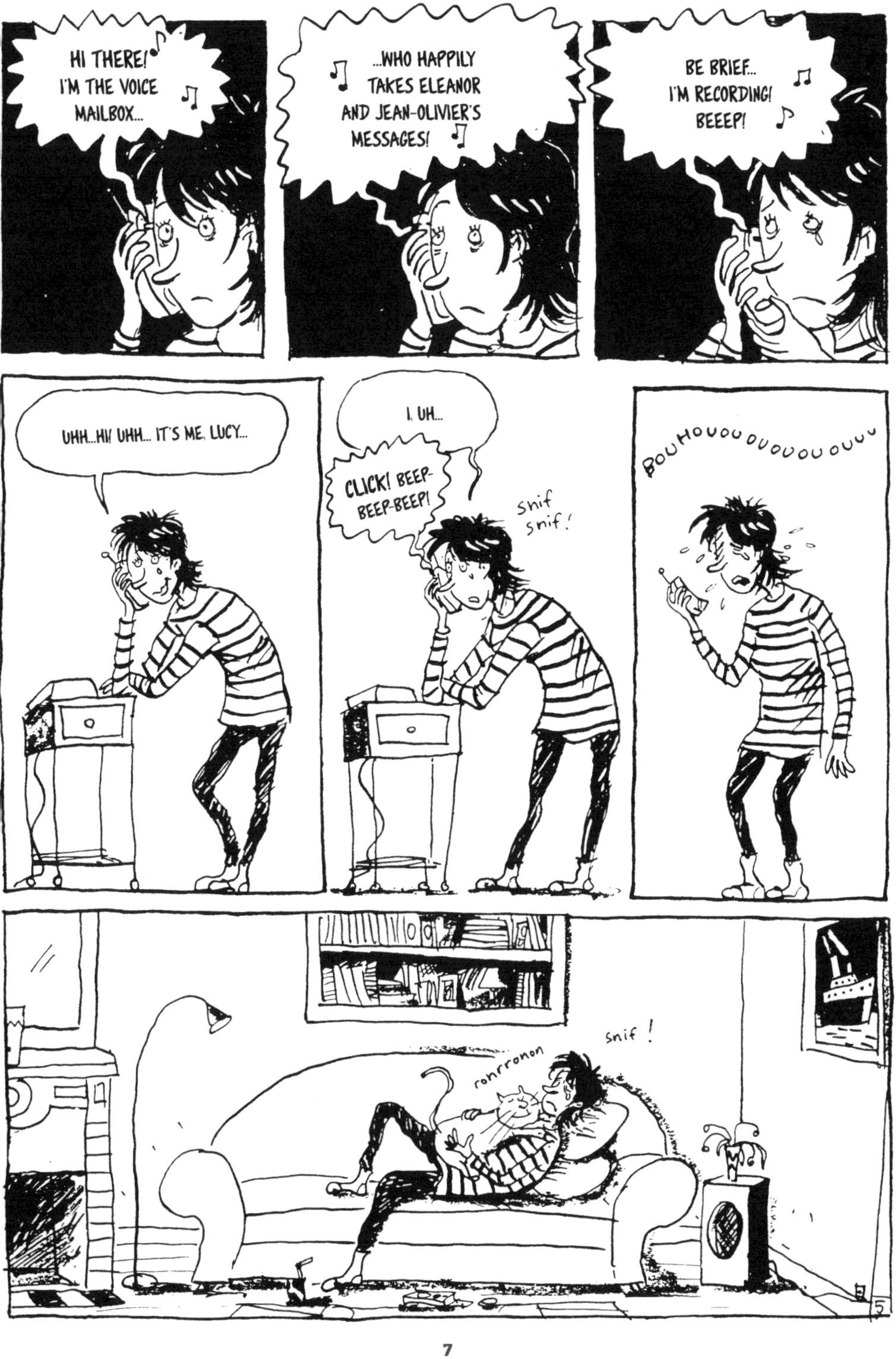
HI THERE! I'M THE VOICE MAILBOX...
...WHO HAPPILY TAKES ELEANOR AND JEAN-OLIVIER'S MESSAGES!
BE BRIEF... I'M RECORDING! BEEEP!
UHH...HI! UHH... IT'S ME, LUCY...
I, UH...
CLICK! BEEP-BEEP-BEEP!
snif snif!
BOUHOUOUOUOUOUOUOUOUUU
ronronon
snif !

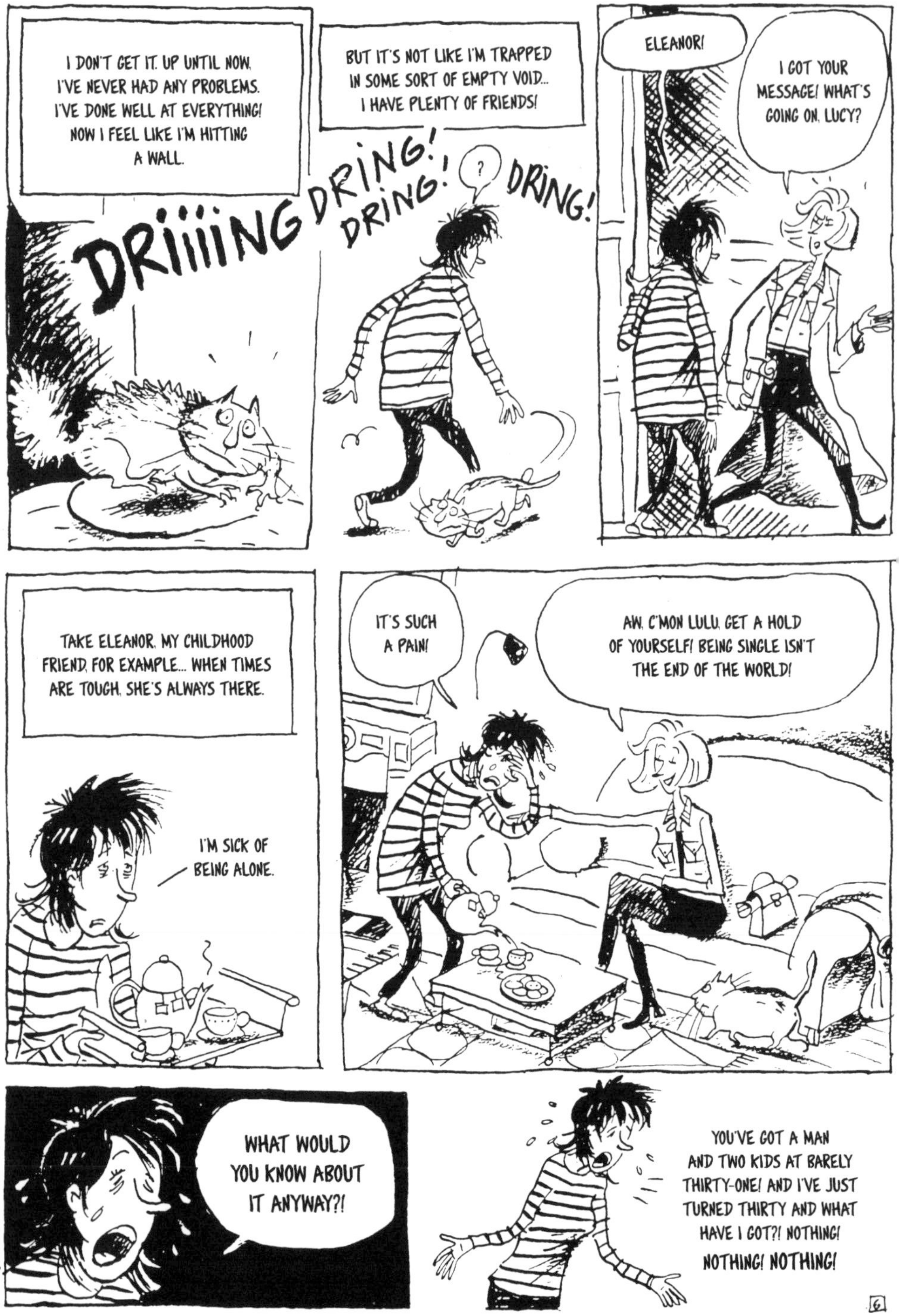
I DON'T GET IT. UP UNTIL NOW, I'VE NEVER HAD ANY PROBLEMS. I'VE DONE WELL AT EVERYTHING! NOW I FEEL LIKE I'M HITTING A WALL.
DRIiiiING
BUT IT'S NOT LIKE I'M TRAPPED IN SOME SORT OF EMPTY VOID... I HAVE PLENTY OF FRIENDS!
DRING!
DRING!
?
DRING!
ELEANOR!
I GOT YOUR MESSAGE! WHAT'S GOING ON, LUCY?
TAKE ELEANOR, MY CHILDHOOD FRIEND, FOR EXAMPLE... WHEN TIMES ARE TOUGH, SHE'S ALWAYS THERE.
I'M SICK OF BEING ALONE.
IT'S SUCH A PAIN!
AW, C'MON LULU, GET A HOLD OF YOURSELF! BEING SINGLE ISN'T THE END OF THE WORLD!
WHAT WOULD YOU KNOW ABOUT IT ANYWAY?!
YOU'VE GOT A MAN AND TWO KIDS AT BARELY THIRTY-ONE! AND I'VE JUST TURNED THIRTY AND WHAT HAVE I GOT?! NOTHING! NOTHING! NOTHING!
6

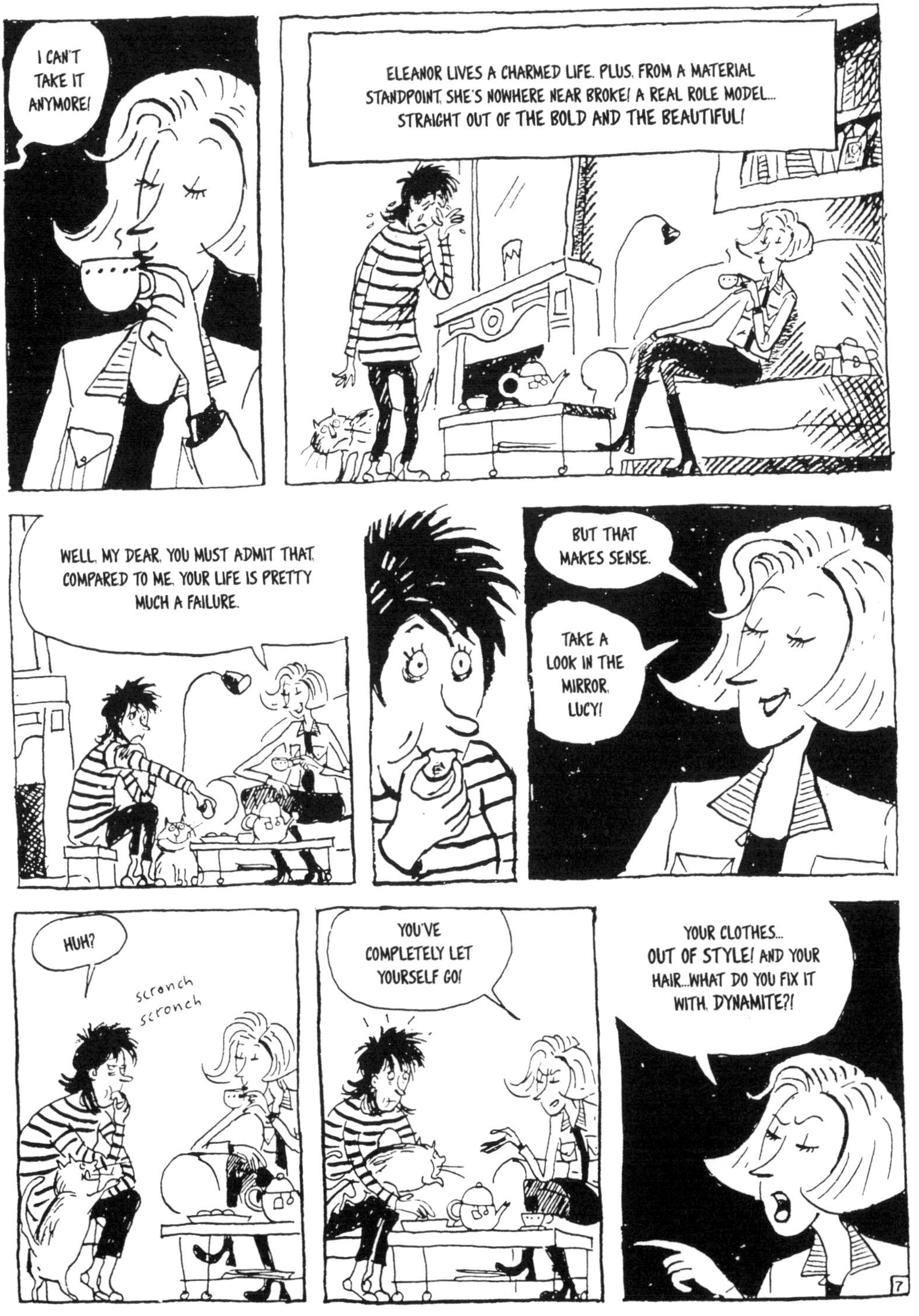
I CAN'T TAKE IT ANYMORE!
ELEANOR LIVES A CHARMED LIFE. PLUS, FROM A MATERIAL STANDPOINT, SHE'S NOWHERE NEAR BROKE! A REAL ROLE MODEL... STRAIGHT OUT OF THE BOLD AND THE BEAUTIFUL!
WELL, MY DEAR, YOU MUST ADMIT THAT, COMPARED TO ME, YOUR LIFE IS PRETTY MUCH A FAILURE.
BUT THAT MAKES SENSE.
TAKE A LOOK IN THE MIRROR, LUCY!
HUH?
scronch scronch
YOU'VE COMPLETELY LET YOURSELF GO!
YOUR CLOTHES... OUT OF STYLE! AND YOUR HAIR...WHAT DO YOU FIX IT WITH, DYNAMITE?!
7

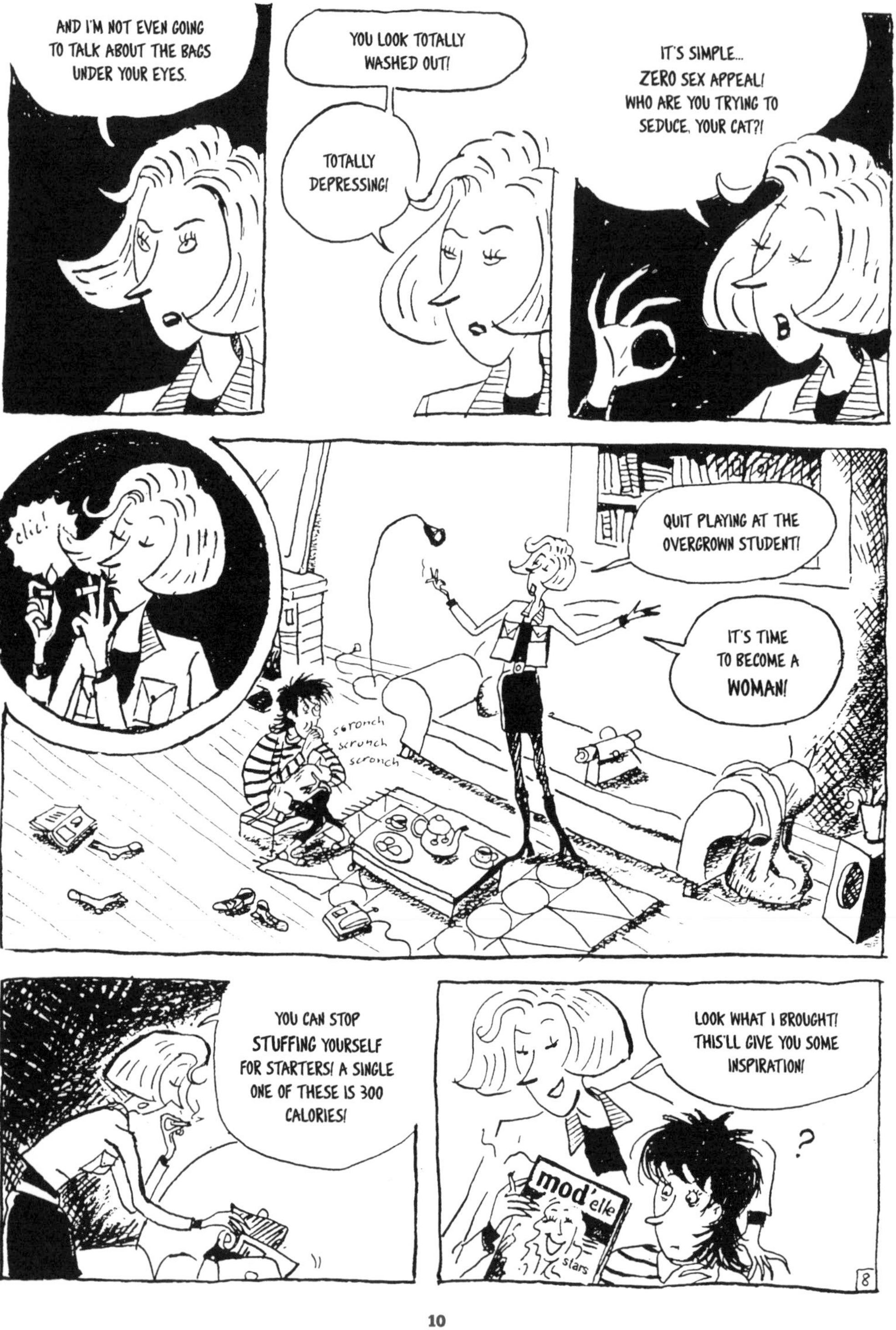
AND I'M NOT EVEN GOING TO TALK ABOUT THE BAGS UNDER YOUR EYES.
YOU LOOK TOTALLY WASHED OUT!
TOTALLY DEPRESSING!
IT'S SIMPLE... ZERO SEX APPEAL! WHO ARE YOU TRYING TO SEDUCE, YOUR CAT?!
clic!
QUIT PLAYING AT THE OVERGROWN STUDENT!
IT'S TIME TO BECOME A WOMAN!
scronch
scrunch
scronch
YOU CAN STOP STUFFING YOURSELF FOR STARTERS! A SINGLE ONE OF THESE IS 300 CALORIES!
LOOK WHAT I BROUGHT! THIS'LL GIVE YOU SOME INSPIRATION!
?
mod'elle
stars
8

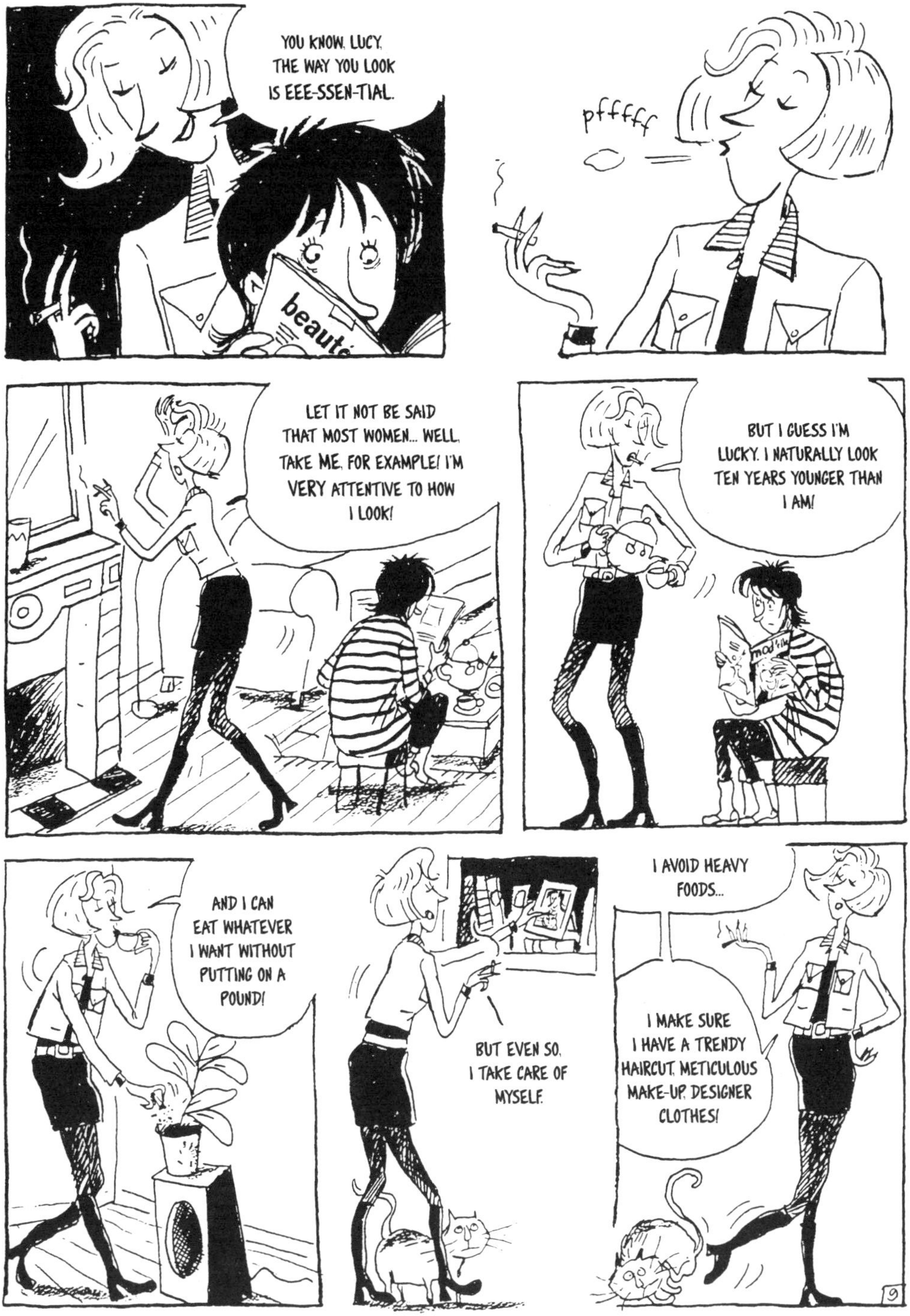

YOU KNOW, LUCY, THE WAY YOU LOOK IS EEE-SSEN-TIAL.
beauté
pfffff
LET IT NOT BE SAID THAT MOST WOMEN... WELL, TAKE ME, FOR EXAMPLE! I'M VERY ATTENTIVE TO HOW I LOOK!
BUT I GUESS I'M LUCKY. I NATURALLY LOOK TEN YEARS YOUNGER THAN I AM!
AND I CAN EAT WHATEVER I WANT WITHOUT PUTTING ON A POUND!
BUT EVEN SO, I TAKE CARE OF MYSELF.
I AVOID HEAVY FOODS...
I MAKE SURE I HAVE A TRENDY HAIRCUT, METICULOUS MAKE-UP, DESIGNER CLOTHES!
9

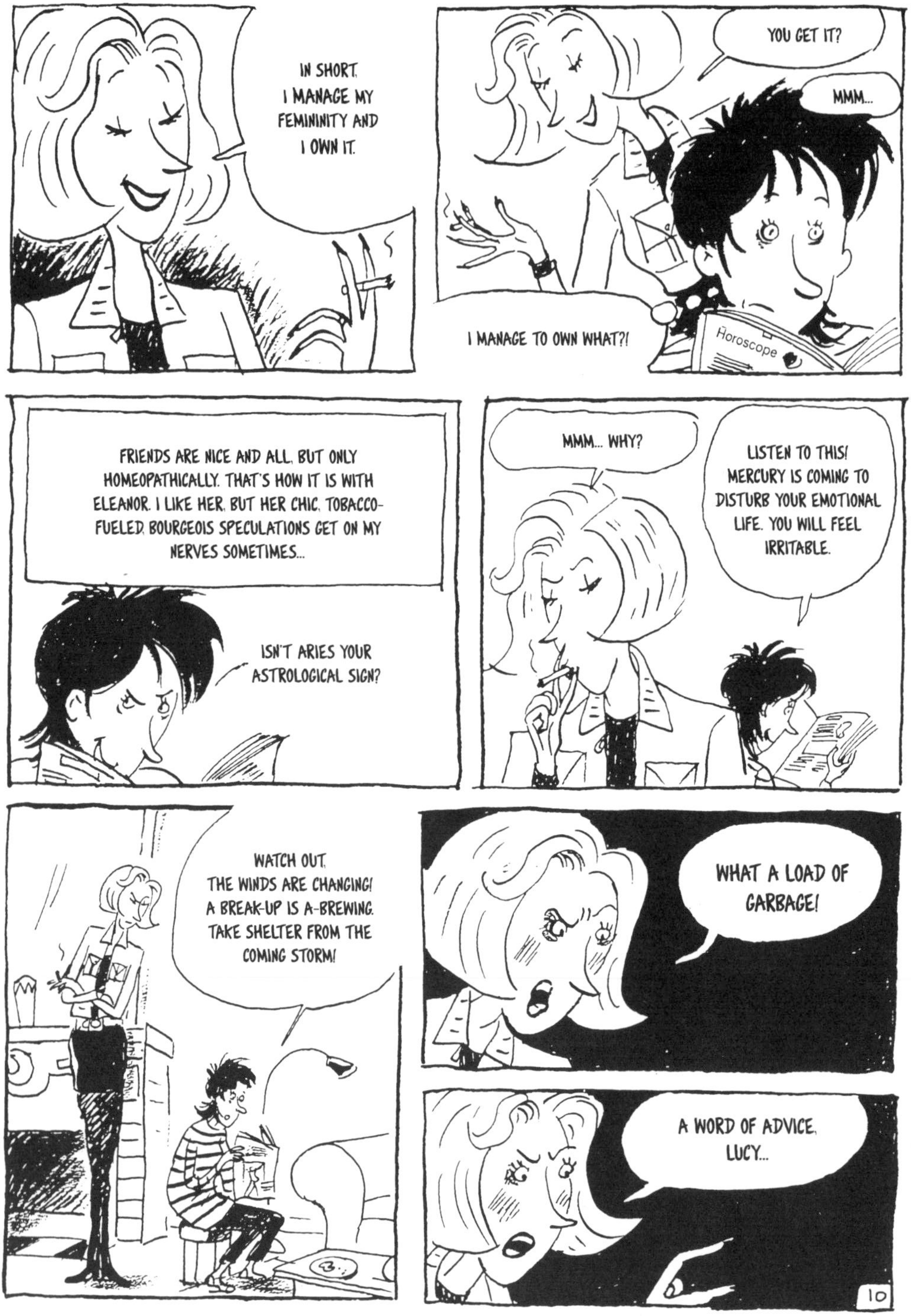
IN SHORT, I MANAGE MY FEMININITY AND I OWN IT.
YOU GET IT?
MMM...
I MANAGE TO OWN WHAT?!
Horoscope
FRIENDS ARE NICE AND ALL, BUT ONLY HOMEOPATHICALLY. THAT'S HOW IT IS WITH ELEANOR. I LIKE HER, BUT HER CHIC, TOBACCO-FUELED, BOURGEOIS SPECULATIONS GET ON MY NERVES SOMETIMES...
ISN'T ARIES YOUR ASTROLOGICAL SIGN?
MMM... WHY?
LISTEN TO THIS! MERCURY IS COMING TO DISTURB YOUR EMOTIONAL LIFE. YOU WILL FEEL IRRITABLE.
WATCH OUT, THE WINDS ARE CHANGING! A BREAK-UP IS A-BREWING. TAKE SHELTER FROM THE COMING STORM!
WHAT A LOAD OF GARBAGE!
A WORD OF ADVICE, LUCY...
10

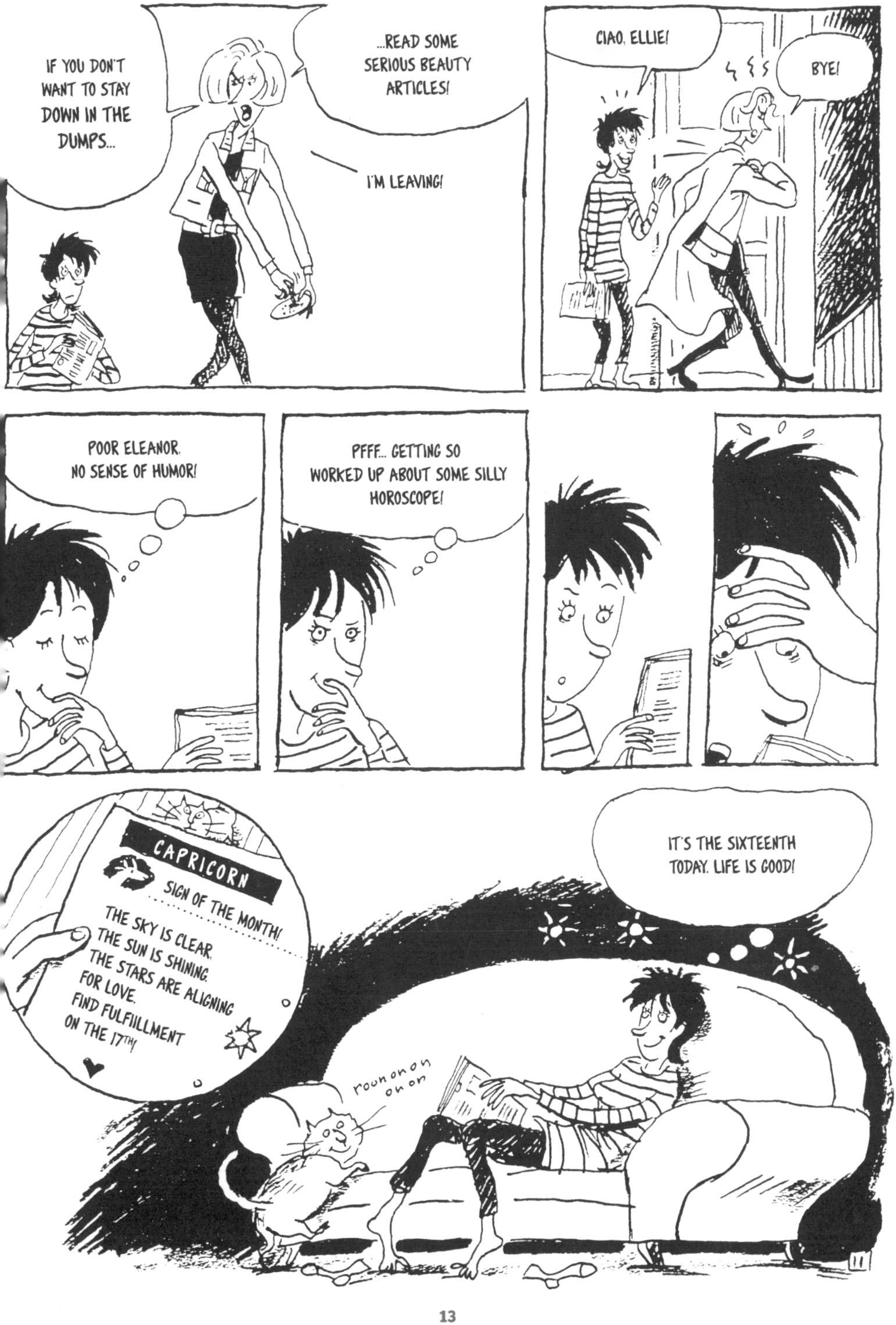
IF YOU DON'T WANT TO STAY DOWN IN THE DUMPS...
...READ SOME SERIOUS BEAUTY ARTICLES!
I'M LEAVING!
CIAO, ELLIE!
BYE!
POOR ELEANOR. NO SENSE OF HUMOR!
PFFF... GETTING SO WORKED UP ABOUT SOME SILLY HOROSCOPE!
CAPRICORN
SIGN OF THE MONTH!
THE SKY IS CLEAR.
THE SUN IS SHINING.
THE STARS ARE ALIGNING FOR LOVE.
FIND FULFILLMENT ON THE 17TH!
IT'S THE SIXTEENTH TODAY. LIFE IS GOOD!
roonononon onon

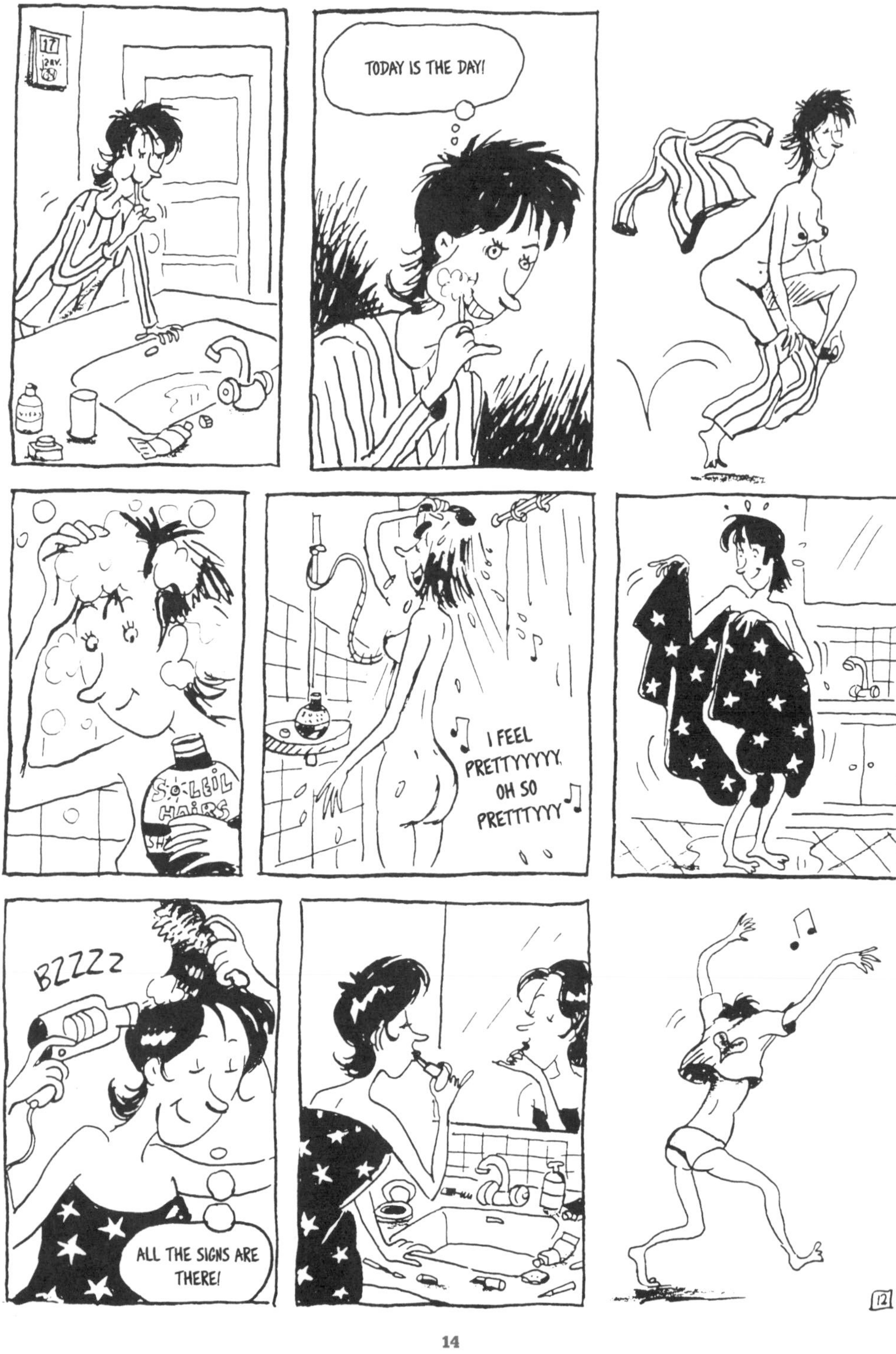
TODAY IS THE DAY!
I FEEL PRETTYYYYY, OH SO PRETTTYYY
BZZZz
ALL THE SIGNS ARE THERE!
12

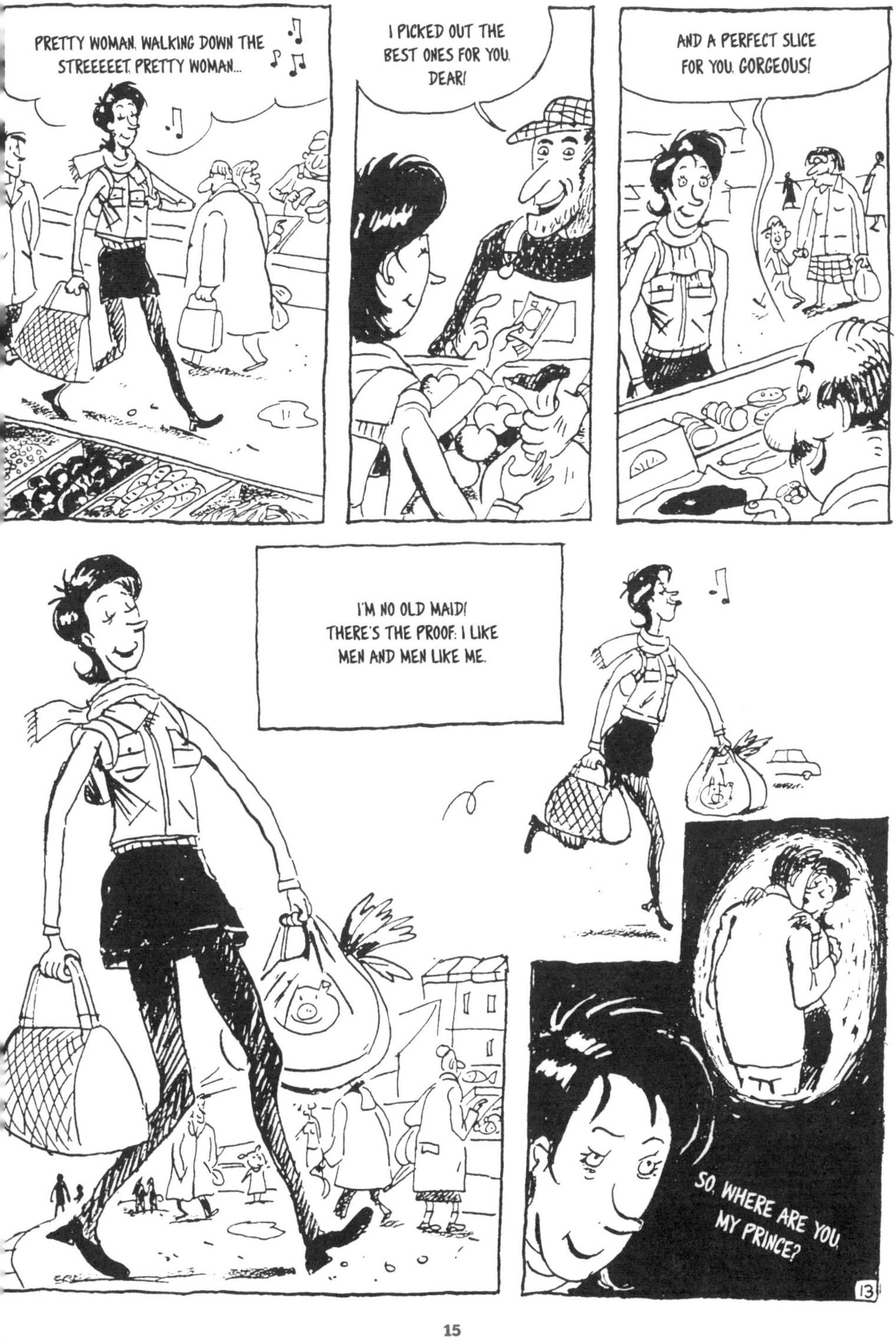
PRETTY WOMAN, WALKING DOWN THE STREEEEET, PRETTY WOMAN...
I PICKED OUT THE BEST ONES FOR YOU, DEAR!
AND A PERFECT SLICE FOR YOU, GORGEOUS!
I'M NO OLD MAID! THERE'S THE PROOF: I LIKE MEN AND MEN LIKE ME.
SO, WHERE ARE YOU, MY PRINCE?
13

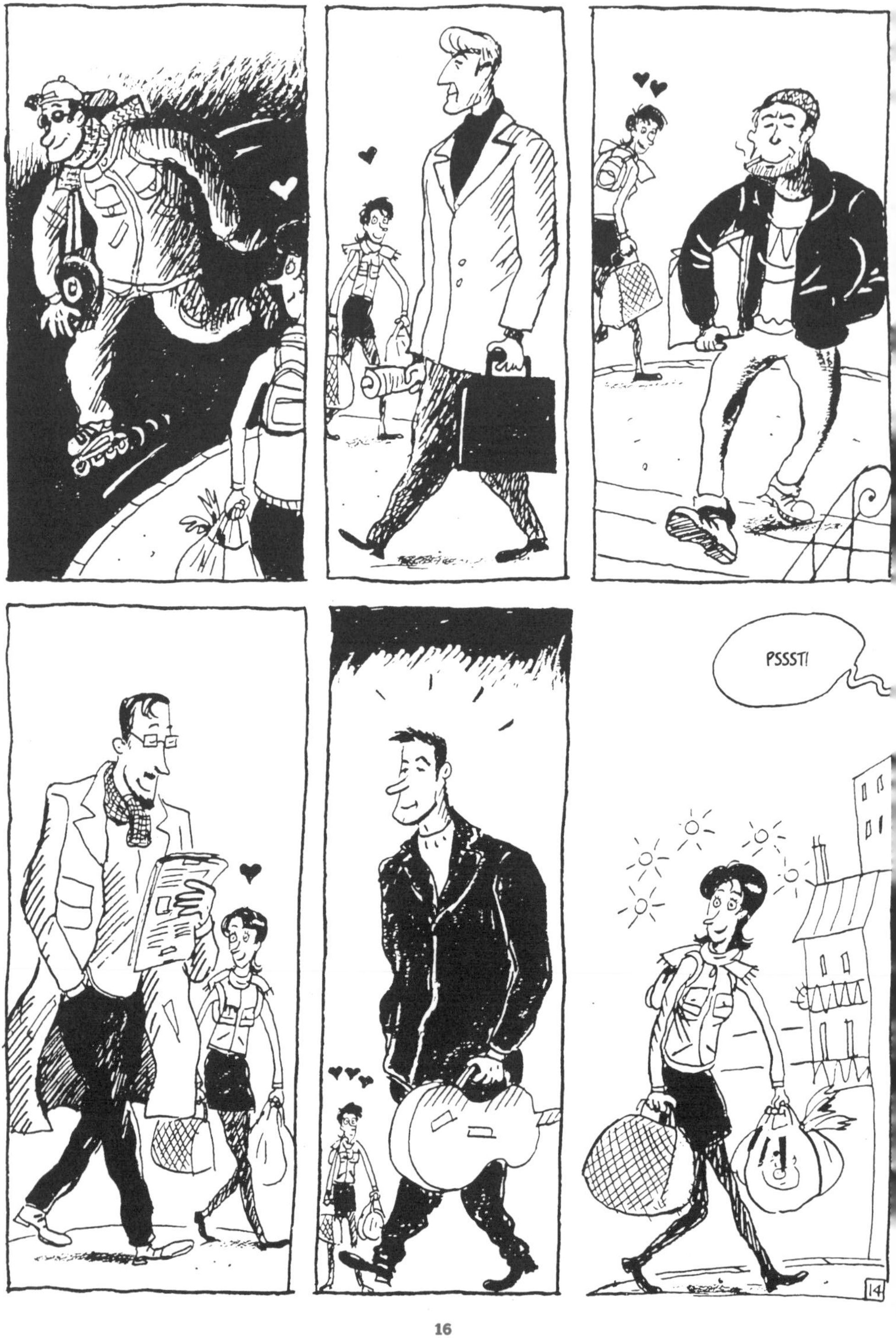
PSSST!
14

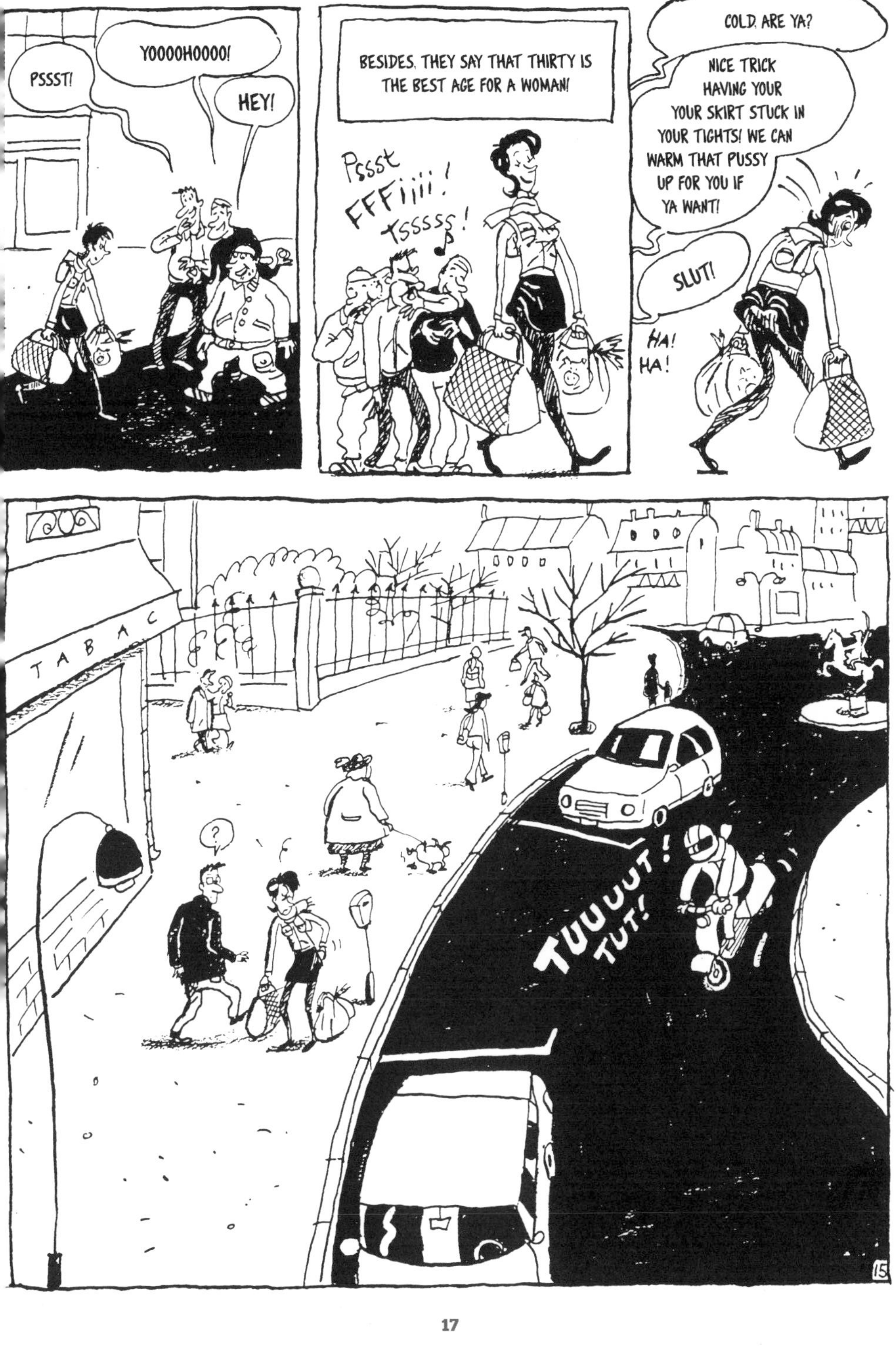
PSSST!
YOOOOHOOOO!
HEY!
BESIDES, THEY SAY THAT THIRTY IS THE BEST AGE FOR A WOMAN!
Pssst
FFFiiii!
Tsssss!
COLD, ARE YA?
NICE TRICK HAVING YOUR YOUR SKIRT STUCK IN YOUR TIGHTS! WE CAN WARM THAT PUSSY UP FOR YOU IF YA WANT!
SLUT!
HA! HA!
TABAC
?
TUUUUT!
TUT!
15

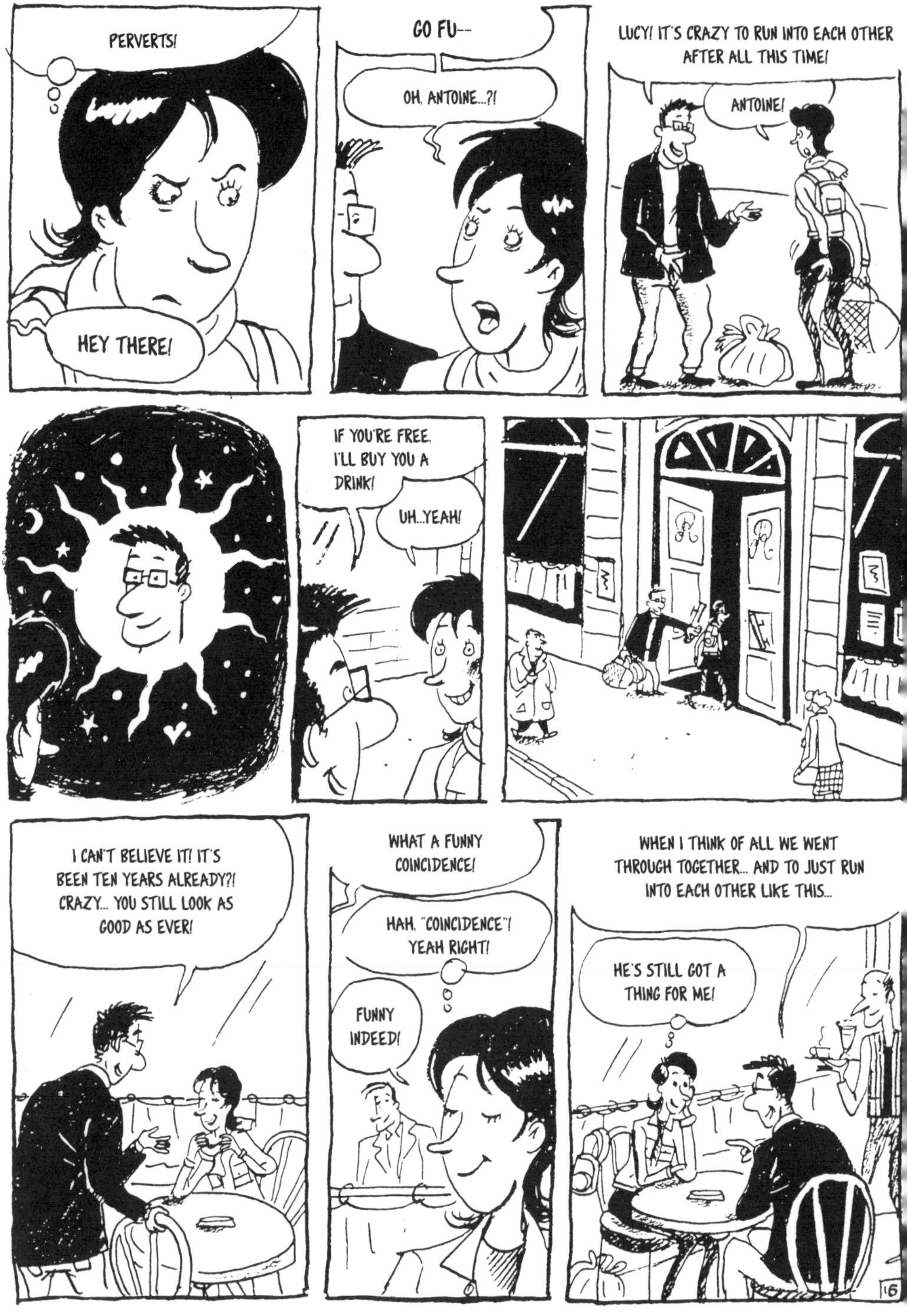
PERVERTS!
HEY THERE!
GO FU--
OH, ANTOINE...?!
LUCY! IT'S CRAZY TO RUN INTO EACH OTHER AFTER ALL THIS TIME!
ANTOINE!
IF YOU'RE FREE, I'LL BUY YOU A DRINK!
UH...YEAH!
I CAN'T BELIEVE IT! IT'S BEEN TEN YEARS ALREADY?! CRAZY... YOU STILL LOOK AS GOOD AS EVER!
WHAT A FUNNY COINCIDENCE!
HAH, "COINCIDENCE"! YEAH RIGHT!
FUNNY INDEED!
WHEN I THINK OF ALL WE WENT THROUGH TOGETHER... AND TO JUST RUN INTO EACH OTHER LIKE THIS...
HE'S STILL GOT A THING FOR ME!
16

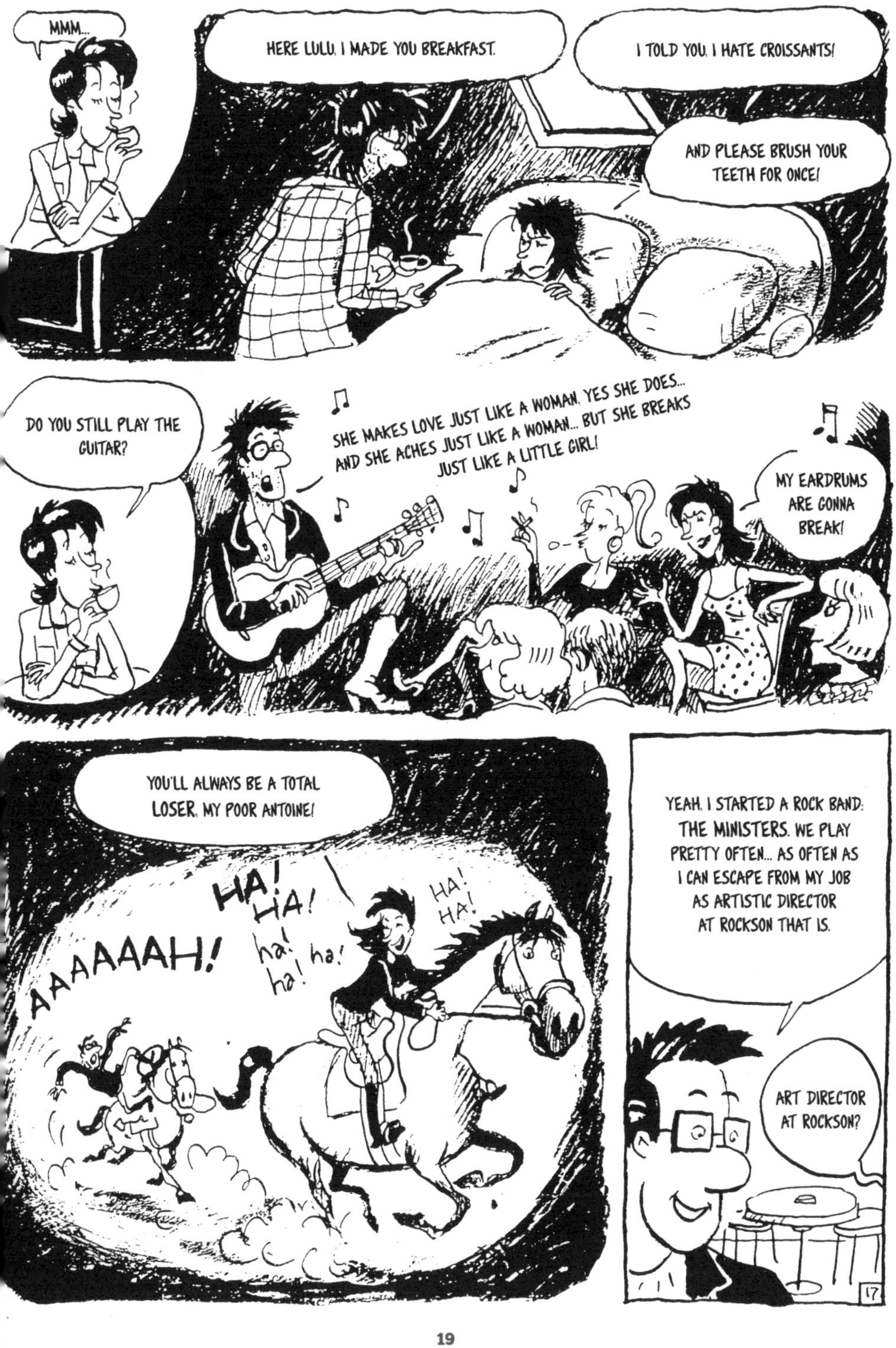
MMM...
HERE LULU, I MADE YOU BREAKFAST.
I TOLD YOU, I HATE CROISSANTS!
AND PLEASE BRUSH YOUR TEETH FOR ONCE!
DO YOU STILL PLAY THE GUITAR?
SHE MAKES LOVE JUST LIKE A WOMAN, YES SHE DOES... AND SHE ACHES JUST LIKE A WOMAN... BUT SHE BREAKS JUST LIKE A LITTLE GIRL!
MY EARDRUMS ARE GONNA BREAK!
YOU'LL ALWAYS BE A TOTAL LOSER, MY POOR ANTOINE!
HA! HA! ha! ha! ha!
HA! HA!
AAAAAAH!
YEAH, I STARTED A ROCK BAND: THE MINISTERS. WE PLAY PRETTY OFTEN... AS OFTEN AS I CAN ESCAPE FROM MY JOB AS ARTISTIC DIRECTOR AT ROCKSON THAT IS.
ART DIRECTOR AT ROCKSON?
17

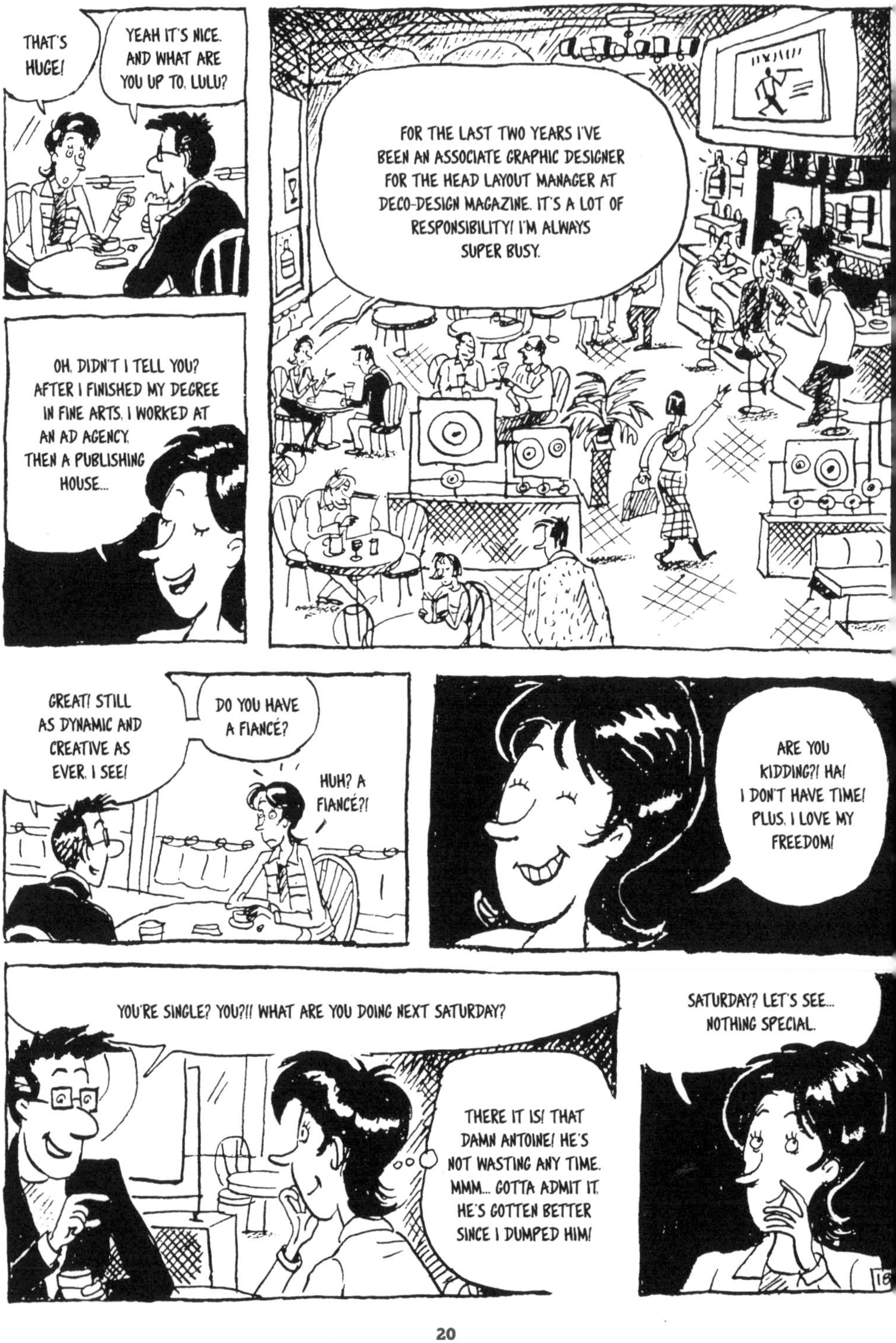
THAT'S HUGE!
YEAH IT'S NICE. AND WHAT ARE YOU UP TO, LULU?
FOR THE LAST TWO YEARS I'VE BEEN AN ASSOCIATE GRAPHIC DESIGNER FOR THE HEAD LAYOUT MANAGER AT DECO-DESIGN MAGAZINE. IT'S A LOT OF RESPONSIBILITY! I'M ALWAYS SUPER BUSY.
OH, DIDN'T I TELL YOU? AFTER I FINISHED MY DEGREE IN FINE ARTS, I WORKED AT AN AD AGENCY, THEN A PUBLISHING HOUSE...
GREAT! STILL AS DYNAMIC AND CREATIVE AS EVER, I SEE!
DO YOU HAVE A FIANCÉ?
HUH? A FIANCÉ?!
ARE YOU KIDDING?! HA! I DON'T HAVE TIME! PLUS, I LOVE MY FREEDOM!
YOU'RE SINGLE? YOU?!! WHAT ARE YOU DOING NEXT SATURDAY?
THERE IT IS! THAT DAMN ANTOINE! HE'S NOT WASTING ANY TIME. MMM... GOTTA ADMIT IT, HE'S GOTTEN BETTER SINCE I DUMPED HIM!
SATURDAY? LET'S SEE... NOTHING SPECIAL.

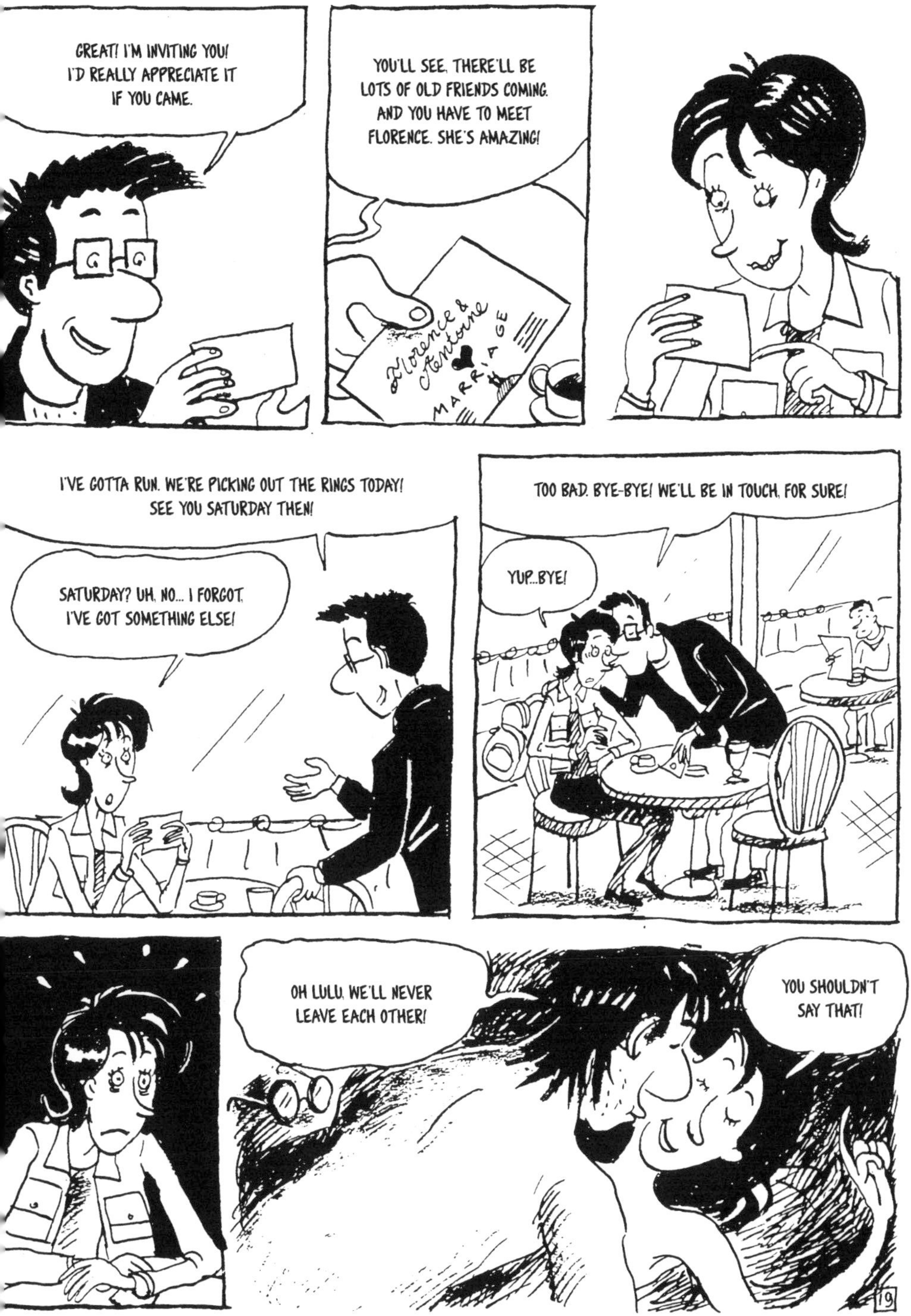
GREAT! I'M INVITING YOU! I'D REALLY APPRECIATE IT IF YOU CAME.
YOU'LL SEE. THERE'LL BE LOTS OF OLD FRIENDS COMING. AND YOU HAVE TO MEET FLORENCE. SHE'S AMAZING!
Florence & Antoine
MARRIAGE
I'VE GOTTA RUN. WE'RE PICKING OUT THE RINGS TODAY! SEE YOU SATURDAY THEN!
SATURDAY? UH, NO... I FORGOT, I'VE GOT SOMETHING ELSE!
TOO BAD. BYE-BYE! WE'LL BE IN TOUCH, FOR SURE!
YUP...BYE!
OH LULU, WE'LL NEVER LEAVE EACH OTHER!
YOU SHOULDN'T SAY THAT!
19

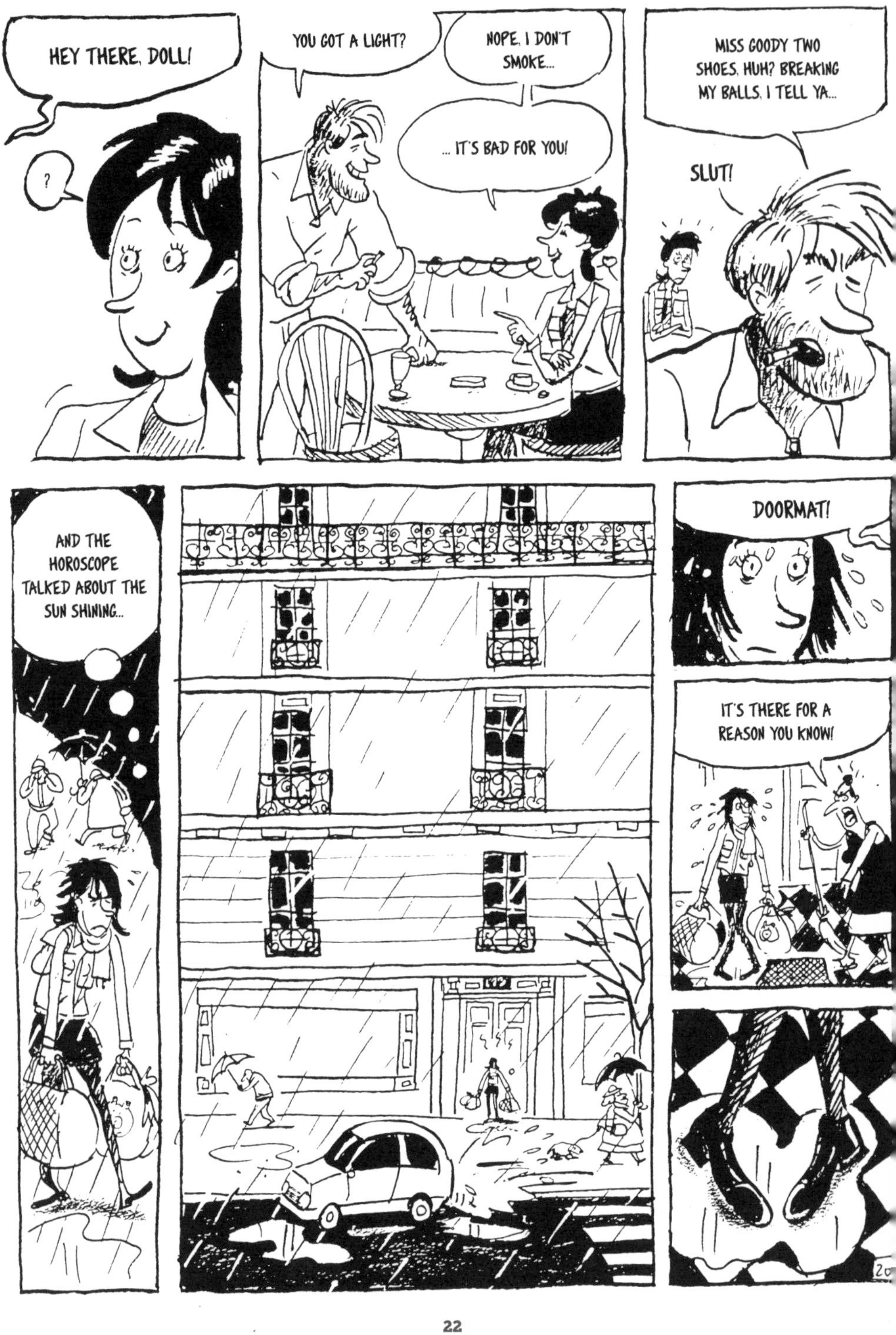
HEY THERE, DOLL!
?
YOU GOT A LIGHT?
NOPE, I DON'T SMOKE...
... IT'S BAD FOR YOU!
MISS GOODY TWO SHOES, HUH? BREAKING MY BALLS, I TELL YA...
SLUT!
AND THE HOROSCOPE TALKED ABOUT THE SUN SHINING...
DOORMAT!
IT'S THERE FOR A REASON YOU KNOW!

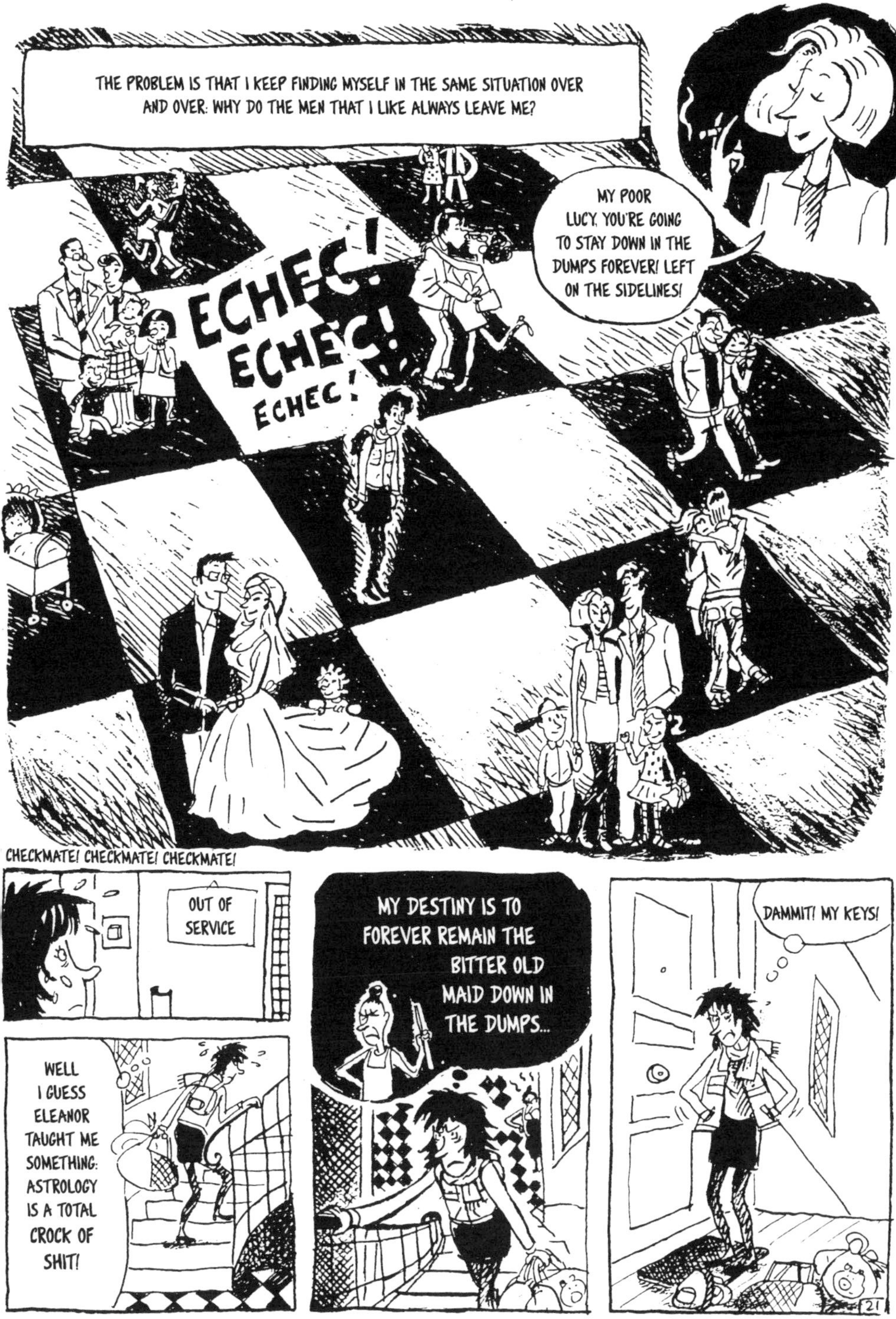
THE PROBLEM IS THAT I KEEP FINDING MYSELF IN THE SAME SITUATION OVER AND OVER: WHY DO THE MEN THAT I LIKE ALWAYS LEAVE ME?
MY POOR LUCY, YOU'RE GOING TO STAY DOWN IN THE DUMPS FOREVER! LEFT ON THE SIDELINES!
ECHEC! ECHEC! ECHEC!
CHECKMATE! CHECKMATE! CHECKMATE!
OUT OF SERVICE
WELL I GUESS ELEANOR TAUGHT ME SOMETHING: ASTROLOGY IS A TOTAL CROCK OF SHIT!
MY DESTINY IS TO FOREVER REMAIN THE BITTER OLD MAID DOWN IN THE DUMPS...
DAMMIT! MY KEYS!
21

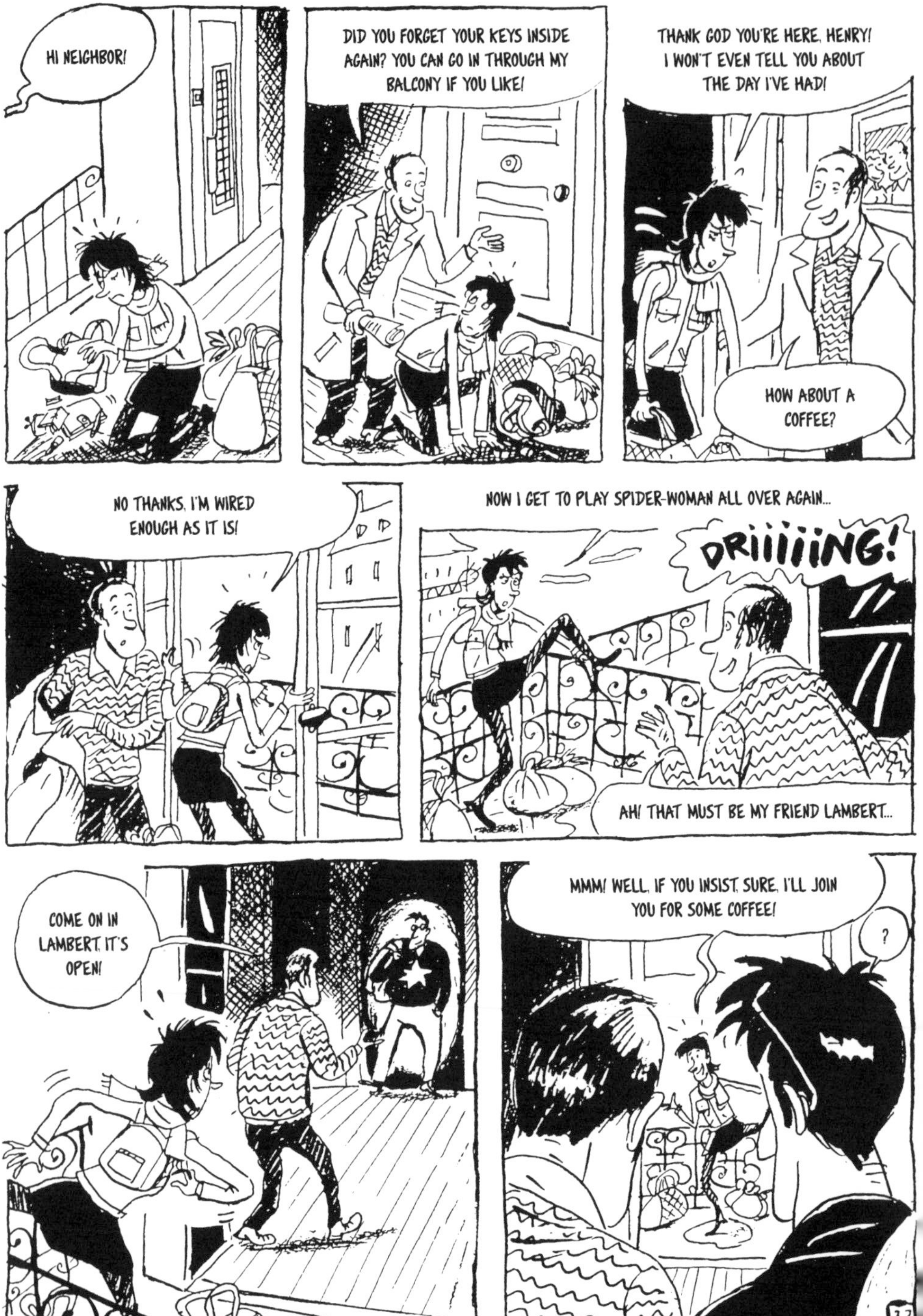
HI NEIGHBOR!
DID YOU FORGET YOUR KEYS INSIDE AGAIN? YOU CAN GO IN THROUGH MY BALCONY IF YOU LIKE!
THANK GOD YOU'RE HERE, HENRY! I WON'T EVEN TELL YOU ABOUT THE DAY I'VE HAD!
HOW ABOUT A COFFEE?
NO THANKS, I'M WIRED ENOUGH AS IT IS!
NOW I GET TO PLAY SPIDER-WOMAN ALL OVER AGAIN...
DRIIIIING!
AH! THAT MUST BE MY FRIEND LAMBERT...
COME ON IN LAMBERT, IT'S OPEN!
MMM! WELL, IF YOU INSIST, SURE, I'LL JOIN YOU FOR SOME COFFEE!
?
22

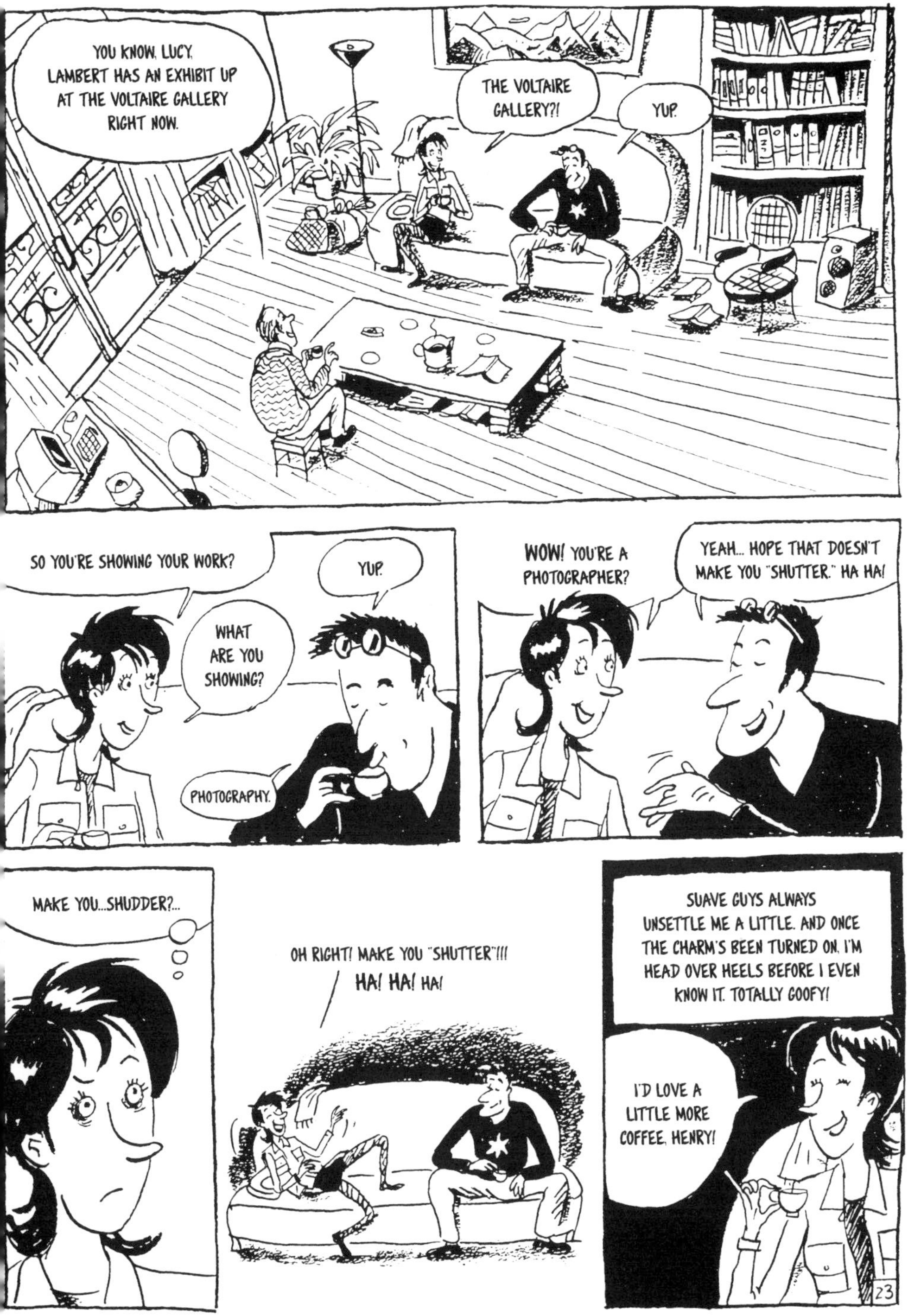
YOU KNOW, LUCY, LAMBERT HAS AN EXHIBIT UP AT THE VOLTAIRE GALLERY RIGHT NOW.
THE VOLTAIRE GALLERY?!
YUP.
SO YOU'RE SHOWING YOUR WORK?
YUP.
WHAT ARE YOU SHOWING?
PHOTOGRAPHY.
WOW! YOU'RE A PHOTOGRAPHER?
YEAH... HOPE THAT DOESN'T MAKE YOU "SHUTTER." HA HA!
MAKE YOU...SHUDDER?...
OH RIGHT! MAKE YOU "SHUTTER"!!!
HA! HA! HA!
SUAVE GUYS ALWAYS UNSETTLE ME A LITTLE. AND ONCE THE CHARM'S BEEN TURNED ON, I'M HEAD OVER HEELS BEFORE I EVEN KNOW IT. TOTALLY GOOFY!
I'D LOVE A LITTLE MORE COFFEE, HENRY!
23

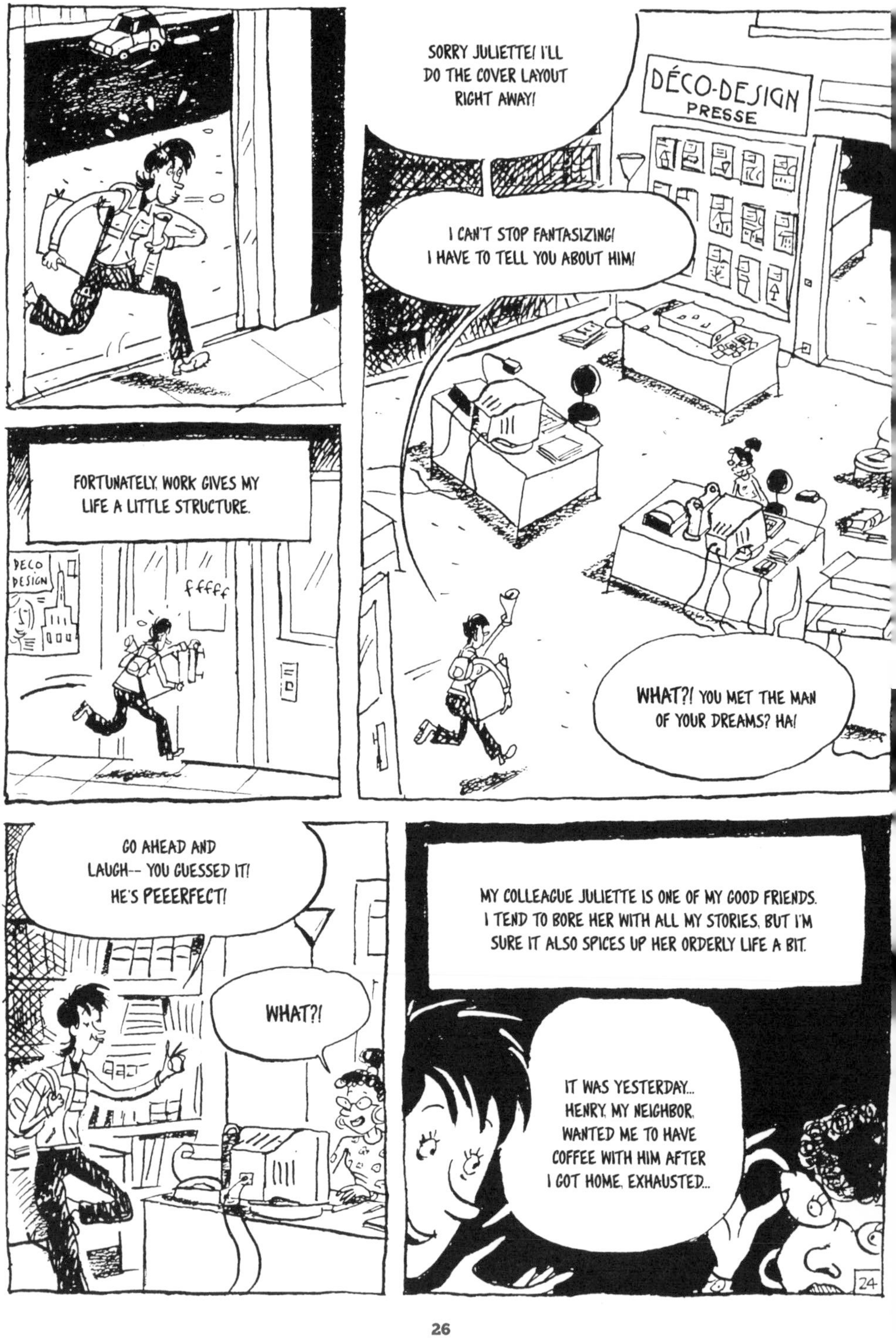

SORRY JULIETTE! I'LL DO THE COVER LAYOUT RIGHT AWAY!
DÉCO-DESIGN PRESSE
I CAN'T STOP FANTASIZING! I HAVE TO TELL YOU ABOUT HIM!
FORTUNATELY, WORK GIVES MY LIFE A LITTLE STRUCTURE.
DECO DESIGN
fffff
WHAT?! YOU MET THE MAN OF YOUR DREAMS? HA!
GO AHEAD AND LAUGH-- YOU GUESSED IT! HE'S PEEERFECT!
WHAT?!
MY COLLEAGUE JULIETTE IS ONE OF MY GOOD FRIENDS. I TEND TO BORE HER WITH ALL MY STORIES, BUT I'M SURE IT ALSO SPICES UP HER ORDERLY LIFE A BIT.
IT WAS YESTERDAY... HENRY, MY NEIGHBOR, WANTED ME TO HAVE COFFEE WITH HIM AFTER I GOT HOME, EXHAUSTED...
24

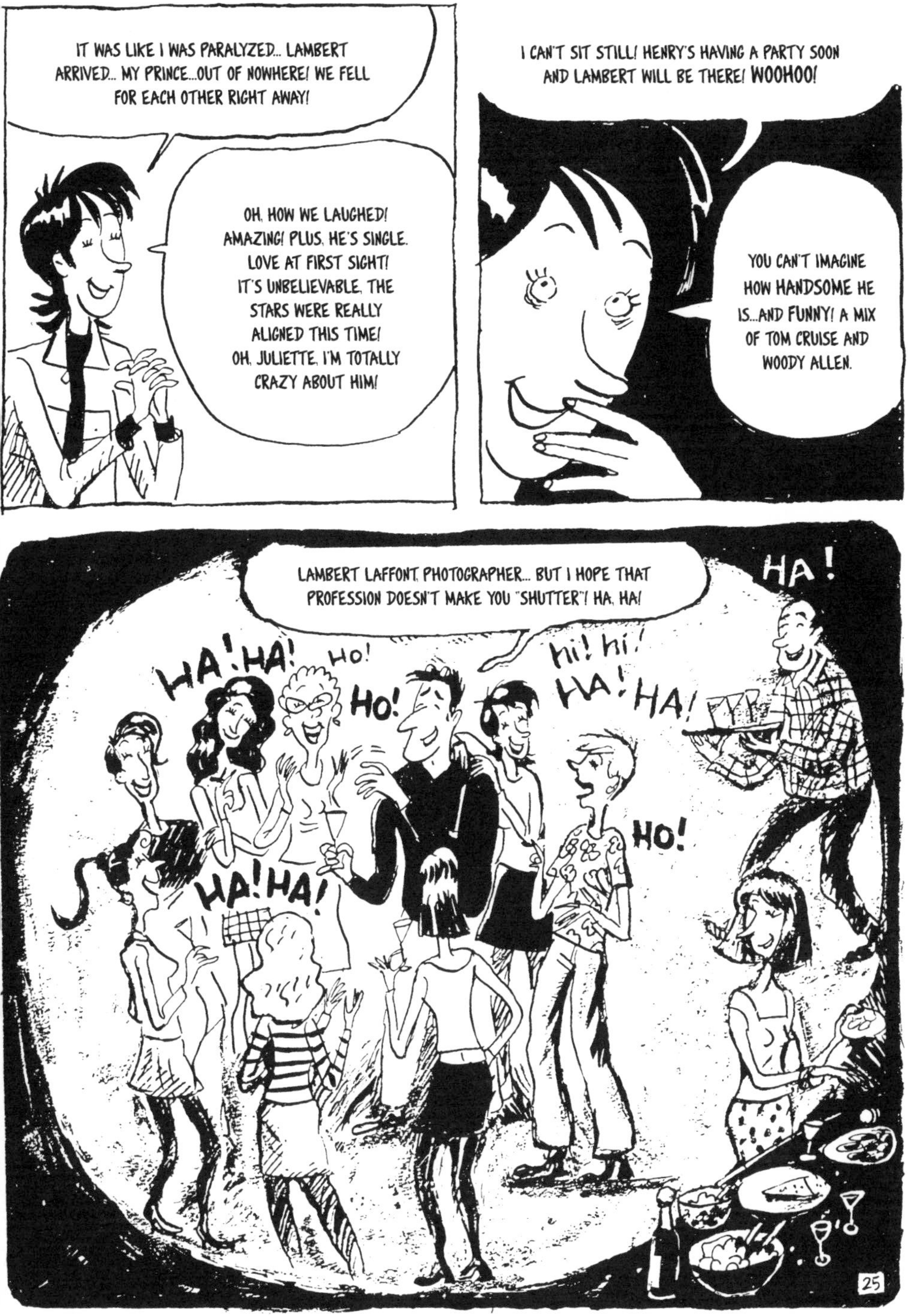
IT WAS LIKE I WAS PARALYZED... LAMBERT ARRIVED... MY PRINCE...OUT OF NOWHERE! WE FELL FOR EACH OTHER RIGHT AWAY!
OH, HOW WE LAUGHED! AMAZING! PLUS, HE'S SINGLE. LOVE AT FIRST SIGHT! IT'S UNBELIEVABLE, THE STARS WERE REALLY ALIGNED THIS TIME! OH, JULIETTE, I'M TOTALLY CRAZY ABOUT HIM!
I CAN'T SIT STILL! HENRY'S HAVING A PARTY SOON AND LAMBERT WILL BE THERE! WOOHOO!
YOU CAN'T IMAGINE HOW HANDSOME HE IS...AND FUNNY! A MIX OF TOM CRUISE AND WOODY ALLEN.
LAMBERT LAFFONT, PHOTOGRAPHER... BUT I HOPE THAT PROFESSION DOESN'T MAKE YOU "SHUTTER"! HA, HA!
HA!
HA! HA!
HO!
HO!
hi! hi!
HA! HA!
HO!
HA! HA!
25

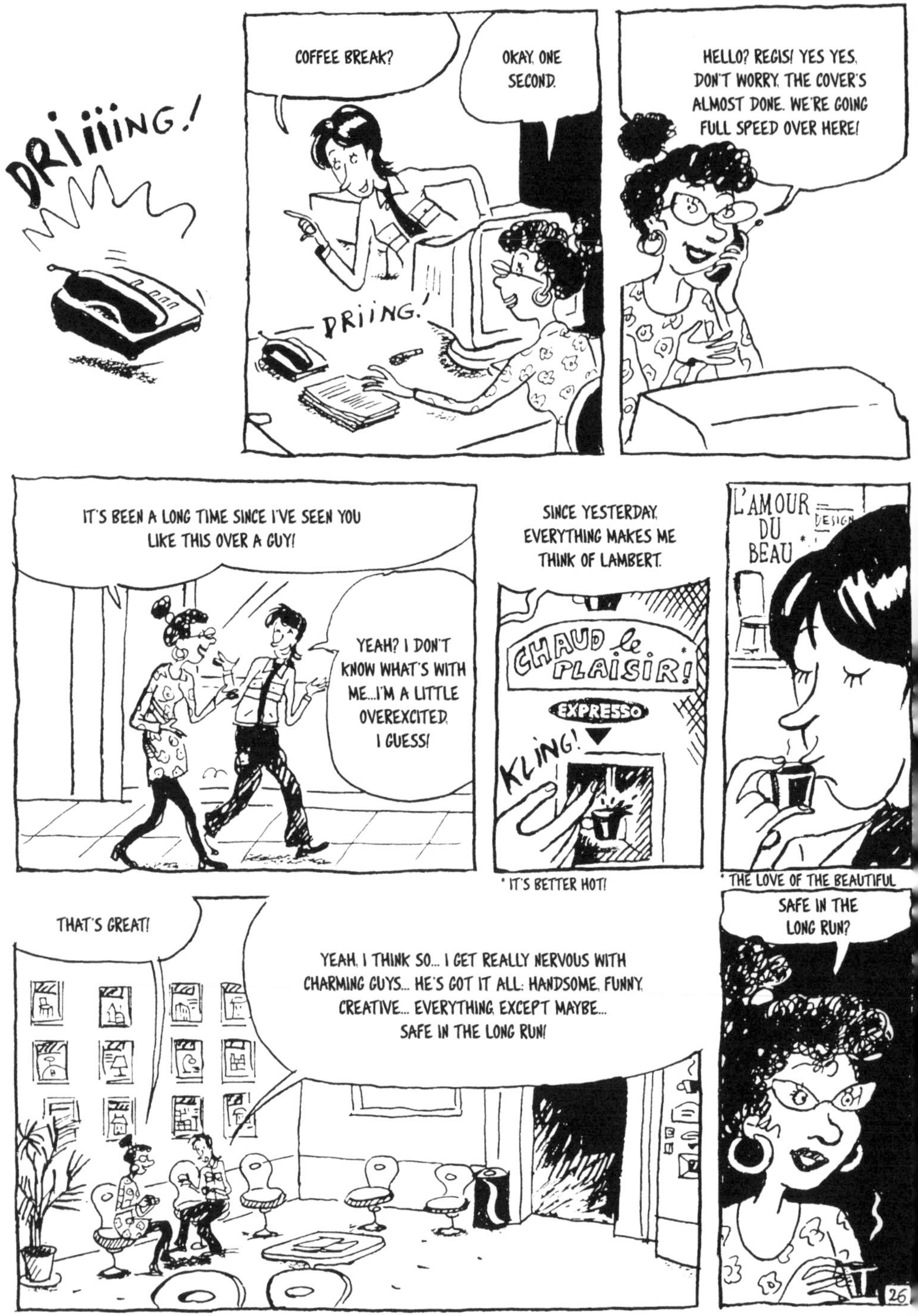
DRIiiiNG!
COFFEE BREAK?
OKAY, ONE SECOND.
DRIiNG!
HELLO? REGIS! YES YES, DON'T WORRY, THE COVER'S ALMOST DONE. WE'RE GOING FULL SPEED OVER HERE!
IT'S BEEN A LONG TIME SINCE I'VE SEEN YOU LIKE THIS OVER A GUY!
YEAH? I DON'T KNOW WHAT'S WITH ME...I'M A LITTLE OVEREXCITED, I GUESS!
SINCE YESTERDAY, EVERYTHING MAKES ME THINK OF LAMBERT.
CHAUD le PLAISIR!*
EXPRESSO
KLING!
* IT'S BETTER HOT!
L'AMOUR DU BEAU*
DESIGN
* THE LOVE OF THE BEAUTIFUL
THAT'S GREAT!
YEAH, I THINK SO... I GET REALLY NERVOUS WITH CHARMING GUYS... HE'S GOT IT ALL: HANDSOME, FUNNY, CREATIVE... EVERYTHING, EXCEPT MAYBE... SAFE IN THE LONG RUN!
SAFE IN THE LONG RUN?
26

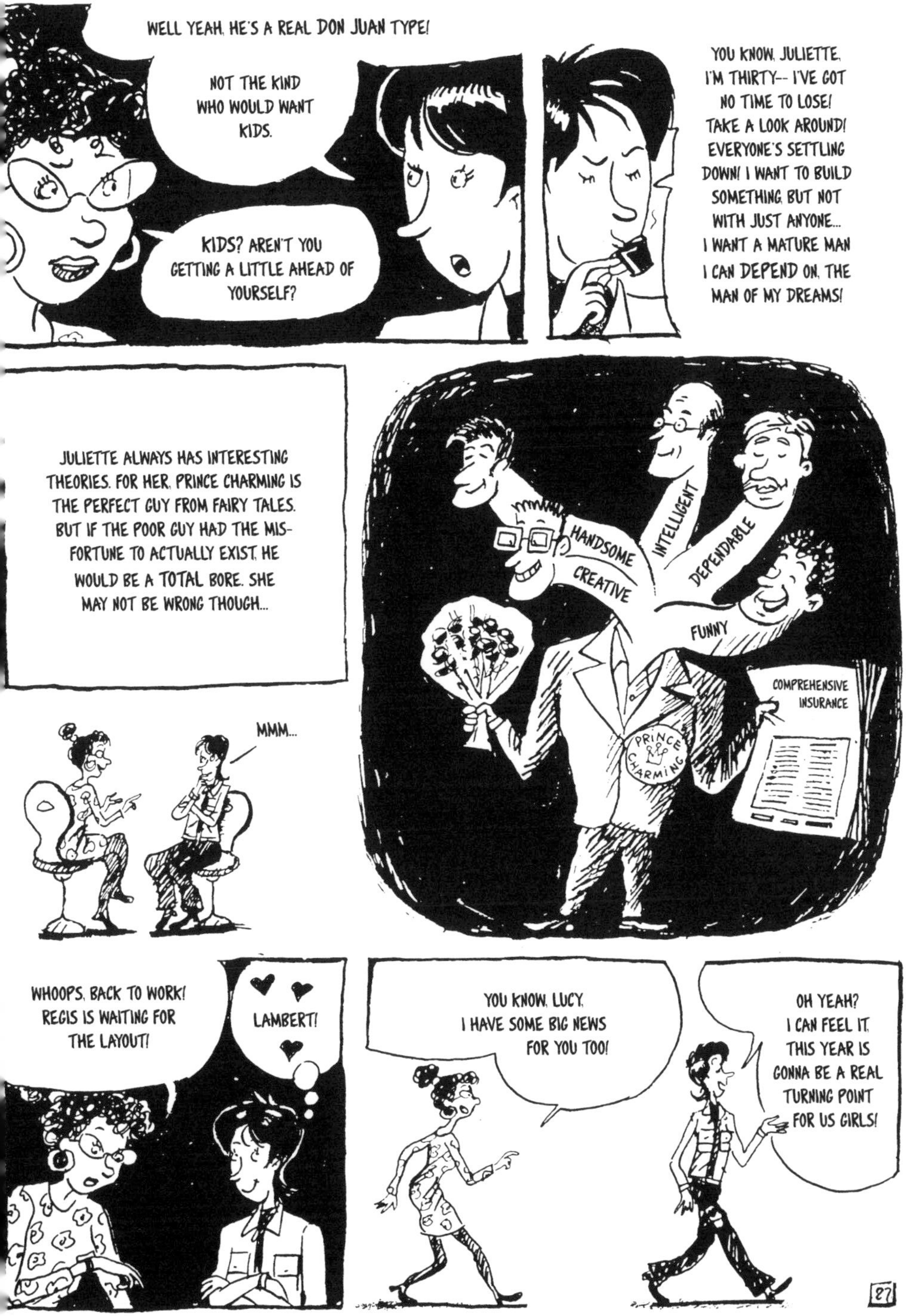
WELL YEAH, HE'S A REAL DON JUAN TYPE!
NOT THE KIND WHO WOULD WANT KIDS.
KIDS? AREN'T YOU GETTING A LITTLE AHEAD OF YOURSELF?
YOU KNOW, JULIETTE, I'M THIRTY-- I'VE GOT NO TIME TO LOSE! TAKE A LOOK AROUND! EVERYONE'S SETTLING DOWN! I WANT TO BUILD SOMETHING, BUT NOT WITH JUST ANYONE... I WANT A MATURE MAN I CAN DEPEND ON, THE MAN OF MY DREAMS!
JULIETTE ALWAYS HAS INTERESTING THEORIES. FOR HER, PRINCE CHARMING IS THE PERFECT GUY FROM FAIRY TALES. BUT IF THE POOR GUY HAD THE MISFORTUNE TO ACTUALLY EXIST, HE WOULD BE A TOTAL BORE. SHE MAY NOT BE WRONG THOUGH...
HANDSOME
INTELLIGENT
DEPENDABLE
CREATIVE
FUNNY
COMPREHENSIVE INSURANCE
PRINCE CHARMING
MMM...
WHOOPS, BACK TO WORK! REGIS IS WAITING FOR THE LAYOUT!
LAMBERT!
YOU KNOW, LUCY, I HAVE SOME BIG NEWS FOR YOU TOO!
OH YEAH? I CAN FEEL IT, THIS YEAR IS GONNA BE A REAL TURNING POINT FOR US GIRLS!
27

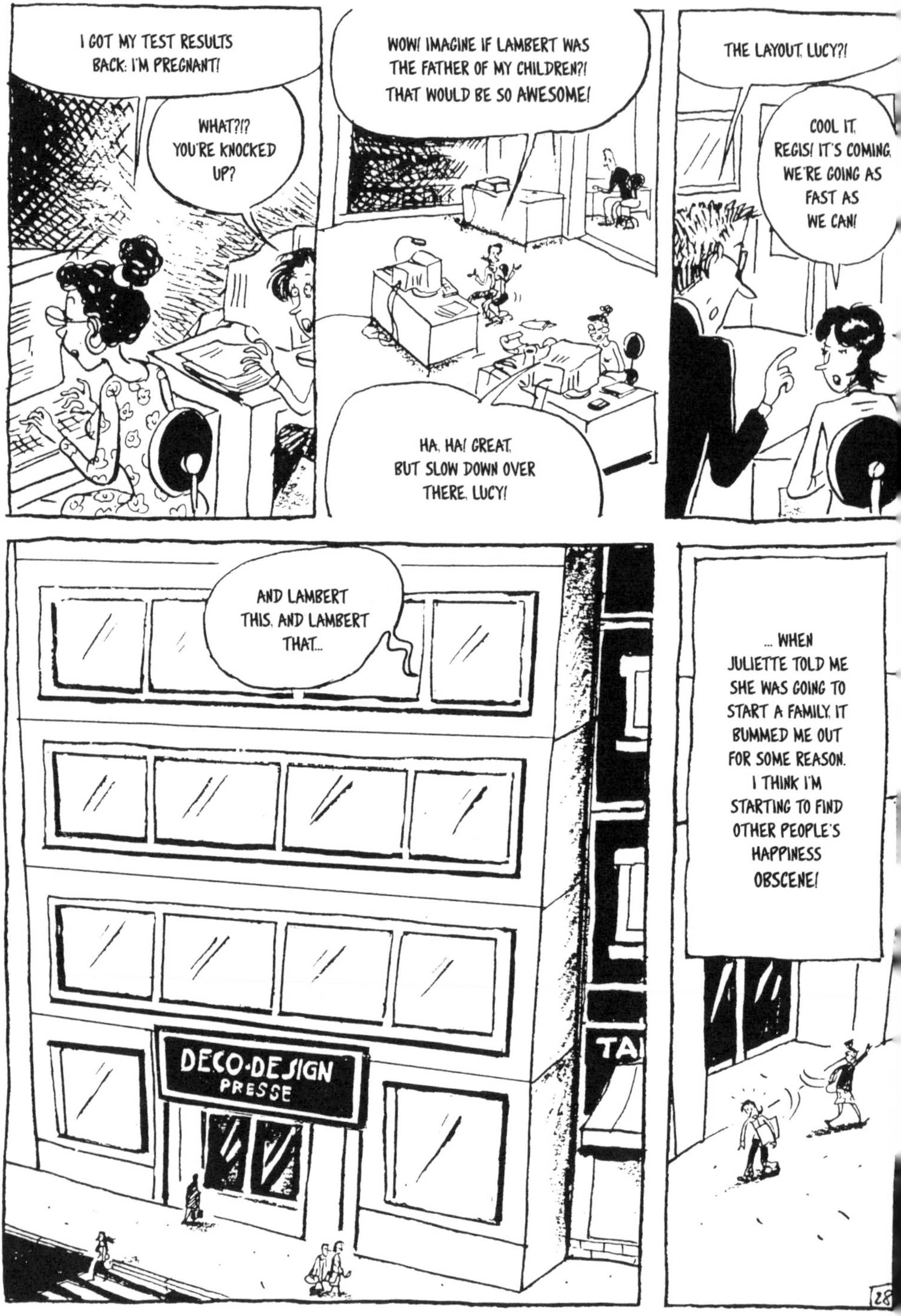
I GOT MY TEST RESULTS BACK: I'M PREGNANT!
WHAT?!? YOU'RE KNOCKED UP?
WOW! IMAGINE IF LAMBERT WAS THE FATHER OF MY CHILDREN?! THAT WOULD BE SO AWESOME!
HA, HA! GREAT, BUT SLOW DOWN OVER THERE, LUCY!
THE LAYOUT, LUCY?!
COOL IT, REGIS! IT'S COMING, WE'RE GOING AS FAST AS WE CAN!
AND LAMBERT THIS, AND LAMBERT THAT...
DECO-DESIGN PRESSE
... WHEN JULIETTE TOLD ME SHE WAS GOING TO START A FAMILY, IT BUMMED ME OUT FOR SOME REASON. I THINK I'M STARTING TO FIND OTHER PEOPLE'S HAPPINESS OBSCENE!
28

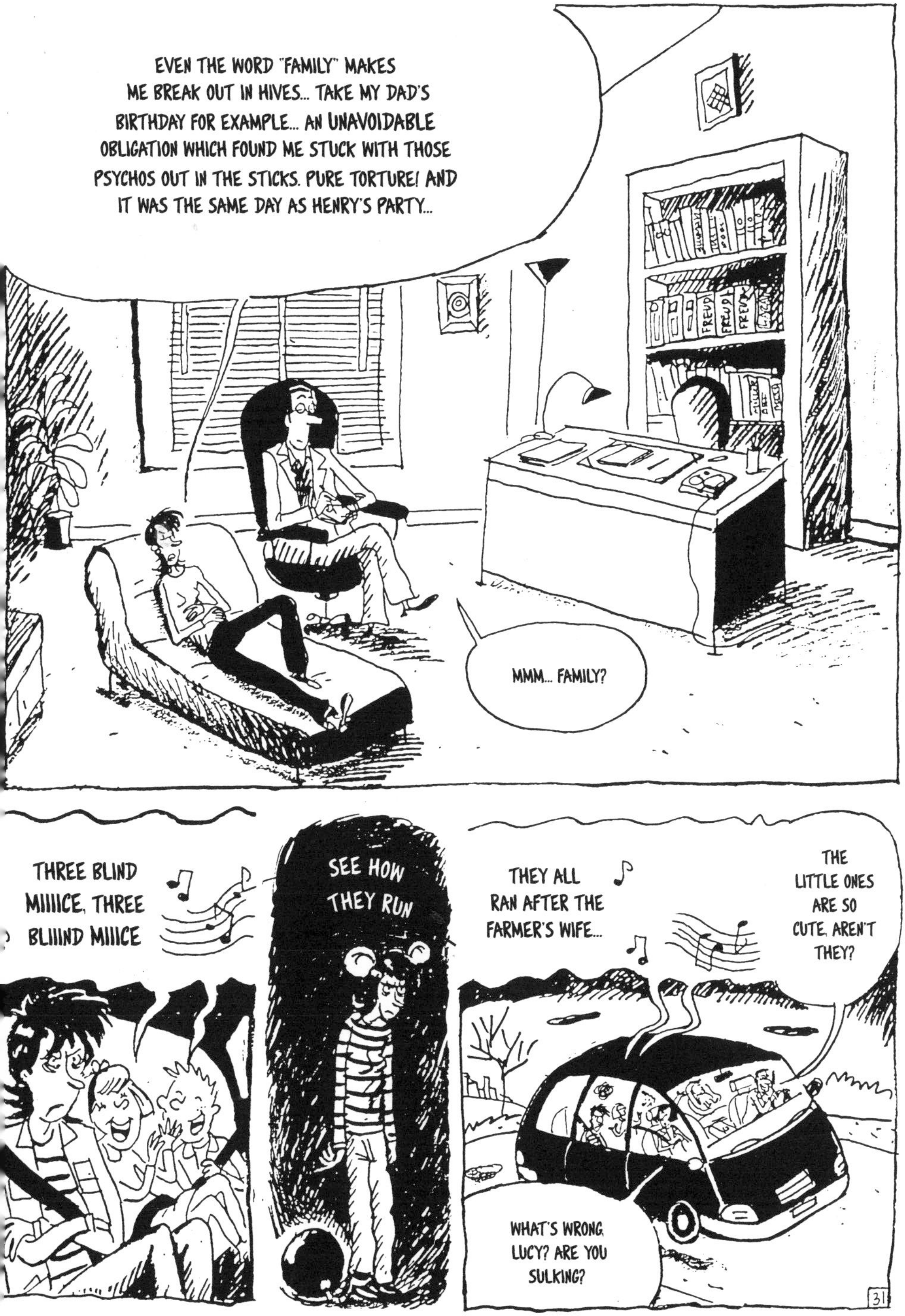
EVEN THE WORD "FAMILY" MAKES ME BREAK OUT IN HIVES... TAKE MY DAD'S BIRTHDAY FOR EXAMPLE... AN UNAVOIDABLE OBLIGATION WHICH FOUND ME STUCK WITH THOSE PSYCHOS OUT IN THE STICKS. PURE TORTURE! AND IT WAS THE SAME DAY AS HENRY'S PARTY...
FREUD
FREUD
FREUD
MMM... FAMILY?
THREE BLIND MIIIICE, THREE BLIIIND MIIICE
SEE HOW THEY RUN
THEY ALL RAN AFTER THE FARMER'S WIFE...
THE LITTLE ONES ARE SO CUTE, AREN'T THEY?
WHAT'S WRONG, LUCY? ARE YOU SULKING?
31

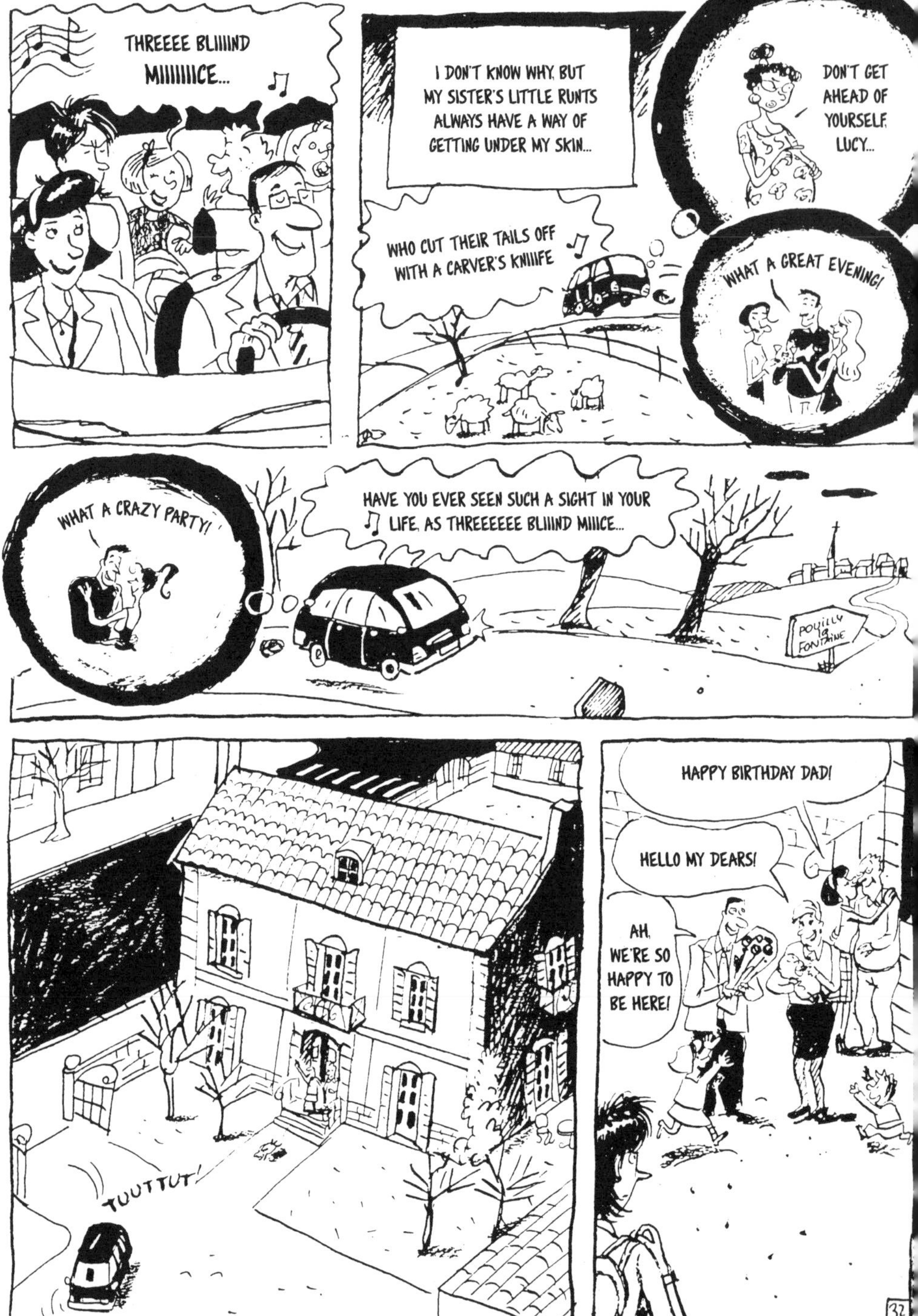
THREEEE BLIIIND MIIIIIICE...
I DON'T KNOW WHY, BUT MY SISTER'S LITTLE RUNTS ALWAYS HAVE A WAY OF GETTING UNDER MY SKIN...
DON'T GET AHEAD OF YOURSELF, LUCY...
WHO CUT THEIR TAILS OFF WITH A CARVER'S KNIIIFE
WHAT A GREAT EVENING!
WHAT A CRAZY PARTY!
HAVE YOU EVER SEEN SUCH A SIGHT IN YOUR LIFE, AS THREEEEEE BLIIIND MIIICE...
POUILLY LA FONTAINE
TUUTTUT!
HAPPY BIRTHDAY DAD!
HELLO MY DEARS!
AH, WE'RE SO HAPPY TO BE HERE!
32

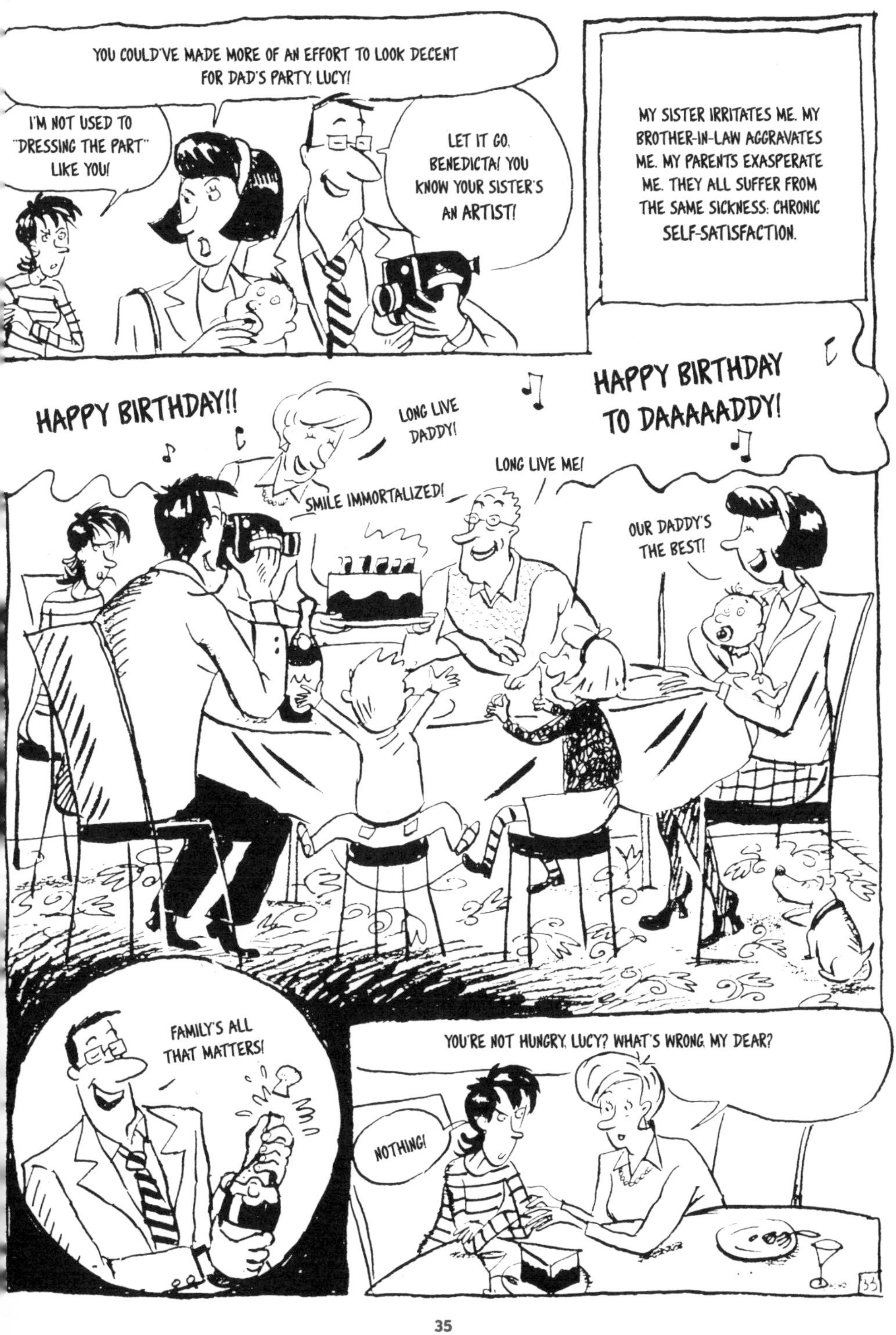

YOU COULD'VE MADE MORE OF AN EFFORT TO LOOK DECENT FOR DAD'S PARTY, LUCY!
I'M NOT USED TO "DRESSING THE PART" LIKE YOU!
LET IT GO, BENEDICTA! YOU KNOW YOUR SISTER'S AN ARTIST!
MY SISTER IRRITATES ME. MY BROTHER-IN-LAW AGGRAVATES ME. MY PARENTS EXASPERATE ME. THEY ALL SUFFER FROM THE SAME SICKNESS: CHRONIC SELF-SATISFACTION.
HAPPY BIRTHDAY!!
LONG LIVE DADDY!
HAPPY BIRTHDAY TO DAAAAADDY!
SMILE IMMORTALIZED!
LONG LIVE ME!
OUR DADDY'S THE BEST!
FAMILY'S ALL THAT MATTERS!
YOU'RE NOT HUNGRY, LUCY? WHAT'S WRONG, MY DEAR?
NOTHING!

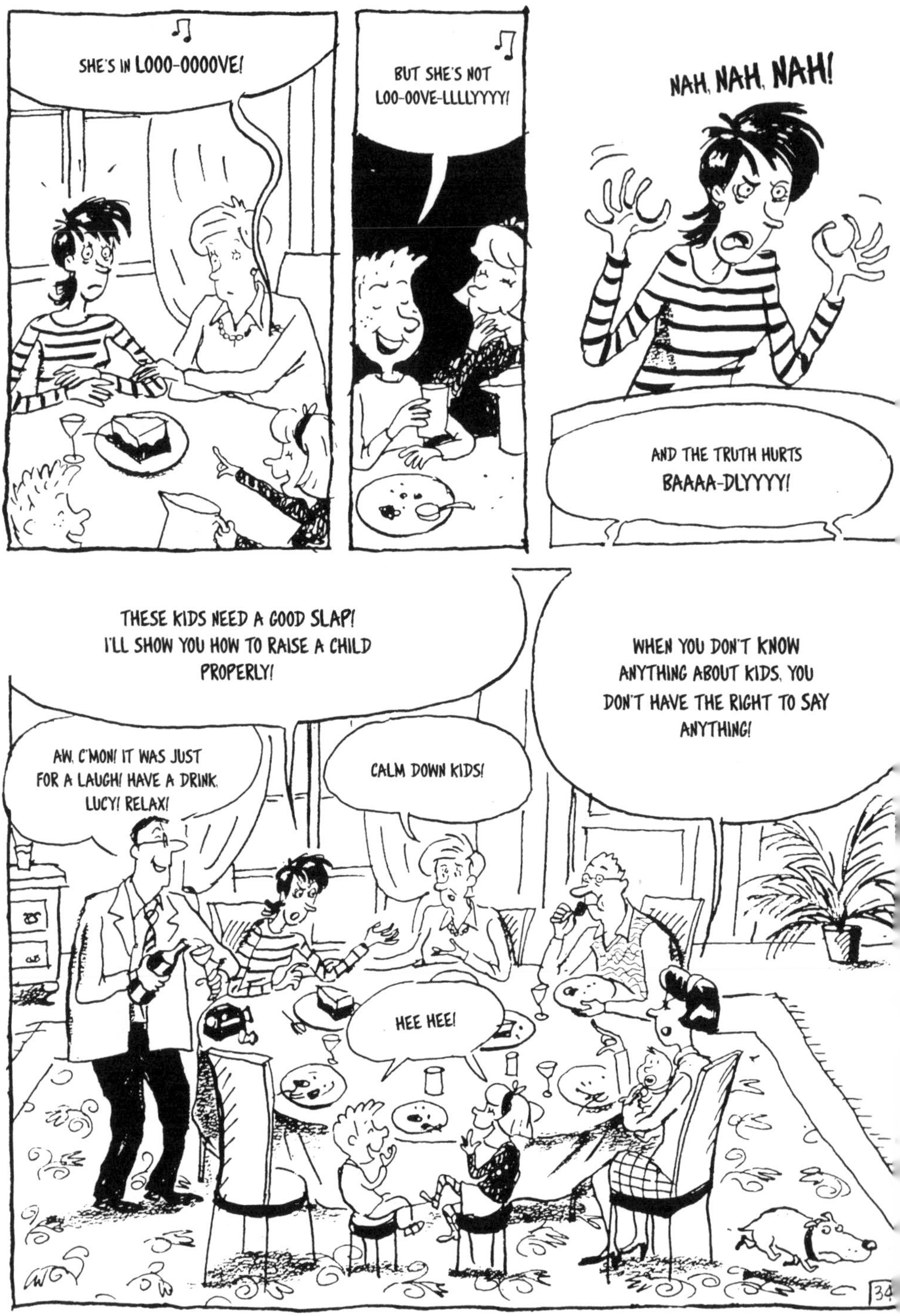
SHE'S IN LOOO-OOOOVE!
BUT SHE'S NOT LOO-OOVE-LLLLYYYY!
NAH, NAH, NAH!
AND THE TRUTH HURTS BAAAA-DLYYYY!
THESE KIDS NEED A GOOD SLAP! I'LL SHOW YOU HOW TO RAISE A CHILD PROPERLY!
WHEN YOU DON'T KNOW ANYTHING ABOUT KIDS, YOU DON'T HAVE THE RIGHT TO SAY ANYTHING!
AW, C'MON! IT WAS JUST FOR A LAUGH! HAVE A DRINK, LUCY! RELAX!
CALM DOWN KIDS!
HEE HEE!
34

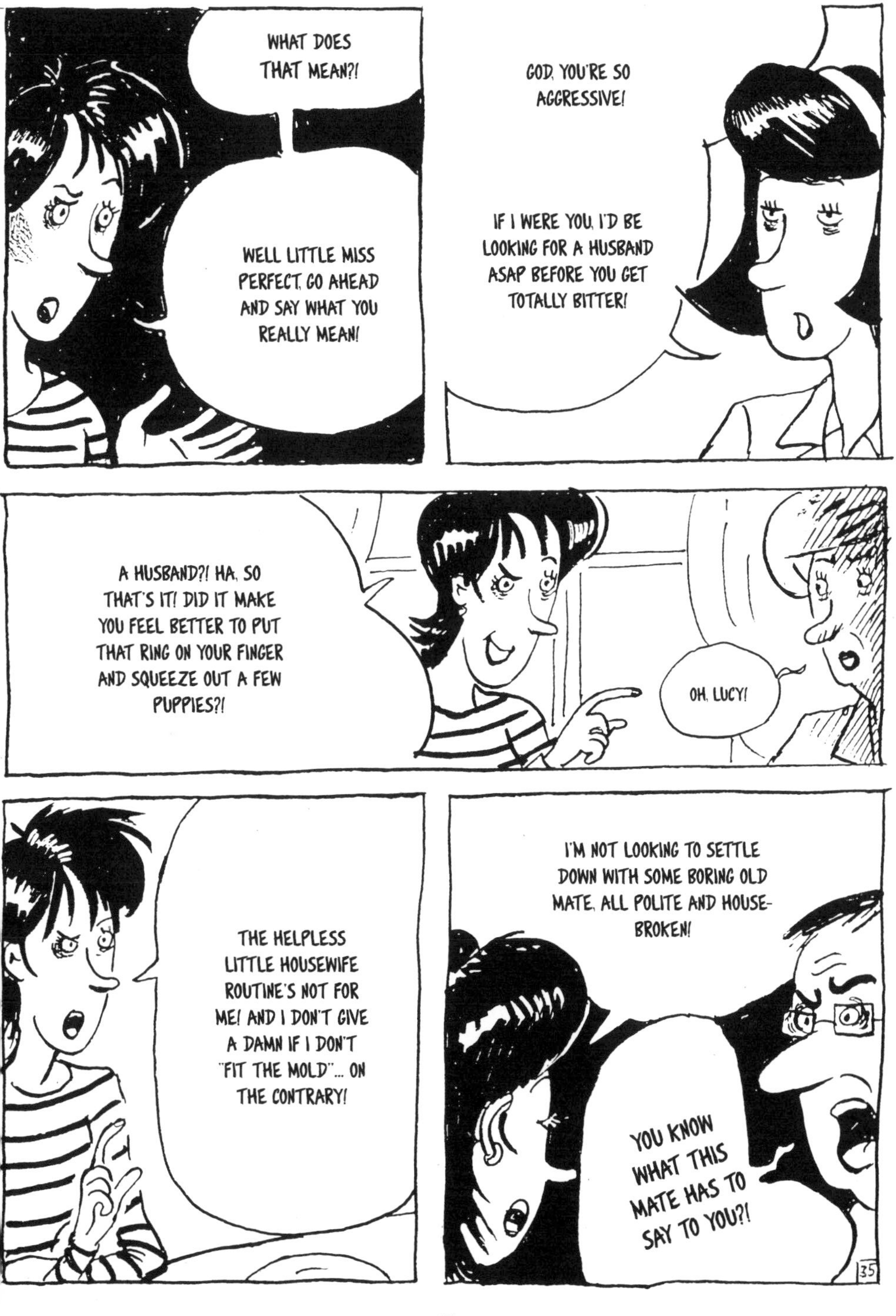
WHAT DOES THAT MEAN?!
WELL LITTLE MISS PERFECT, GO AHEAD AND SAY WHAT YOU REALLY MEAN!
GOD, YOU'RE SO AGGRESSIVE!
IF I WERE YOU, I'D BE LOOKING FOR A HUSBAND ASAP BEFORE YOU GET TOTALLY BITTER!
A HUSBAND?! HA, SO THAT'S IT! DID IT MAKE YOU FEEL BETTER TO PUT THAT RING ON YOUR FINGER AND SQUEEZE OUT A FEW PUPPIES?!
OH, LUCY!
THE HELPLESS LITTLE HOUSEWIFE ROUTINE'S NOT FOR ME! AND I DON'T GIVE A DAMN IF I DON'T "FIT THE MOLD"... ON THE CONTRARY!
I'M NOT LOOKING TO SETTLE DOWN WITH SOME BORING OLD MATE, ALL POLITE AND HOUSE-BROKEN!
YOU KNOW WHAT THIS MATE HAS TO SAY TO YOU?!
35

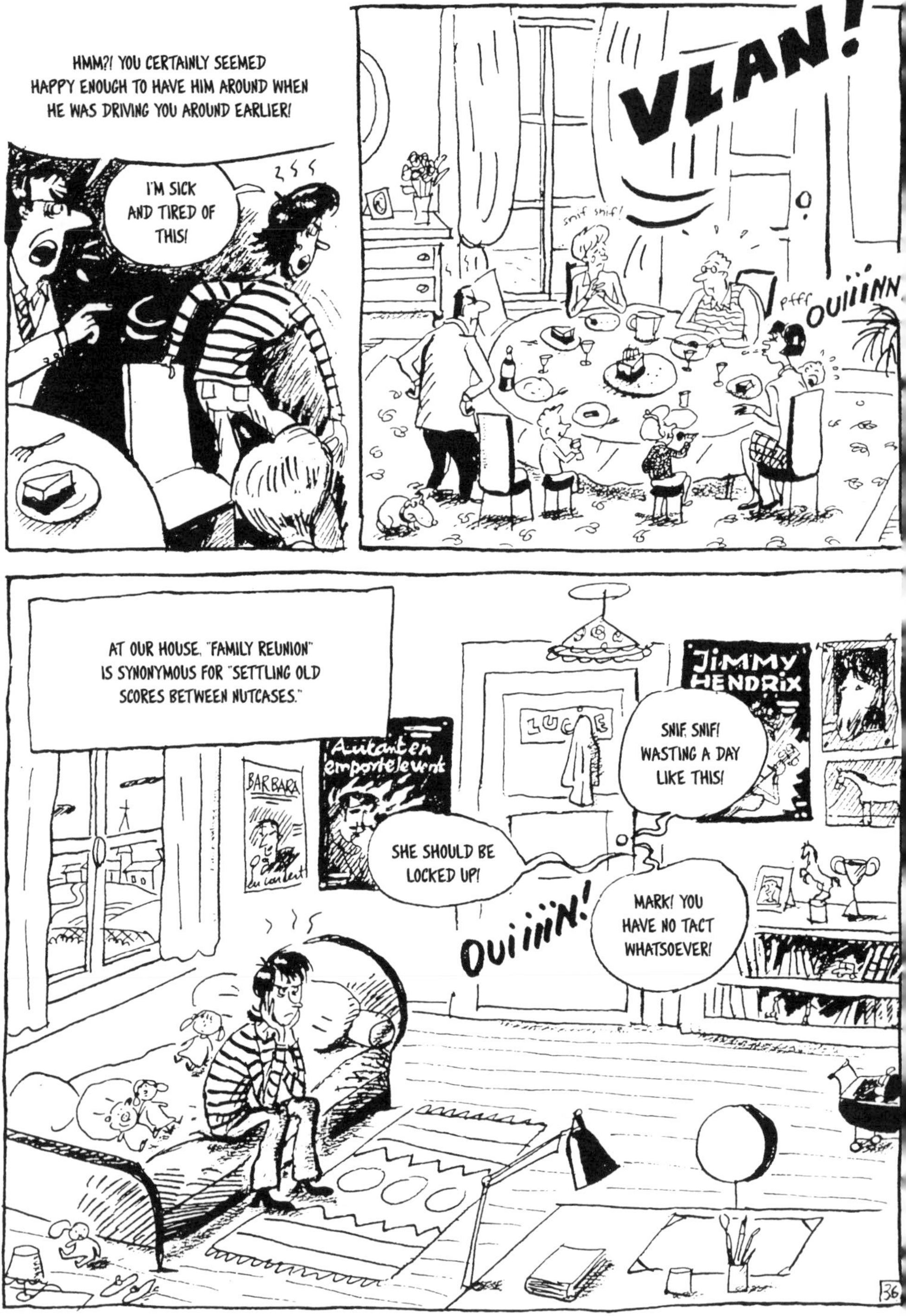
HMM?! YOU CERTAINLY SEEMED HAPPY ENOUGH TO HAVE HIM AROUND WHEN HE WAS DRIVING YOU AROUND EARLIER!
I'M SICK AND TIRED OF THIS!
VLAN!
snif snif!
pfff
OUIIINN
AT OUR HOUSE, "FAMILY REUNION" IS SYNONYMOUS FOR "SETTLING OLD SCORES BETWEEN NUTCASES."
BARBARA
Autant en emporte le vent
JIMMY HENDRIX
LUCIE
SNIF, SNIF! WASTING A DAY LIKE THIS!
SHE SHOULD BE LOCKED UP!
OUIIIIN!
MARK! YOU HAVE NO TACT WHATSOEVER!
36

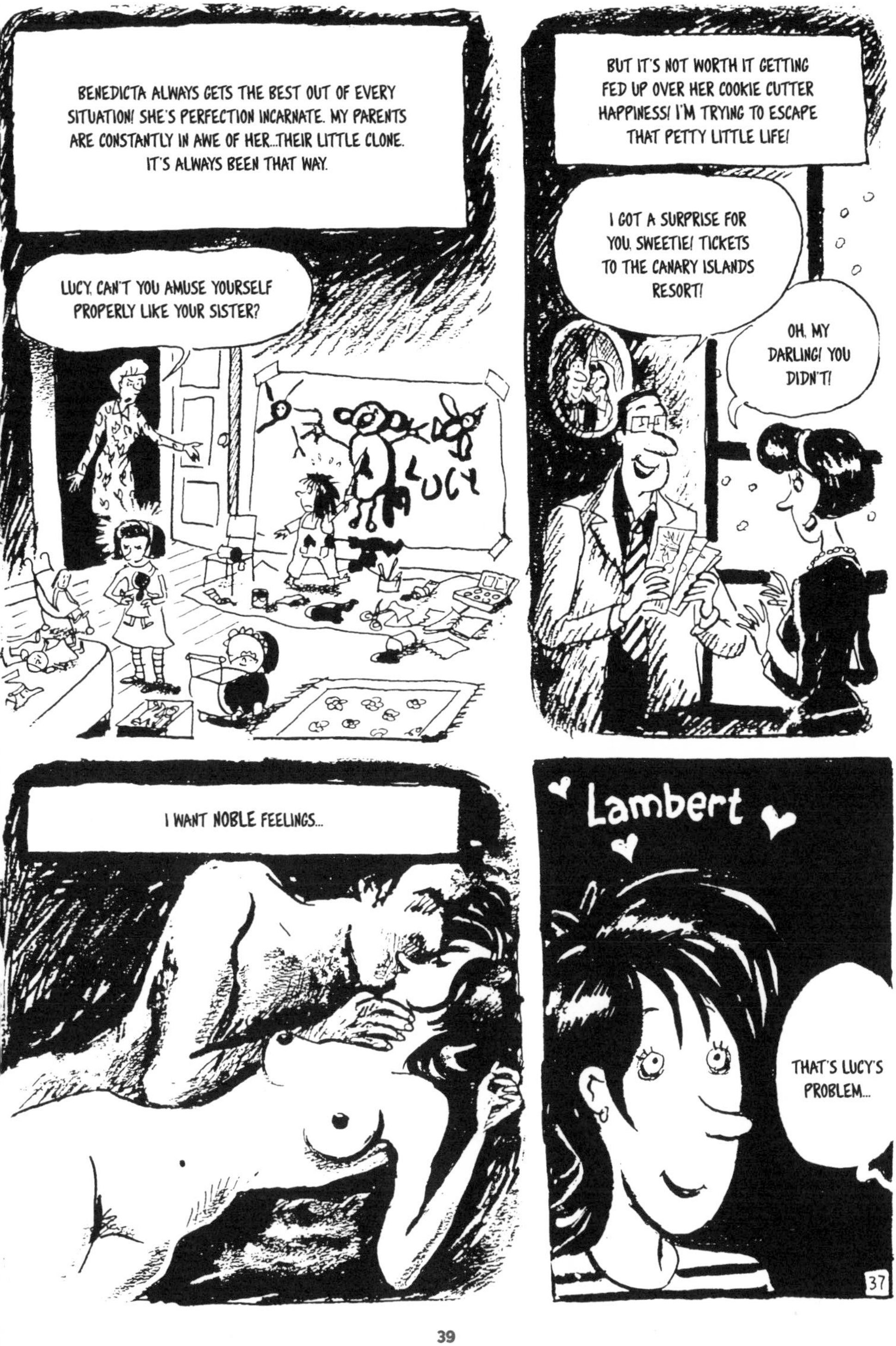

BENEDICTA ALWAYS GETS THE BEST OUT OF EVERY SITUATION! SHE'S PERFECTION INCARNATE. MY PARENTS ARE CONSTANTLY IN AWE OF HER...THEIR LITTLE CLONE. IT'S ALWAYS BEEN THAT WAY.
LUCY, CAN'T YOU AMUSE YOURSELF PROPERLY LIKE YOUR SISTER?
LUCY
BUT IT'S NOT WORTH IT GETTING FED UP OVER HER COOKIE CUTTER HAPPINESS! I'M TRYING TO ESCAPE THAT PETTY LITTLE LIFE!
I GOT A SURPRISE FOR YOU, SWEETIE! TICKETS TO THE CANARY ISLANDS RESORT!
OH, MY DARLING! YOU DIDN'T!
I WANT NOBLE FEELINGS...
Lambert
THAT'S LUCY'S PROBLEM...
37

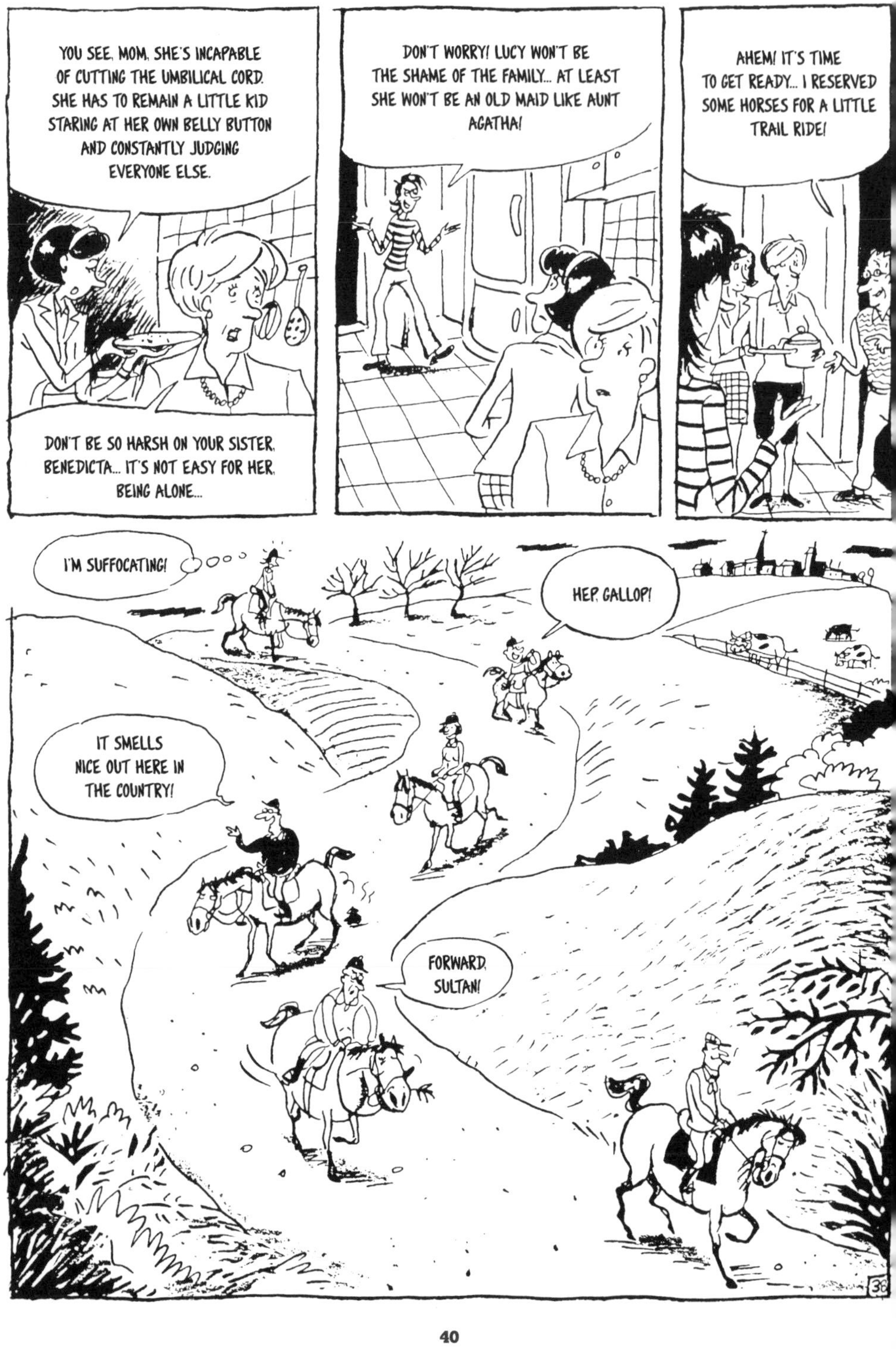
YOU SEE, MOM, SHE'S INCAPABLE OF CUTTING THE UMBILICAL CORD. SHE HAS TO REMAIN A LITTLE KID STARING AT HER OWN BELLY BUTTON AND CONSTANTLY JUDGING EVERYONE ELSE.
DON'T BE SO HARSH ON YOUR SISTER, BENEDICTA... IT'S NOT EASY FOR HER, BEING ALONE...
DON'T WORRY! LUCY WON'T BE THE SHAME OF THE FAMILY... AT LEAST SHE WON'T BE AN OLD MAID LIKE AUNT AGATHA!
AHEM! IT'S TIME TO GET READY... I RESERVED SOME HORSES FOR A LITTLE TRAIL RIDE!
I'M SUFFOCATING!
HEP, GALLOP!
IT SMELLS NICE OUT HERE IN THE COUNTRY!
FORWARD, SULTAN!
38

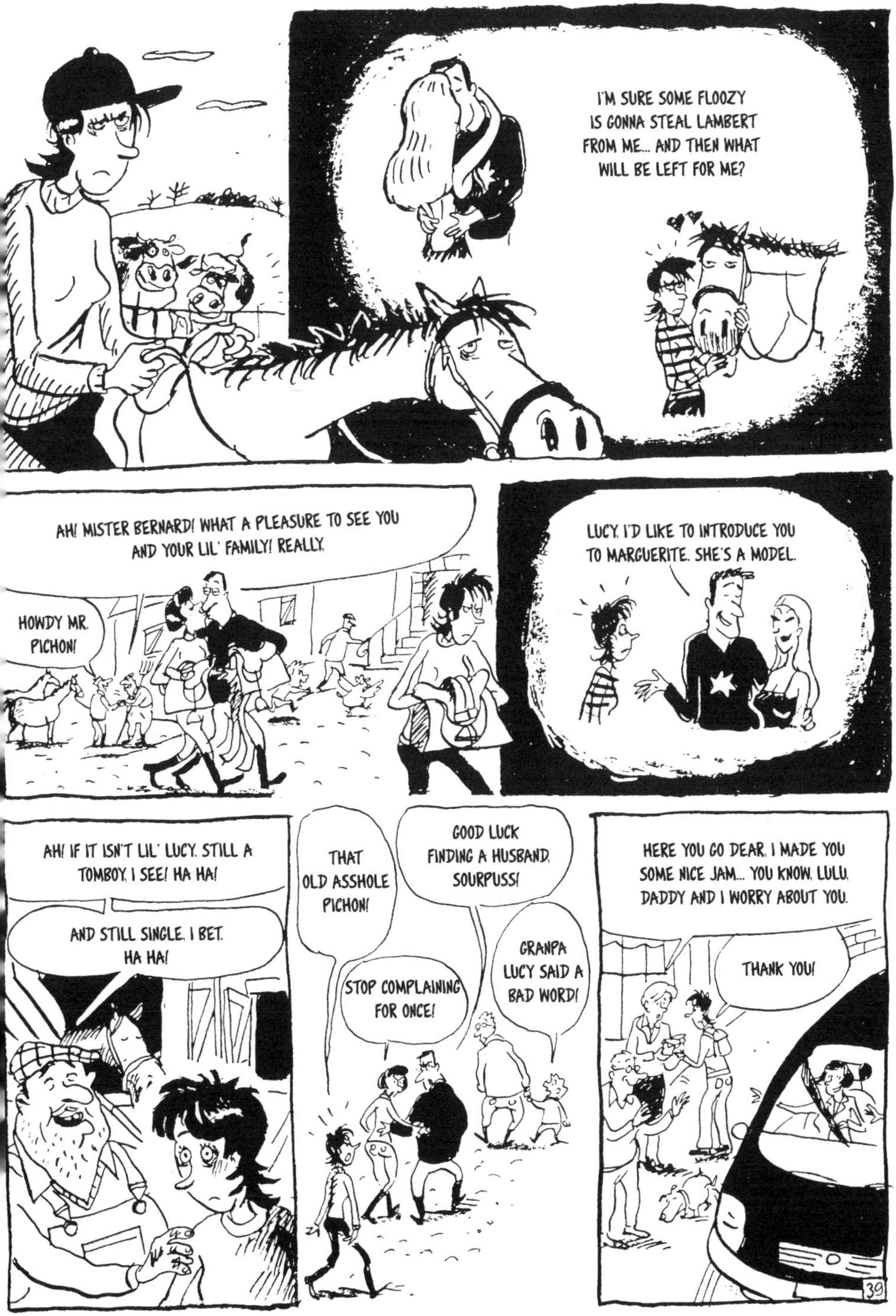
I'M SURE SOME FLOOZY IS GONNA STEAL LAMBERT FROM ME... AND THEN WHAT WILL BE LEFT FOR ME?
AH! MISTER BERNARD! WHAT A PLEASURE TO SEE YOU AND YOUR LIL' FAMILY! REALLY.
HOWDY MR. PICHON!
LUCY, I'D LIKE TO INTRODUCE YOU TO MARGUERITE. SHE'S A MODEL.
AH! IF IT ISN'T LIL' LUCY. STILL A TOMBOY, I SEE! HA HA!
AND STILL SINGLE, I BET. HA HA!
THAT OLD ASSHOLE PICHON!
GOOD LUCK FINDING A HUSBAND, SOURPUSS!
STOP COMPLAINING FOR ONCE!
GRANPA LUCY SAID A BAD WORD!
HERE YOU GO DEAR, I MADE YOU SOME NICE JAM... YOU KNOW, LULU, DADDY AND I WORRY ABOUT YOU.
THANK YOU!
39

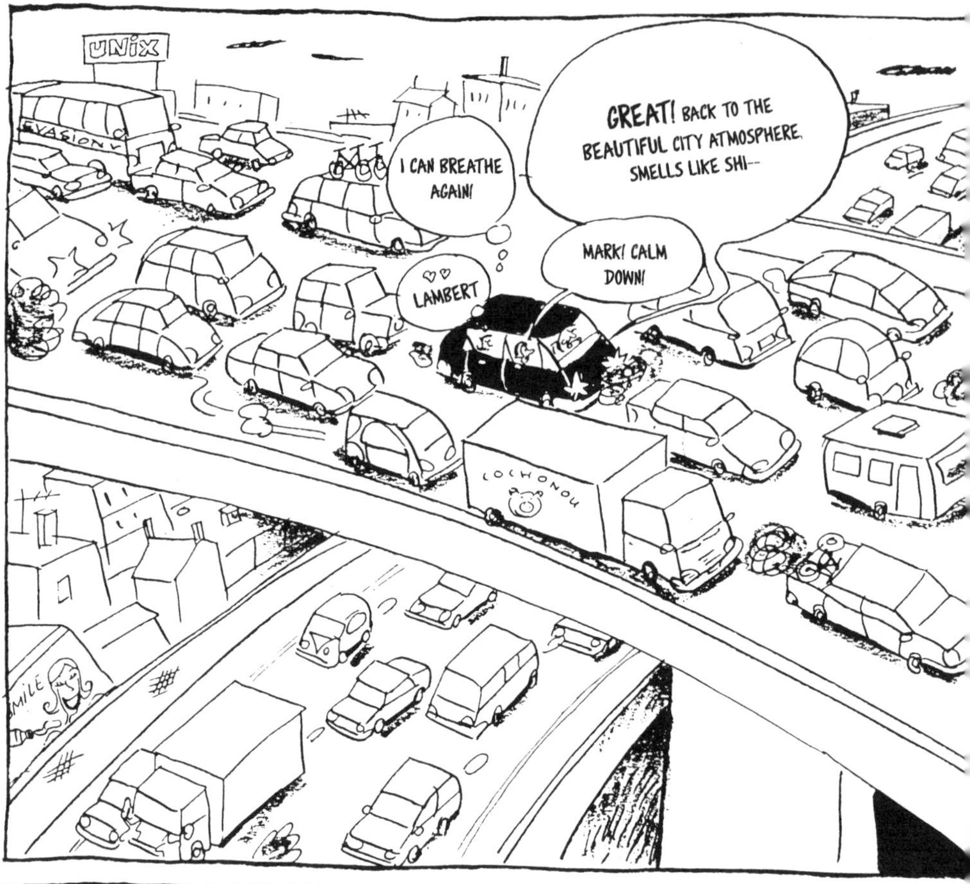
UNIX
EVASION
I CAN BREATHE AGAIN!
GREAT! BACK TO THE BEAUTIFUL CITY ATMOSPHERE. SMELLS LIKE SHI--
LAMBERT
MARK! CALM DOWN!
COCHONOU
SMILE

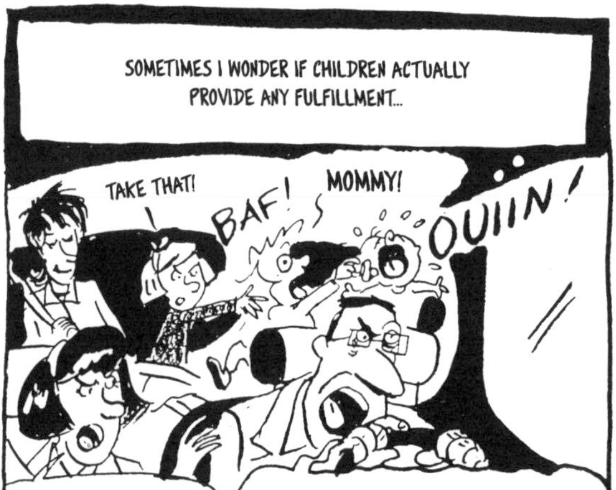
SOMETIMES I WONDER IF CHILDREN ACTUALLY PROVIDE ANY FULFILLMENT...
TAKE THAT!
BAF!
MOMMY!
OUIIN!
BE QUIET BACK THERE!
KEEP IT UP AND I'LL THROW YOU ALL OUT THE WINDOW!

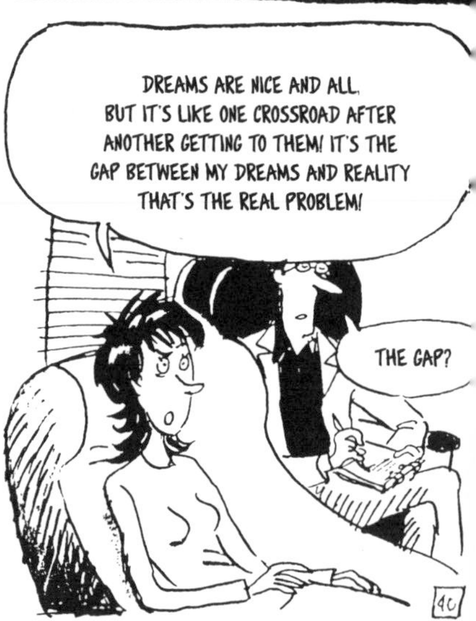
DREAMS ARE NICE AND ALL, BUT IT'S LIKE ONE CROSSROAD AFTER ANOTHER GETTING TO THEM! IT'S THE GAP BETWEEN MY DREAMS AND REALITY THAT'S THE REAL PROBLEM!
THE GAP?

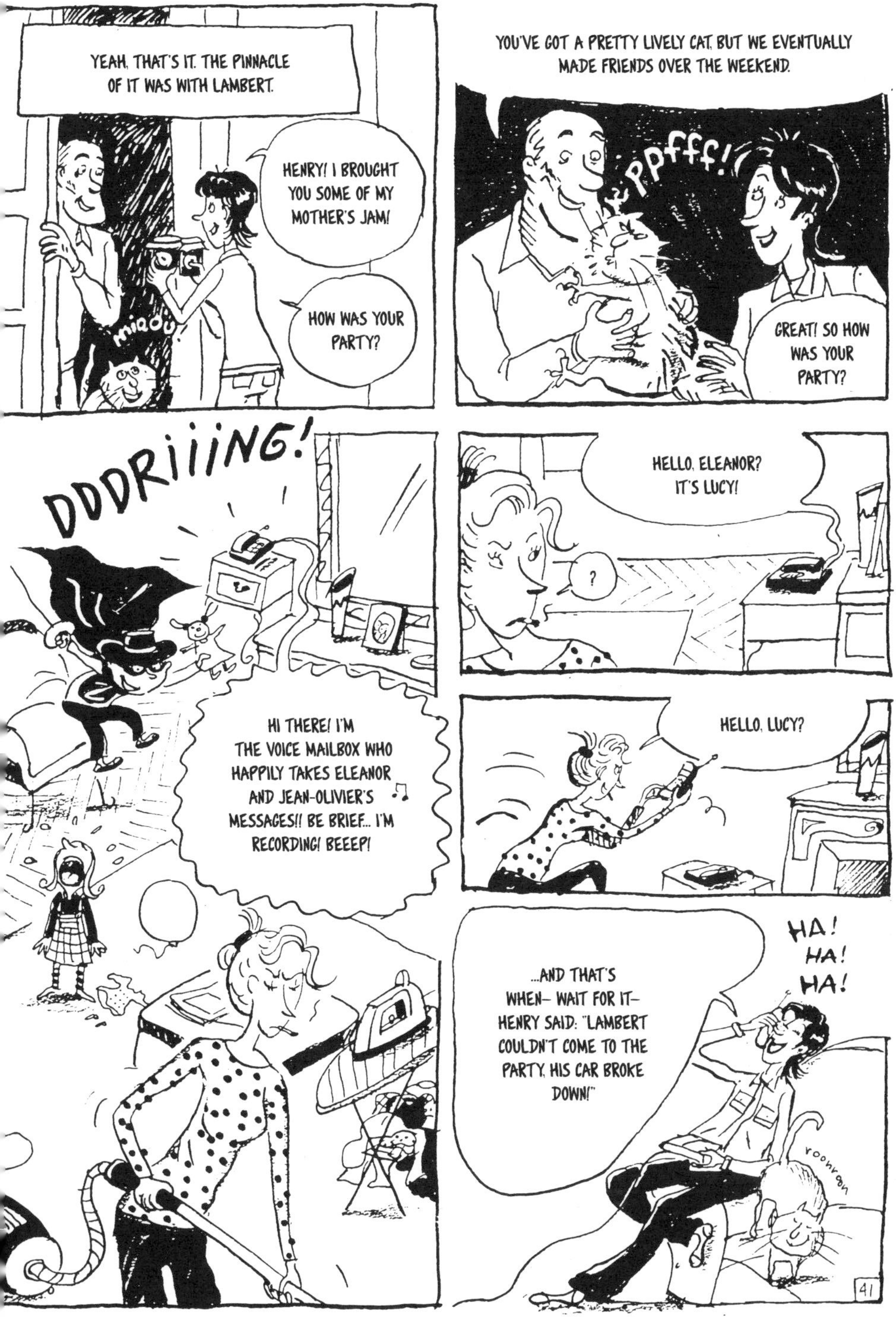
YEAH, THAT'S IT. THE PINNACLE OF IT WAS WITH LAMBERT.
HENRY! I BROUGHT YOU SOME OF MY MOTHER'S JAM!
miaou
HOW WAS YOUR PARTY?
YOU'VE GOT A PRETTY LIVELY CAT, BUT WE EVENTUALLY MADE FRIENDS OVER THE WEEKEND.
PPFFF!
GREAT! SO HOW WAS YOUR PARTY?
DDDRiiiNG!
HI THERE! I'M THE VOICE MAILBOX WHO HAPPILY TAKES ELEANOR AND JEAN-OLIVIER'S MESSAGES!! BE BRIEF... I'M RECORDING! BEEEP!
HELLO, ELEANOR? IT'S LUCY!
?
HELLO, LUCY?
...AND THAT'S WHEN— WAIT FOR IT— HENRY SAID: "LAMBERT COULDN'T COME TO THE PARTY, HIS CAR BROKE DOWN!"
HA! HA! HA!
roonroon
41

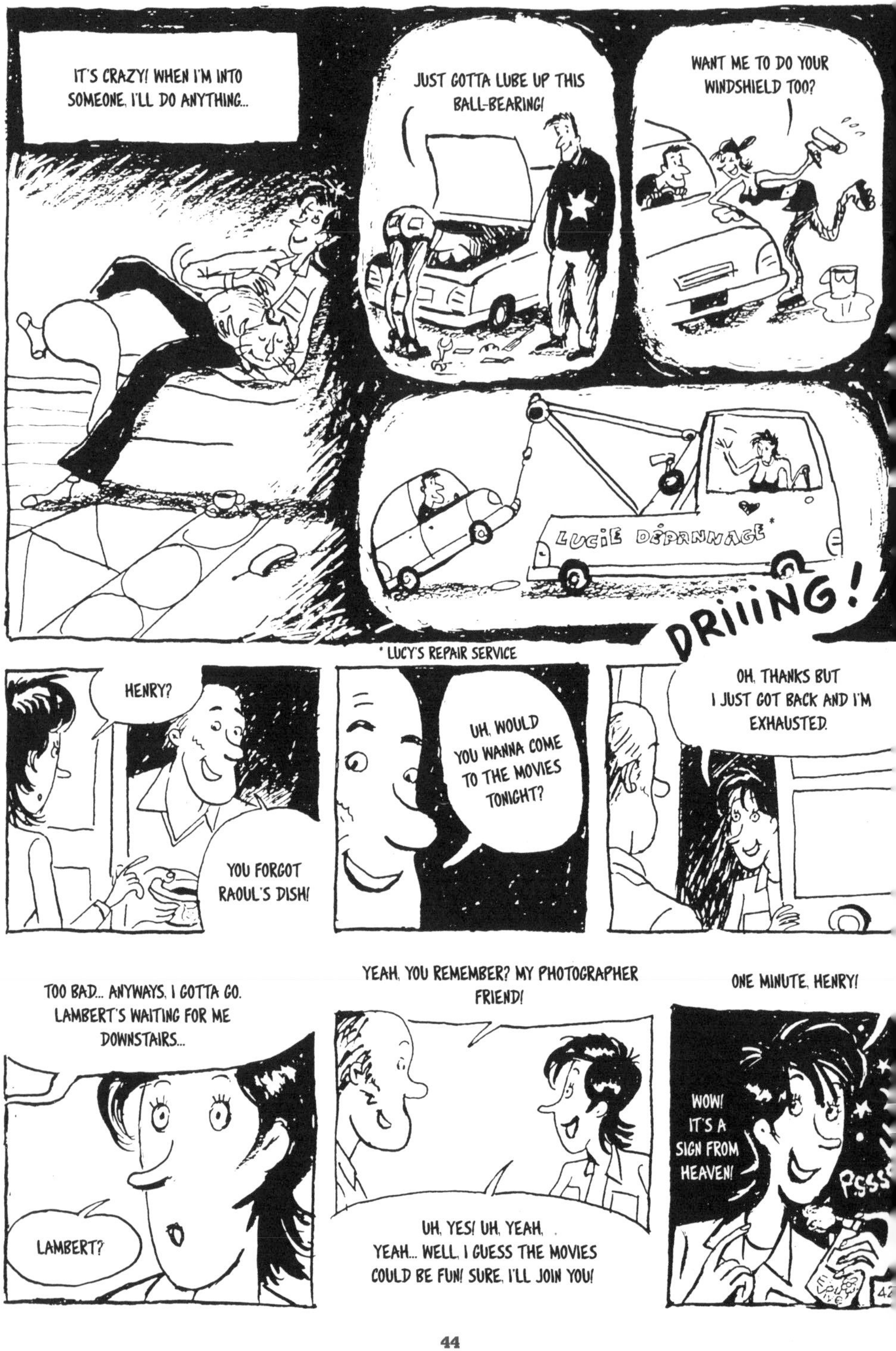
IT'S CRAZY! WHEN I'M INTO SOMEONE, I'LL DO ANYTHING...
JUST GOTTA LUBE UP THIS BALL-BEARING!
WANT ME TO DO YOUR WINDSHIELD TOO?
LUCIE DÉPANNAGE*
DRIIING!
* LUCY'S REPAIR SERVICE
HENRY?
YOU FORGOT RAOUL'S DISH!
UH, WOULD YOU WANNA COME TO THE MOVIES TONIGHT?
OH, THANKS BUT I JUST GOT BACK AND I'M EXHAUSTED.
TOO BAD... ANYWAYS, I GOTTA GO. LAMBERT'S WAITING FOR ME DOWNSTAIRS...
LAMBERT?
YEAH, YOU REMEMBER? MY PHOTOGRAPHER FRIEND!
UH, YES! UH, YEAH, YEAH... WELL, I GUESS THE MOVIES COULD BE FUN! SURE, I'LL JOIN YOU!
ONE MINUTE, HENRY!
WOW! IT'S A SIGN FROM HEAVEN!

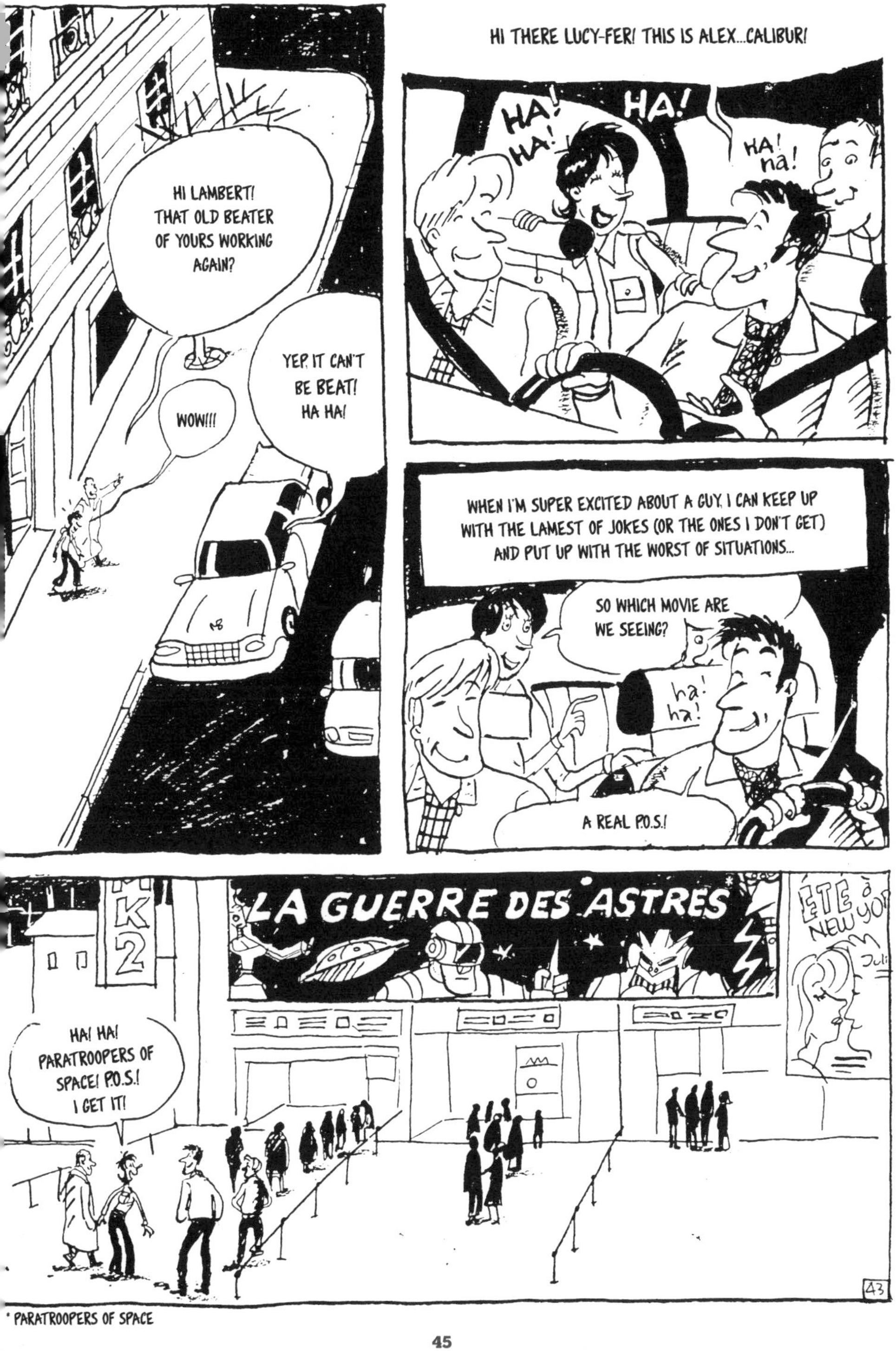
HI LAMBERT! THAT OLD BEATER OF YOURS WORKING AGAIN?
WOW!!!
YEP. IT CAN'T BE BEAT! HA HA!
HI THERE LUCY-FER! THIS IS ALEX...CALIBUR!
HA! HA!
HA!
HA! na!
WHEN I'M SUPER EXCITED ABOUT A GUY, I CAN KEEP UP WITH THE LAMEST OF JOKES (OR THE ONES I DON'T GET) AND PUT UP WITH THE WORST OF SITUATIONS...
SO WHICH MOVIE ARE WE SEEING?
ha! ha!
A REAL P.O.S.!
LA GUERRE DES ASTRES*
MK2
HA! HA! PARATROOPERS OF SPACE! P.O.S.! I GET IT!
43

* PARATROOPERS OF SPACE

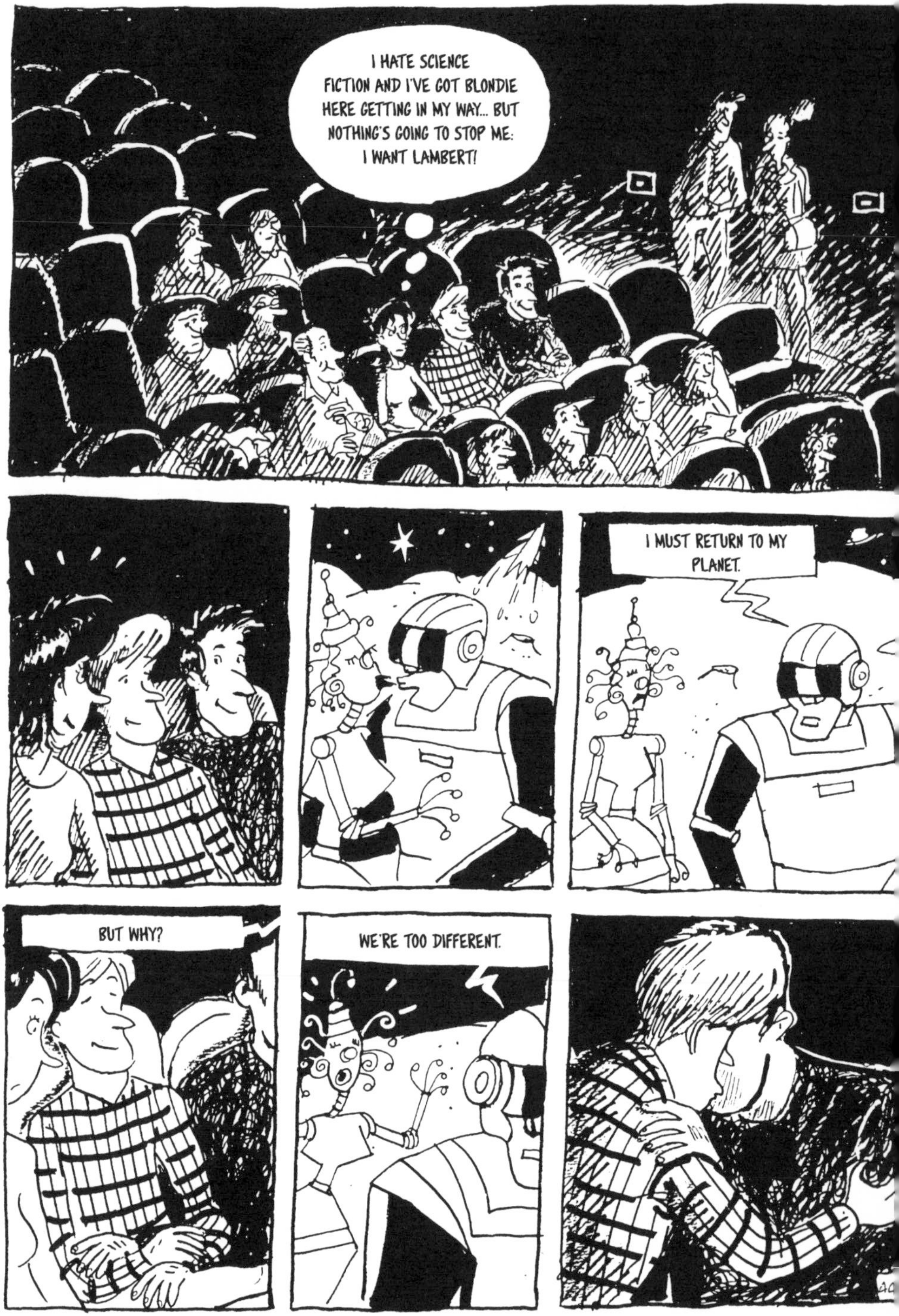
I HATE SCIENCE FICTION AND I'VE GOT BLONDIE HERE GETTING IN MY WAY... BUT NOTHING'S GOING TO STOP ME: I WANT LAMBERT!
I MUST RETURN TO MY PLANET.
BUT WHY?
WE'RE TOO DIFFERENT.

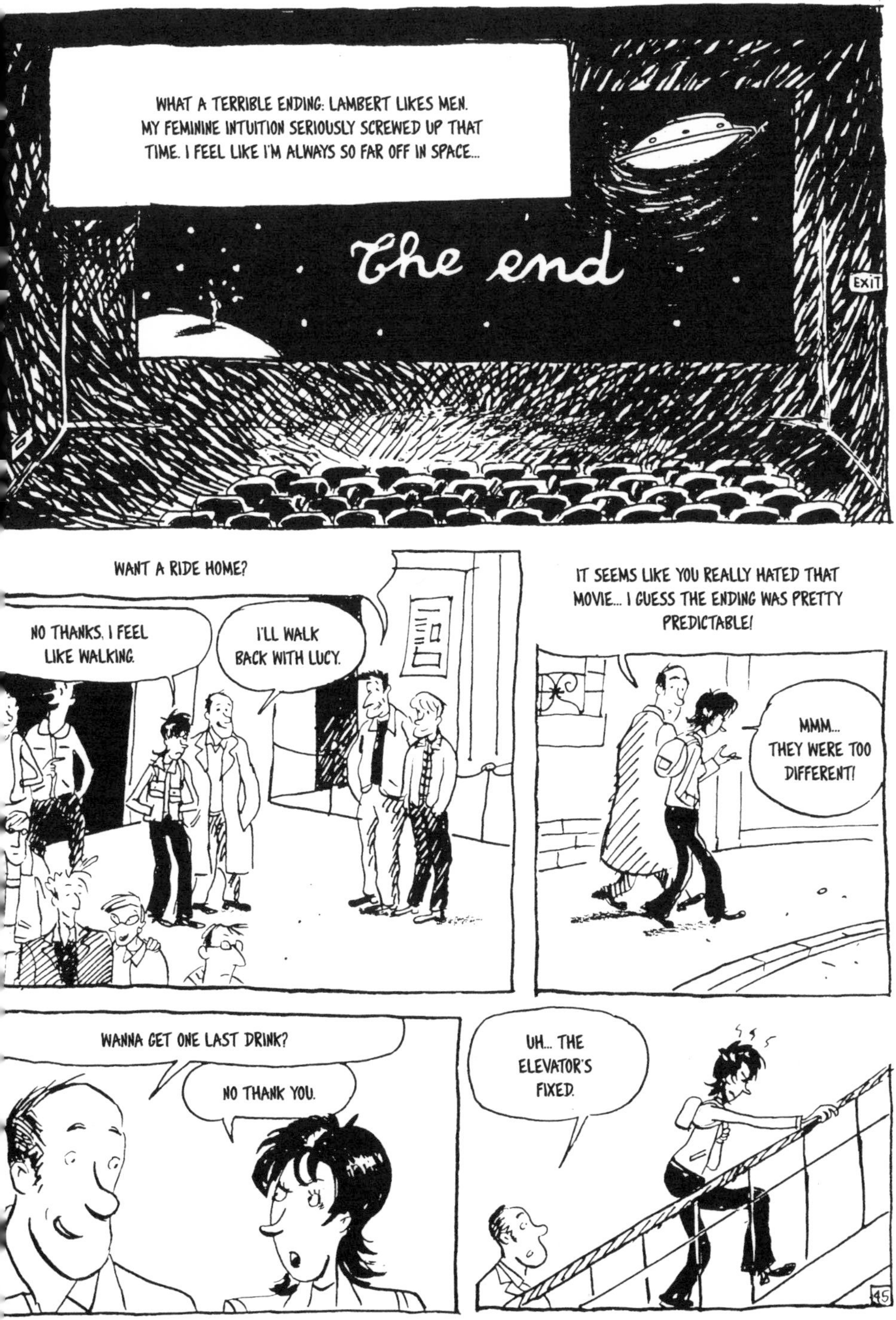
WHAT A TERRIBLE ENDING: LAMBERT LIKES MEN. MY FEMININE INTUITION SERIOUSLY SCREWED UP THAT TIME. I FEEL LIKE I'M ALWAYS SO FAR OFF IN SPACE...
The end
EXIT
WANT A RIDE HOME?
NO THANKS, I FEEL LIKE WALKING.
I'LL WALK BACK WITH LUCY.
IT SEEMS LIKE YOU REALLY HATED THAT MOVIE... I GUESS THE ENDING WAS PRETTY PREDICTABLE!
MMM... THEY WERE TOO DIFFERENT!
WANNA GET ONE LAST DRINK?
NO THANK YOU.
UH... THE ELEVATOR'S FIXED.
45

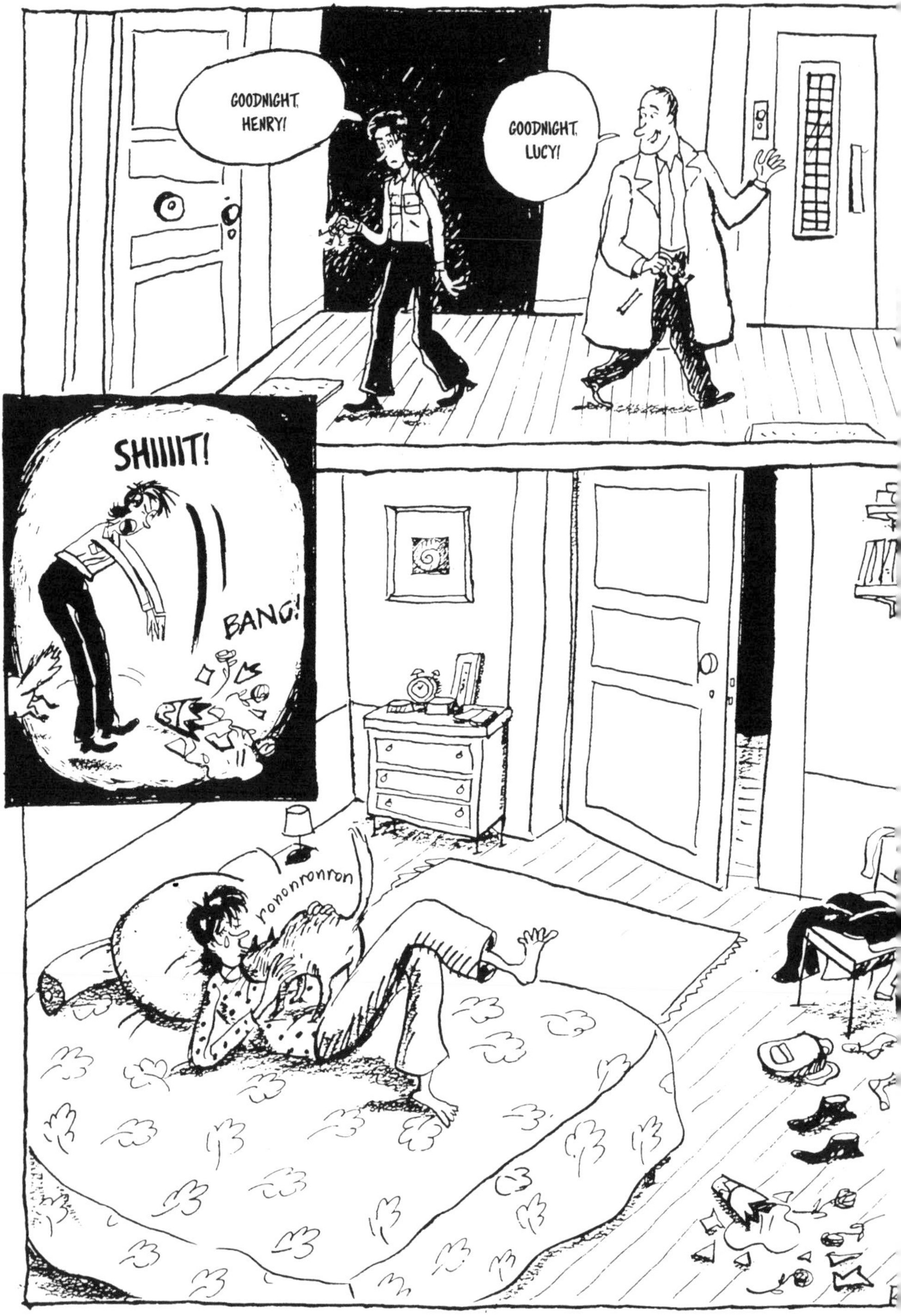
GOODNIGHT, HENRY!
GOODNIGHT, LUCY!
SHIIIIT!
BANG!
ronronronron

KNIGHT

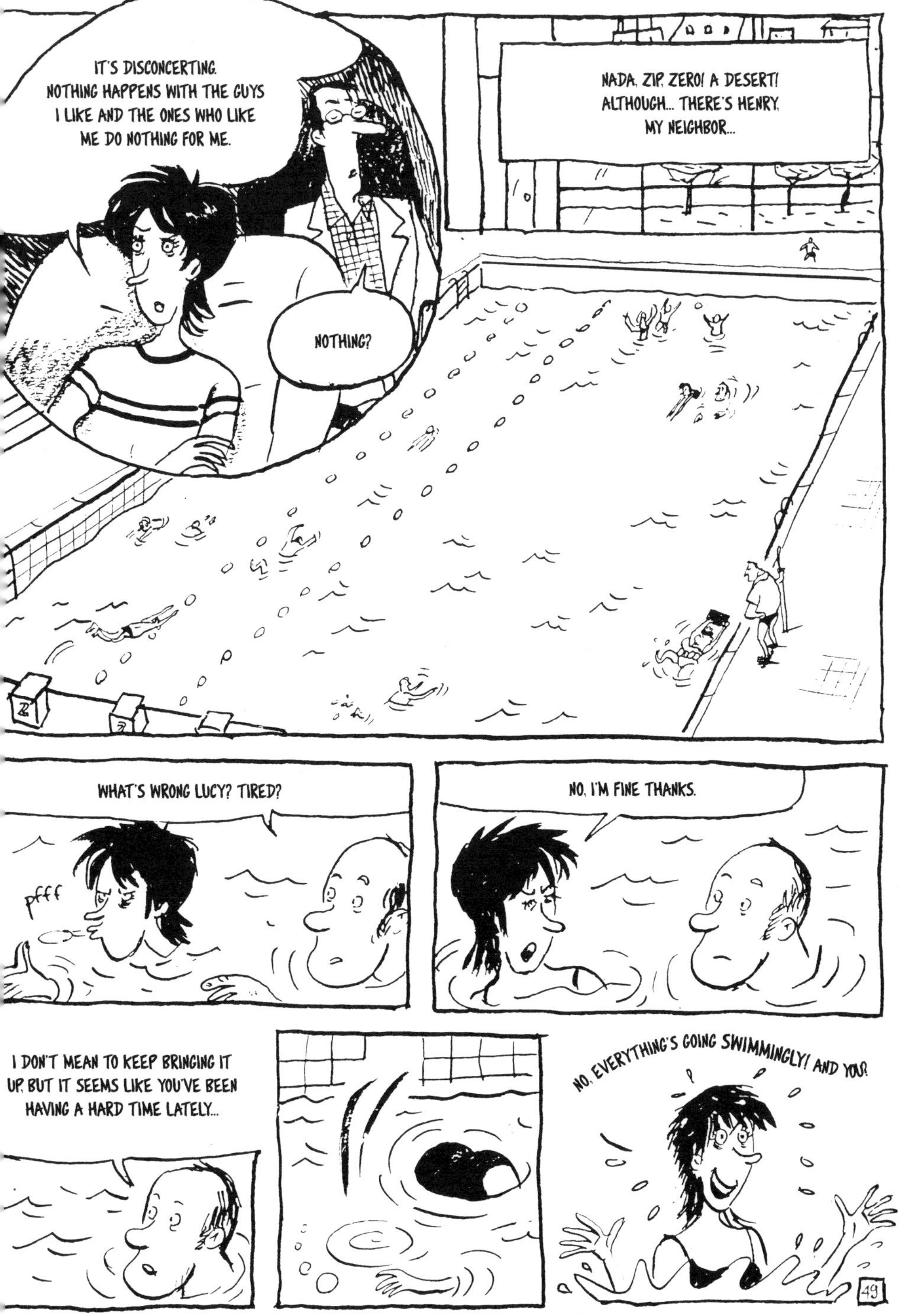
IT'S DISCONCERTING.
NOTHING HAPPENS WITH THE GUYS I LIKE AND THE ONES WHO LIKE ME DO NOTHING FOR ME.
NOTHING?
NADA, ZIP, ZERO! A DESERT! ALTHOUGH... THERE'S HENRY, MY NEIGHBOR...
WHAT'S WRONG LUCY? TIRED?
pfff
NO, I'M FINE THANKS.
I DON'T MEAN TO KEEP BRINGING IT UP, BUT IT SEEMS LIKE YOU'VE BEEN HAVING A HARD TIME LATELY...
NO, EVERYTHING'S GOING SWIMMINGLY! AND YOU?
49

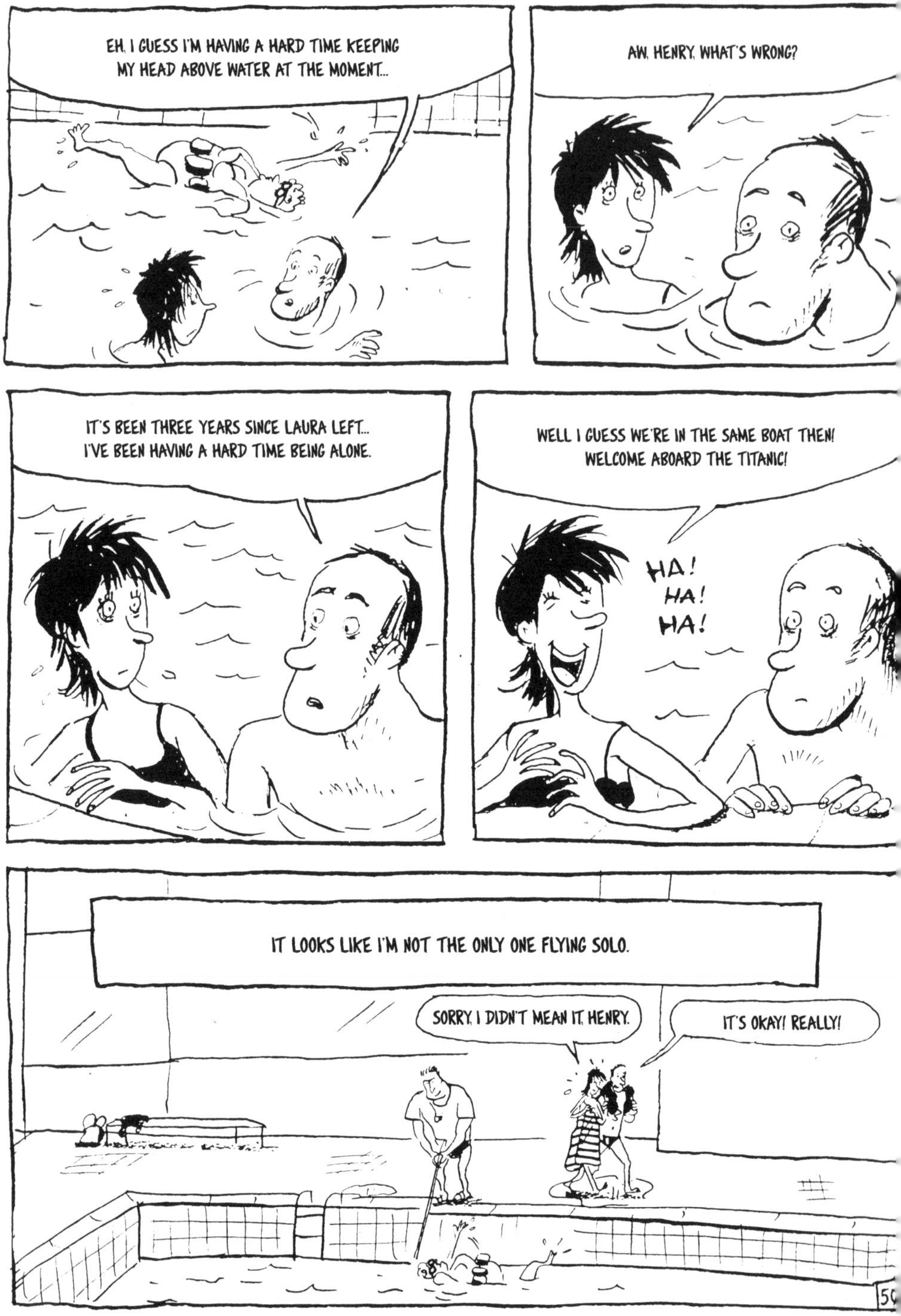
EH, I GUESS I'M HAVING A HARD TIME KEEPING MY HEAD ABOVE WATER AT THE MOMENT...
AW, HENRY, WHAT'S WRONG?
IT'S BEEN THREE YEARS SINCE LAURA LEFT... I'VE BEEN HAVING A HARD TIME BEING ALONE.
WELL I GUESS WE'RE IN THE SAME BOAT THEN! WELCOME ABOARD THE TITANIC!
HA! HA! HA!
IT LOOKS LIKE I'M NOT THE ONLY ONE FLYING SOLO.
SORRY, I DIDN'T MEAN IT, HENRY.
IT'S OKAY! REALLY!

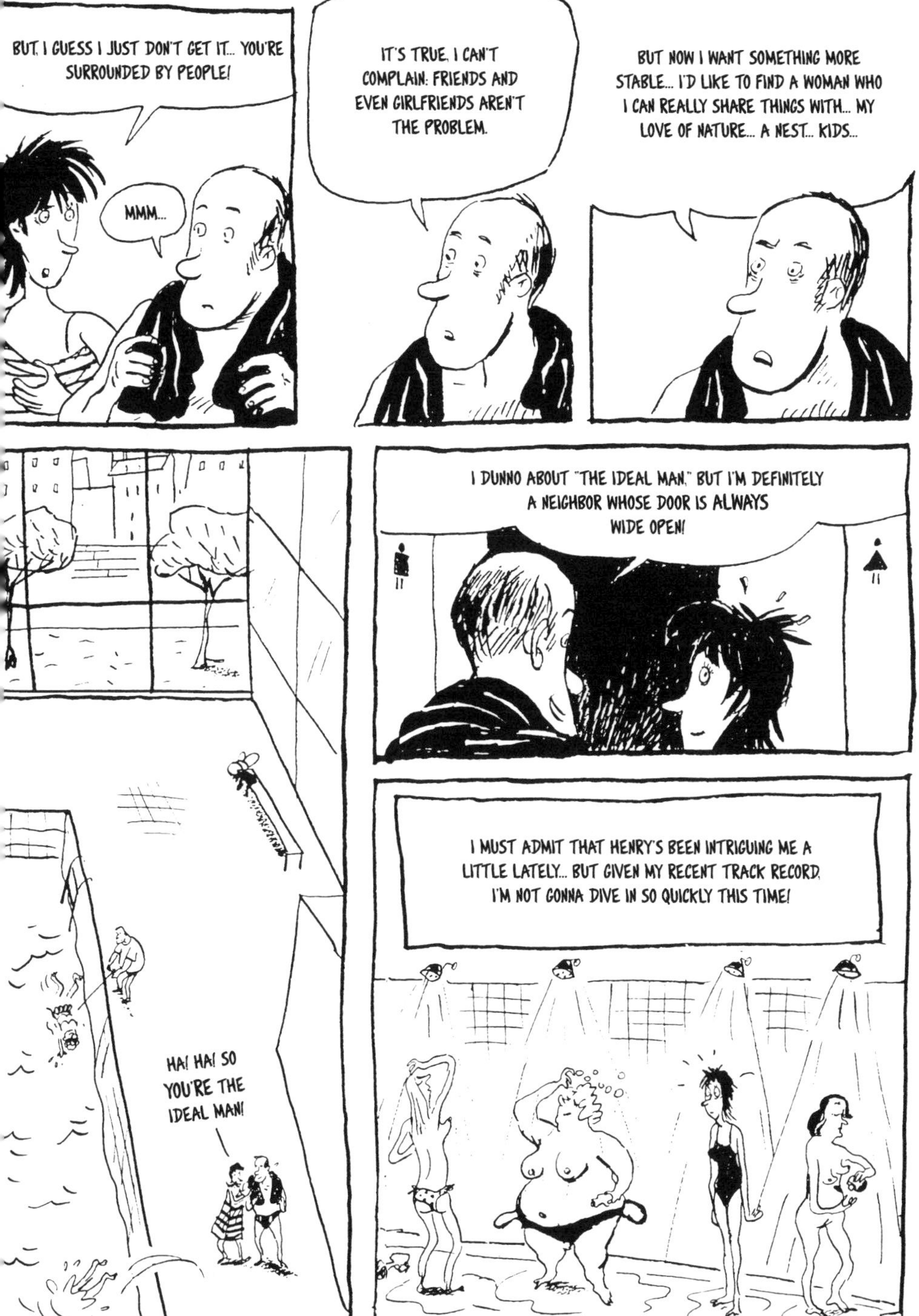
BUT, I GUESS I JUST DON'T GET IT... YOU'RE SURROUNDED BY PEOPLE!
MMM...
IT'S TRUE, I CAN'T COMPLAIN: FRIENDS AND EVEN GIRLFRIENDS AREN'T THE PROBLEM.
BUT NOW I WANT SOMETHING MORE STABLE... I'D LIKE TO FIND A WOMAN WHO I CAN REALLY SHARE THINGS WITH... MY LOVE OF NATURE... A NEST... KIDS...
HA! HA! SO YOU'RE THE IDEAL MAN!
I DUNNO ABOUT "THE IDEAL MAN," BUT I'M DEFINITELY A NEIGHBOR WHOSE DOOR IS ALWAYS WIDE OPEN!
I MUST ADMIT THAT HENRY'S BEEN INTRIGUING ME A LITTLE LATELY... BUT GIVEN MY RECENT TRACK RECORD, I'M NOT GONNA DIVE IN SO QUICKLY THIS TIME!
51

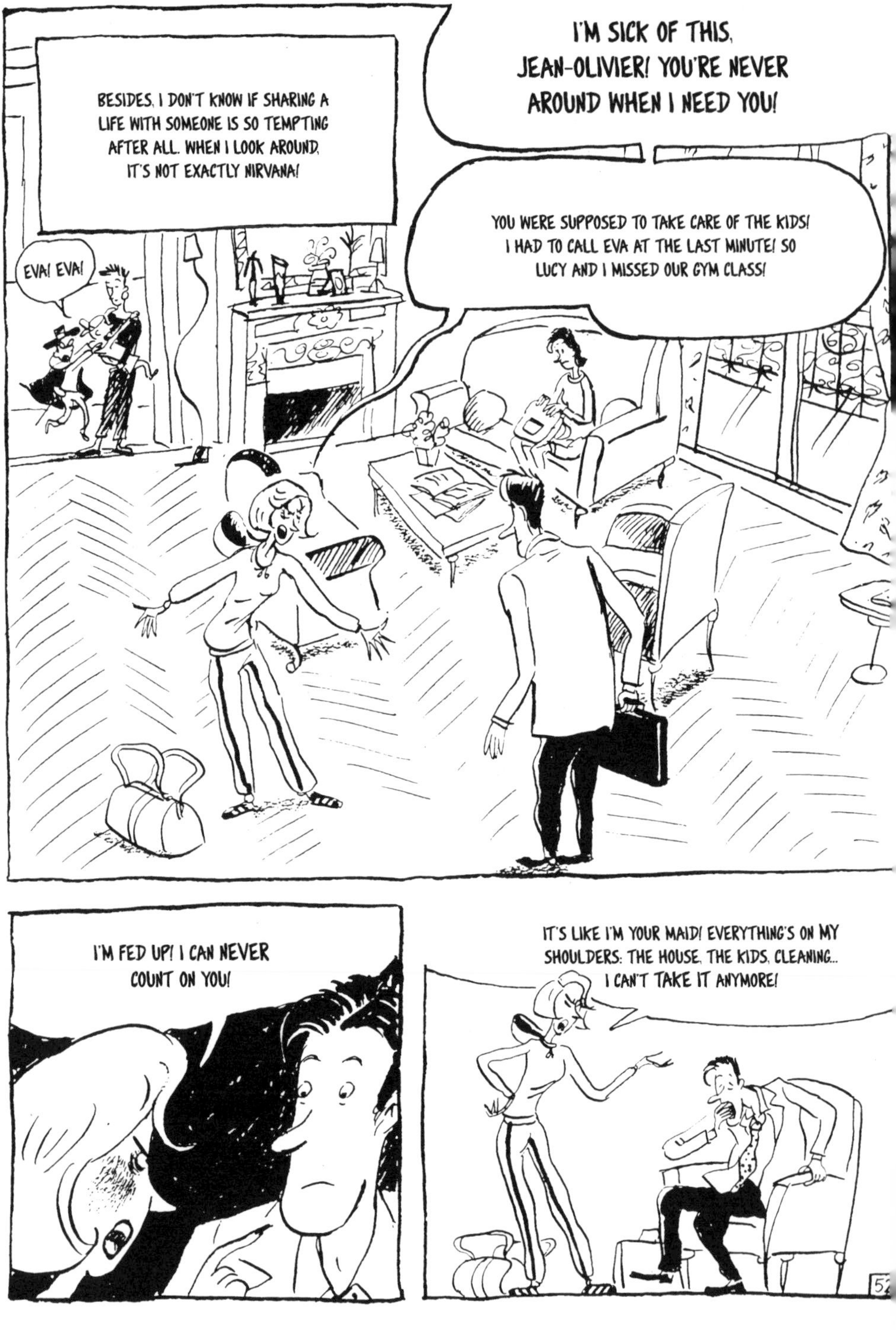
BESIDES, I DON'T KNOW IF SHARING A LIFE WITH SOMEONE IS SO TEMPTING AFTER ALL. WHEN I LOOK AROUND, IT'S NOT EXACTLY NIRVANA!
I'M SICK OF THIS, JEAN-OLIVIER! YOU'RE NEVER AROUND WHEN I NEED YOU!
EVA! EVA!
YOU WERE SUPPOSED TO TAKE CARE OF THE KIDS! I HAD TO CALL EVA AT THE LAST MINUTE! SO LUCY AND I MISSED OUR GYM CLASS!
I'M FED UP! I CAN NEVER COUNT ON YOU!
IT'S LIKE I'M YOUR MAID! EVERYTHING'S ON MY SHOULDERS: THE HOUSE, THE KIDS, CLEANING... I CAN'T TAKE IT ANYMORE!

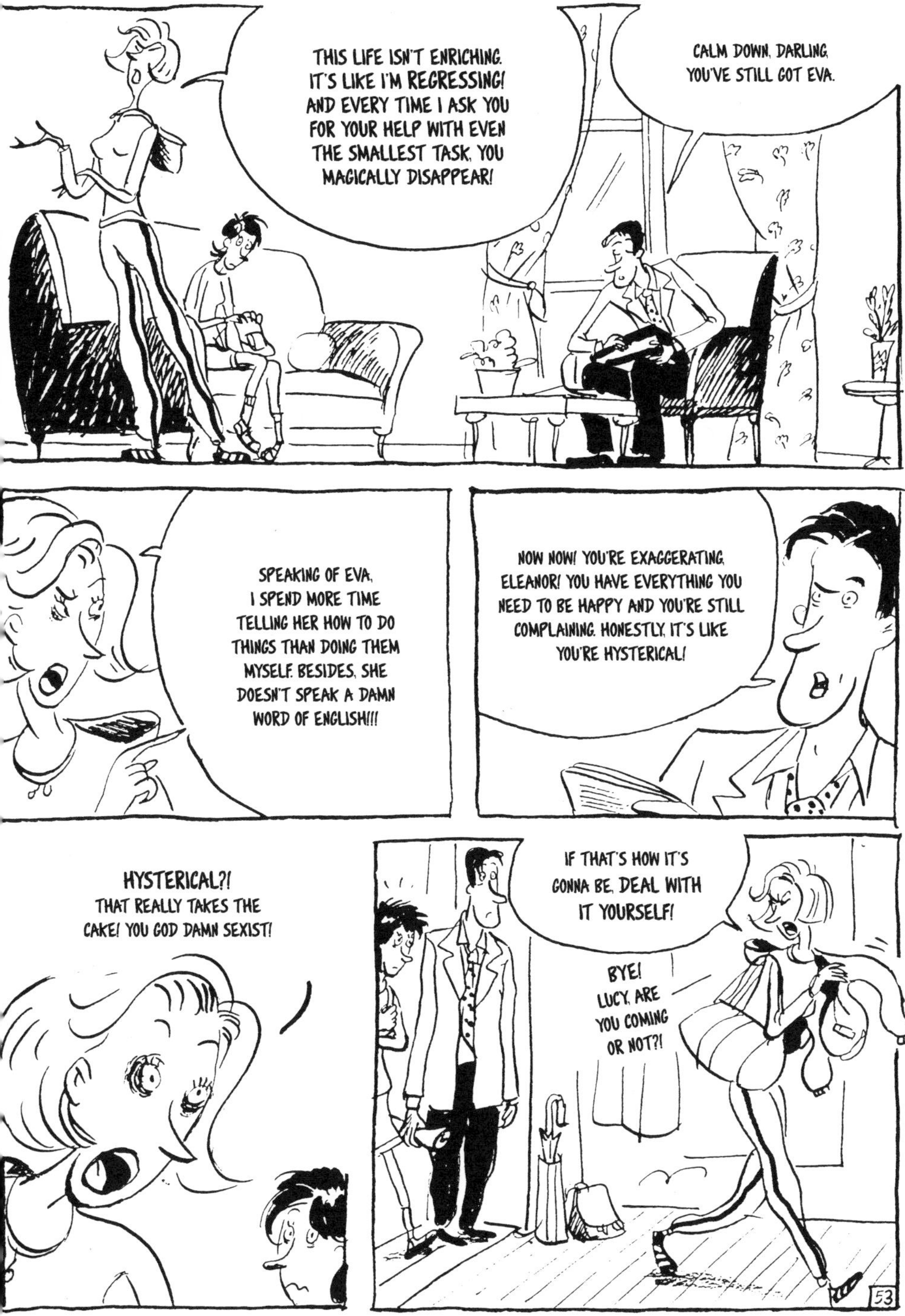
THIS LIFE ISN'T ENRICHING. IT'S LIKE I'M REGRESSING! AND EVERY TIME I ASK YOU FOR YOUR HELP WITH EVEN THE SMALLEST TASK, YOU MAGICALLY DISAPPEAR!
CALM DOWN, DARLING. YOU'VE STILL GOT EVA.
SPEAKING OF EVA, I SPEND MORE TIME TELLING HER HOW TO DO THINGS THAN DOING THEM MYSELF. BESIDES, SHE DOESN'T SPEAK A DAMN WORD OF ENGLISH!!!
NOW NOW! YOU'RE EXAGGERATING, ELEANOR! YOU HAVE EVERYTHING YOU NEED TO BE HAPPY AND YOU'RE STILL COMPLAINING. HONESTLY, IT'S LIKE YOU'RE HYSTERICAL!
HYSTERICAL?! THAT REALLY TAKES THE CAKE! YOU GOD DAMN SEXIST!
IF THAT'S HOW IT'S GONNA BE, DEAL WITH IT YOURSELF!
BYE! LUCY, ARE YOU COMING OR NOT?!
53

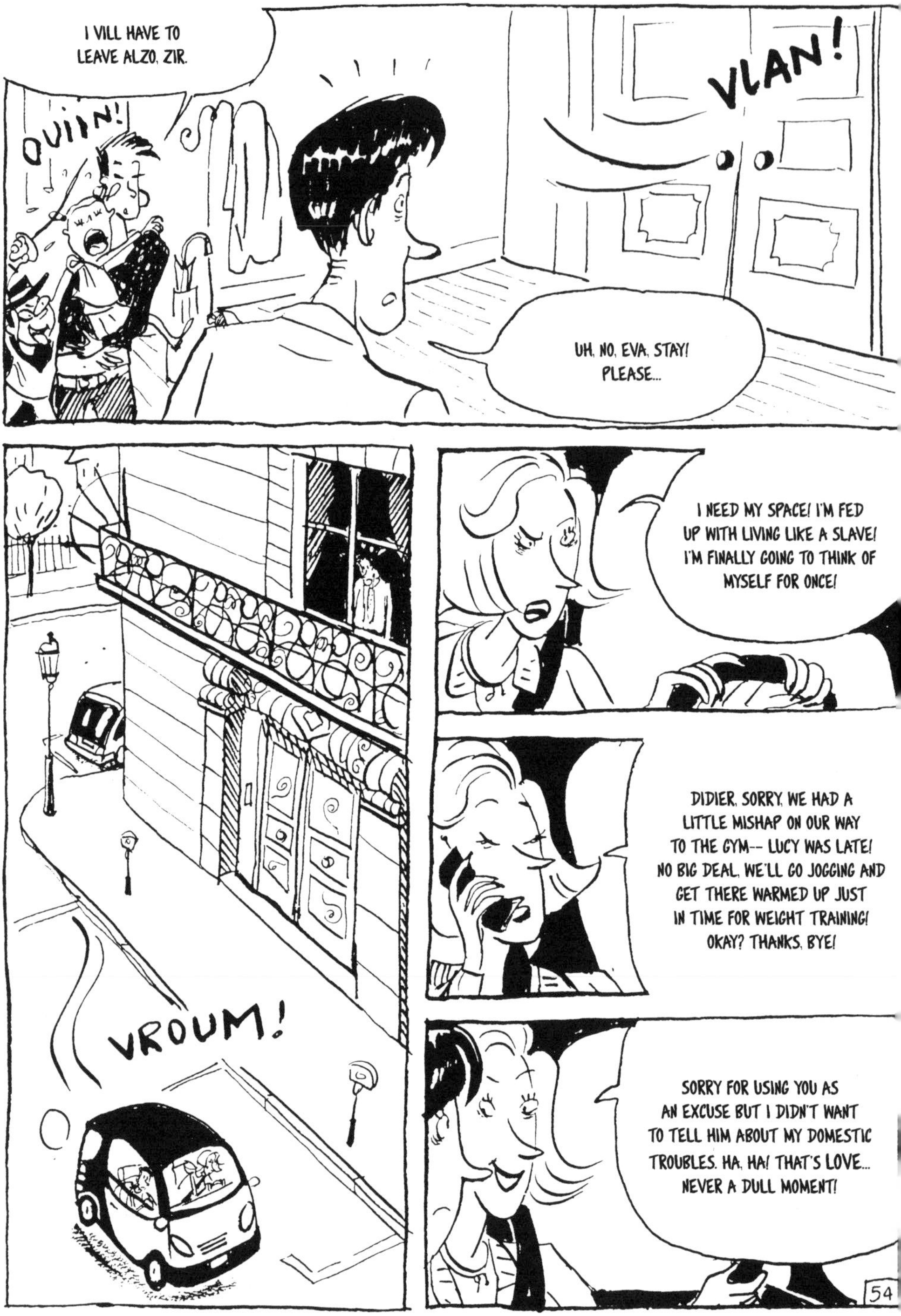
I VILL HAVE TO LEAVE ALZO, ZIR.
OUIIN!
VLAN!
UH, NO, EVA, STAY! PLEASE...
I NEED MY SPACE! I'M FED UP WITH LIVING LIKE A SLAVE! I'M FINALLY GOING TO THINK OF MYSELF FOR ONCE!
DIDIER, SORRY, WE HAD A LITTLE MISHAP ON OUR WAY TO THE GYM-- LUCY WAS LATE! NO BIG DEAL, WE'LL GO JOGGING AND GET THERE WARMED UP JUST IN TIME FOR WEIGHT TRAINING! OKAY? THANKS, BYE!
VROUM!
SORRY FOR USING YOU AS AN EXCUSE BUT I DIDN'T WANT TO TELL HIM ABOUT MY DOMESTIC TROUBLES. HA, HA! THAT'S LOVE... NEVER A DULL MOMENT!
54

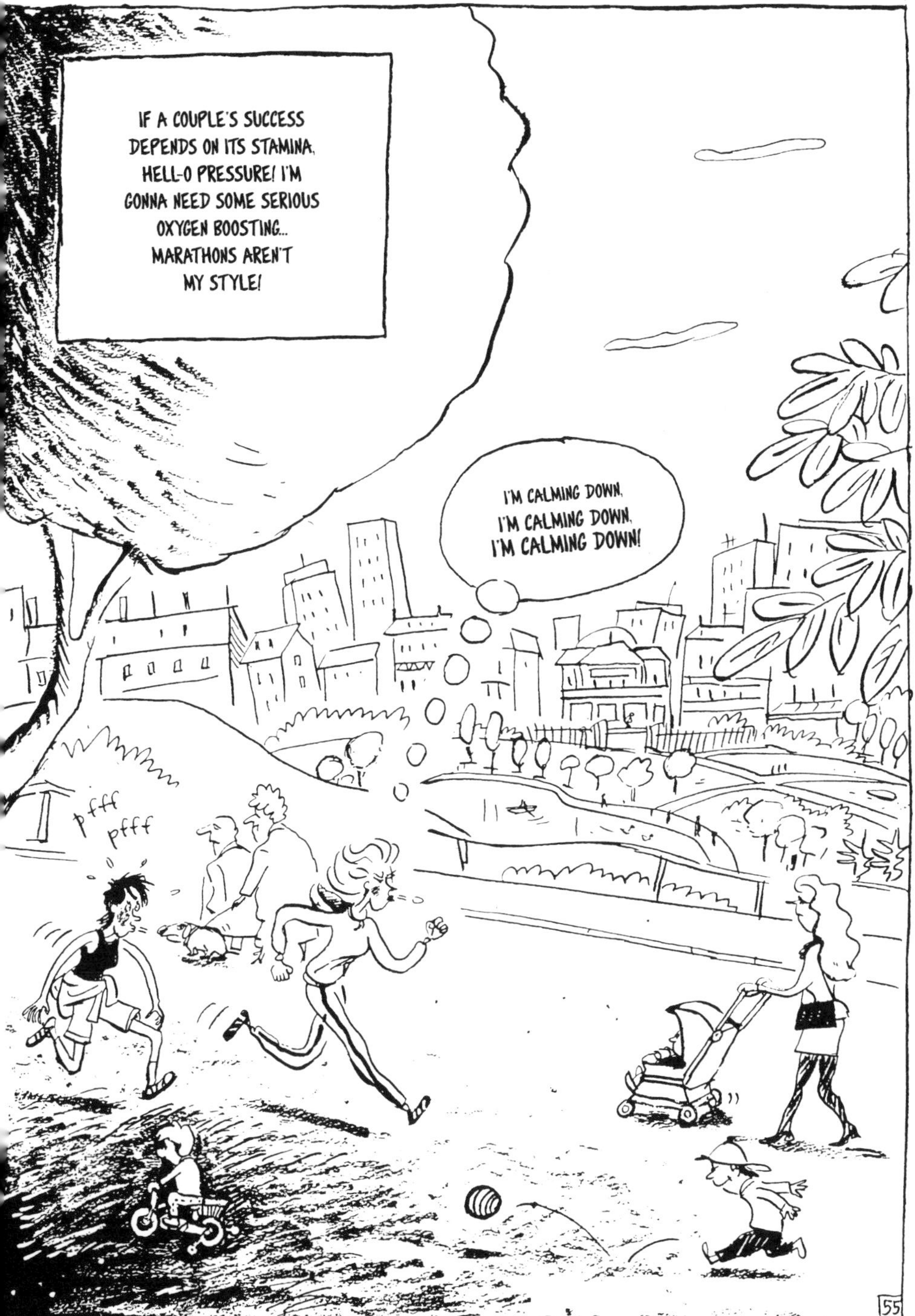
IF A COUPLE'S SUCCESS DEPENDS ON ITS STAMINA, HELL-O PRESSURE! I'M GONNA NEED SOME SERIOUS OXYGEN BOOSTING... MARATHONS AREN'T MY STYLE!
I'M CALMING DOWN, I'M CALMING DOWN, I'M CALMING DOWN!
pfff pfff
55

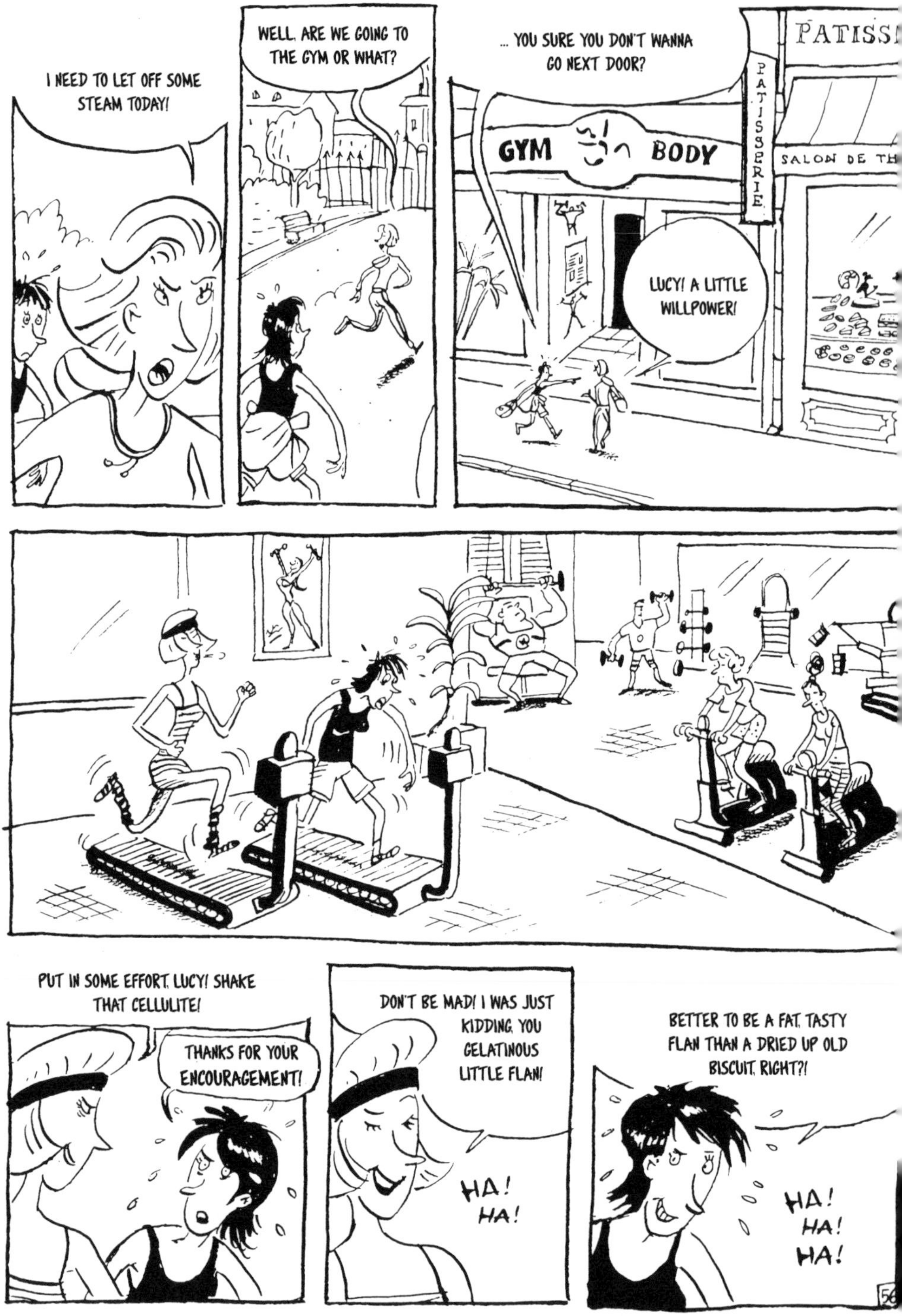
I NEED TO LET OFF SOME STEAM TODAY!
WELL, ARE WE GOING TO THE GYM OR WHAT?
... YOU SURE YOU DON'T WANNA GO NEXT DOOR?
PATISS
GYM BODY
PATISSERIE
SALON DE TH
LUCY! A LITTLE WILLPOWER!
PUT IN SOME EFFORT, LUCY! SHAKE THAT CELLULITE!
THANKS FOR YOUR ENCOURAGEMENT!
DON'T BE MAD! I WAS JUST KIDDING, YOU GELATINOUS LITTLE FLAN!
HA! HA!
BETTER TO BE A FAT, TASTY FLAN THAN A DRIED UP OLD BISCUIT, RIGHT?!
HA! HA! HA!

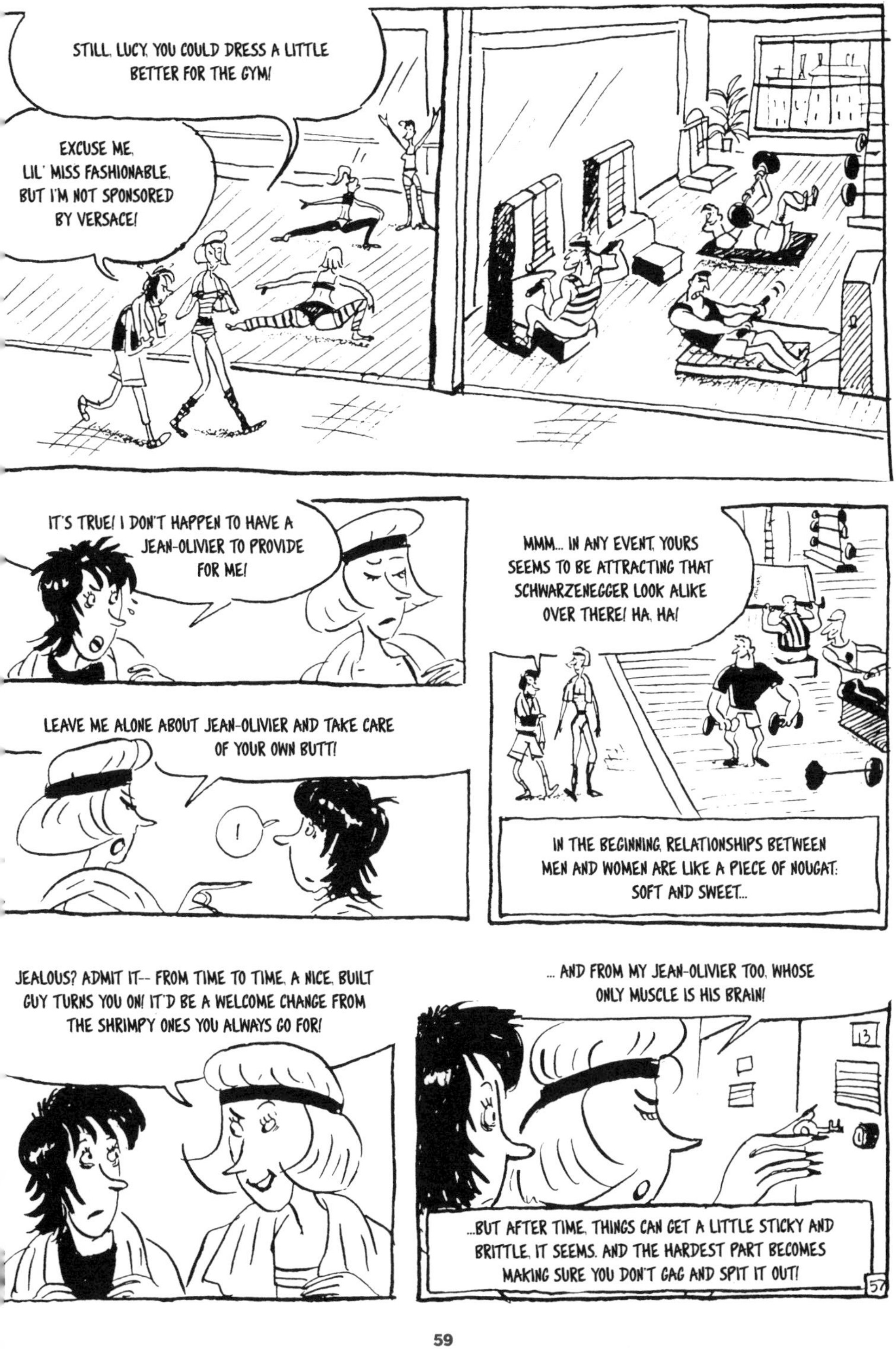
STILL, LUCY, YOU COULD DRESS A LITTLE BETTER FOR THE GYM!
EXCUSE ME, LIL' MISS FASHIONABLE, BUT I'M NOT SPONSORED BY VERSACE!
IT'S TRUE! I DON'T HAPPEN TO HAVE A JEAN-OLIVIER TO PROVIDE FOR ME!
LEAVE ME ALONE ABOUT JEAN-OLIVIER AND TAKE CARE OF YOUR OWN BUTT!
!
MMM... IN ANY EVENT, YOURS SEEMS TO BE ATTRACTING THAT SCHWARZENEGGER LOOK ALIKE OVER THERE! HA, HA!
IN THE BEGINNING, RELATIONSHIPS BETWEEN MEN AND WOMEN ARE LIKE A PIECE OF NOUGAT: SOFT AND SWEET...
JEALOUS? ADMIT IT-- FROM TIME TO TIME, A NICE, BUILT GUY TURNS YOU ON! IT'D BE A WELCOME CHANGE FROM THE SHRIMPY ONES YOU ALWAYS GO FOR!
... AND FROM MY JEAN-OLIVIER TOO, WHOSE ONLY MUSCLE IS HIS BRAIN!
13
...BUT AFTER TIME, THINGS CAN GET A LITTLE STICKY AND BRITTLE, IT SEEMS. AND THE HARDEST PART BECOMES MAKING SURE YOU DON'T GAG AND SPIT IT OUT!
57

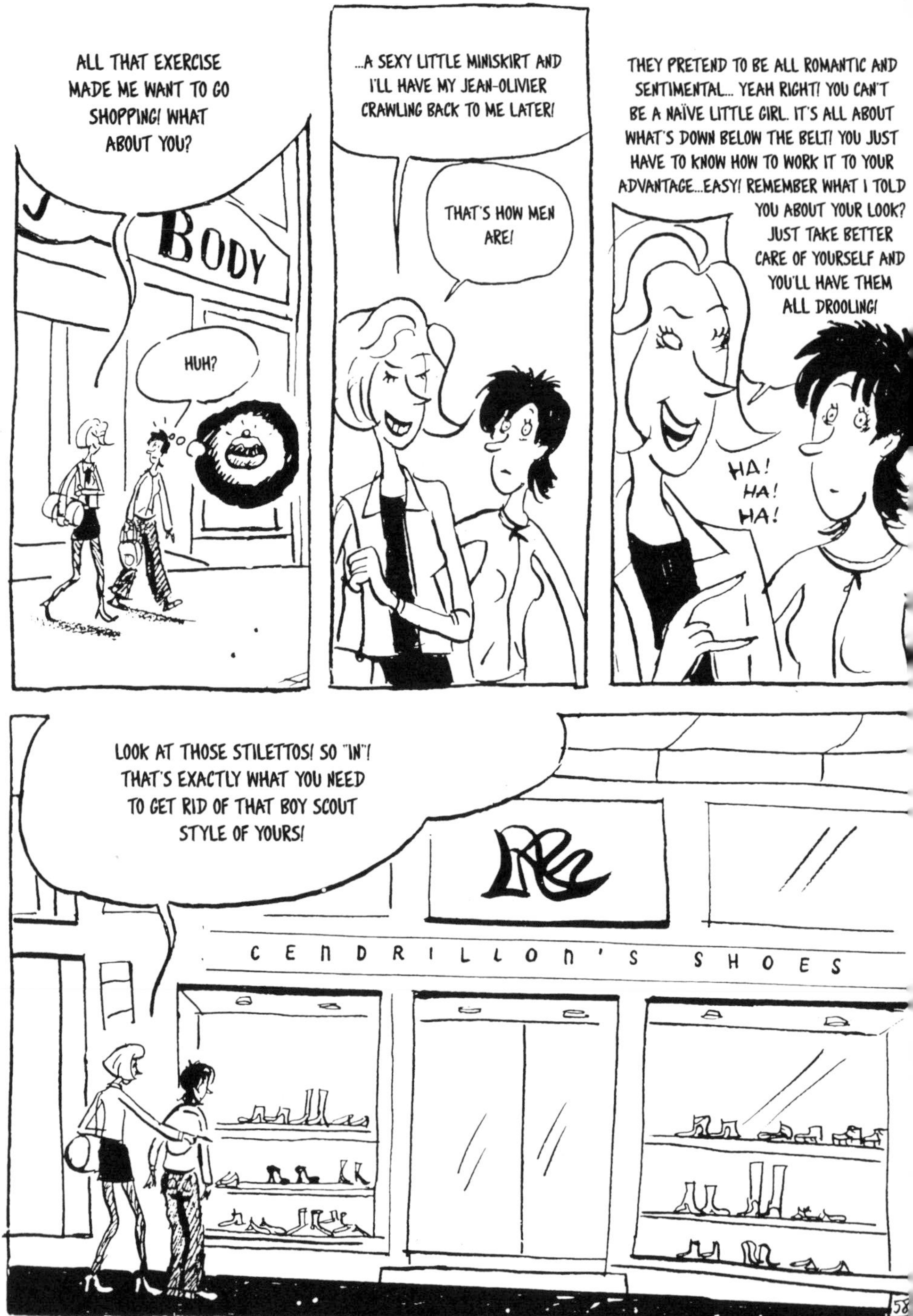

ALL THAT EXERCISE MADE ME WANT TO GO SHOPPING! WHAT ABOUT YOU?
BODY
HUH?
...A SEXY LITTLE MINISKIRT AND I'LL HAVE MY JEAN-OLIVIER CRAWLING BACK TO ME LATER!
THAT'S HOW MEN ARE!
THEY PRETEND TO BE ALL ROMANTIC AND SENTIMENTAL... YEAH RIGHT! YOU CAN'T BE A NAÏVE LITTLE GIRL. IT'S ALL ABOUT WHAT'S DOWN BELOW THE BELT! YOU JUST HAVE TO KNOW HOW TO WORK IT TO YOUR ADVANTAGE...EASY! REMEMBER WHAT I TOLD YOU ABOUT YOUR LOOK? JUST TAKE BETTER CARE OF YOURSELF AND YOU'LL HAVE THEM ALL DROOLING!
HA! HA! HA!
LOOK AT THOSE STILETTOS! SO "IN"! THAT'S EXACTLY WHAT YOU NEED TO GET RID OF THAT BOY SCOUT STYLE OF YOURS!
CENDRILLON'S SHOES
58

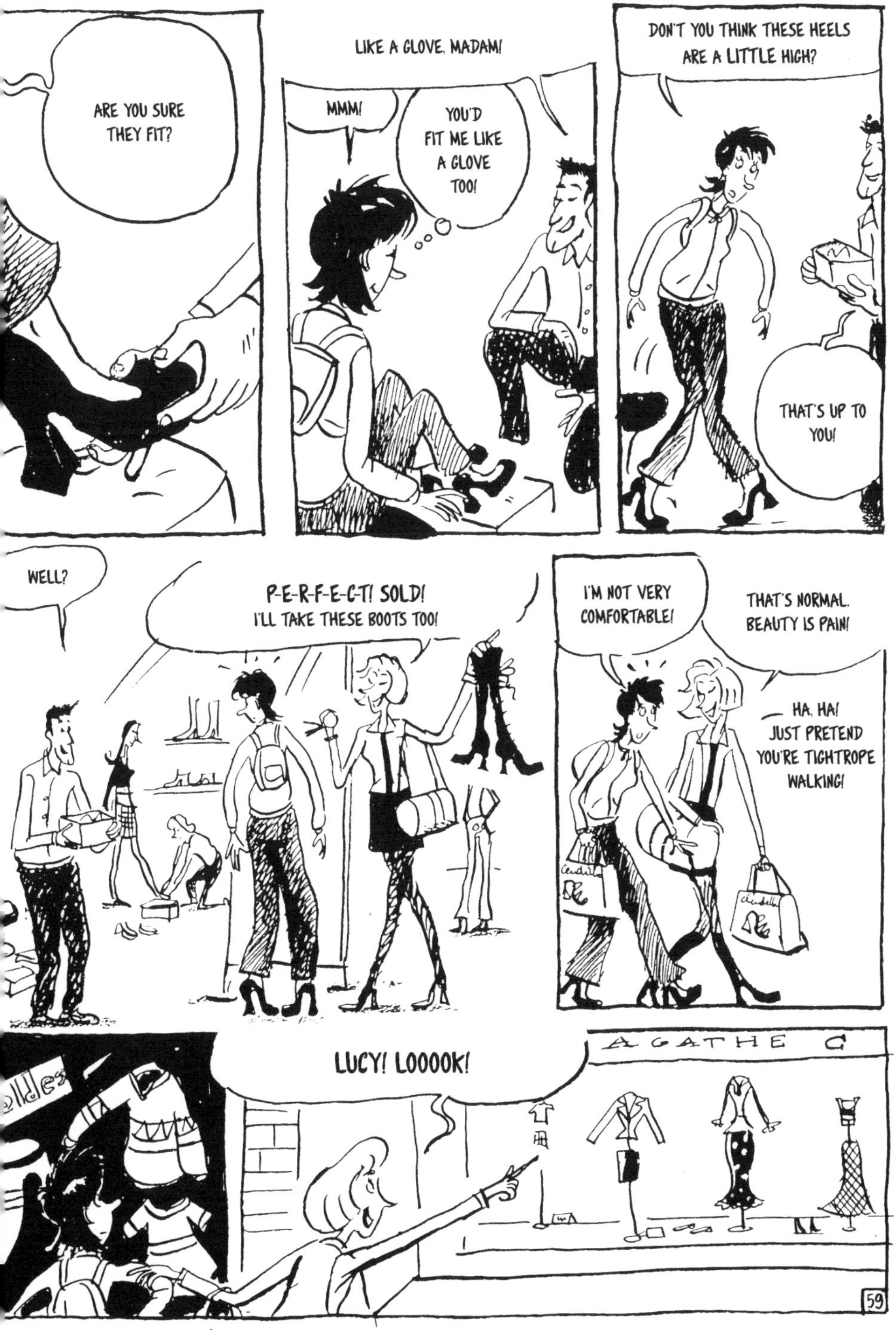
ARE YOU SURE THEY FIT?
LIKE A GLOVE, MADAM!
MMM!
YOU'D FIT ME LIKE A GLOVE TOO!
DON'T YOU THINK THESE HEELS ARE A LITTLE HIGH?
THAT'S UP TO YOU!
WELL?
P-E-R-F-E-C-T! SOLD! I'LL TAKE THESE BOOTS TOO!
I'M NOT VERY COMFORTABLE!
THAT'S NORMAL. BEAUTY IS PAIN!
HA, HA! JUST PRETEND YOU'RE TIGHTROPE WALKING!
LUCY! LOOOOK!
AGATHE C
59

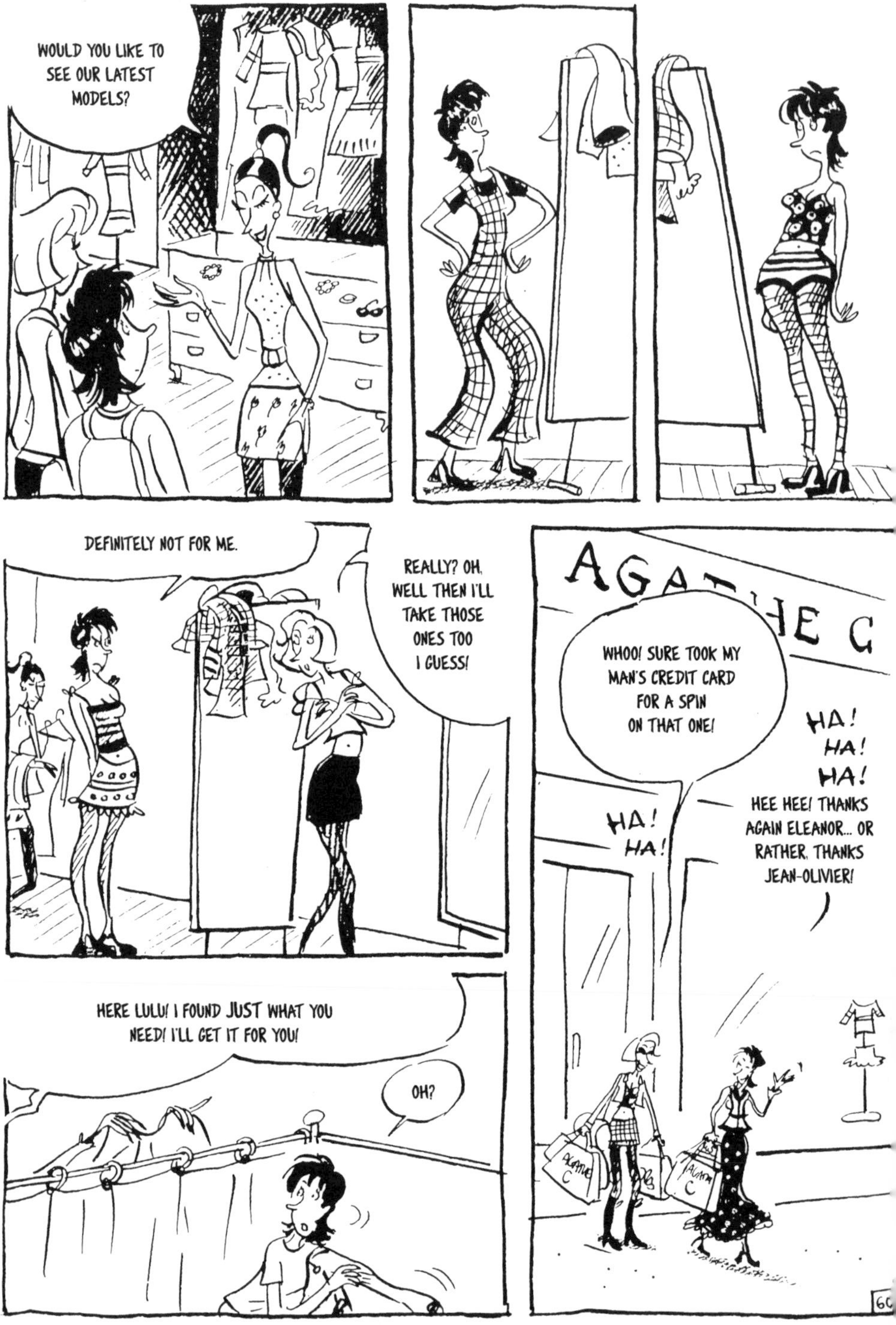

WOULD YOU LIKE TO SEE OUR LATEST MODELS?
DEFINITELY NOT FOR ME.
REALLY? OH, WELL THEN I'LL TAKE THOSE ONES TOO I GUESS!
HERE LULU! I FOUND JUST WHAT YOU NEED! I'LL GET IT FOR YOU!
OH?
AGA HE C
WHOO! SURE TOOK MY MAN'S CREDIT CARD FOR A SPIN ON THAT ONE!
HA! HA! HA!
HA! HA!
HEE HEE! THANKS AGAIN ELEANOR... OR RATHER, THANKS JEAN-OLIVIER!

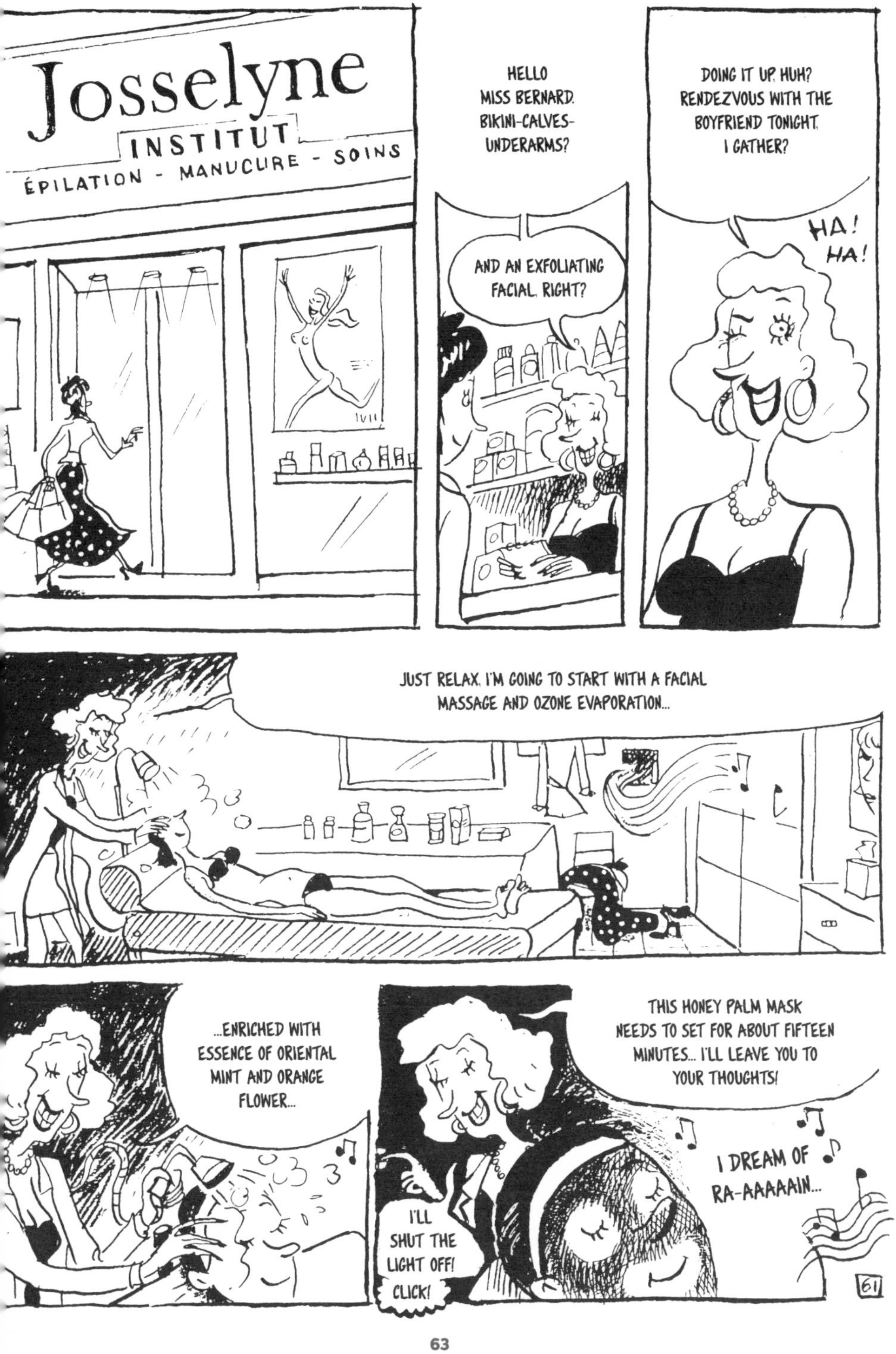
Josselyne
INSTITUT
ÉPILATION - MANUCURE - SOINS
HELLO MISS BERNARD. BIKINI-CALVES-UNDERARMS?
AND AN EXFOLIATING FACIAL, RIGHT?
DOING IT UP, HUH? RENDEZVOUS WITH THE BOYFRIEND TONIGHT, I GATHER?
HA! HA!
JUST RELAX, I'M GOING TO START WITH A FACIAL MASSAGE AND OZONE EVAPORATION...
...ENRICHED WITH ESSENCE OF ORIENTAL MINT AND ORANGE FLOWER...
THIS HONEY PALM MASK NEEDS TO SET FOR ABOUT FIFTEEN MINUTES... I'LL LEAVE YOU TO YOUR THOUGHTS!
I'LL SHUT THE LIGHT OFF!
CLICK!
I DREAM OF RA-AAAAAIN...
61

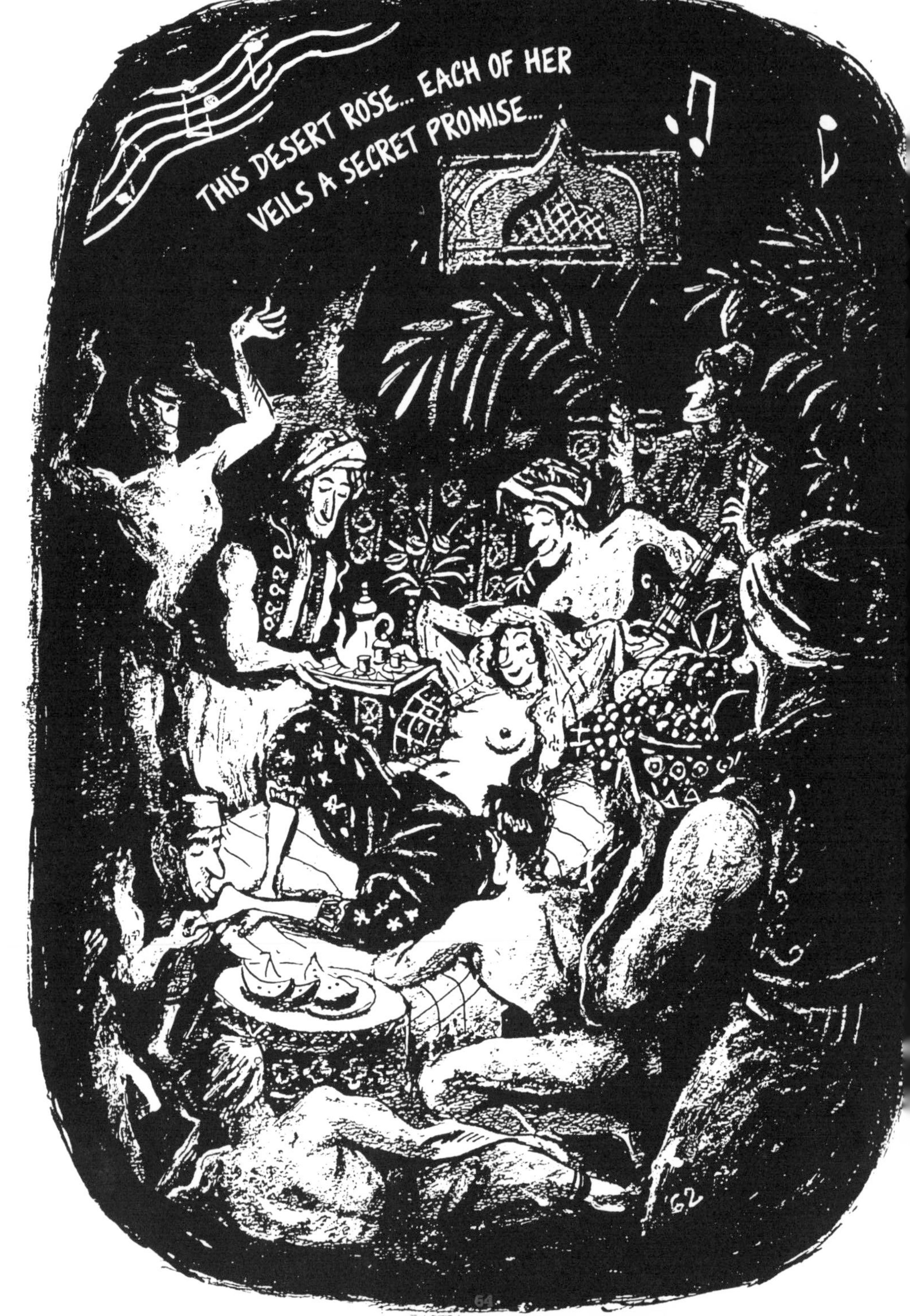
THIS DESERT ROSE... EACH OF HER
VEILS A SECRET PROMISE...
62

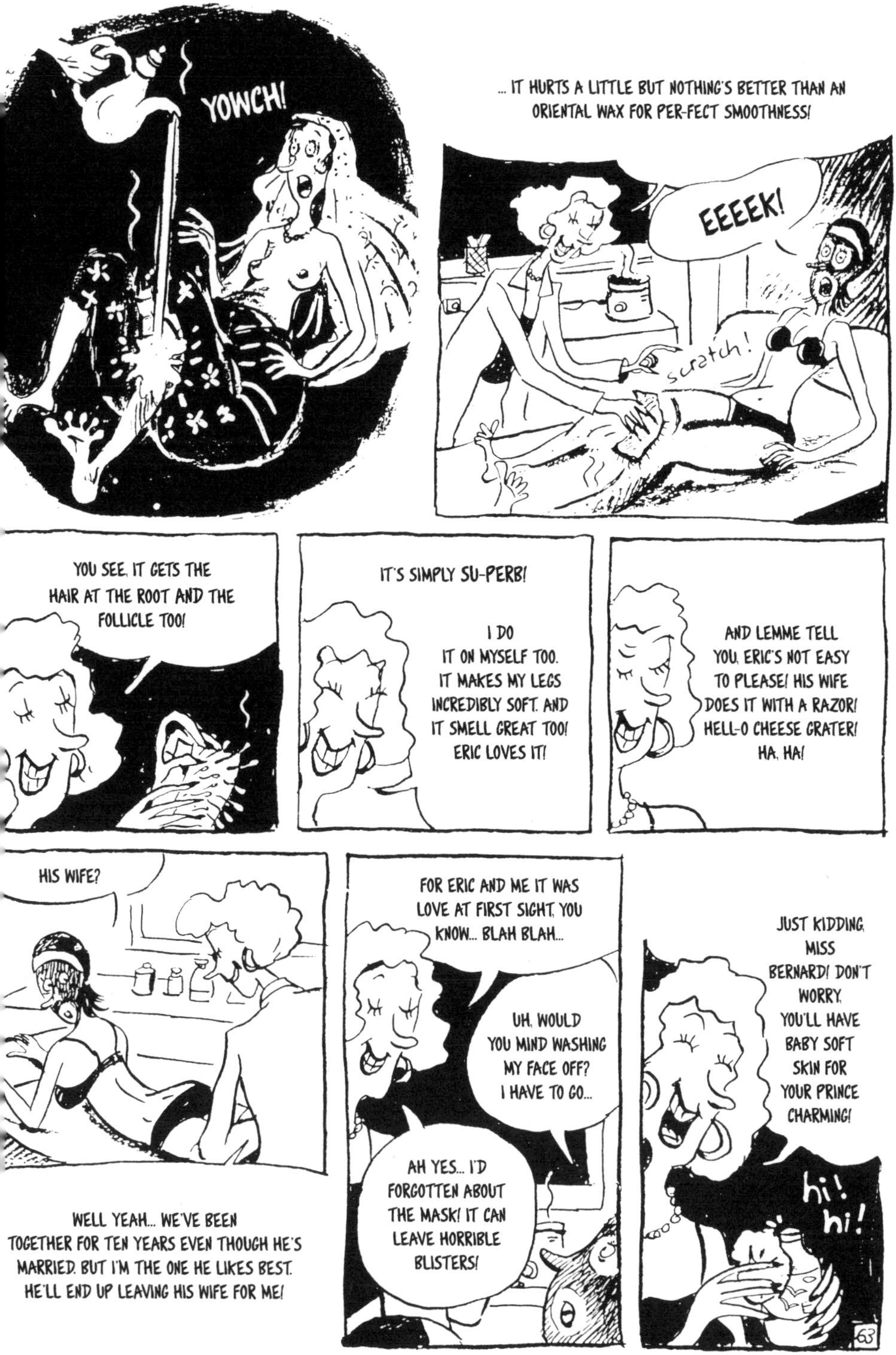
YOWCH!
... IT HURTS A LITTLE BUT NOTHING'S BETTER THAN AN ORIENTAL WAX FOR PER-FECT SMOOTHNESS!
EEEEK!
scratch!
YOU SEE, IT GETS THE HAIR AT THE ROOT AND THE FOLLICLE TOO!
IT'S SIMPLY SU-PERB!
I DO IT ON MYSELF TOO. IT MAKES MY LEGS INCREDIBLY SOFT. AND IT SMELL GREAT TOO! ERIC LOVES IT!
AND LEMME TELL YOU, ERIC'S NOT EASY TO PLEASE! HIS WIFE DOES IT WITH A RAZOR! HELL-O CHEESE GRATER! HA, HA!
HIS WIFE?
WELL YEAH... WE'VE BEEN TOGETHER FOR TEN YEARS EVEN THOUGH HE'S MARRIED. BUT I'M THE ONE HE LIKES BEST. HE'LL END UP LEAVING HIS WIFE FOR ME!
FOR ERIC AND ME IT WAS LOVE AT FIRST SIGHT, YOU KNOW... BLAH BLAH...
UH, WOULD YOU MIND WASHING MY FACE OFF? I HAVE TO GO...
AH YES... I'D FORGOTTEN ABOUT THE MASK! IT CAN LEAVE HORRIBLE BLISTERS!
JUST KIDDING, MISS BERNARD! DON'T WORRY, YOU'LL HAVE BABY SOFT SKIN FOR YOUR PRINCE CHARMING!
hi! hi!
63

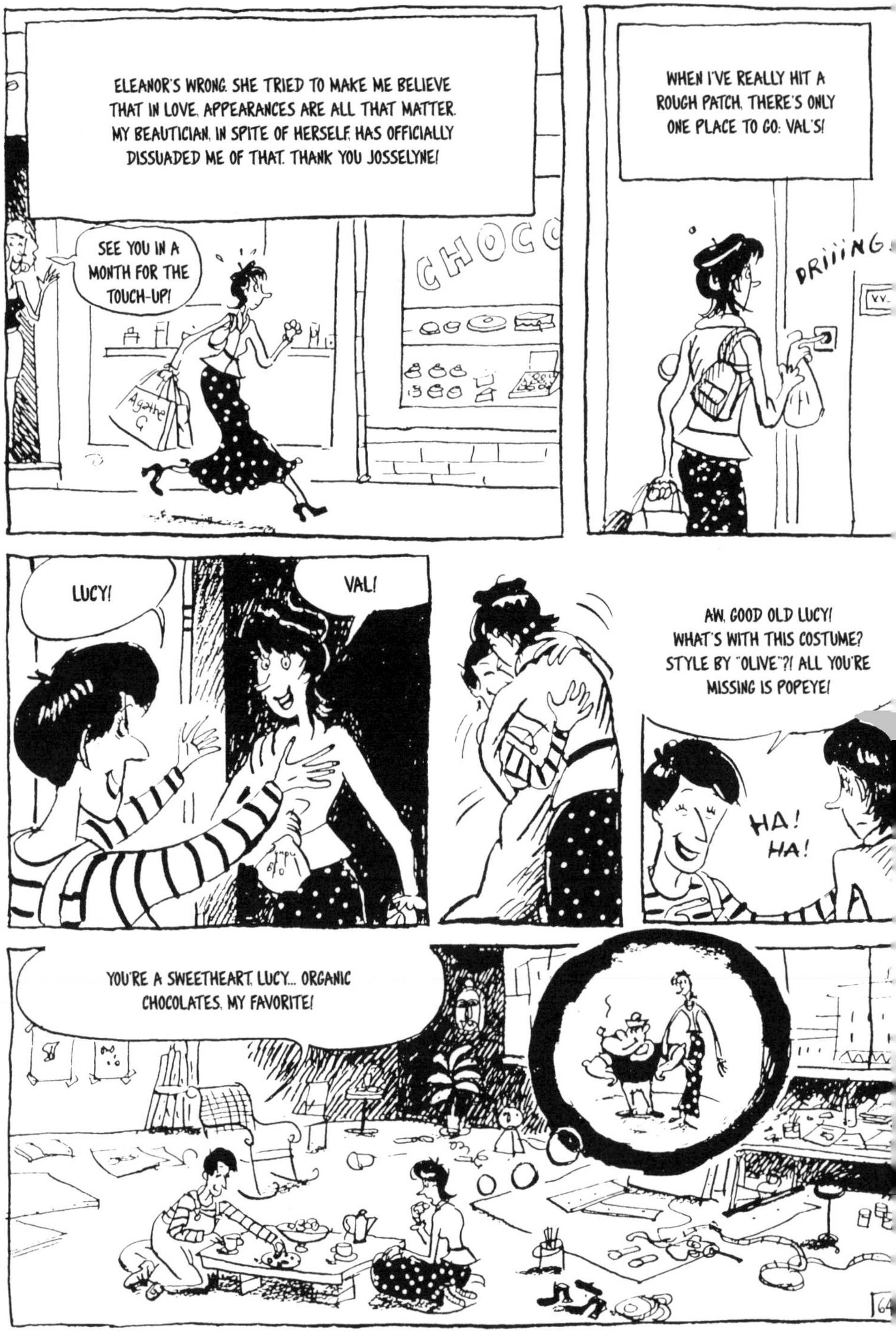
ELEANOR'S WRONG. SHE TRIED TO MAKE ME BELIEVE THAT IN LOVE, APPEARANCES ARE ALL THAT MATTER. MY BEAUTICIAN, IN SPITE OF HERSELF, HAS OFFICIALLY DISSUADED ME OF THAT. THANK YOU JOSSELYNE!
SEE YOU IN A MONTH FOR THE TOUCH-UP!
CHOCO
Agathe G
WHEN I'VE REALLY HIT A ROUGH PATCH, THERE'S ONLY ONE PLACE TO GO: VAL'S!
DRIIING
LUCY!
VAL!
AW, GOOD OLD LUCY! WHAT'S WITH THIS COSTUME? STYLE BY "OLIVE"?! ALL YOU'RE MISSING IS POPEYE!
HA! HA!
YOU'RE A SWEETHEART, LUCY... ORGANIC CHOCOLATES, MY FAVORITE!
64

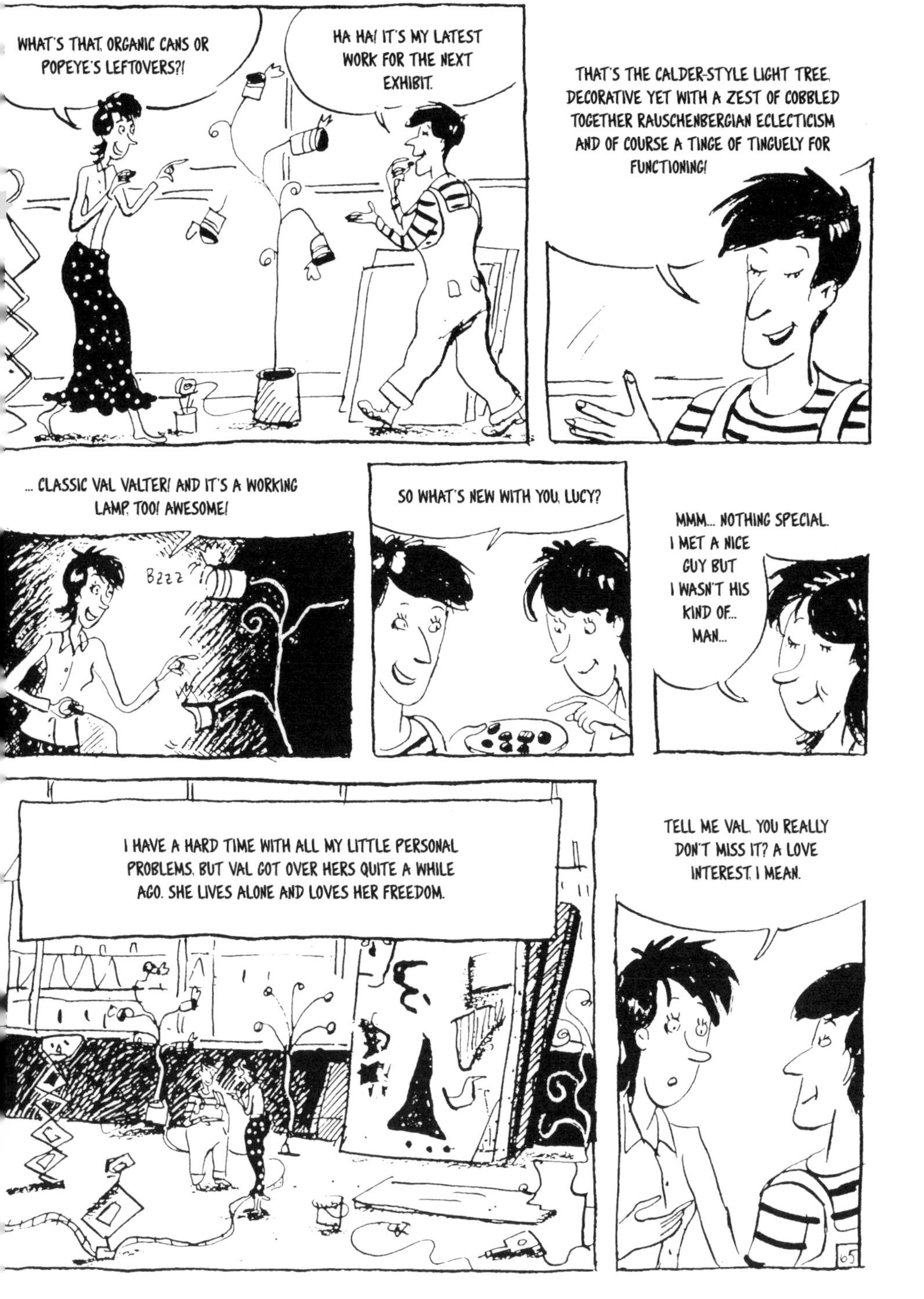
WHAT'S THAT, ORGANIC CANS OR POPEYE'S LEFTOVERS?!
HA HA! IT'S MY LATEST WORK FOR THE NEXT EXHIBIT.
THAT'S THE CALDER-STYLE LIGHT TREE, DECORATIVE YET WITH A ZEST OF COBBLED TOGETHER RAUSCHENBERGIAN ECLECTICISM AND OF COURSE A TINGE OF TINGUELY FOR FUNCTIONING!
... CLASSIC VAL VALTER! AND IT'S A WORKING LAMP, TOO! AWESOME!
BZZZ
SO WHAT'S NEW WITH YOU, LUCY?
MMM... NOTHING SPECIAL. I MET A NICE GUY BUT I WASN'T HIS KIND OF... MAN...
I HAVE A HARD TIME WITH ALL MY LITTLE PERSONAL PROBLEMS, BUT VAL GOT OVER HERS QUITE A WHILE AGO. SHE LIVES ALONE AND LOVES HER FREEDOM.
TELL ME VAL, YOU REALLY DON'T MISS IT? A LOVE INTEREST, I MEAN.
65

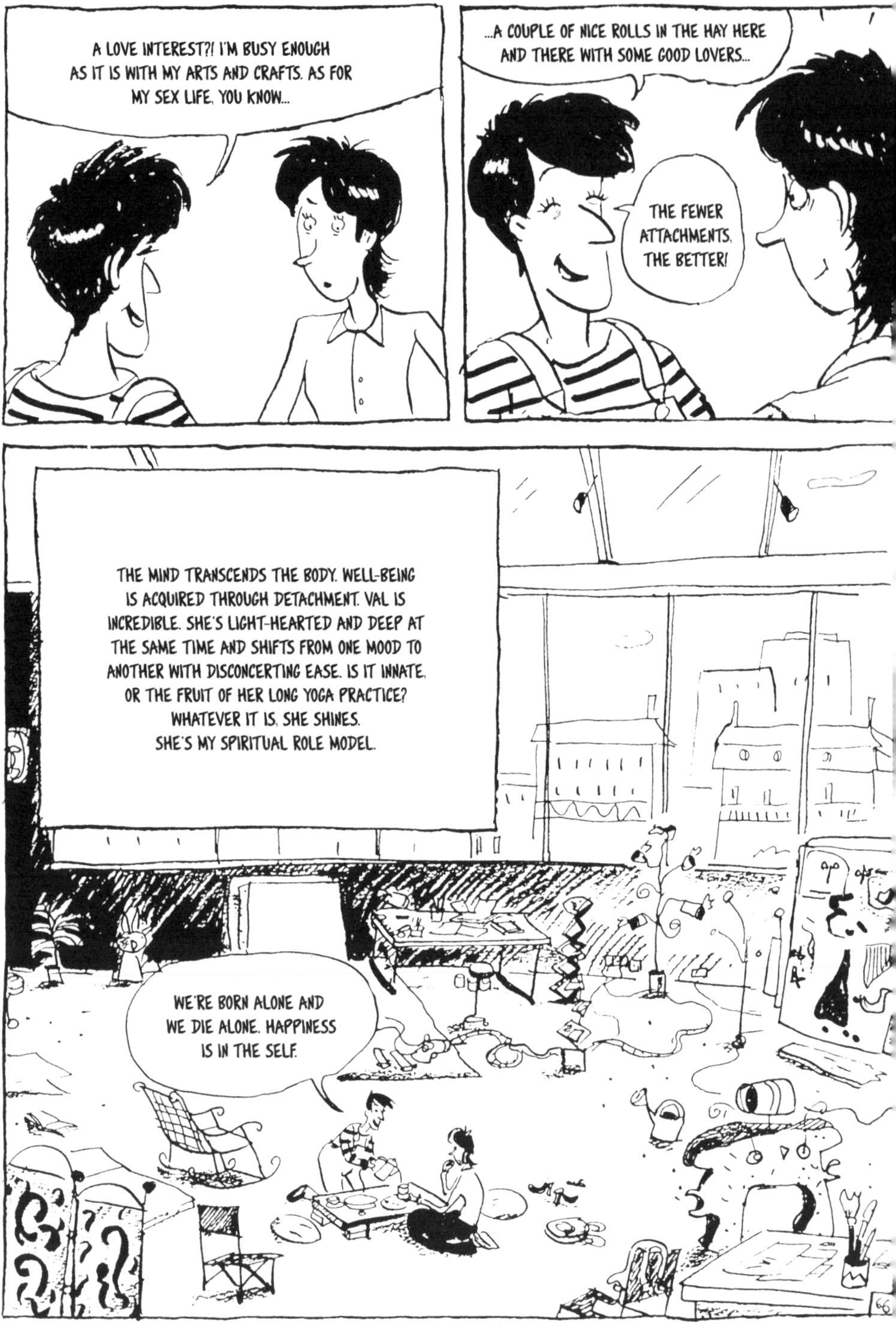

A LOVE INTEREST?! I'M BUSY ENOUGH AS IT IS WITH MY ARTS AND CRAFTS. AS FOR MY SEX LIFE, YOU KNOW...
...A COUPLE OF NICE ROLLS IN THE HAY HERE AND THERE WITH SOME GOOD LOVERS...
THE FEWER ATTACHMENTS, THE BETTER!
THE MIND TRANSCENDS THE BODY. WELL-BEING IS ACQUIRED THROUGH DETACHMENT. VAL IS INCREDIBLE. SHE'S LIGHT-HEARTED AND DEEP AT THE SAME TIME AND SHIFTS FROM ONE MOOD TO ANOTHER WITH DISCONCERTING EASE. IS IT INNATE, OR THE FRUIT OF HER LONG YOGA PRACTICE? WHATEVER IT IS, SHE SHINES. SHE'S MY SPIRITUAL ROLE MODEL.
WE'RE BORN ALONE AND WE DIE ALONE. HAPPINESS IS IN THE SELF.

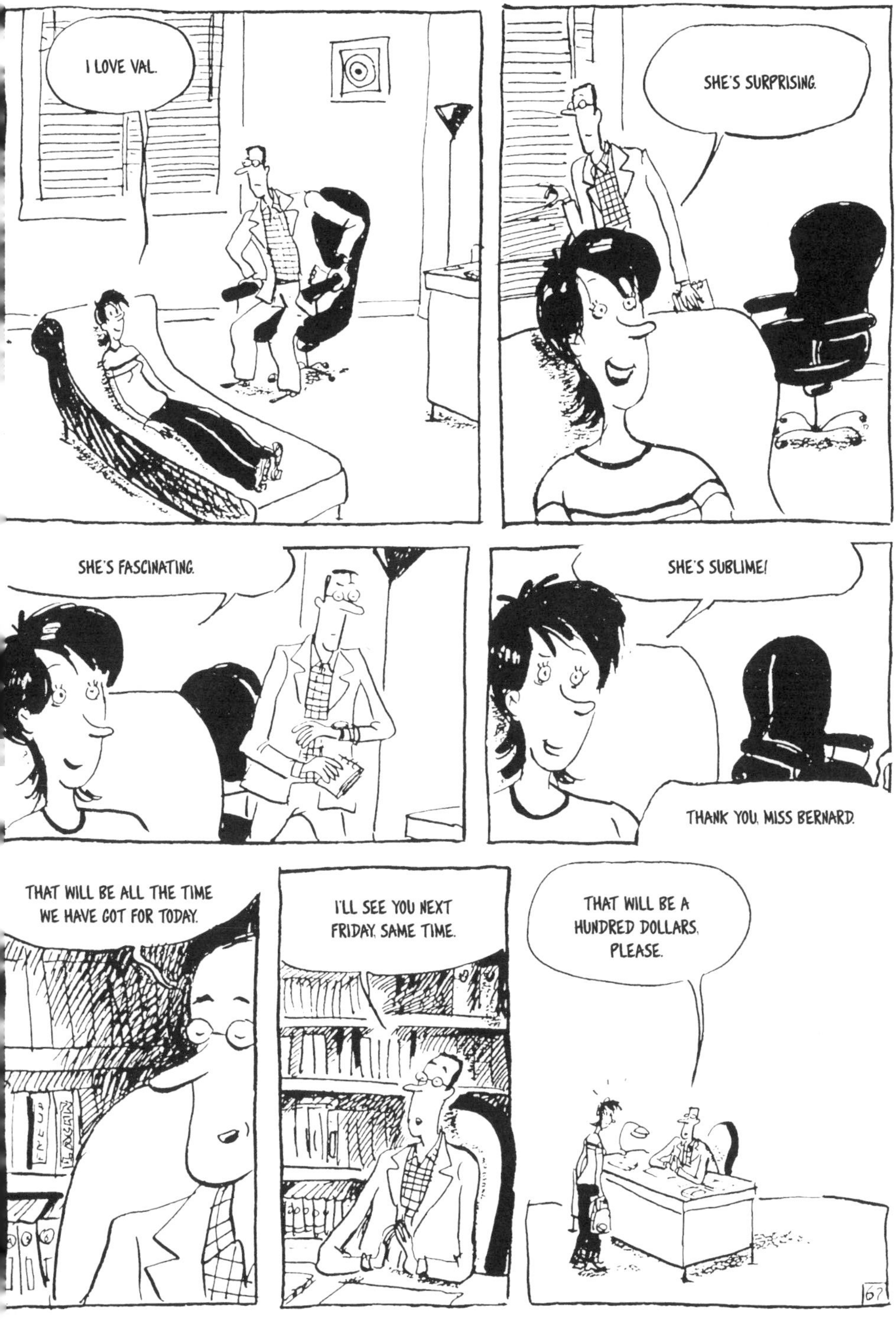
I LOVE VAL.
SHE'S SURPRISING.
SHE'S FASCINATING.
SHE'S SUBLIME!
THANK YOU, MISS BERNARD.
THAT WILL BE ALL THE TIME WE HAVE GOT FOR TODAY.
I'LL SEE YOU NEXT FRIDAY, SAME TIME.
THAT WILL BE A HUNDRED DOLLARS, PLEASE.

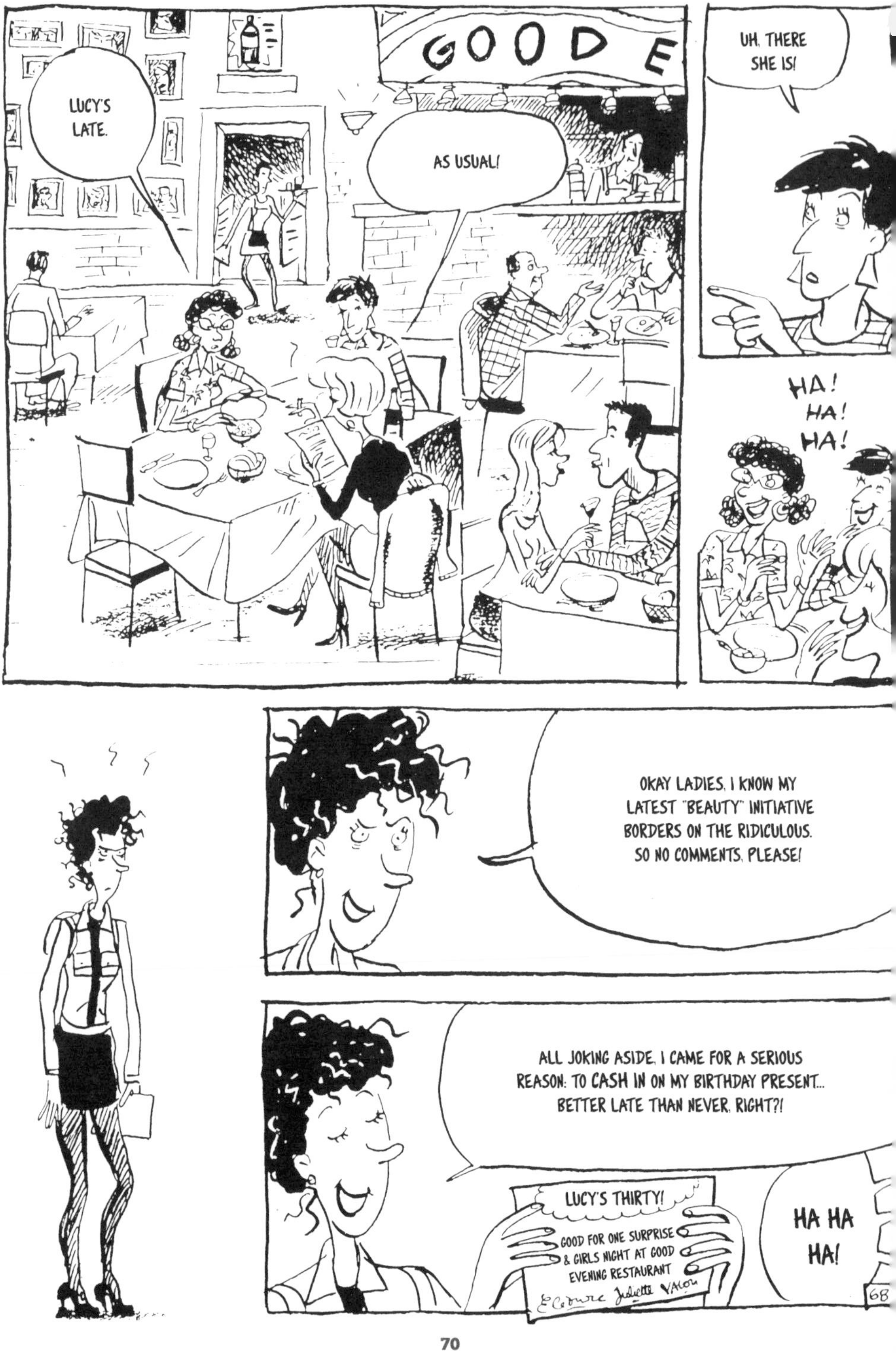
GOODE
LUCY'S LATE.
AS USUAL!
UH, THERE SHE IS!
HA! HA! HA!
OKAY LADIES, I KNOW MY LATEST "BEAUTY" INITIATIVE BORDERS ON THE RIDICULOUS. SO NO COMMENTS, PLEASE!
ALL JOKING ASIDE, I CAME FOR A SERIOUS REASON: TO CASH IN ON MY BIRTHDAY PRESENT... BETTER LATE THAN NEVER, RIGHT?!
LUCY'S THIRTY!
GOOD FOR ONE SURPRISE & GIRLS NIGHT AT GOOD EVENING RESTAURANT
HA HA HA!
68

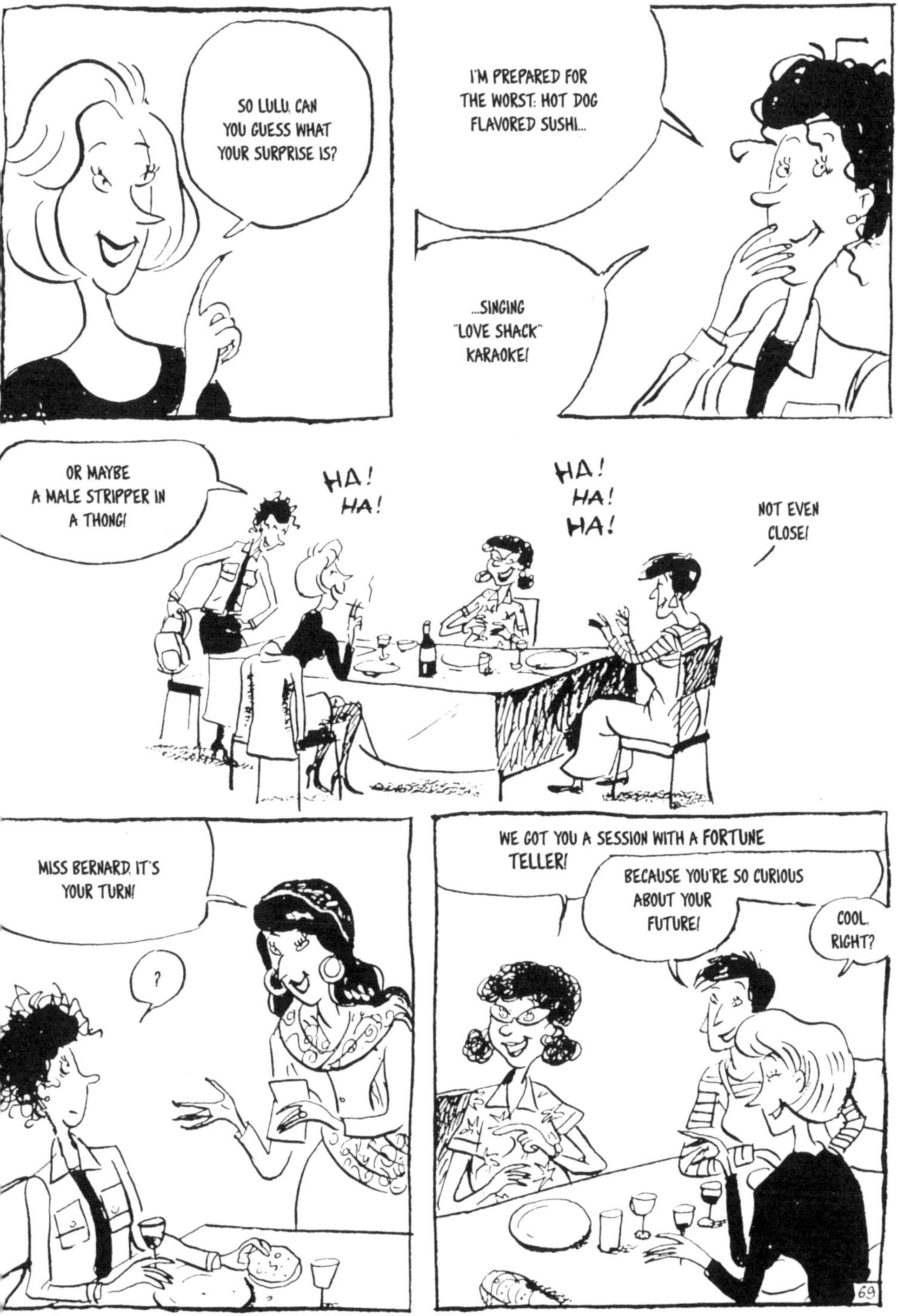
SO LULU, CAN YOU GUESS WHAT YOUR SURPRISE IS?
I'M PREPARED FOR THE WORST: HOT DOG FLAVORED SUSHI...
...SINGING "LOVE SHACK" KARAOKE!
OR MAYBE A MALE STRIPPER IN A THONG!
HA! HA!
HA! HA! HA!
NOT EVEN CLOSE!
MISS BERNARD, IT'S YOUR TURN!
?
WE GOT YOU A SESSION WITH A FORTUNE TELLER!
BECAUSE YOU'RE SO CURIOUS ABOUT YOUR FUTURE!
COOL, RIGHT?
69

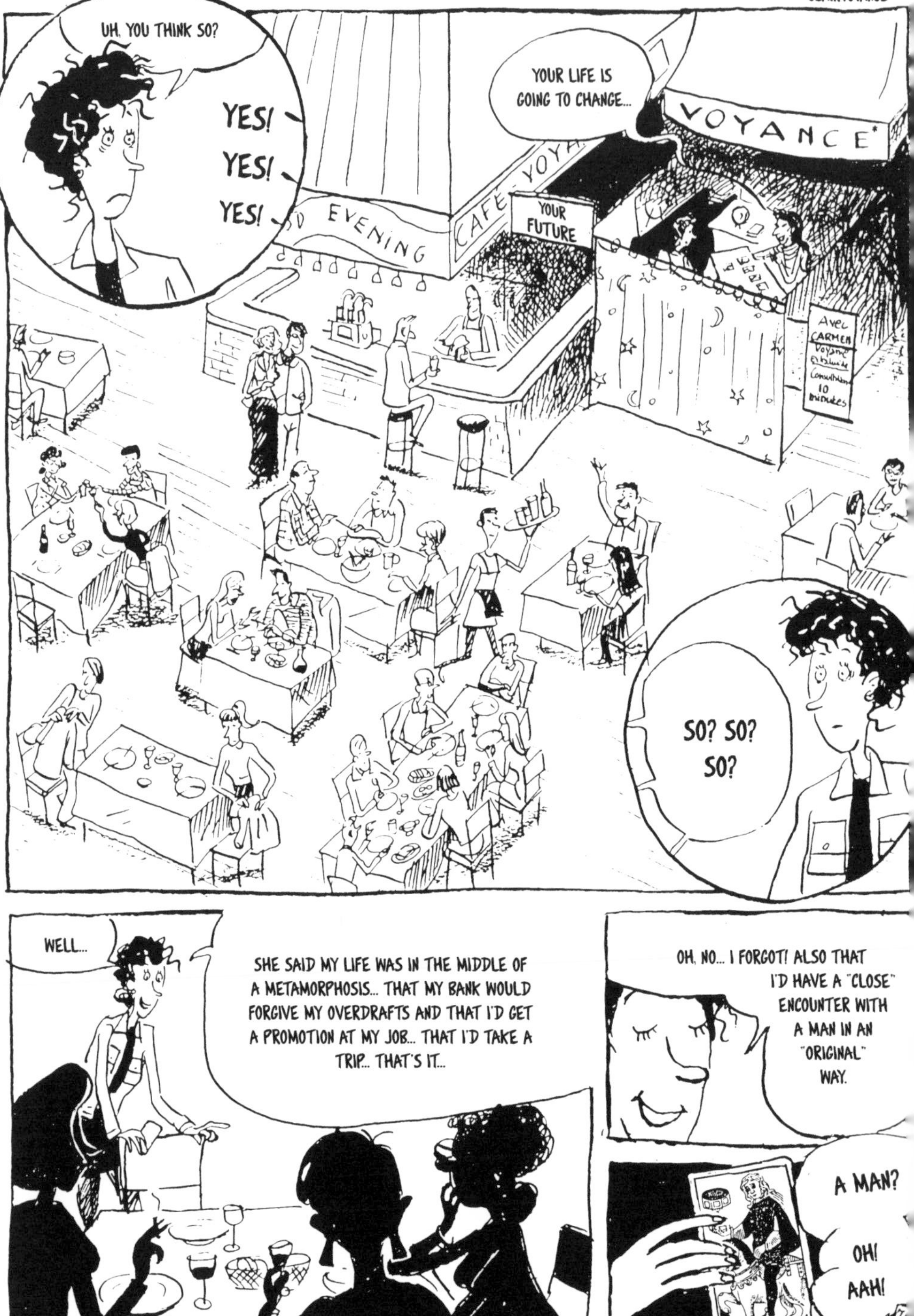
UH, YOU THINK SO?
YES!
YES!
YES!
YOUR LIFE IS GOING TO CHANGE...
VOYANCE*
EVENING
CAFÉ VOYA
YOUR FUTURE
SO? SO? SO?
WELL...
SHE SAID MY LIFE WAS IN THE MIDDLE OF A METAMORPHOSIS... THAT MY BANK WOULD FORGIVE MY OVERDRAFTS AND THAT I'D GET A PROMOTION AT MY JOB... THAT I'D TAKE A TRIP... THAT'S IT...
OH, NO... I FORGOT! ALSO THAT I'D HAVE A "CLOSE" ENCOUNTER WITH A MAN IN AN "ORIGINAL" WAY.
A MAN?
OH!
AAH!

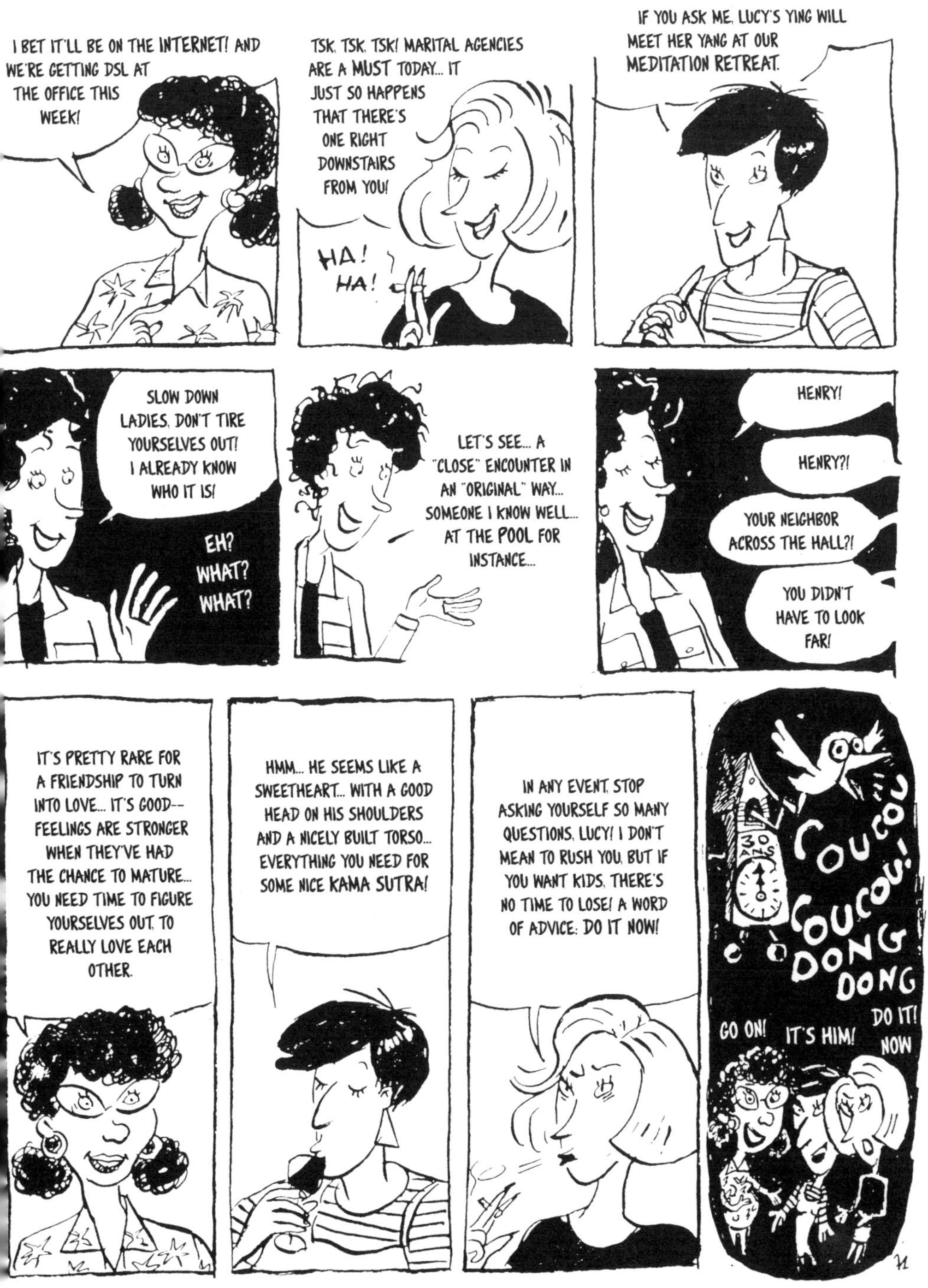

I BET IT'LL BE ON THE INTERNET! AND WE'RE GETTING DSL AT THE OFFICE THIS WEEK!
TSK, TSK, TSK! MARITAL AGENCIES ARE A MUST TODAY... IT JUST SO HAPPENS THAT THERE'S ONE RIGHT DOWNSTAIRS FROM YOU!
HA! HA!
IF YOU ASK ME, LUCY'S YING WILL MEET HER YANG AT OUR MEDITATION RETREAT.
SLOW DOWN LADIES, DON'T TIRE YOURSELVES OUT! I ALREADY KNOW WHO IT IS!
EH? WHAT? WHAT?
LET'S SEE... A "CLOSE" ENCOUNTER IN AN "ORIGINAL" WAY... SOMEONE I KNOW WELL... AT THE POOL FOR INSTANCE...
HENRY!
HENRY?!
YOUR NEIGHBOR ACROSS THE HALL?!
YOU DIDN'T HAVE TO LOOK FAR!
IT'S PRETTY RARE FOR A FRIENDSHIP TO TURN INTO LOVE... IT'S GOOD-- FEELINGS ARE STRONGER WHEN THEY'VE HAD THE CHANCE TO MATURE... YOU NEED TIME TO FIGURE YOURSELVES OUT, TO REALLY LOVE EACH OTHER.
HMM... HE SEEMS LIKE A SWEETHEART... WITH A GOOD HEAD ON HIS SHOULDERS AND A NICELY BUILT TORSO... EVERYTHING YOU NEED FOR SOME NICE KAMA SUTRA!
IN ANY EVENT, STOP ASKING YOURSELF SO MANY QUESTIONS, LUCY! I DON'T MEAN TO RUSH YOU, BUT IF YOU WANT KIDS, THERE'S NO TIME TO LOSE! A WORD OF ADVICE: DO IT NOW!
30 ANS
COUCOU! COUCOU!
DONG DONG
GO ON!
IT'S HIM!
DO IT! NOW

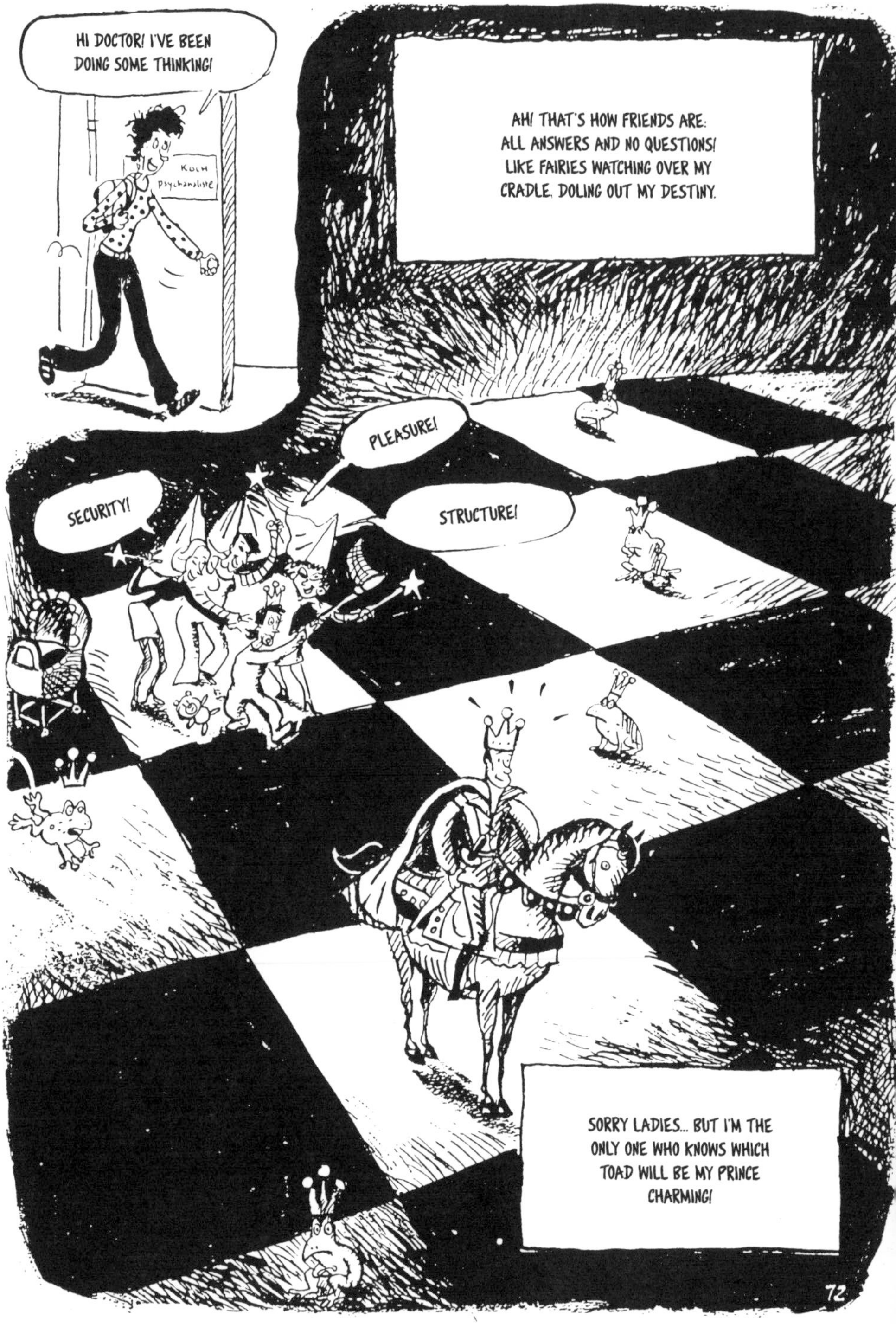
HI DOCTOR! I'VE BEEN DOING SOME THINKING!
KOCH Psychanalyste
AH! THAT'S HOW FRIENDS ARE: ALL ANSWERS AND NO QUESTIONS! LIKE FAIRIES WATCHING OVER MY CRADLE, DOLING OUT MY DESTINY.
SECURITY!
PLEASURE!
STRUCTURE!
SORRY LADIES... BUT I'M THE ONLY ONE WHO KNOWS WHICH TOAD WILL BE MY PRINCE CHARMING!
72

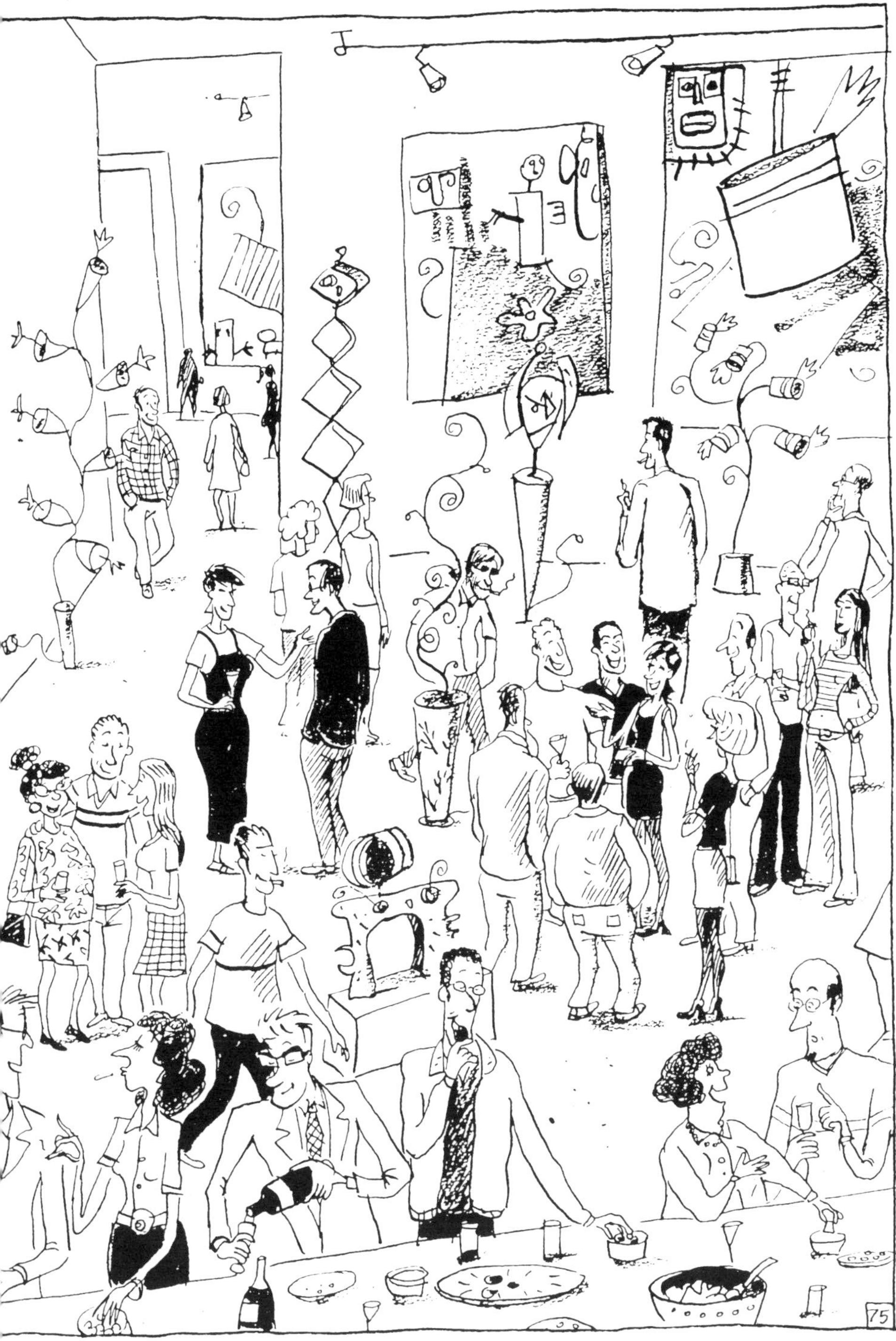
75

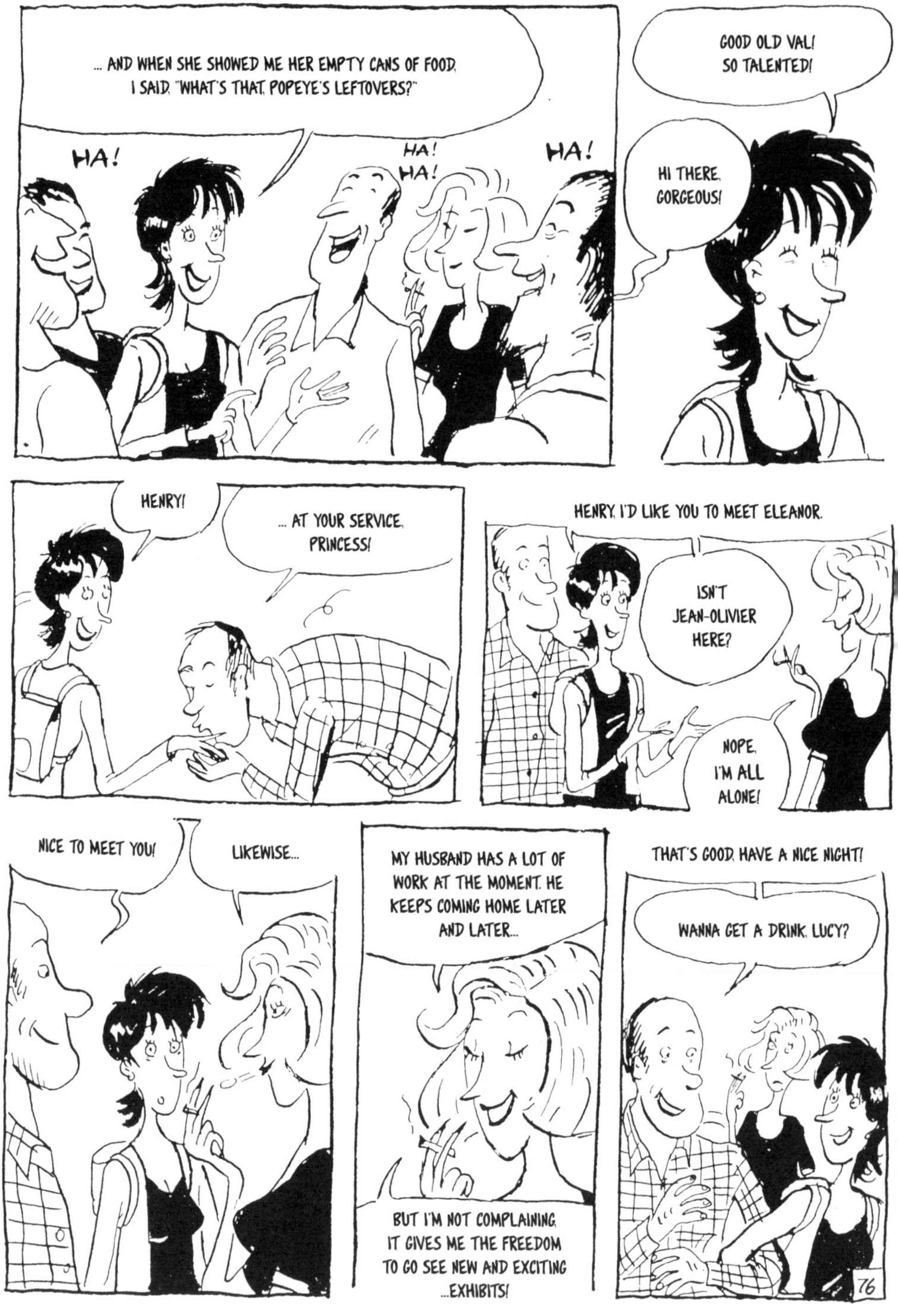
... AND WHEN SHE SHOWED ME HER EMPTY CANS OF FOOD, I SAID, "WHAT'S THAT, POPEYE'S LEFTOVERS?"
HA!
HA! HA!
HA!
GOOD OLD VAL! SO TALENTED!
HI THERE, GORGEOUS!
HENRY!
... AT YOUR SERVICE, PRINCESS!
HENRY, I'D LIKE YOU TO MEET ELEANOR.
ISN'T JEAN-OLIVIER HERE?
NOPE, I'M ALL ALONE!
NICE TO MEET YOU!
LIKEWISE...
MY HUSBAND HAS A LOT OF WORK AT THE MOMENT. HE KEEPS COMING HOME LATER AND LATER...
BUT I'M NOT COMPLAINING, IT GIVES ME THE FREEDOM TO GO SEE NEW AND EXCITING ...EXHIBITS!
THAT'S GOOD, HAVE A NICE NIGHT!
WANNA GET A DRINK, LUCY?
76

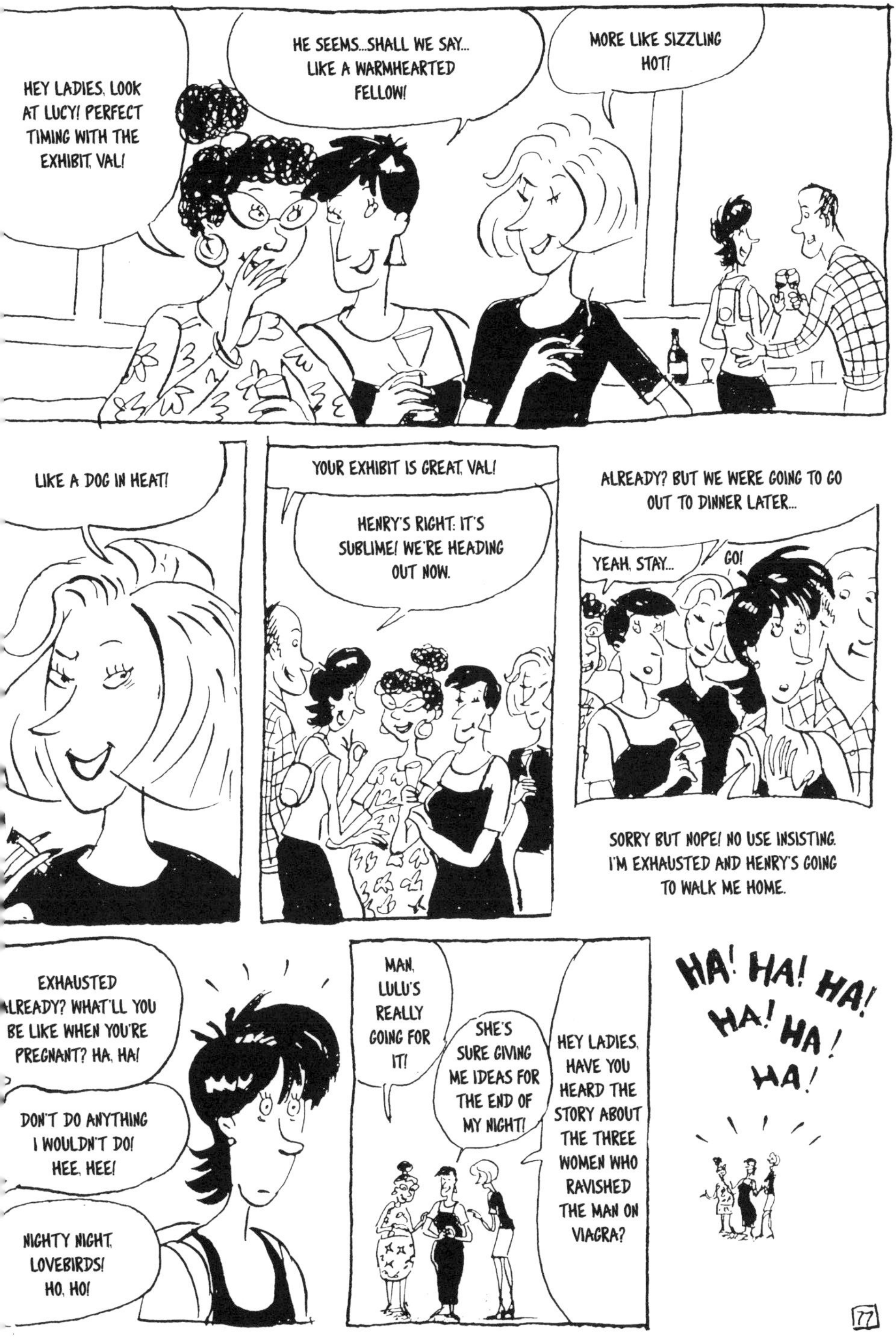
HEY LADIES, LOOK AT LUCY! PERFECT TIMING WITH THE EXHIBIT, VAL!
HE SEEMS...SHALL WE SAY... LIKE A WARMHEARTED FELLOW!
MORE LIKE SIZZLING HOT!
LIKE A DOG IN HEAT!
YOUR EXHIBIT IS GREAT, VAL!
HENRY'S RIGHT: IT'S SUBLIME! WE'RE HEADING OUT NOW.
ALREADY? BUT WE WERE GOING TO GO OUT TO DINNER LATER...
YEAH, STAY...
GO!
SORRY BUT NOPE! NO USE INSISTING. I'M EXHAUSTED AND HENRY'S GOING TO WALK ME HOME.
EXHAUSTED ALREADY? WHAT'LL YOU BE LIKE WHEN YOU'RE PREGNANT? HA, HA!
DON'T DO ANYTHING I WOULDN'T DO! HEE, HEE!
NIGHTY NIGHT, LOVEBIRDS! HO, HO!
MAN, LULU'S REALLY GOING FOR IT!
SHE'S SURE GIVING ME IDEAS FOR THE END OF MY NIGHT!
HEY LADIES, HAVE YOU HEARD THE STORY ABOUT THE THREE WOMEN WHO RAVISHED THE MAN ON VIAGRA?
HA! HA! HA! HA! HA! HA!
77

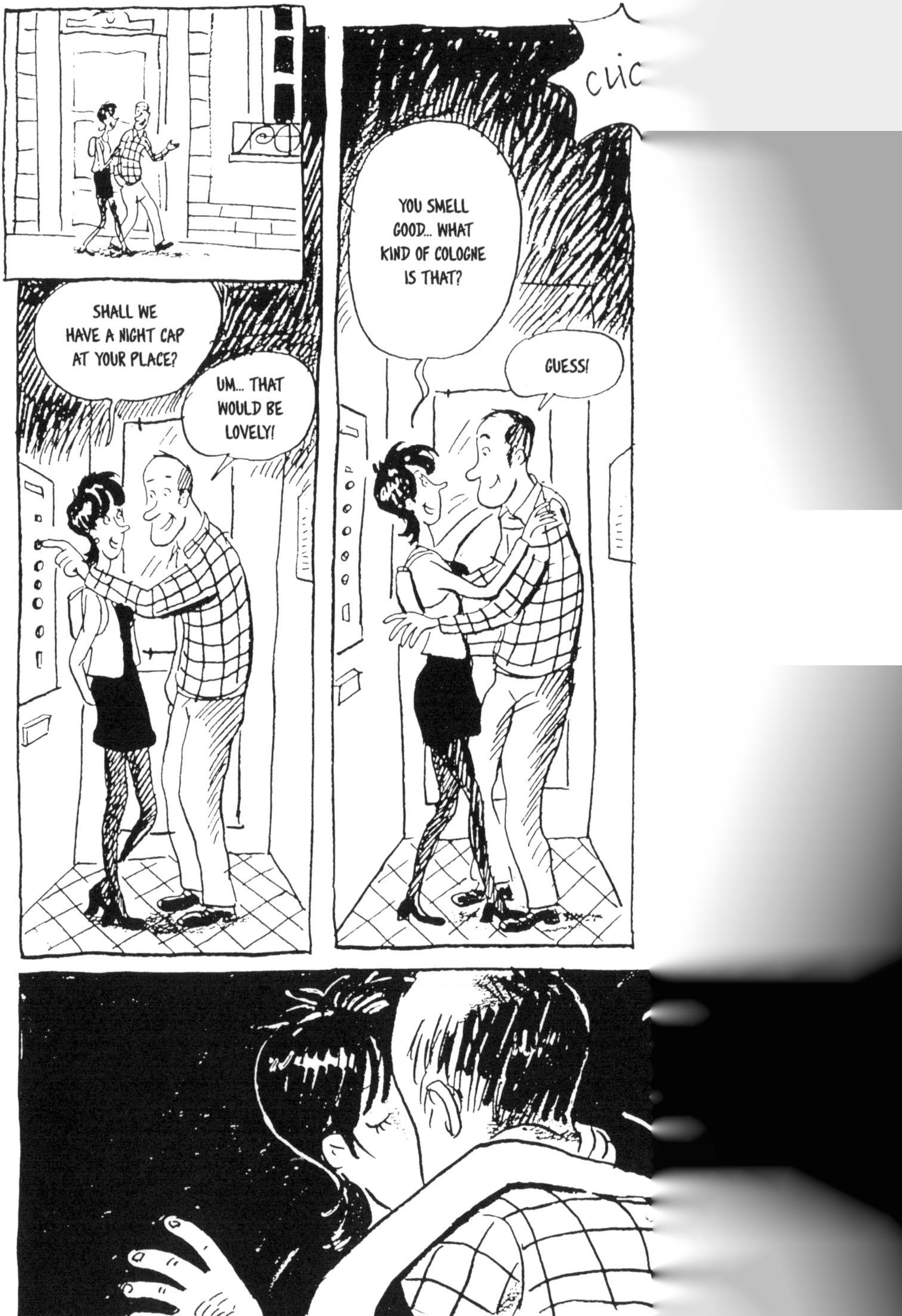
CLIC
SHALL WE HAVE A NIGHT CAP AT YOUR PLACE?
UM... THAT WOULD BE LOVELY!
YOU SMELL GOOD... WHAT KIND OF COLOGNE IS THAT?
GUESS!

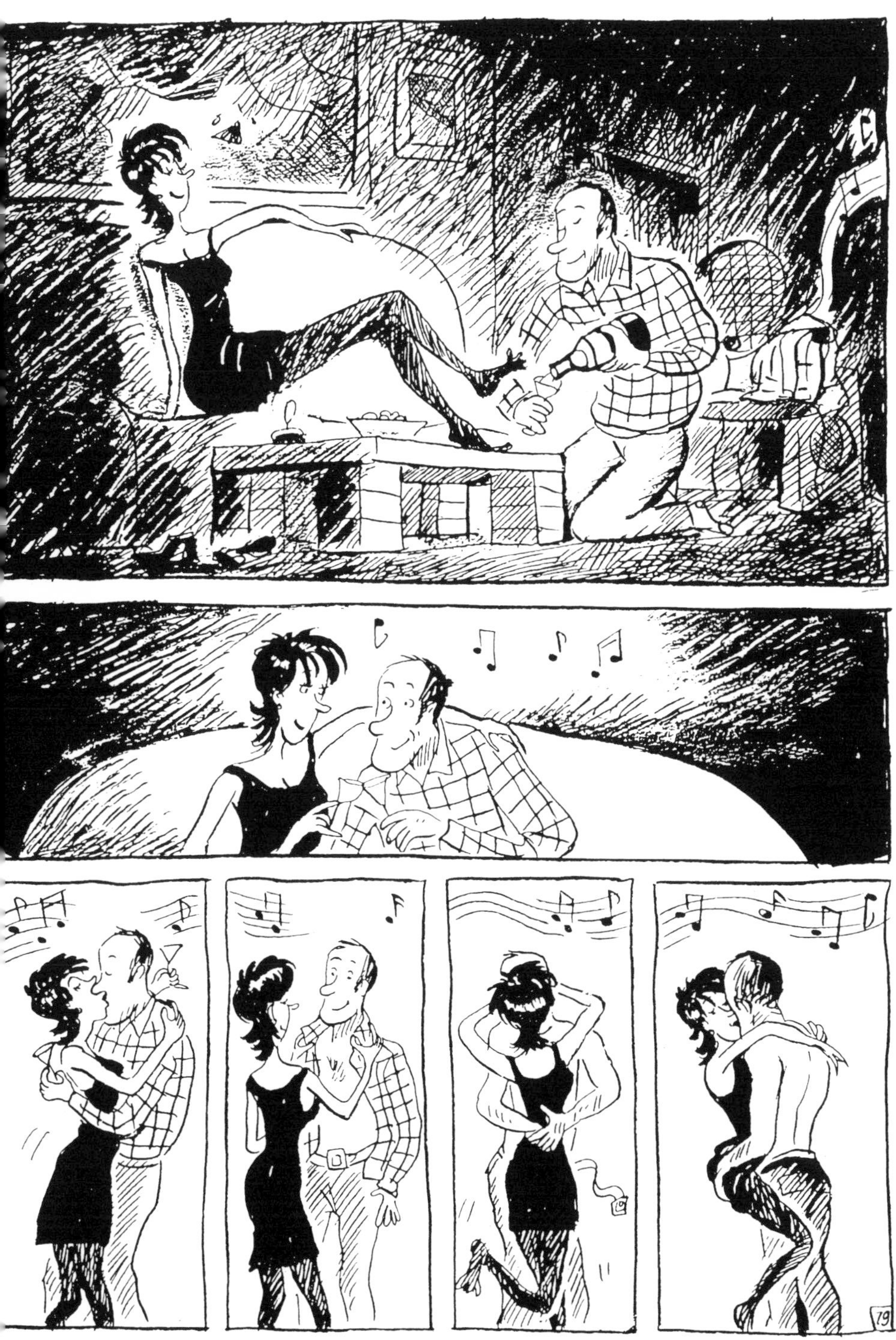
19

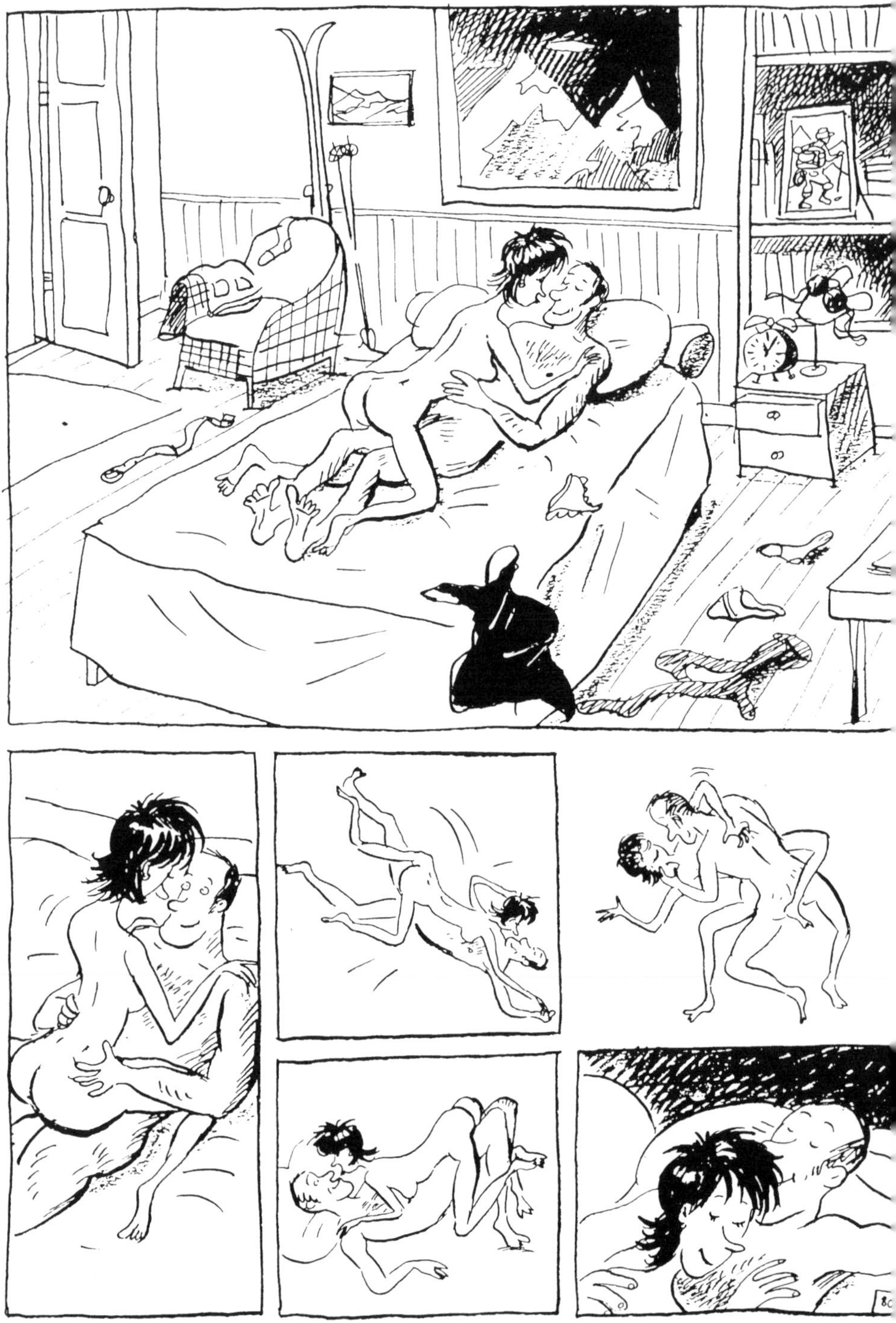

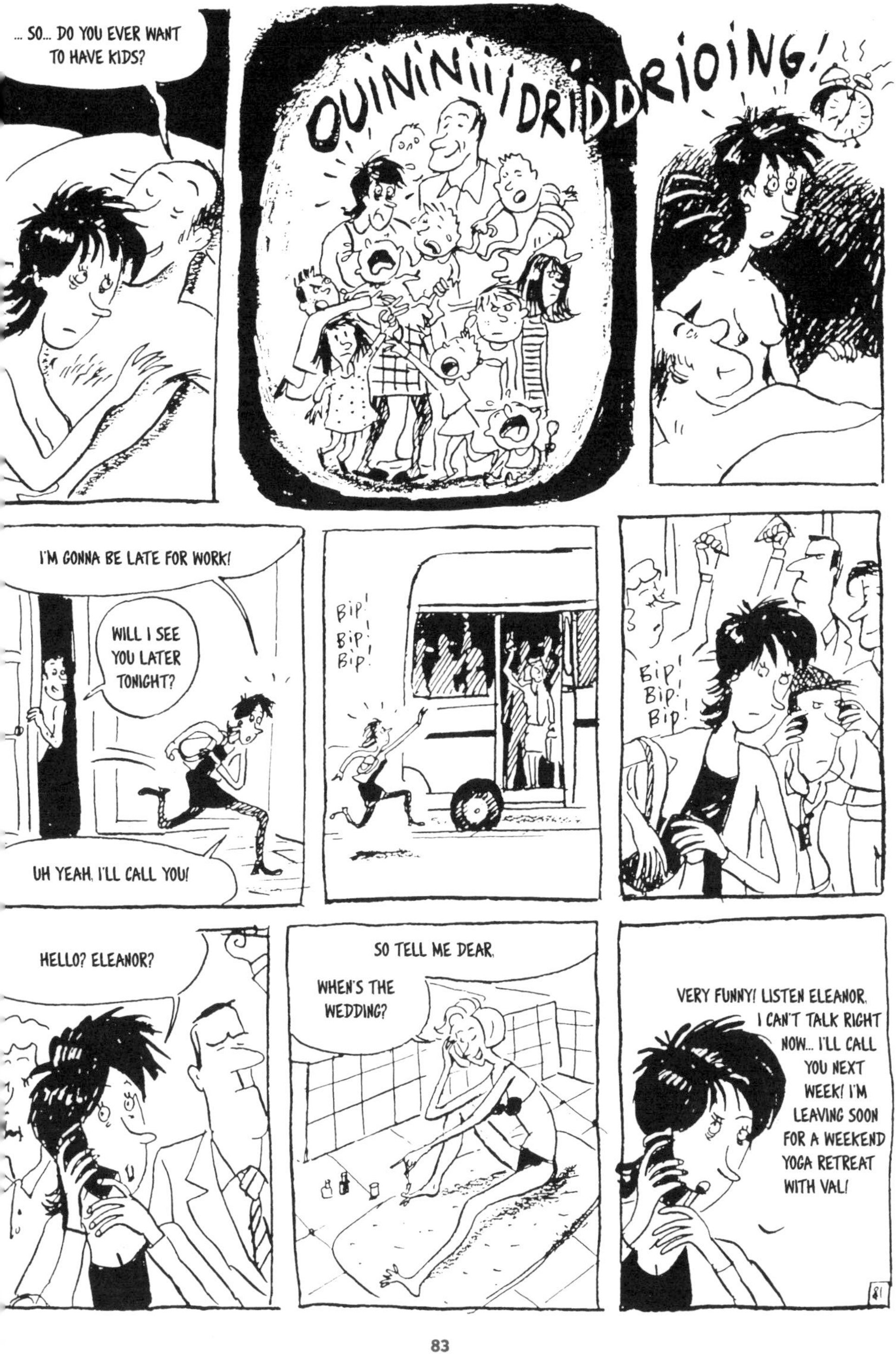
... SO... DO YOU EVER WANT TO HAVE KIDS?
OUINININIII DRIDDRIOING!
I'M GONNA BE LATE FOR WORK!
WILL I SEE YOU LATER TONIGHT?
UH YEAH, I'LL CALL YOU!
Bip! Bip! Bip!
Bip! Bip! Bip!
HELLO? ELEANOR?
SO TELL ME DEAR,
WHEN'S THE WEDDING?
VERY FUNNY! LISTEN ELEANOR, I CAN'T TALK RIGHT NOW... I'LL CALL YOU NEXT WEEK! I'M LEAVING SOON FOR A WEEKEND YOGA RETREAT WITH VAL!
81

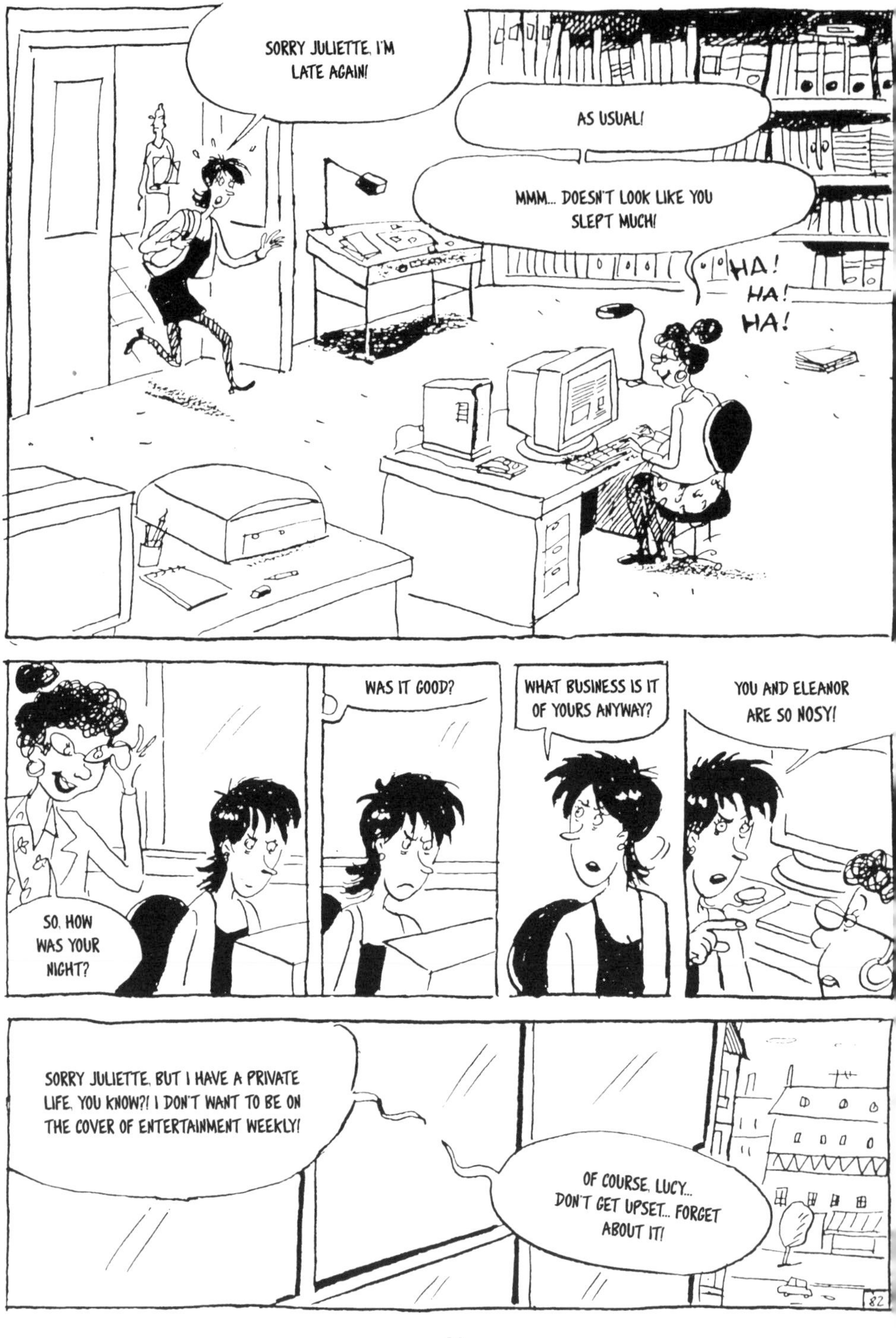
SORRY JULIETTE, I'M LATE AGAIN!
AS USUAL!
MMM... DOESN'T LOOK LIKE YOU SLEPT MUCH!
HA! HA! HA!
SO, HOW WAS YOUR NIGHT?
WAS IT GOOD?
WHAT BUSINESS IS IT OF YOURS ANYWAY?
YOU AND ELEANOR ARE SO NOSY!
SORRY JULIETTE, BUT I HAVE A PRIVATE LIFE, YOU KNOW?! I DON'T WANT TO BE ON THE COVER OF ENTERTAINMENT WEEKLY!
OF COURSE, LUCY... DON'T GET UPSET... FORGET ABOUT IT!
82

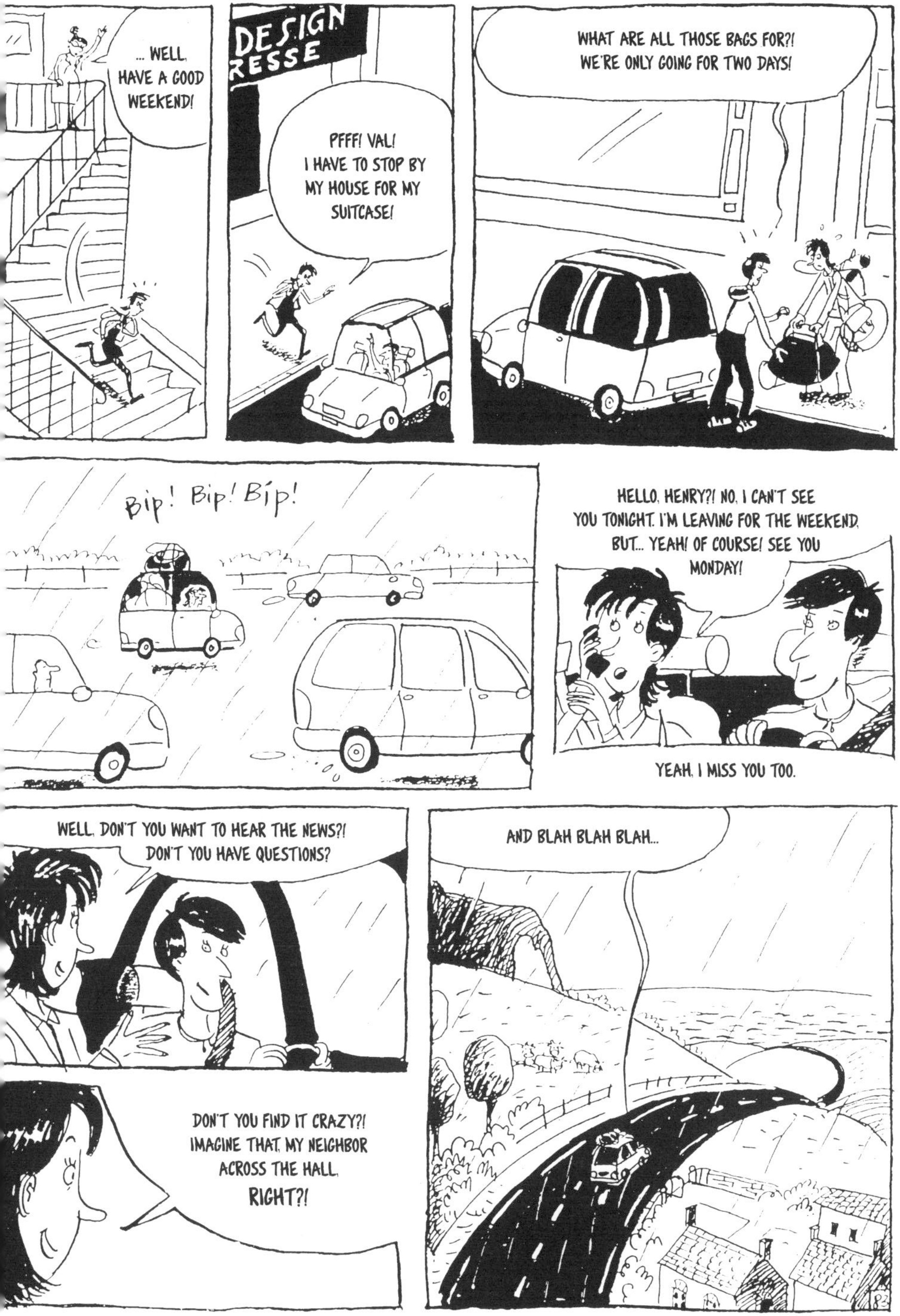
... WELL, HAVE A GOOD WEEKEND!
DESIGN
RESSE
PFFF! VAL! I HAVE TO STOP BY MY HOUSE FOR MY SUITCASE!
WHAT ARE ALL THOSE BAGS FOR?! WE'RE ONLY GOING FOR TWO DAYS!
Bip! Bip! Bip!
HELLO, HENRY?! NO, I CAN'T SEE YOU TONIGHT. I'M LEAVING FOR THE WEEKEND, BUT... YEAH! OF COURSE! SEE YOU MONDAY!
YEAH, I MISS YOU TOO.
WELL, DON'T YOU WANT TO HEAR THE NEWS?! DON'T YOU HAVE QUESTIONS?
AND BLAH BLAH BLAH...
DON'T YOU FIND IT CRAZY?! IMAGINE THAT, MY NEIGHBOR ACROSS THE HALL, RIGHT?!

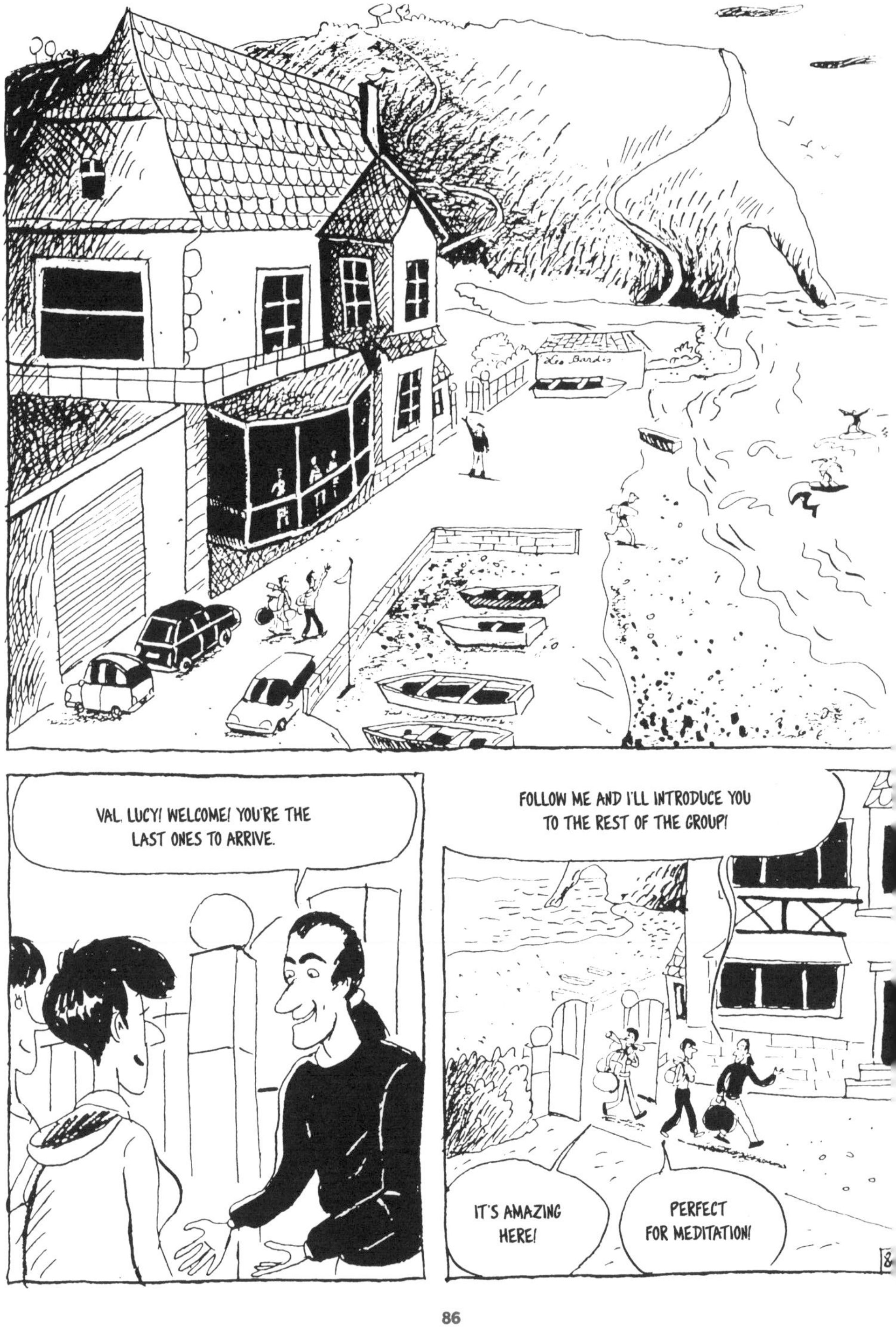
VAL, LUCY! WELCOME! YOU'RE THE LAST ONES TO ARRIVE.
FOLLOW ME AND I'LL INTRODUCE YOU TO THE REST OF THE GROUP!
IT'S AMAZING HERE!
PERFECT FOR MEDITATION!

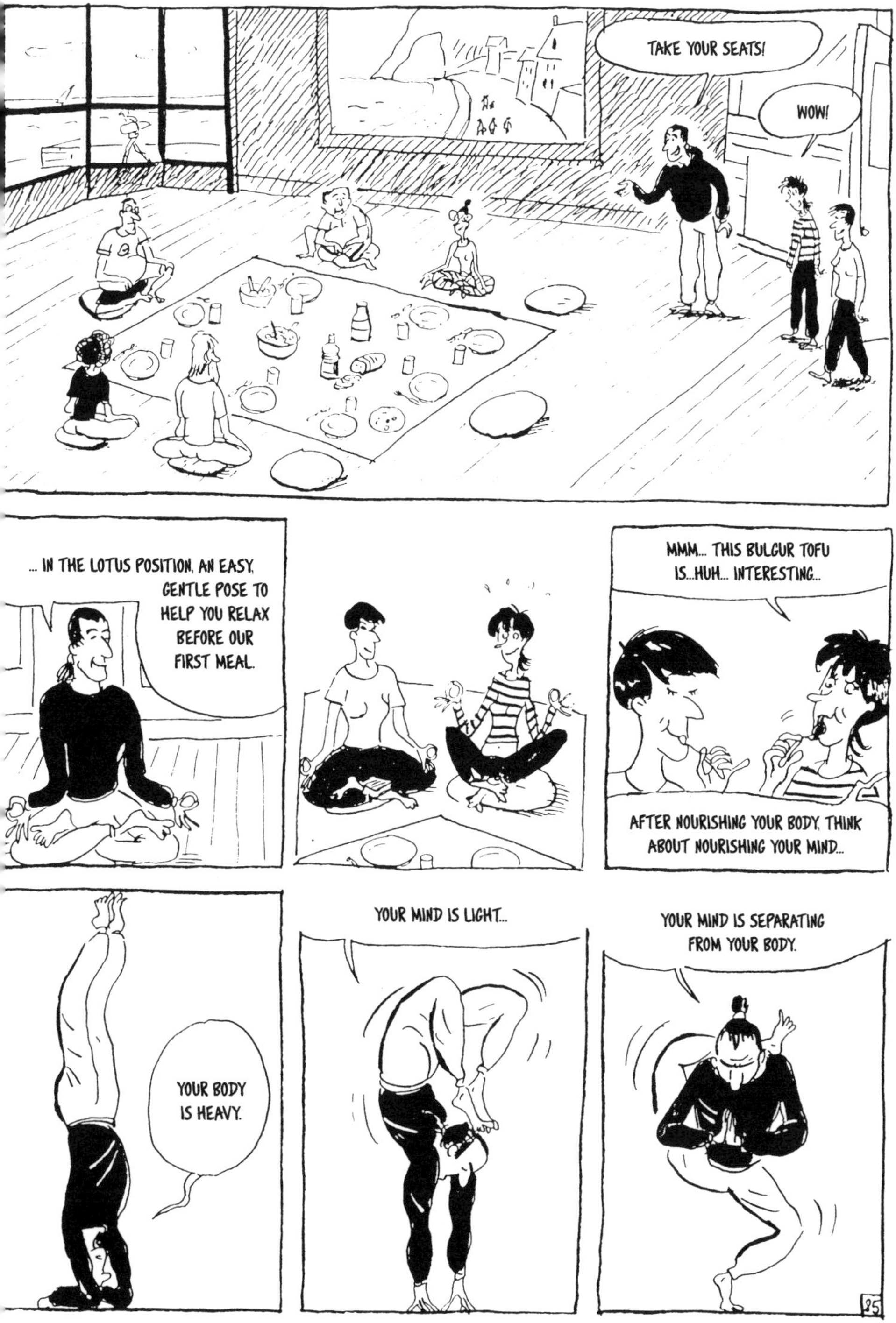
TAKE YOUR SEATS!
WOW!
... IN THE LOTUS POSITION, AN EASY, GENTLE POSE TO HELP YOU RELAX BEFORE OUR FIRST MEAL.
MMM... THIS BULGUR TOFU IS...HUH... INTERESTING...
AFTER NOURISHING YOUR BODY, THINK ABOUT NOURISHING YOUR MIND...
YOUR BODY IS HEAVY.
YOUR MIND IS LIGHT...
YOUR MIND IS SEPARATING FROM YOUR BODY.
85

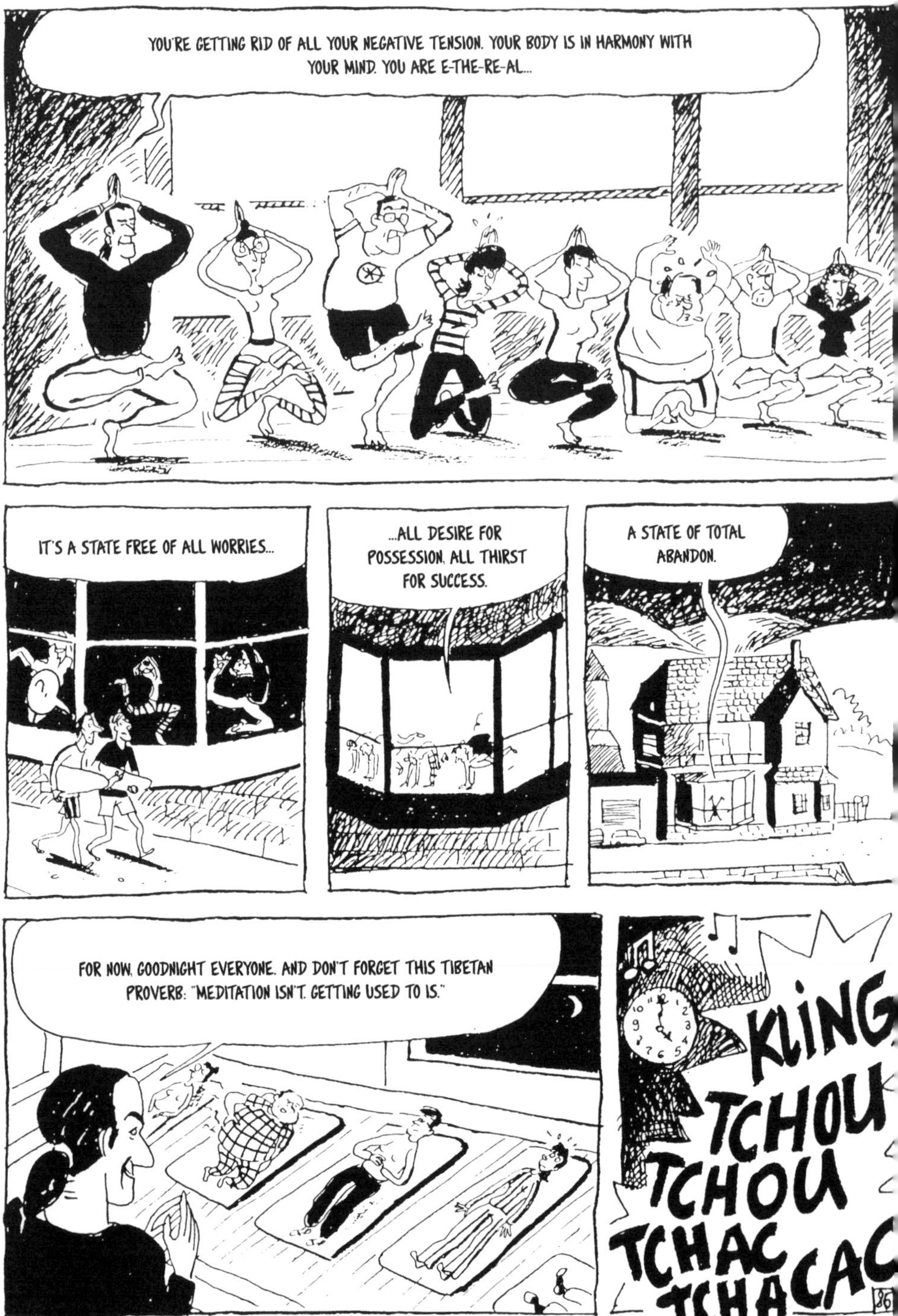
YOU'RE GETTING RID OF ALL YOUR NEGATIVE TENSION. YOUR BODY IS IN HARMONY WITH YOUR MIND. YOU ARE E-THE-RE-AL...
IT'S A STATE FREE OF ALL WORRIES...
...ALL DESIRE FOR POSSESSION, ALL THIRST FOR SUCCESS.
A STATE OF TOTAL ABANDON.
FOR NOW, GOODNIGHT EVERYONE. AND DON'T FORGET THIS TIBETAN PROVERB: "MEDITATION ISN'T. GETTING USED TO IS."
KLING
TCHOU
TCHOU
TCHAC
TCHACAC

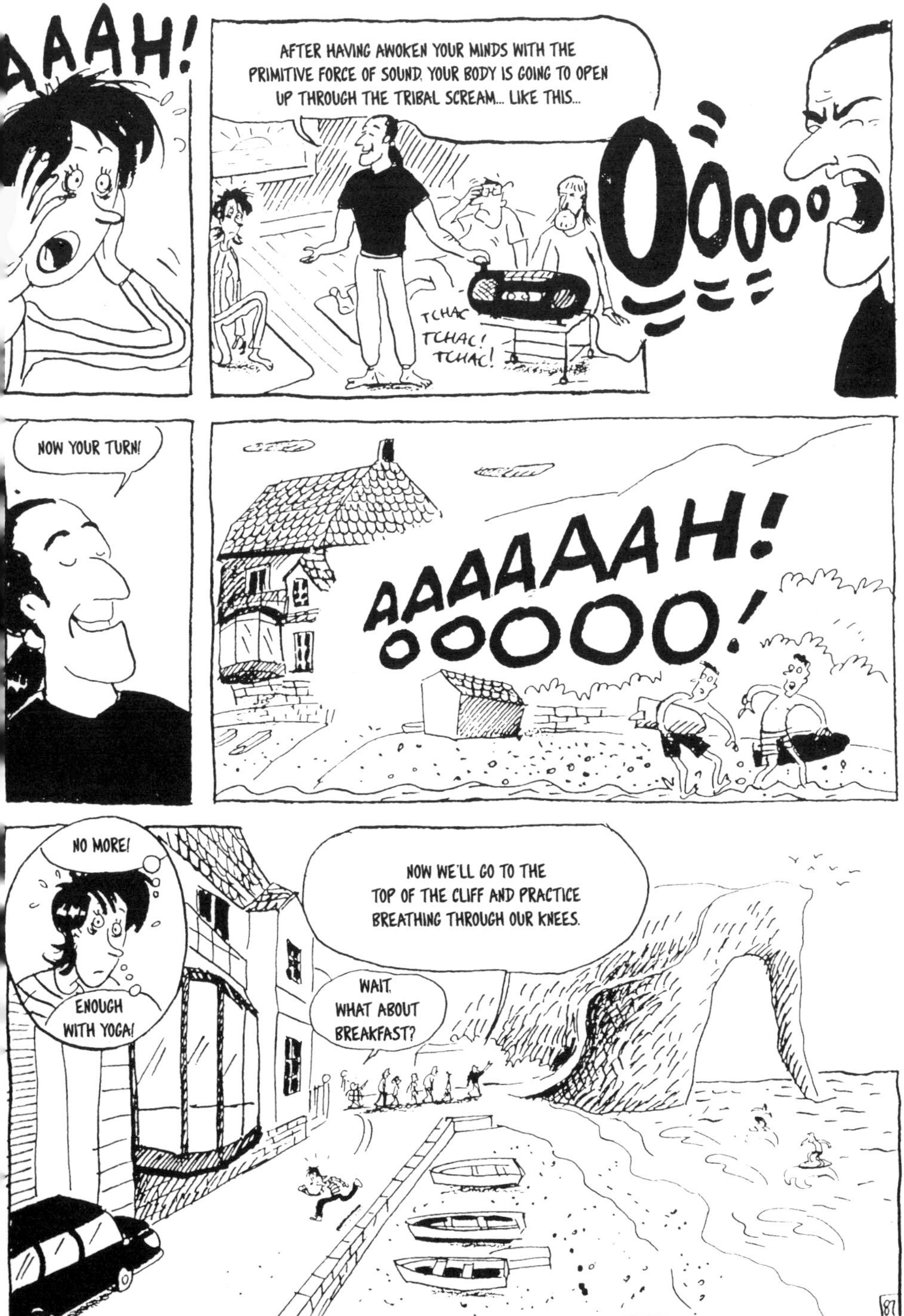
AAAH!
AFTER HAVING AWOKEN YOUR MINDS WITH THE PRIMITIVE FORCE OF SOUND, YOUR BODY IS GOING TO OPEN UP THROUGH THE TRIBAL SCREAM... LIKE THIS...
TCHAC TCHAC! TCHAC!
OOOOOO
NOW YOUR TURN!
AAAAAH! OOOOOO!
NO MORE!
ENOUGH WITH YOGA!
NOW WE'LL GO TO THE TOP OF THE CLIFF AND PRACTICE BREATHING THROUGH OUR KNEES.
WAIT, WHAT ABOUT BREAKFAST?
87

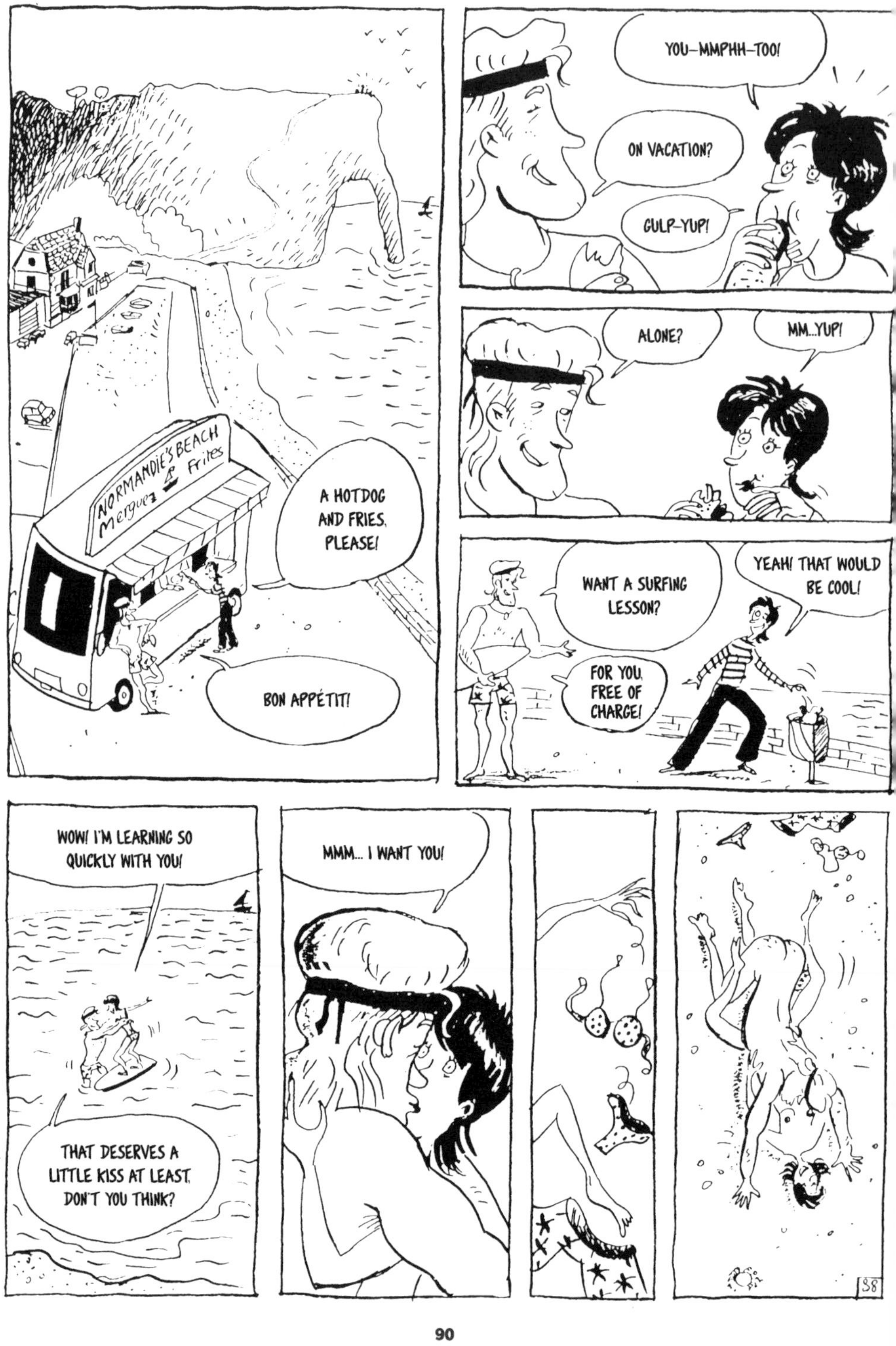
NORMANDIE'S BEACH
Merguez Frites
A HOTDOG AND FRIES, PLEASE!
BON APPÉTIT!
YOU—MMPHH—TOO!
ON VACATION?
GULP—YUP!
ALONE?
MM...YUP!
WANT A SURFING LESSON?
FOR YOU, FREE OF CHARGE!
YEAH! THAT WOULD BE COOL!
WOW! I'M LEARNING SO QUICKLY WITH YOU!
THAT DESERVES A LITTLE KISS AT LEAST, DON'T YOU THINK?
MMM... I WANT YOU!
38

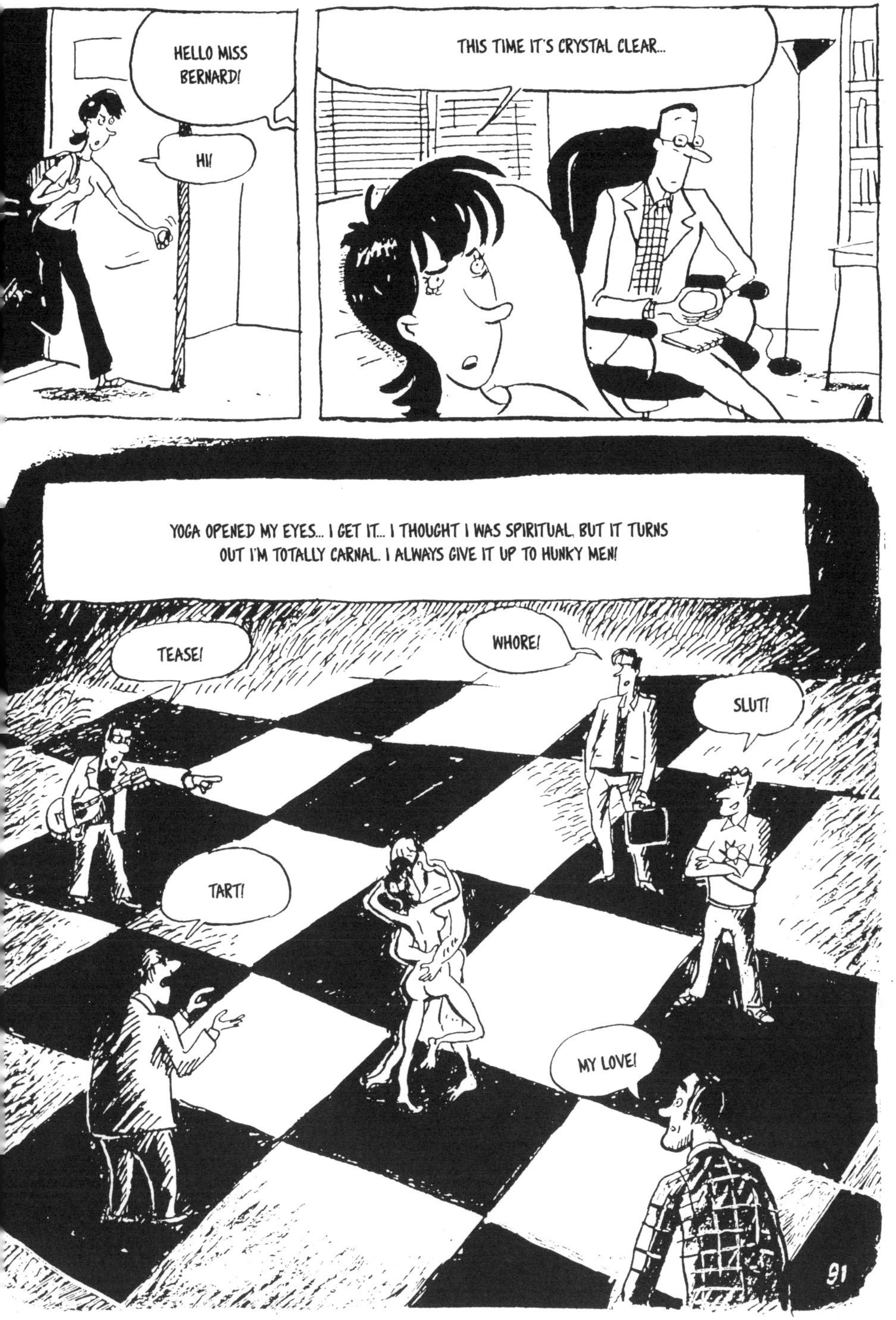
HELLO MISS BERNARD!
HI!
THIS TIME IT'S CRYSTAL CLEAR...
YOGA OPENED MY EYES... I GET IT... I THOUGHT I WAS SPIRITUAL, BUT IT TURNS OUT I'M TOTALLY CARNAL. I ALWAYS GIVE IT UP TO HUNKY MEN!
TEASE!
WHORE!
SLUT!
TART!
MY LOVE!
91

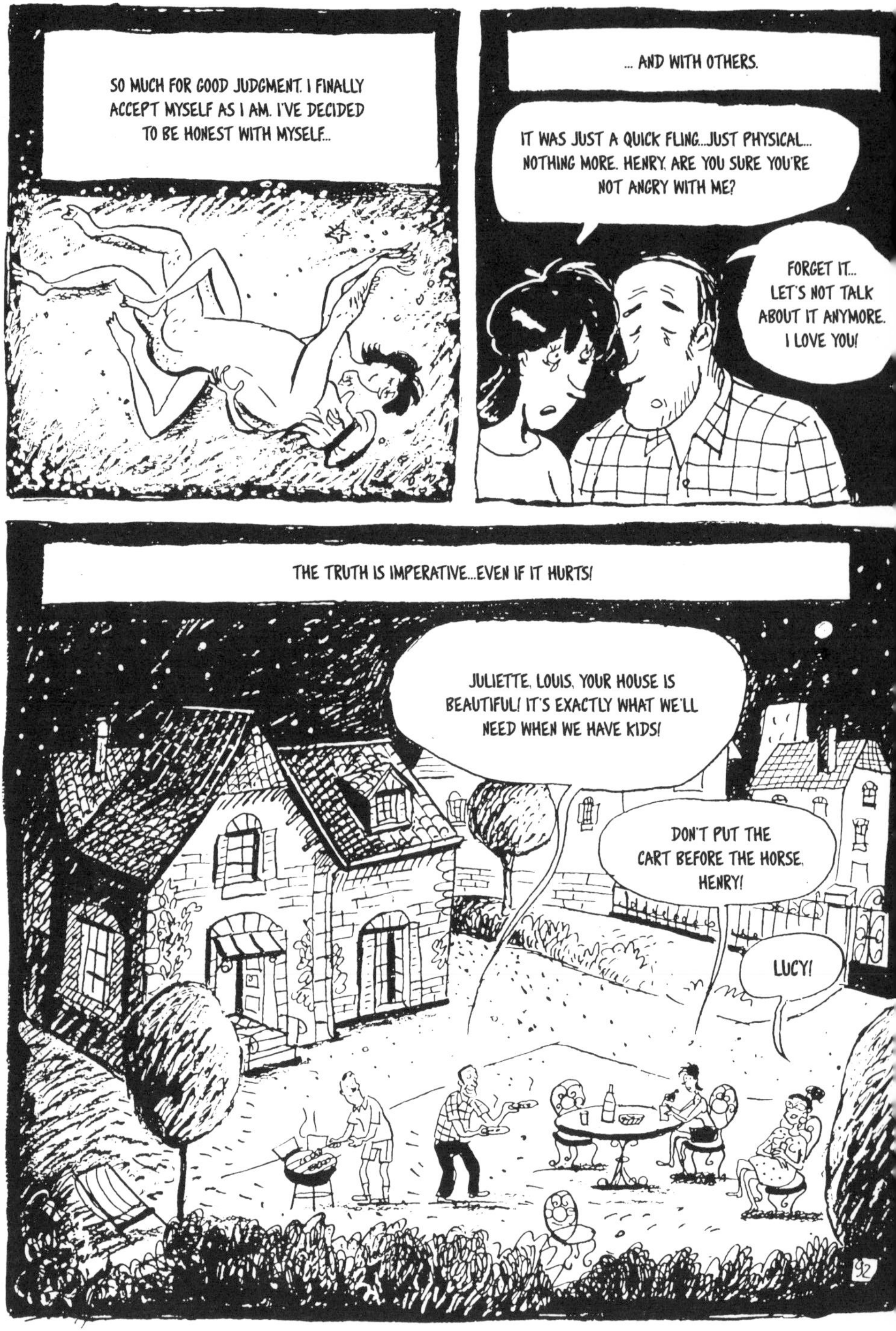
SO MUCH FOR GOOD JUDGMENT. I FINALLY ACCEPT MYSELF AS I AM. I'VE DECIDED TO BE HONEST WITH MYSELF...
... AND WITH OTHERS.
IT WAS JUST A QUICK FLING...JUST PHYSICAL... NOTHING MORE. HENRY, ARE YOU SURE YOU'RE NOT ANGRY WITH ME?
FORGET IT... LET'S NOT TALK ABOUT IT ANYMORE. I LOVE YOU!
THE TRUTH IS IMPERATIVE...EVEN IF IT HURTS!
JULIETTE, LOUIS, YOUR HOUSE IS BEAUTIFUL! IT'S EXACTLY WHAT WE'LL NEED WHEN WE HAVE KIDS!
DON'T PUT THE CART BEFORE THE HORSE, HENRY!
LUCY!
92

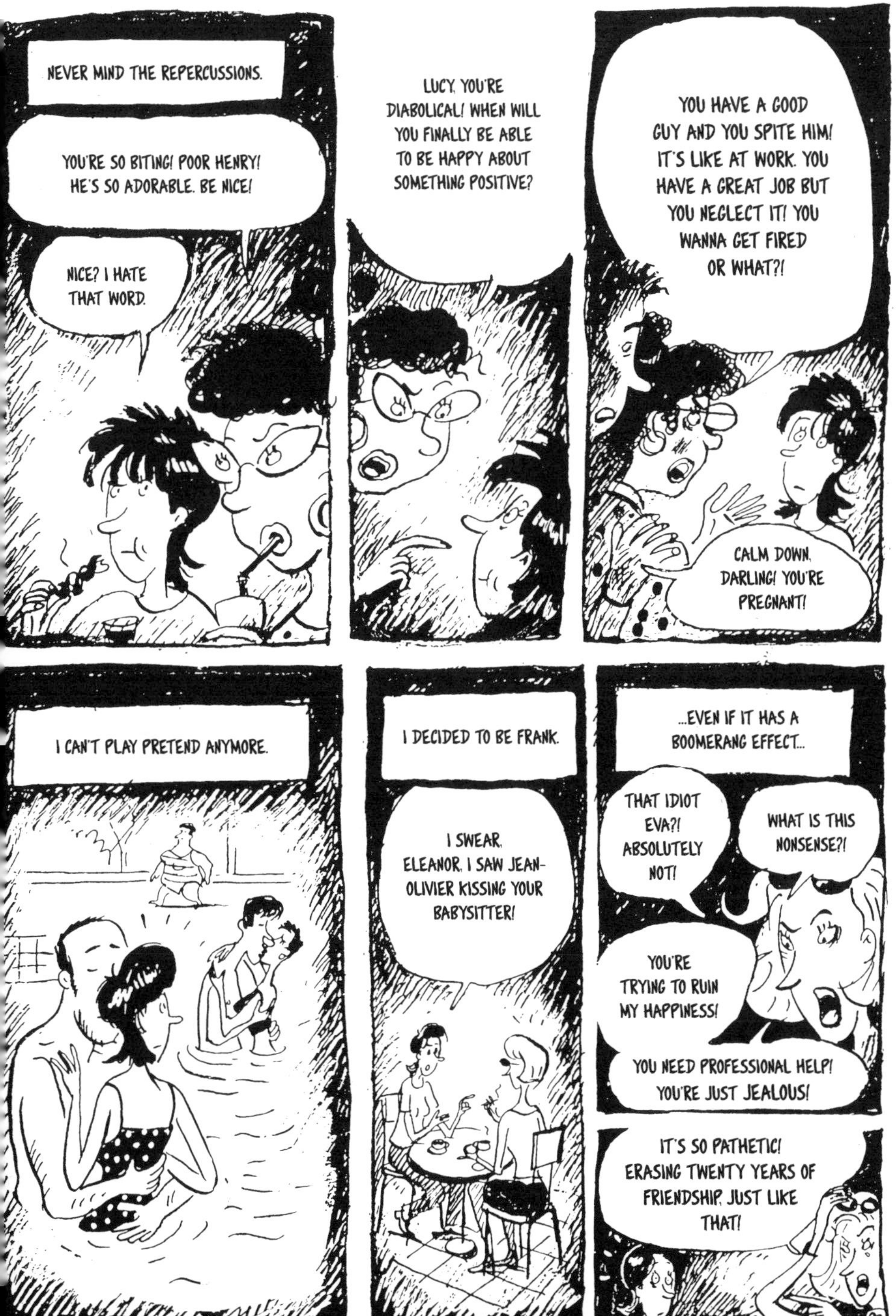
NEVER MIND THE REPERCUSSIONS.
YOU'RE SO BITING! POOR HENRY! HE'S SO ADORABLE. BE NICE!
NICE? I HATE THAT WORD.
LUCY, YOU'RE DIABOLICAL! WHEN WILL YOU FINALLY BE ABLE TO BE HAPPY ABOUT SOMETHING POSITIVE?
YOU HAVE A GOOD GUY AND YOU SPITE HIM! IT'S LIKE AT WORK. YOU HAVE A GREAT JOB BUT YOU NEGLECT IT! YOU WANNA GET FIRED OR WHAT?!
CALM DOWN, DARLING! YOU'RE PREGNANT!
I CAN'T PLAY PRETEND ANYMORE.
I DECIDED TO BE FRANK.
I SWEAR, ELEANOR, I SAW JEAN-OLIVIER KISSING YOUR BABYSITTER!
...EVEN IF IT HAS A BOOMERANG EFFECT...
THAT IDIOT EVA?! ABSOLUTELY NOT!
WHAT IS THIS NONSENSE?!
YOU'RE TRYING TO RUIN MY HAPPINESS!
YOU NEED PROFESSIONAL HELP! YOU'RE JUST JEALOUS!
IT'S SO PATHETIC! ERASING TWENTY YEARS OF FRIENDSHIP, JUST LIKE THAT!
93

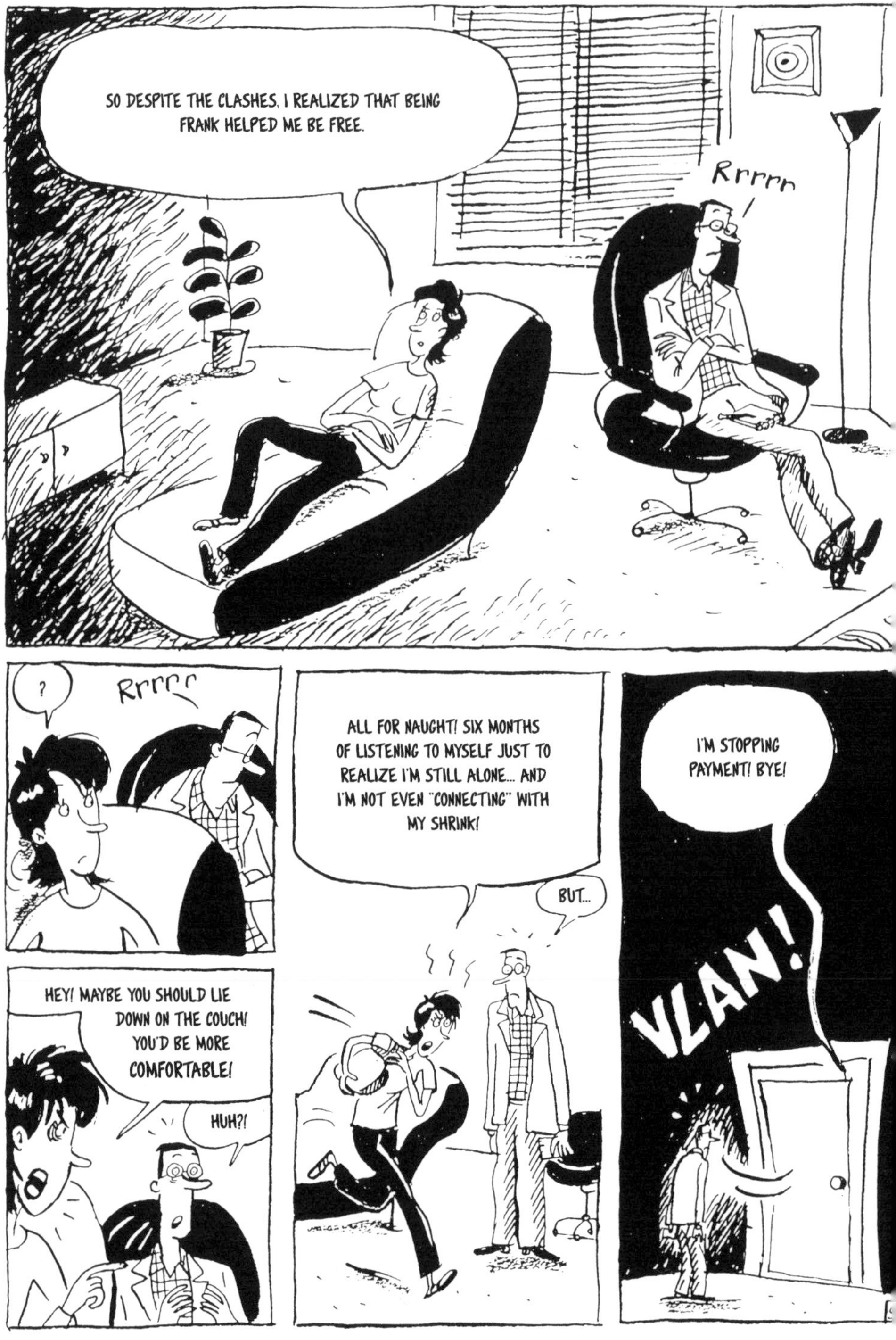
SO DESPITE THE CLASHES, I REALIZED THAT BEING FRANK HELPED ME BE FREE.
Rrrrr
?
Rrrrr
ALL FOR NAUGHT! SIX MONTHS OF LISTENING TO MYSELF JUST TO REALIZE I'M STILL ALONE... AND I'M NOT EVEN "CONNECTING" WITH MY SHRINK!
BUT...
I'M STOPPING PAYMENT! BYE!
VLAN!
HEY! MAYBE YOU SHOULD LIE DOWN ON THE COUCH! YOU'D BE MORE COMFORTABLE!
HUH?!

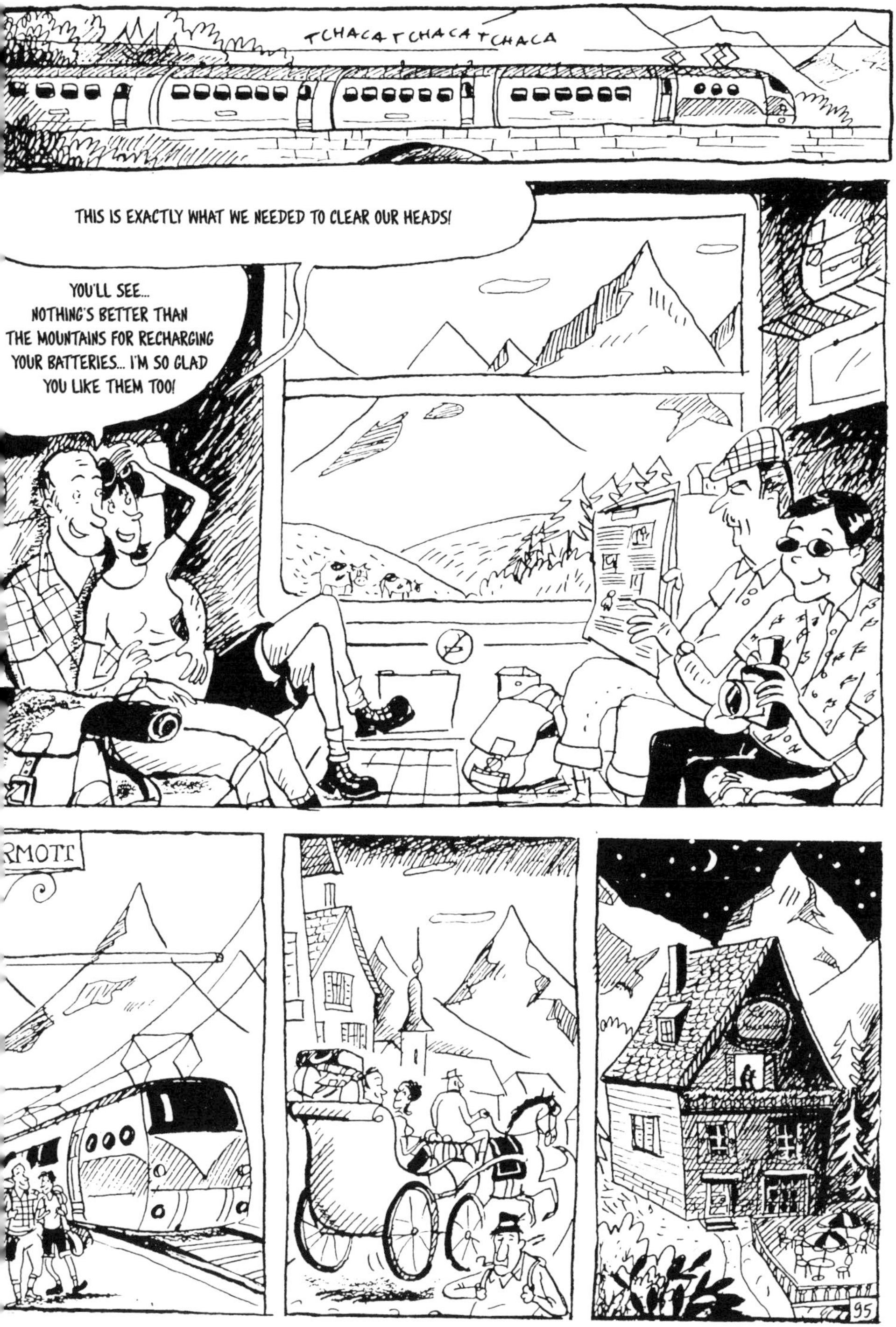
TCHACA TCHACA TCHACA
THIS IS EXACTLY WHAT WE NEEDED TO CLEAR OUR HEADS!
YOU'LL SEE... NOTHING'S BETTER THAN THE MOUNTAINS FOR RECHARGING YOUR BATTERIES... I'M SO GLAD YOU LIKE THEM TOO!
RMOTT
95

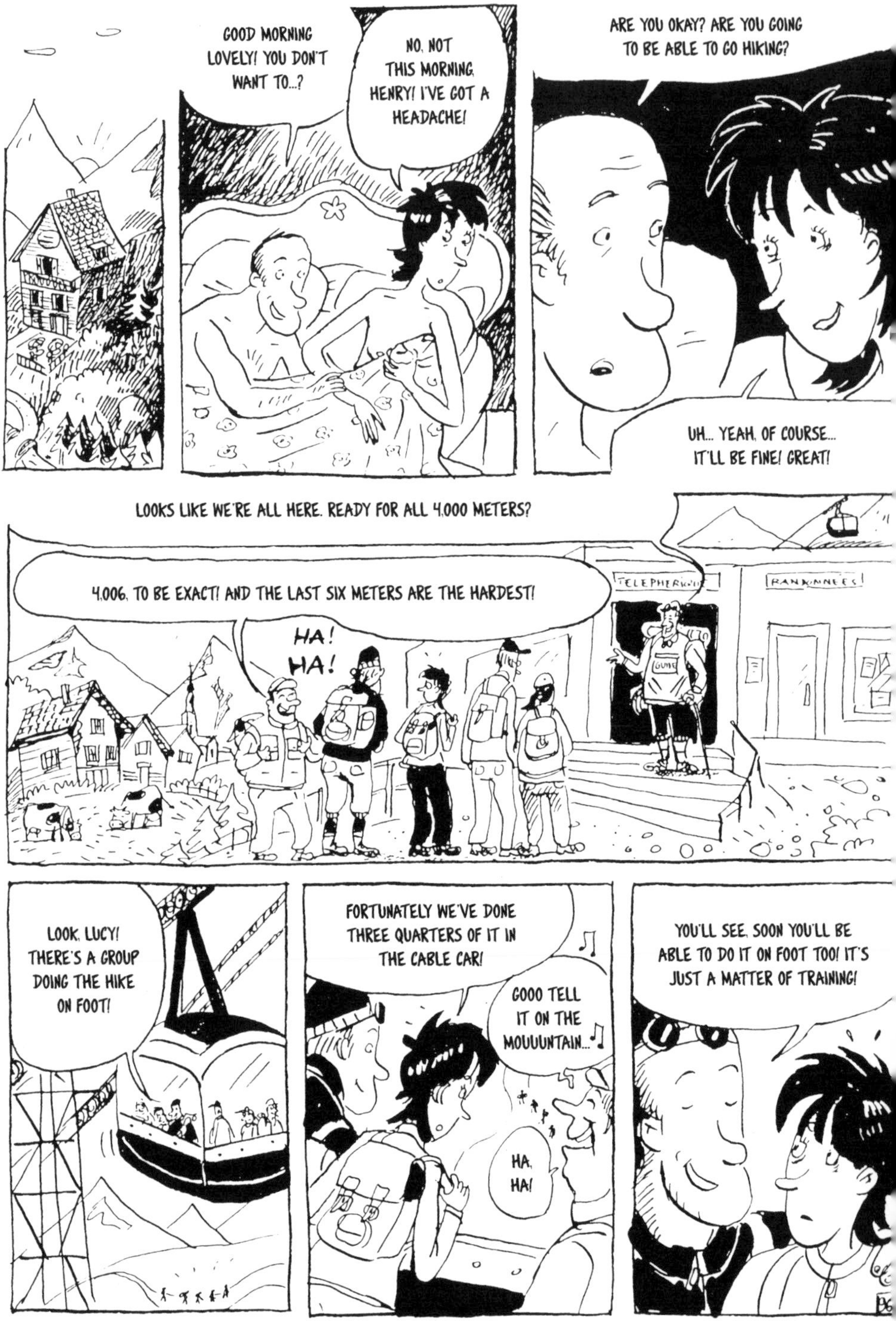
GOOD MORNING LOVELY! YOU DON'T WANT TO...?
NO, NOT THIS MORNING, HENRY! I'VE GOT A HEADACHE!
ARE YOU OKAY? ARE YOU GOING TO BE ABLE TO GO HIKING?
UH... YEAH, OF COURSE... IT'LL BE FINE! GREAT!
LOOKS LIKE WE'RE ALL HERE. READY FOR ALL 4,000 METERS?
4,006, TO BE EXACT! AND THE LAST SIX METERS ARE THE HARDEST!
HA! HA!
TELEPHERIQUE
RANDONNEES
GUIDE
LOOK, LUCY! THERE'S A GROUP DOING THE HIKE ON FOOT!
FORTUNATELY WE'VE DONE THREE QUARTERS OF IT IN THE CABLE CAR!
GOOO TELL IT ON THE MOUUUNTAIN...
HA, HA!
YOU'LL SEE, SOON YOU'LL BE ABLE TO DO IT ON FOOT TOO! IT'S JUST A MATTER OF TRAINING!

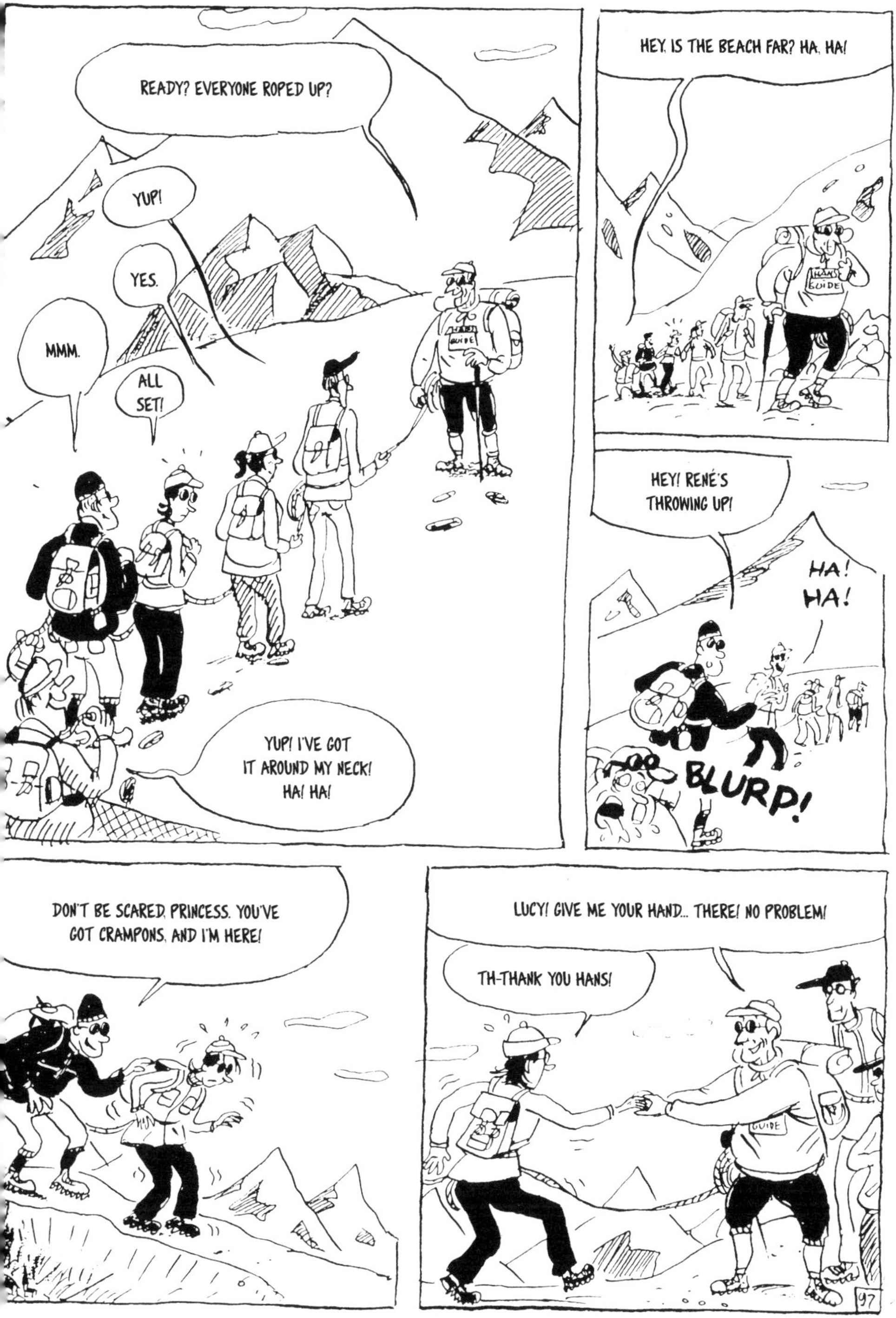
READY? EVERYONE ROPED UP?
YUP!
YES.
MMM.
ALL SET!
YUP! I'VE GOT IT AROUND MY NECK! HA! HA!
HEY, IS THE BEACH FAR? HA, HA!
HEY! RENÉ'S THROWING UP!
HA! HA!
BLURP!
DON'T BE SCARED, PRINCESS. YOU'VE GOT CRAMPONS, AND I'M HERE!
LUCY! GIVE ME YOUR HAND... THERE! NO PROBLEM!
TH-THANK YOU HANS!

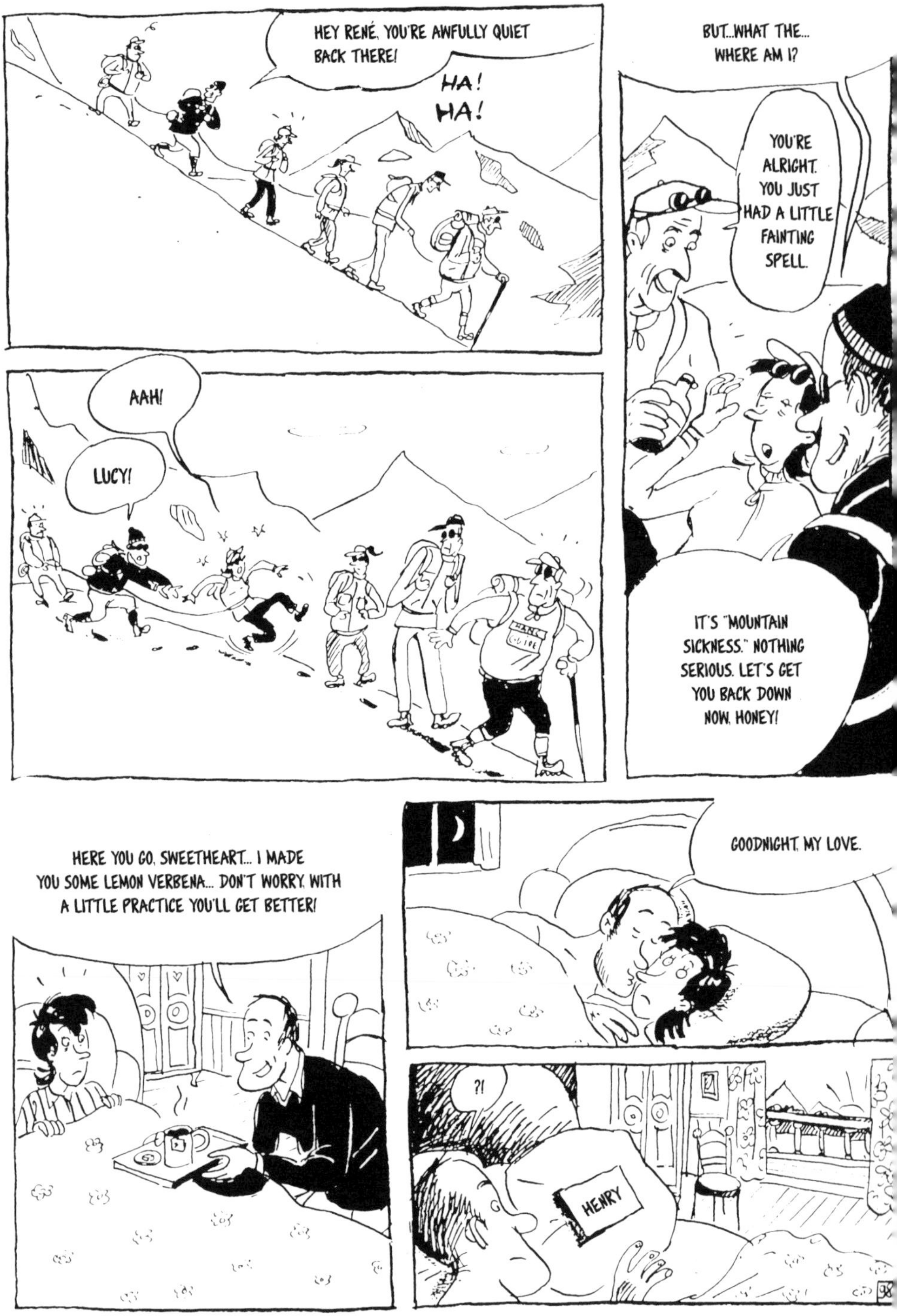
HEY RENÉ, YOU'RE AWFULLY QUIET BACK THERE!
HA! HA!
AAH!
LUCY!
BUT...WHAT THE... WHERE AM I?
YOU'RE ALRIGHT. YOU JUST HAD A LITTLE FAINTING SPELL.
IT'S "MOUNTAIN SICKNESS." NOTHING SERIOUS. LET'S GET YOU BACK DOWN NOW, HONEY!
HERE YOU GO, SWEETHEART... I MADE YOU SOME LEMON VERBENA... DON'T WORRY, WITH A LITTLE PRACTICE YOU'LL GET BETTER!
GOODNIGHT, MY LOVE.
?!
HENRY

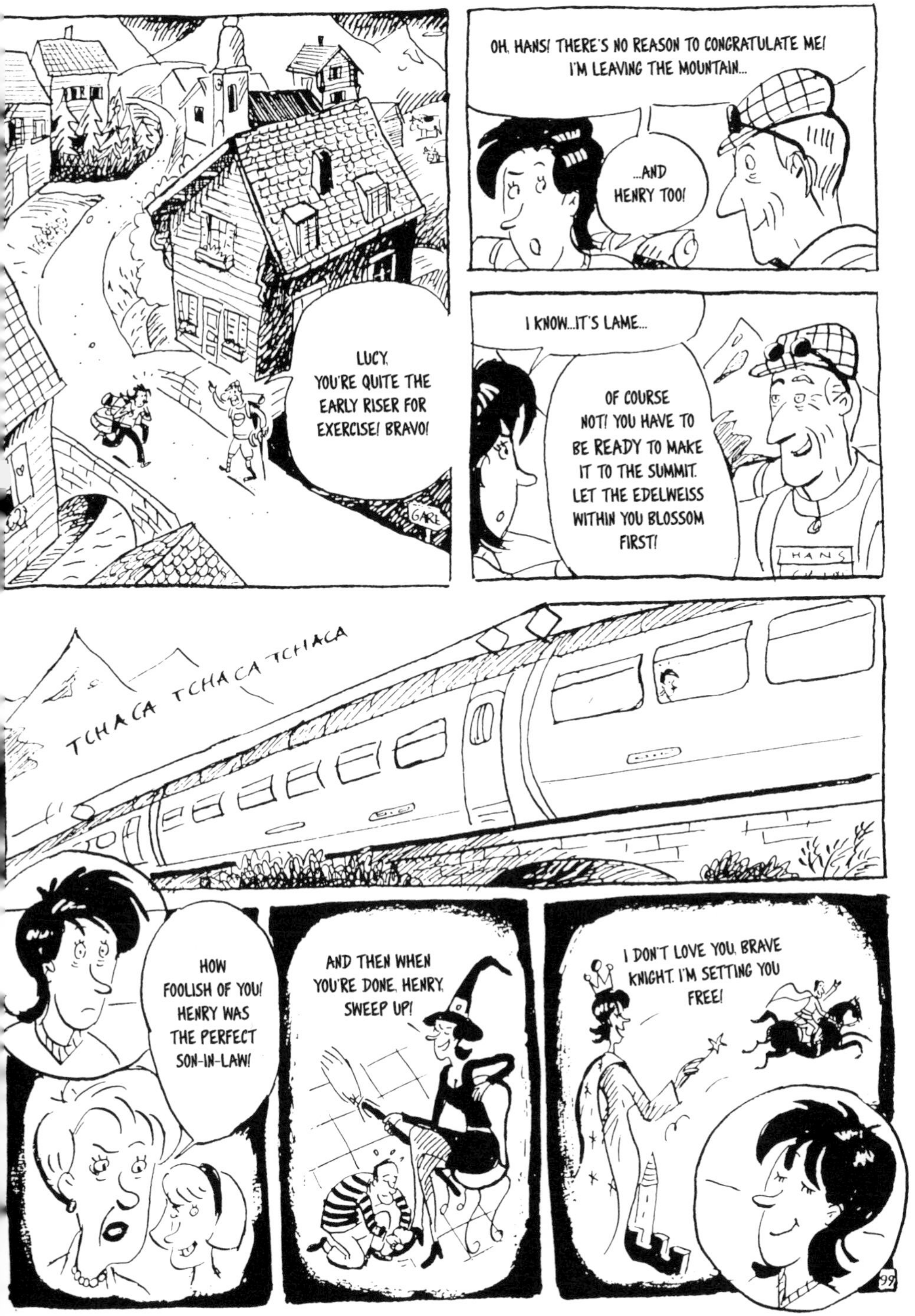
LUCY, YOU'RE QUITE THE EARLY RISER FOR EXERCISE! BRAVO!
GARE
OH, HANS! THERE'S NO REASON TO CONGRATULATE ME! I'M LEAVING THE MOUNTAIN...
...AND HENRY TOO!
I KNOW...IT'S LAME...
OF COURSE NOT! YOU HAVE TO BE READY TO MAKE IT TO THE SUMMIT. LET THE EDELWEISS WITHIN YOU BLOSSOM FIRST!
HANS
TCHACA TCHACA TCHACA TCHACA
HOW FOOLISH OF YOU! HENRY WAS THE PERFECT SON-IN-LAW!
AND THEN WHEN YOU'RE DONE, HENRY, SWEEP UP!
I DON'T LOVE YOU, BRAVE KNIGHT. I'M SETTING YOU FREE!
99

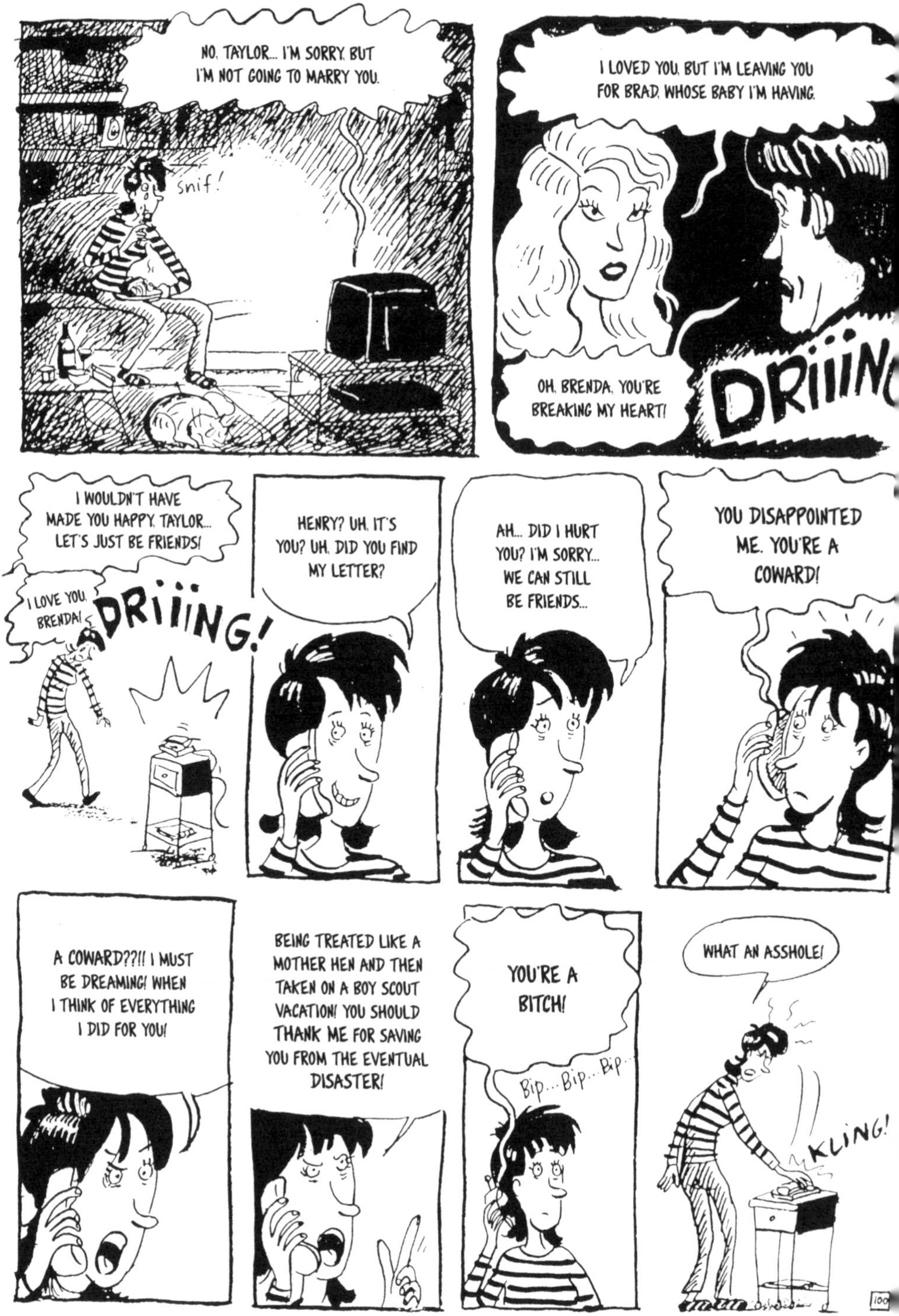
NO, TAYLOR... I'M SORRY, BUT I'M NOT GOING TO MARRY YOU.
snif!
I LOVED YOU, BUT I'M LEAVING YOU FOR BRAD, WHOSE BABY I'M HAVING.
OH, BRENDA, YOU'RE BREAKING MY HEART!
DRIIING
I WOULDN'T HAVE MADE YOU HAPPY, TAYLOR... LET'S JUST BE FRIENDS!
I LOVE YOU, BRENDA!
DRIIING!
HENRY? UH, IT'S YOU? UH, DID YOU FIND MY LETTER?
AH... DID I HURT YOU? I'M SORRY... WE CAN STILL BE FRIENDS...
YOU DISAPPOINTED ME. YOU'RE A COWARD!
A COWARD??!! I MUST BE DREAMING! WHEN I THINK OF EVERYTHING I DID FOR YOU!
BEING TREATED LIKE A MOTHER HEN AND THEN TAKEN ON A BOY SCOUT VACATION! YOU SHOULD THANK ME FOR SAVING YOU FROM THE EVENTUAL DISASTER!
YOU'RE A BITCH!
Bip... Bip... Bip...
WHAT AN ASSHOLE!
KLING!
100

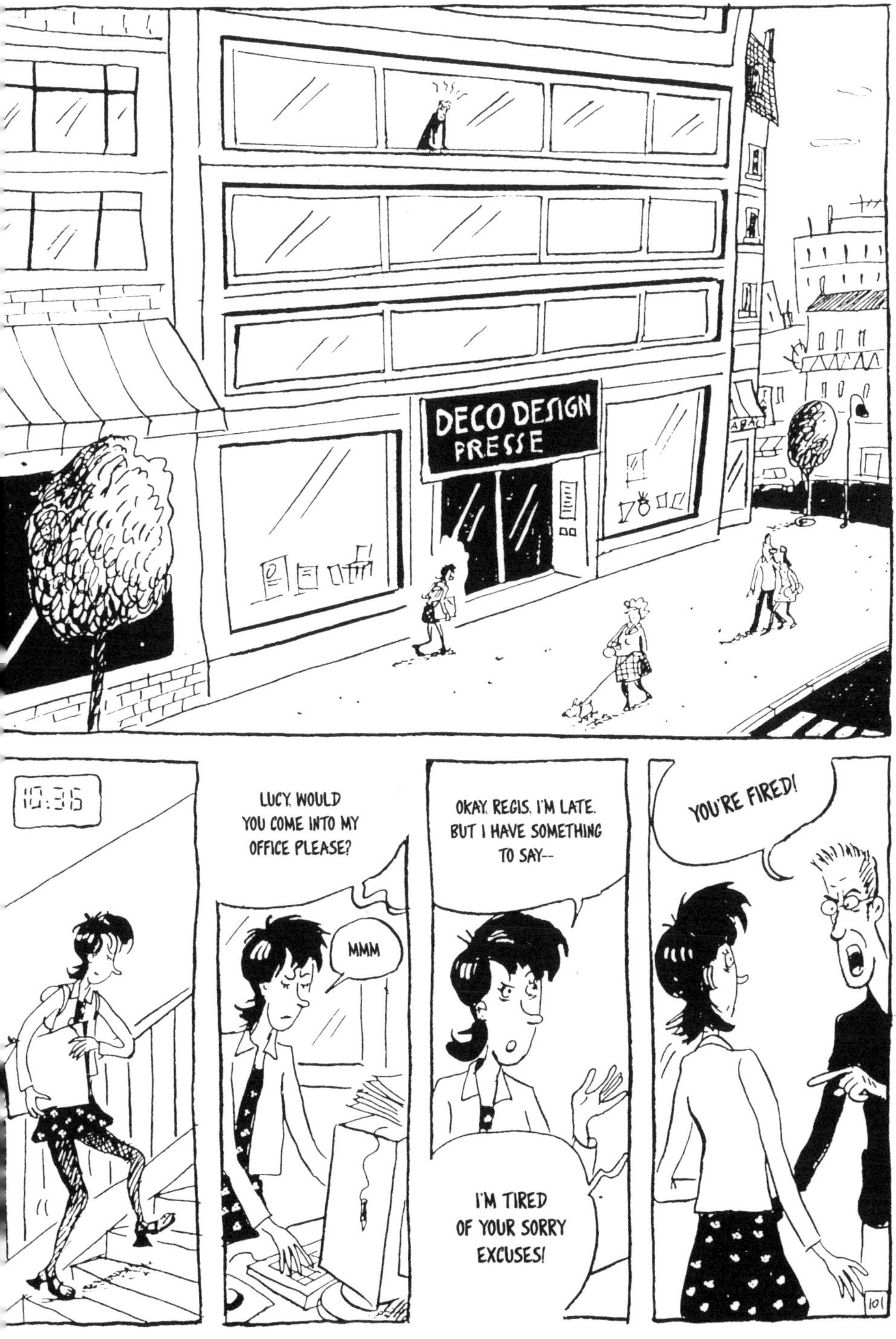
DECO DESIGN
PRESSE
10:36
LUCY, WOULD YOU COME INTO MY OFFICE PLEASE?
MMM
OKAY, REGIS, I'M LATE. BUT I HAVE SOMETHING TO SAY--
I'M TIRED OF YOUR SORRY EXCUSES!
YOU'RE FIRED!
101

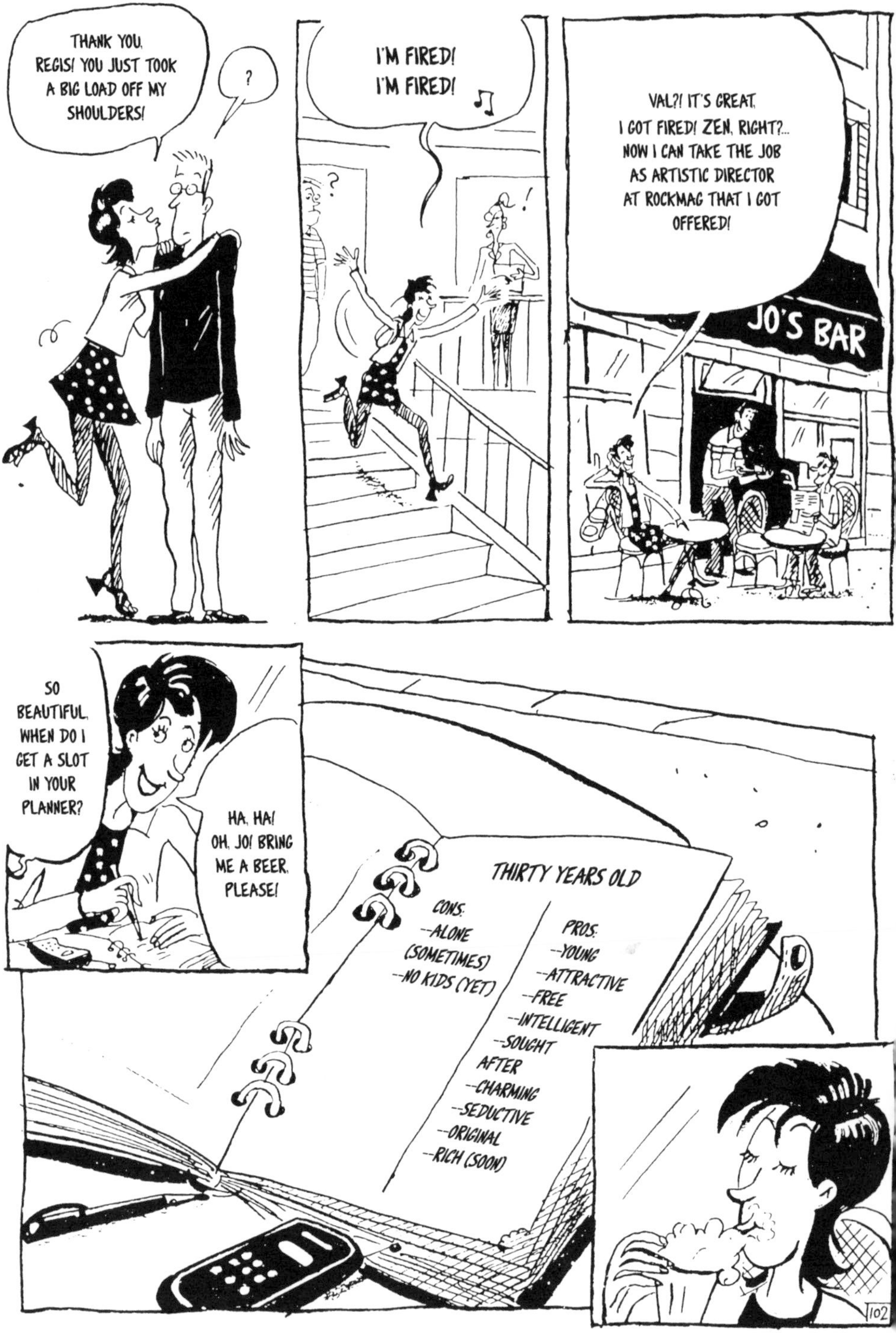
THANK YOU, REGIS! YOU JUST TOOK A BIG LOAD OFF MY SHOULDERS!
?
I'M FIRED! I'M FIRED!
?
!
VAL?! IT'S GREAT, I GOT FIRED! ZEN, RIGHT?... NOW I CAN TAKE THE JOB AS ARTISTIC DIRECTOR AT ROCKMAG THAT I GOT OFFERED!
JO'S BAR
SO BEAUTIFUL, WHEN DO I GET A SLOT IN YOUR PLANNER?
HA, HA! OH, JO! BRING ME A BEER, PLEASE!
THIRTY YEARS OLD
CONS:
--ALONE (SOMETIMES)
--NO KIDS (YET)
PROS:
--YOUNG
--ATTRACTIVE
--FREE
--INTELLIGENT
--SOUGHT AFTER
--CHARMING
--SEDUCTIVE
--ORIGINAL
--RICH (SOON)
102

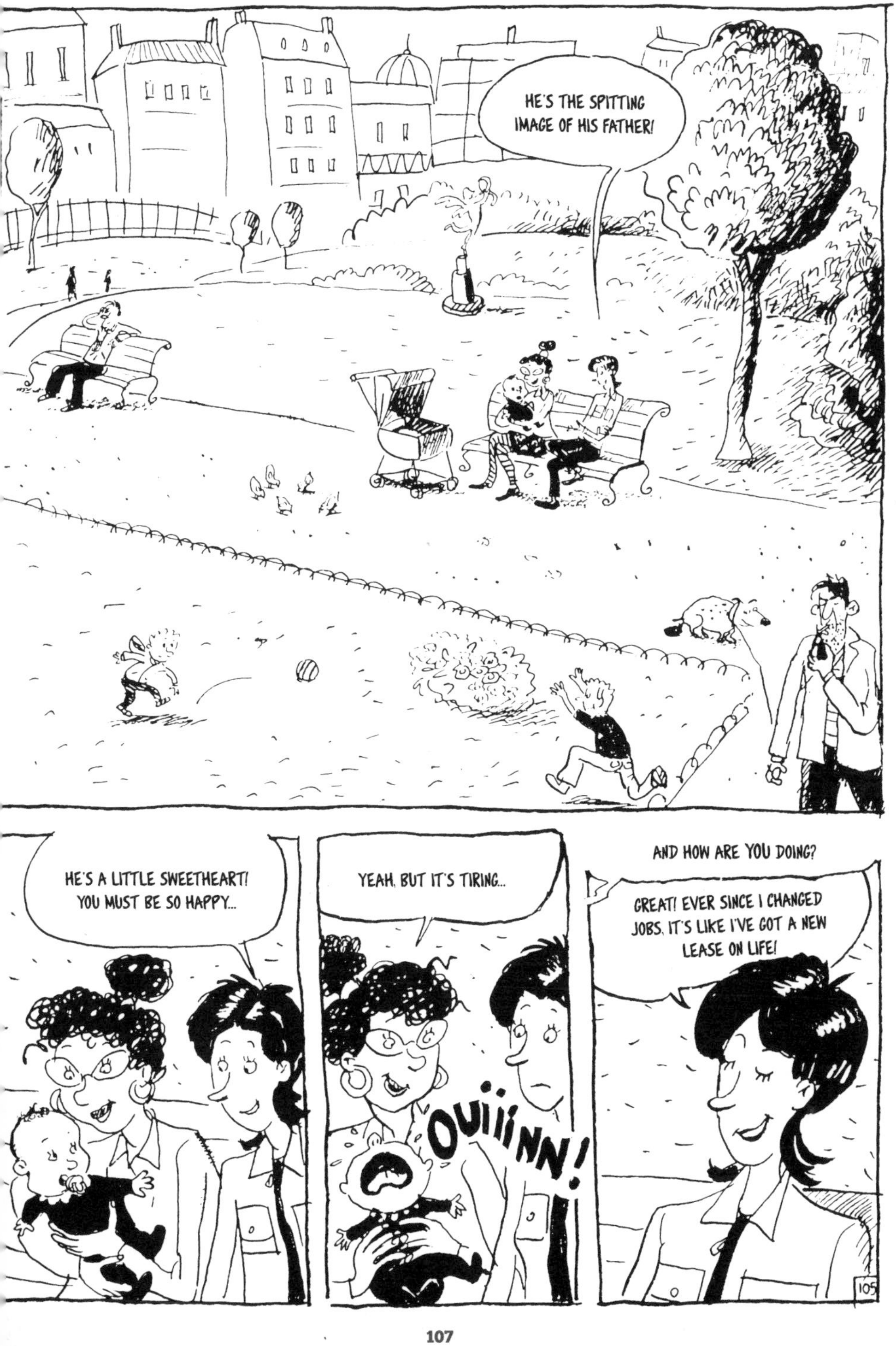

HE'S THE SPITTING IMAGE OF HIS FATHER!
HE'S A LITTLE SWEETHEART! YOU MUST BE SO HAPPY...
YEAH, BUT IT'S TIRING...
OUIIIINN!
AND HOW ARE YOU DOING?
GREAT! EVER SINCE I CHANGED JOBS, IT'S LIKE I'VE GOT A NEW LEASE ON LIFE!
105

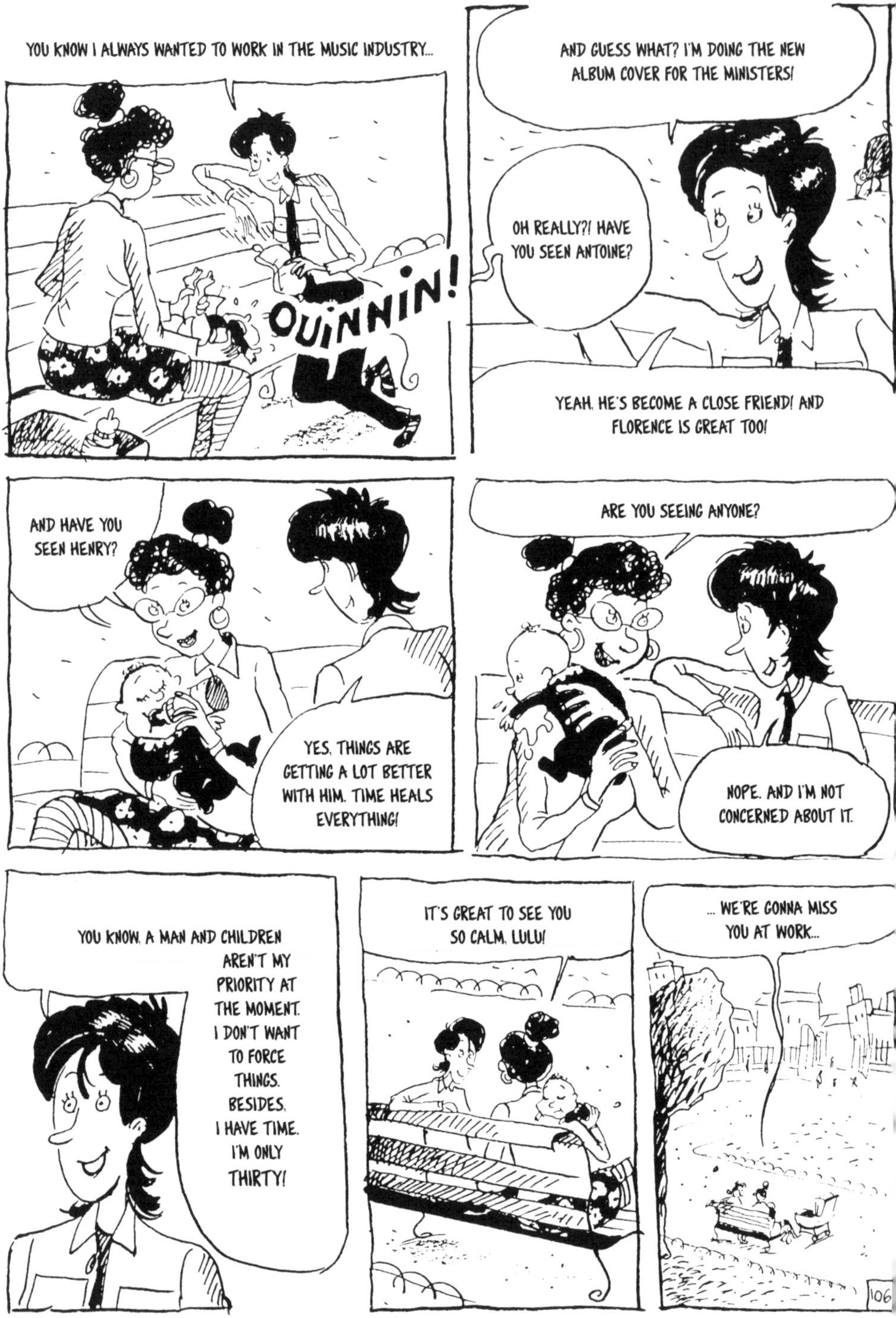
YOU KNOW I ALWAYS WANTED TO WORK IN THE MUSIC INDUSTRY...
OUINNIN!
AND GUESS WHAT? I'M DOING THE NEW ALBUM COVER FOR THE MINISTERS!
OH REALLY?! HAVE YOU SEEN ANTOINE?
YEAH, HE'S BECOME A CLOSE FRIEND! AND FLORENCE IS GREAT TOO!
AND HAVE YOU SEEN HENRY?
YES, THINGS ARE GETTING A LOT BETTER WITH HIM. TIME HEALS EVERYTHING!
ARE YOU SEEING ANYONE?
NOPE. AND I'M NOT CONCERNED ABOUT IT.
YOU KNOW, A MAN AND CHILDREN AREN'T MY PRIORITY AT THE MOMENT. I DON'T WANT TO FORCE THINGS. BESIDES, I HAVE TIME. I'M ONLY THIRTY!
IT'S GREAT TO SEE YOU SO CALM, LULU!
... WE'RE GONNA MISS YOU AT WORK...
106

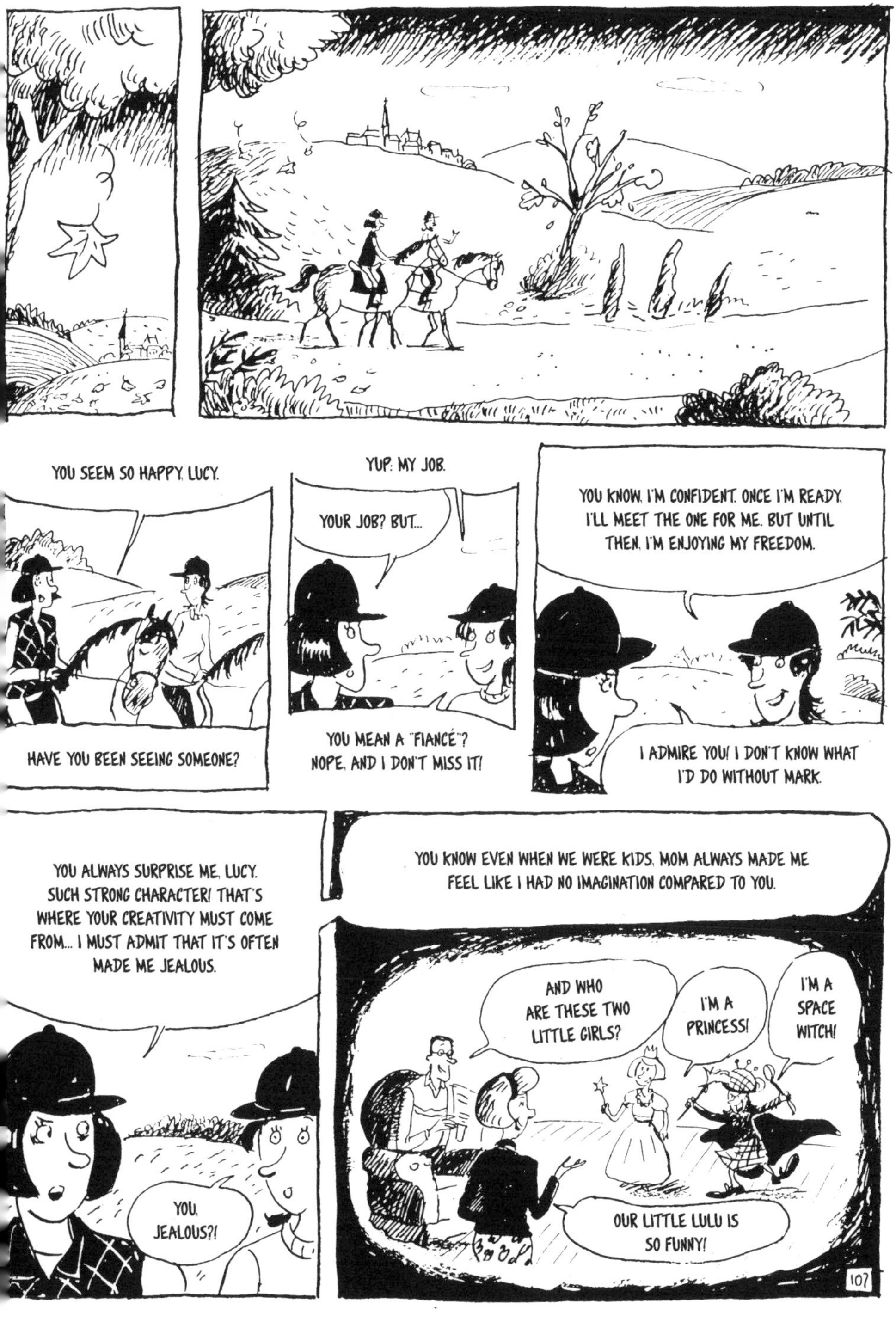
YOU SEEM SO HAPPY, LUCY.
HAVE YOU BEEN SEEING SOMEONE?
YUP: MY JOB.
YOUR JOB? BUT...
YOU MEAN A "FIANCÉ"? NOPE, AND I DON'T MISS IT!
YOU KNOW, I'M CONFIDENT. ONCE I'M READY, I'LL MEET THE ONE FOR ME. BUT UNTIL THEN, I'M ENJOYING MY FREEDOM.
I ADMIRE YOU! I DON'T KNOW WHAT I'D DO WITHOUT MARK.
YOU ALWAYS SURPRISE ME, LUCY. SUCH STRONG CHARACTER! THAT'S WHERE YOUR CREATIVITY MUST COME FROM... I MUST ADMIT THAT IT'S OFTEN MADE ME JEALOUS.
YOU, JEALOUS?!
YOU KNOW EVEN WHEN WE WERE KIDS, MOM ALWAYS MADE ME FEEL LIKE I HAD NO IMAGINATION COMPARED TO YOU.
AND WHO ARE THESE TWO LITTLE GIRLS?
I'M A PRINCESS!
I'M A SPACE WITCH!
OUR LITTLE LULU IS SO FUNNY!
107

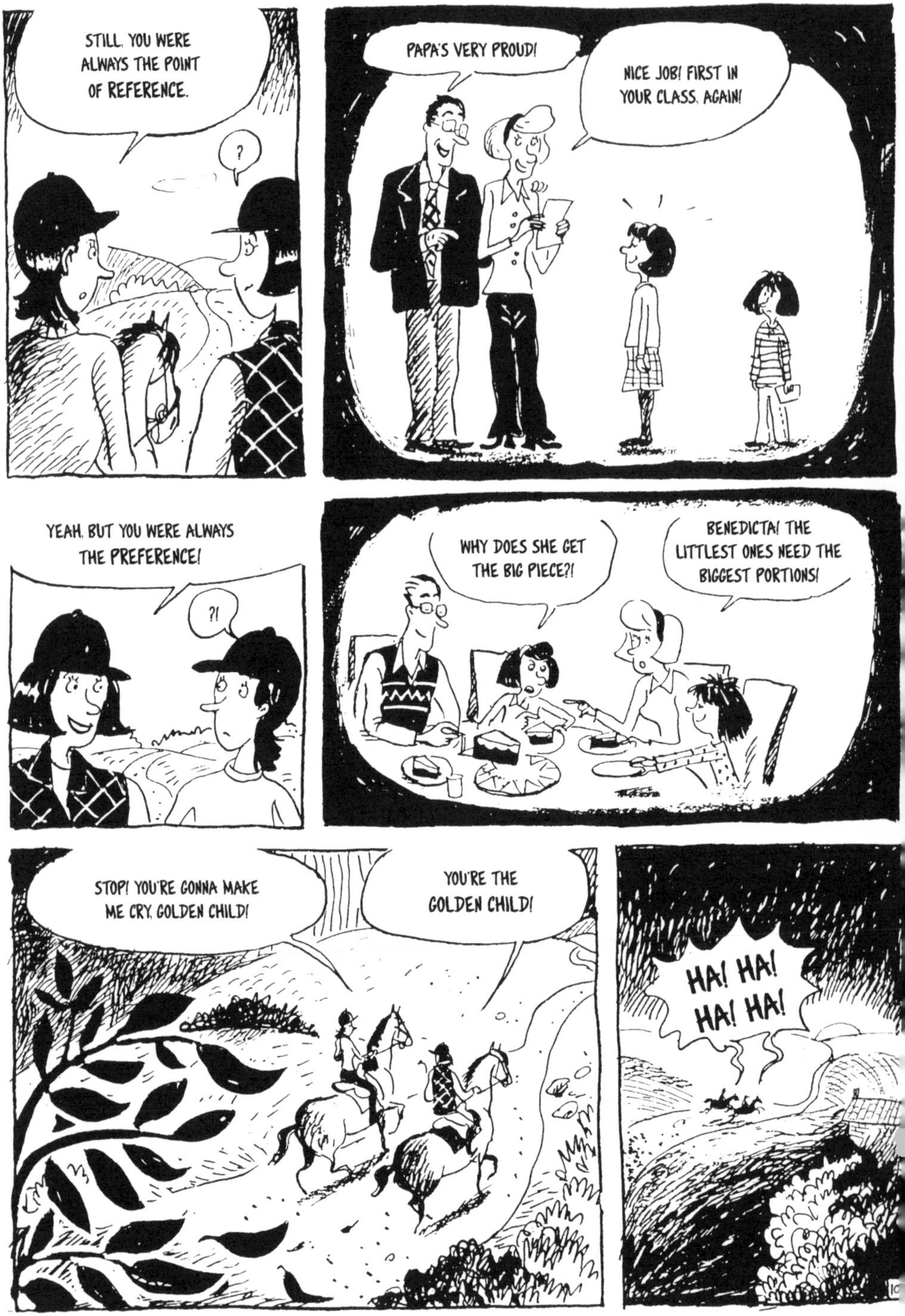
STILL, YOU WERE ALWAYS THE POINT OF REFERENCE.
?
PAPA'S VERY PROUD!
NICE JOB! FIRST IN YOUR CLASS, AGAIN!
YEAH, BUT YOU WERE ALWAYS THE PREFERENCE!
?!
WHY DOES SHE GET THE BIG PIECE?!
BENEDICTA! THE LITTLEST ONES NEED THE BIGGEST PORTIONS!
STOP! YOU'RE GONNA MAKE ME CRY, GOLDEN CHILD!
YOU'RE THE GOLDEN CHILD!
HA! HA! HA! HA!

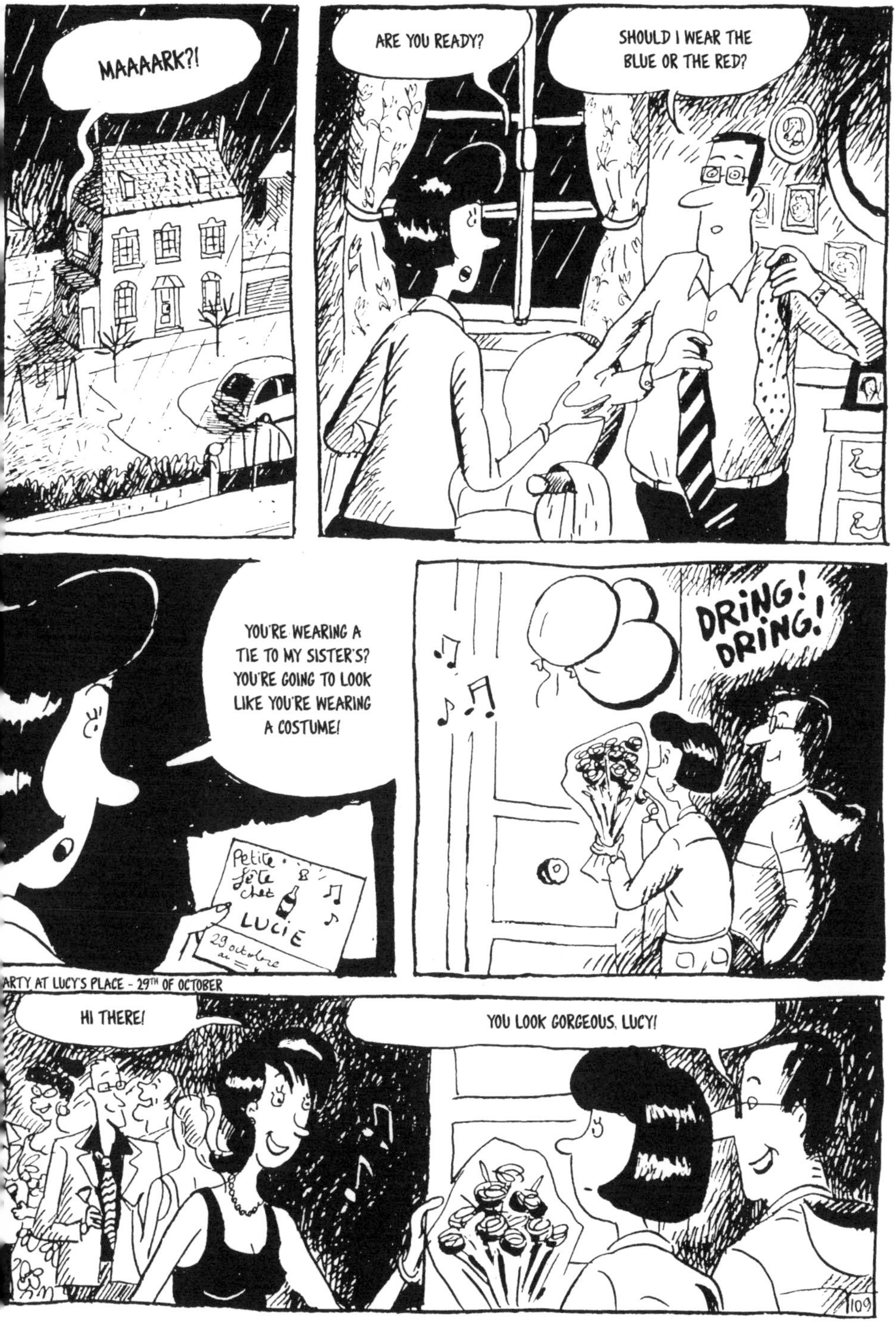
MAAAARK?!
ARE YOU READY?
SHOULD I WEAR THE BLUE OR THE RED?
YOU'RE WEARING A TIE TO MY SISTER'S? YOU'RE GOING TO LOOK LIKE YOU'RE WEARING A COSTUME!
Petite fête
LUCIE
29 octobre
DRING! DRING!
ARTY AT LUCY'S PLACE - 29TH OF OCTOBER
HI THERE!
YOU LOOK GORGEOUS, LUCY!
109

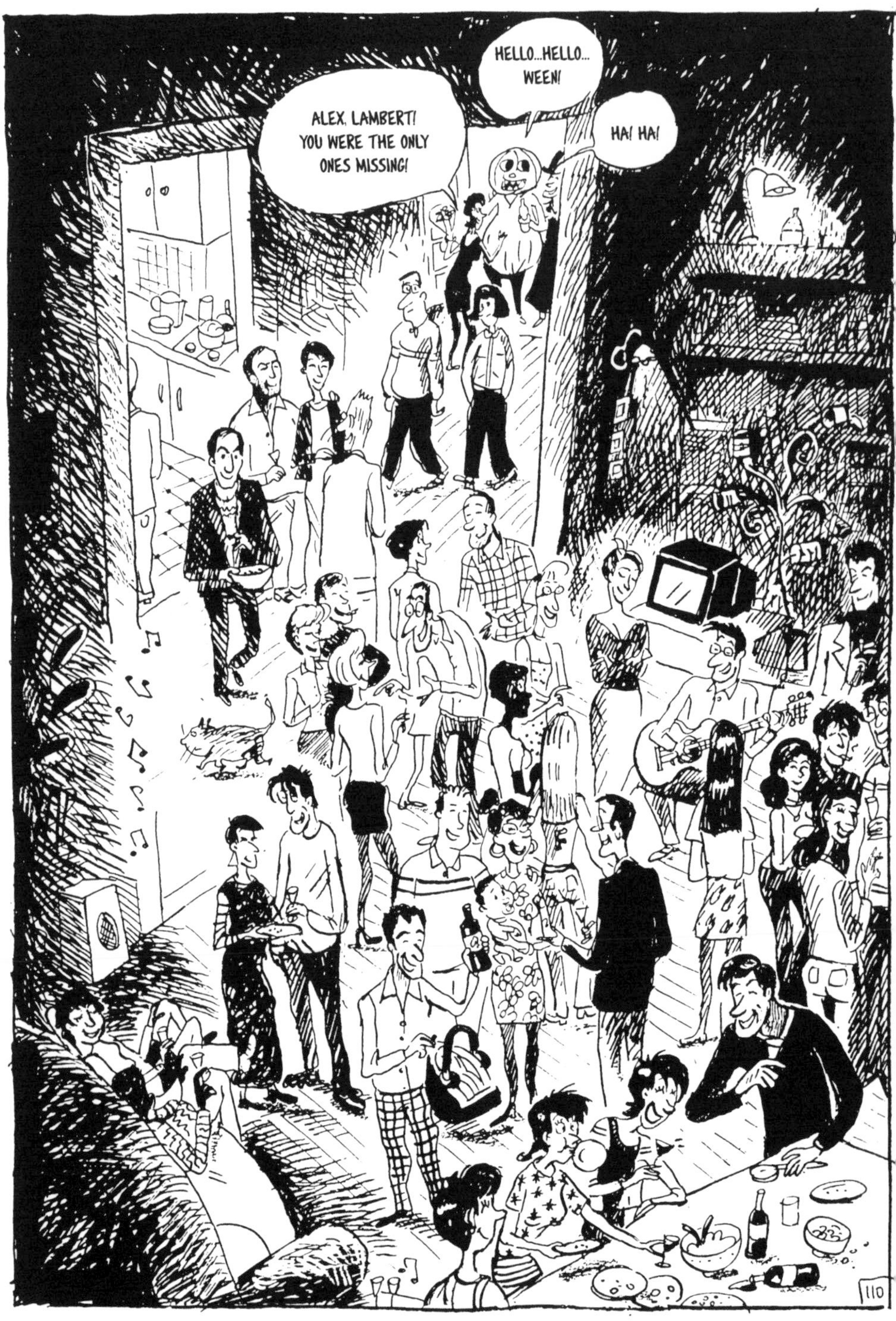
HELLO...HELLO... WEEN!
ALEX, LAMBERT! YOU WERE THE ONLY ONES MISSING!
HA! HA!
110

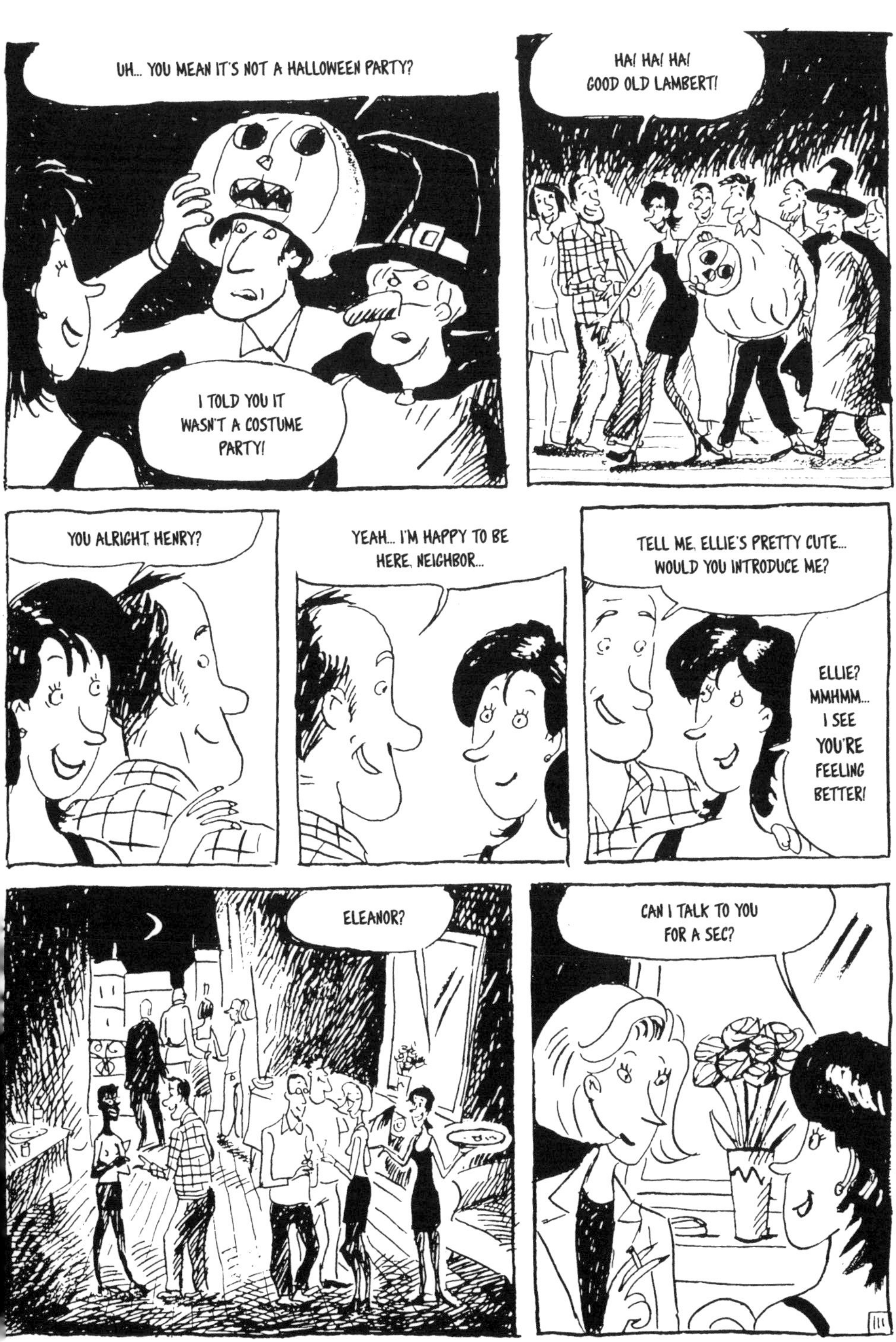
UH... YOU MEAN IT'S NOT A HALLOWEEN PARTY?
I TOLD YOU IT WASN'T A COSTUME PARTY!
HA! HA! HA! GOOD OLD LAMBERT!
YOU ALRIGHT, HENRY?
YEAH... I'M HAPPY TO BE HERE, NEIGHBOR...
TELL ME, ELLIE'S PRETTY CUTE... WOULD YOU INTRODUCE ME?
ELLIE? MMHMM... I SEE YOU'RE FEELING BETTER!
ELEANOR?
CAN I TALK TO YOU FOR A SEC?

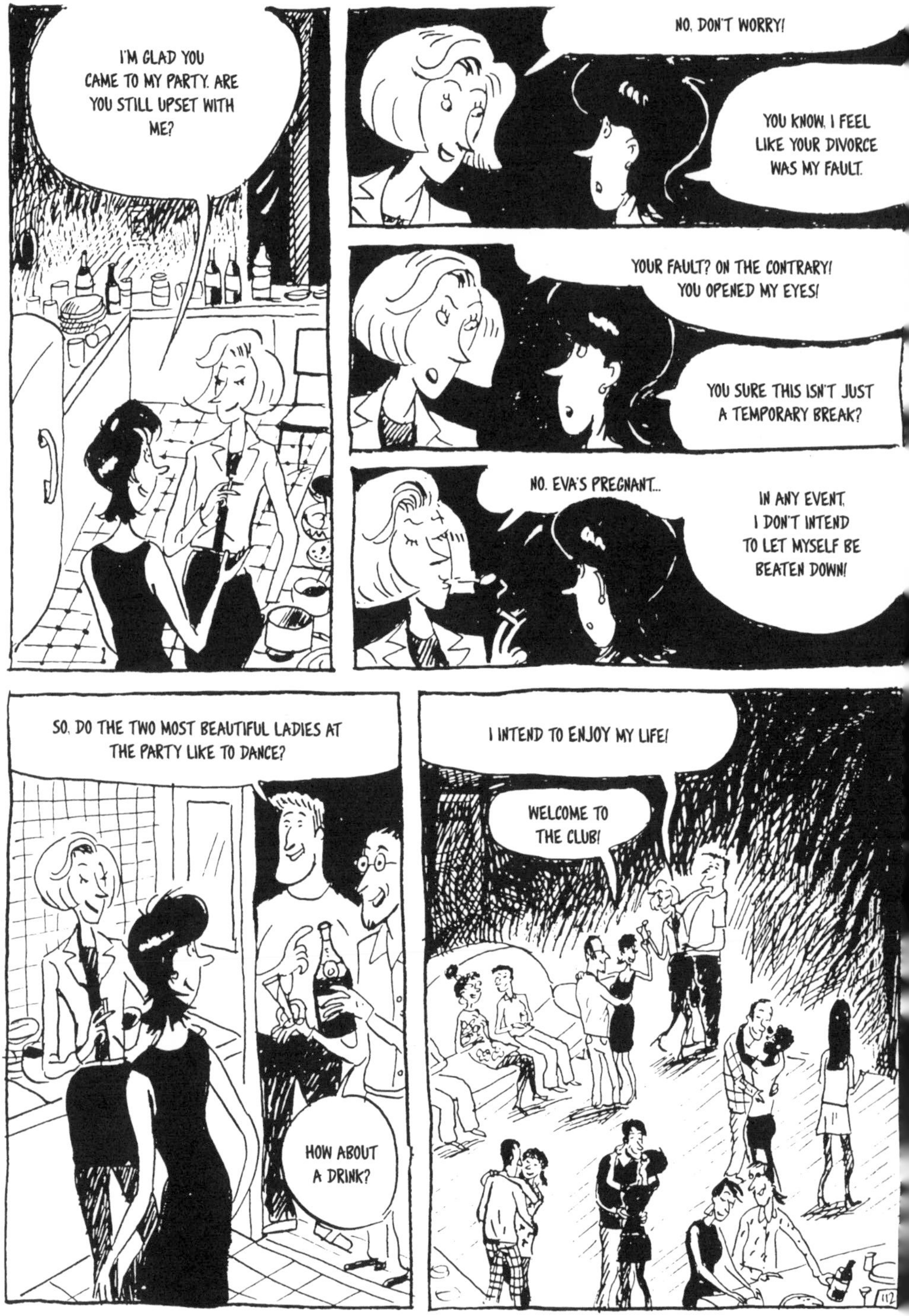
I'M GLAD YOU CAME TO MY PARTY. ARE YOU STILL UPSET WITH ME?
NO, DON'T WORRY!
YOU KNOW, I FEEL LIKE YOUR DIVORCE WAS MY FAULT.
YOUR FAULT? ON THE CONTRARY! YOU OPENED MY EYES!
YOU SURE THIS ISN'T JUST A TEMPORARY BREAK?
NO. EVA'S PREGNANT...
IN ANY EVENT, I DON'T INTEND TO LET MYSELF BE BEATEN DOWN!
SO, DO THE TWO MOST BEAUTIFUL LADIES AT THE PARTY LIKE TO DANCE?
HOW ABOUT A DRINK?
I INTEND TO ENJOY MY LIFE!
WELCOME TO THE CLUB!
112

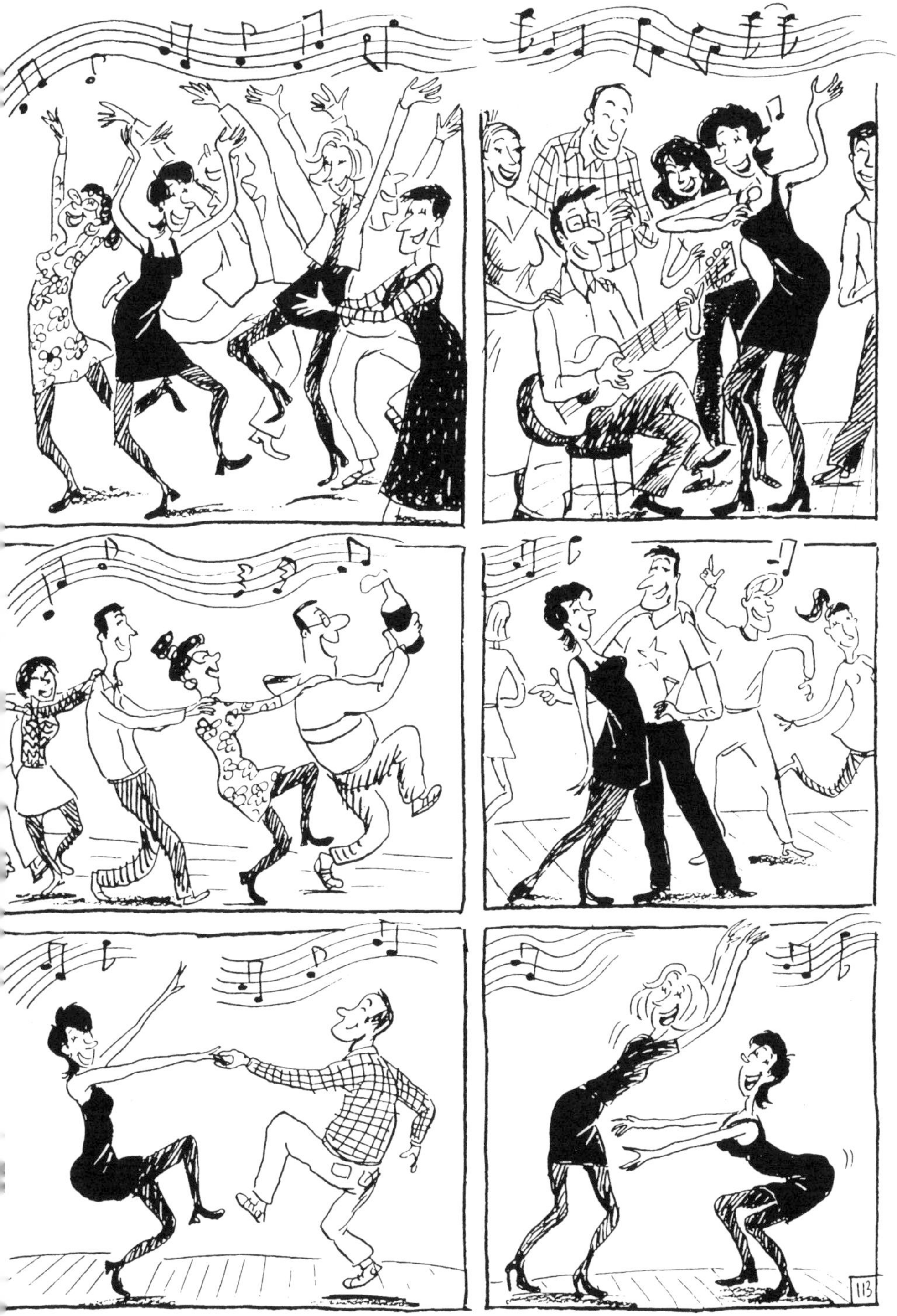
113

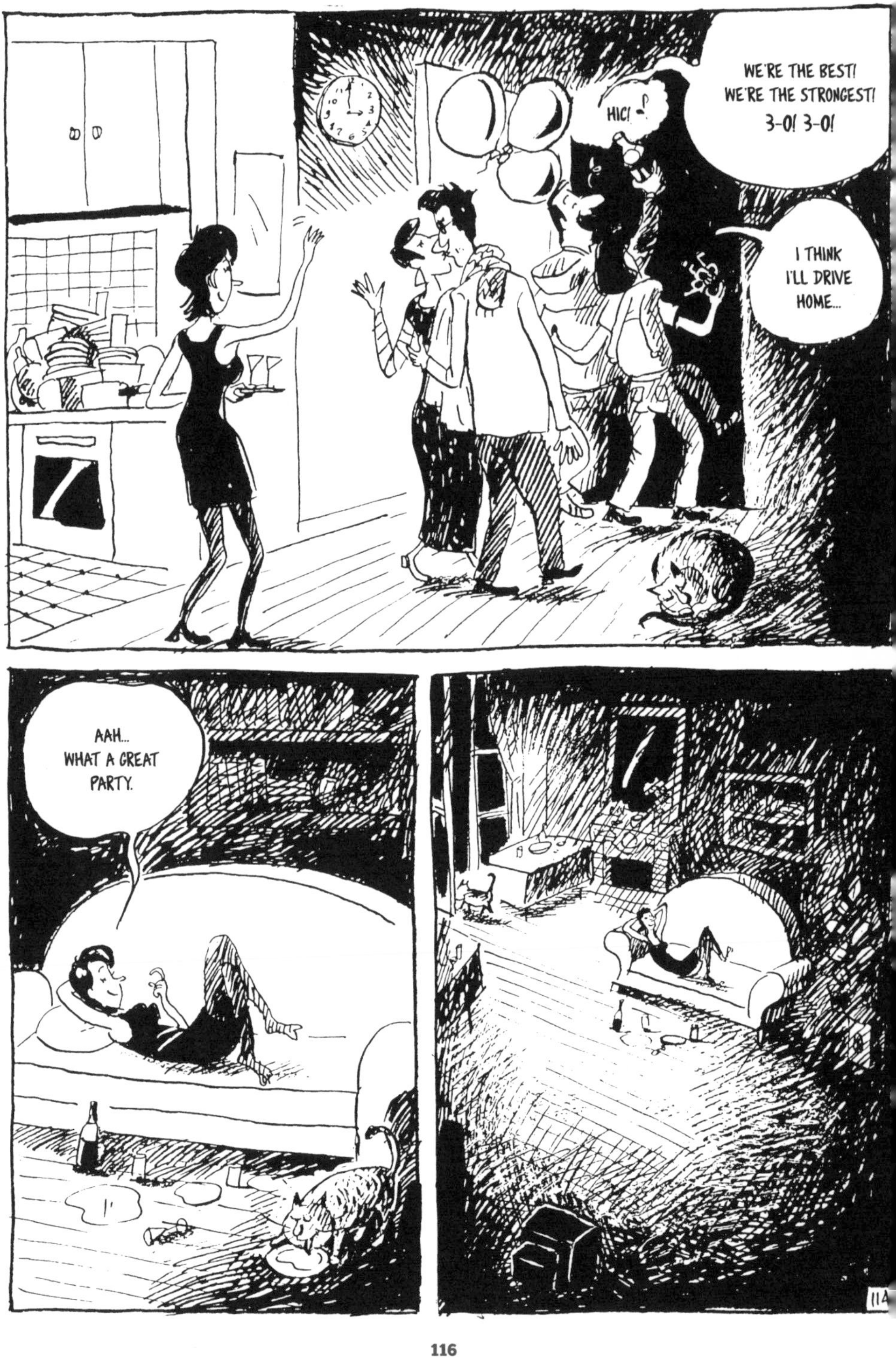

HIC! -!
WE'RE THE BEST! WE'RE THE STRONGEST! 3-0! 3-0!
I THINK I'LL DRIVE HOME...
AAH... WHAT A GREAT PARTY.

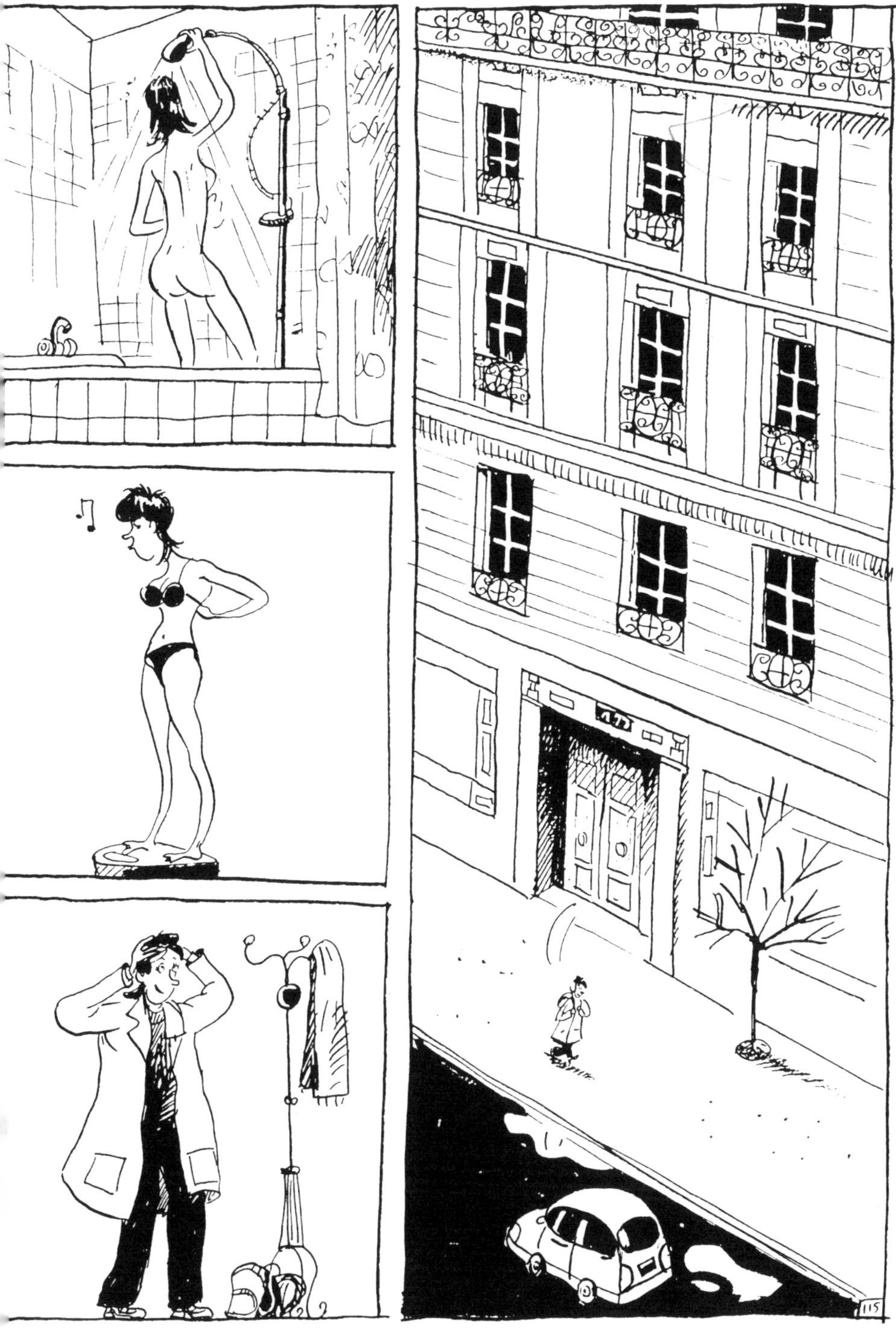

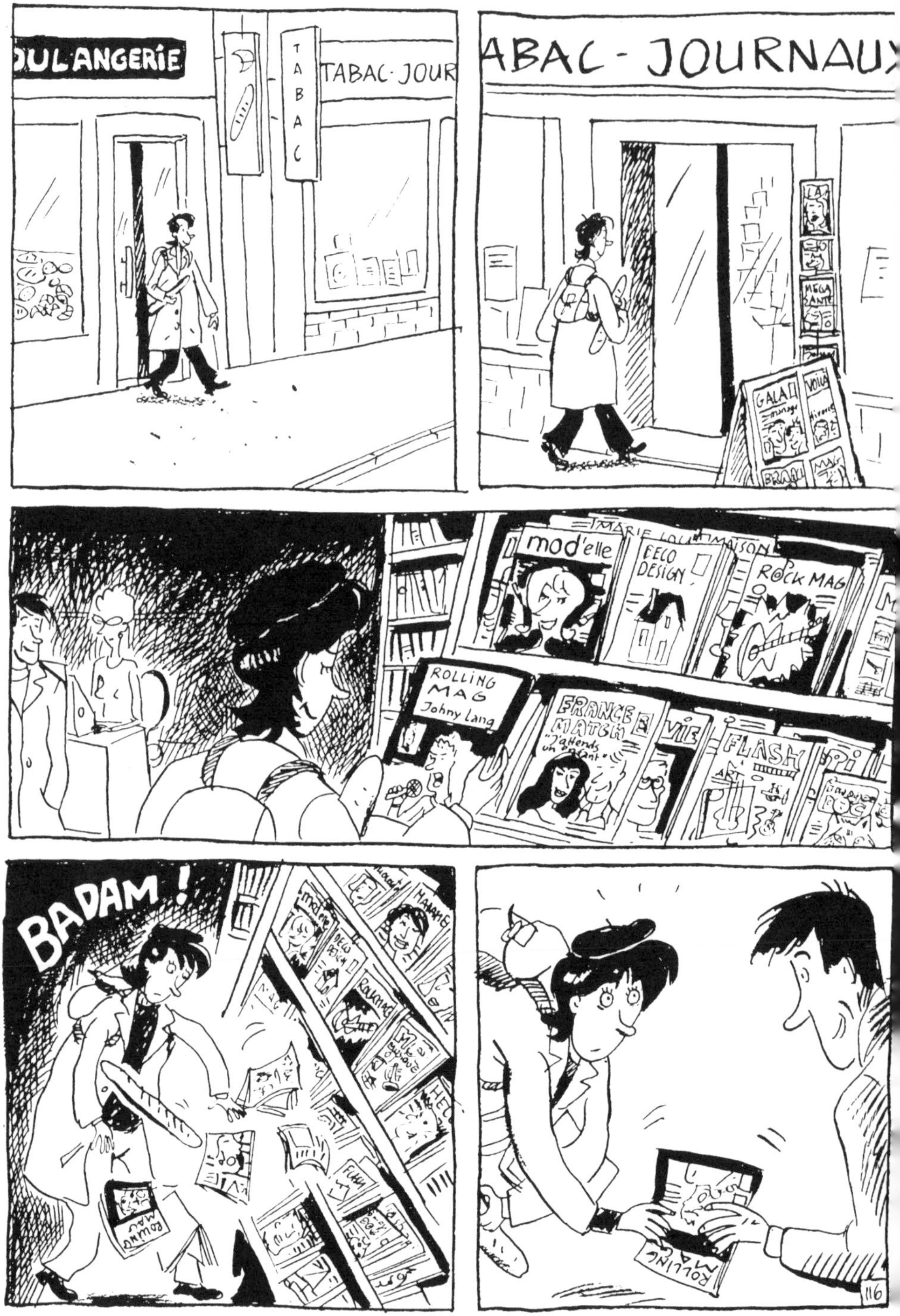
OULANGERIE
TABAC
TABAC-JOUR
ABAC - JOURNAUX
GALA
VOICI
mod'elle
DECO DESIGN
ROCK MAG
ROLLING MAG
Johny Lang
FRANCE MATCH
"J'attends un enfant"
VIE
FLASH
ART
BADAM !
116

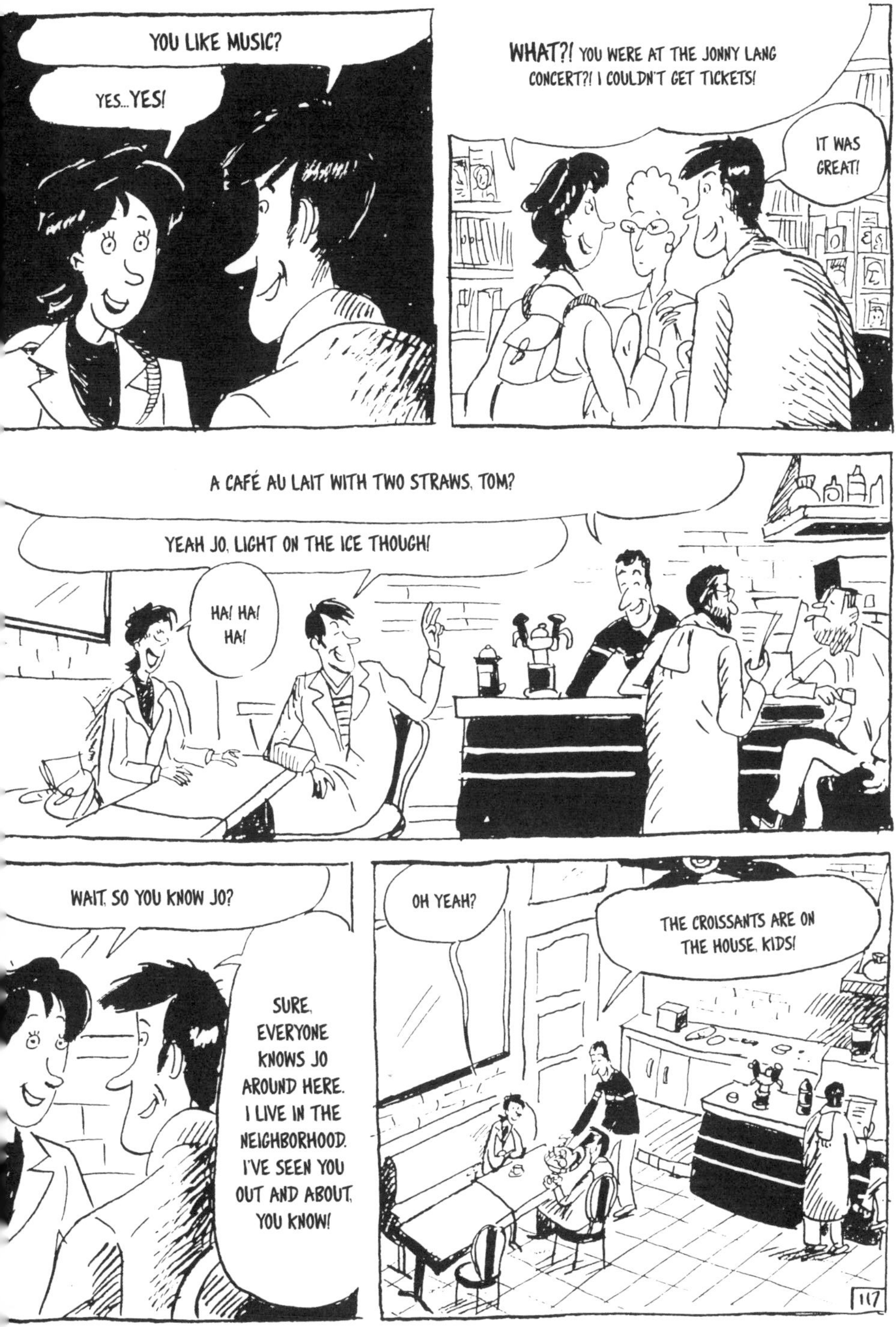
YOU LIKE MUSIC?
YES... YES!
WHAT?! YOU WERE AT THE JONNY LANG CONCERT?! I COULDN'T GET TICKETS!
IT WAS GREAT!
A CAFÉ AU LAIT WITH TWO STRAWS, TOM?
YEAH JO, LIGHT ON THE ICE THOUGH!
HA! HA! HA!
WAIT, SO YOU KNOW JO?
SURE, EVERYONE KNOWS JO AROUND HERE. I LIVE IN THE NEIGHBORHOOD. I'VE SEEN YOU OUT AND ABOUT, YOU KNOW!
OH YEAH?
THE CROISSANTS ARE ON THE HOUSE, KIDS!
117

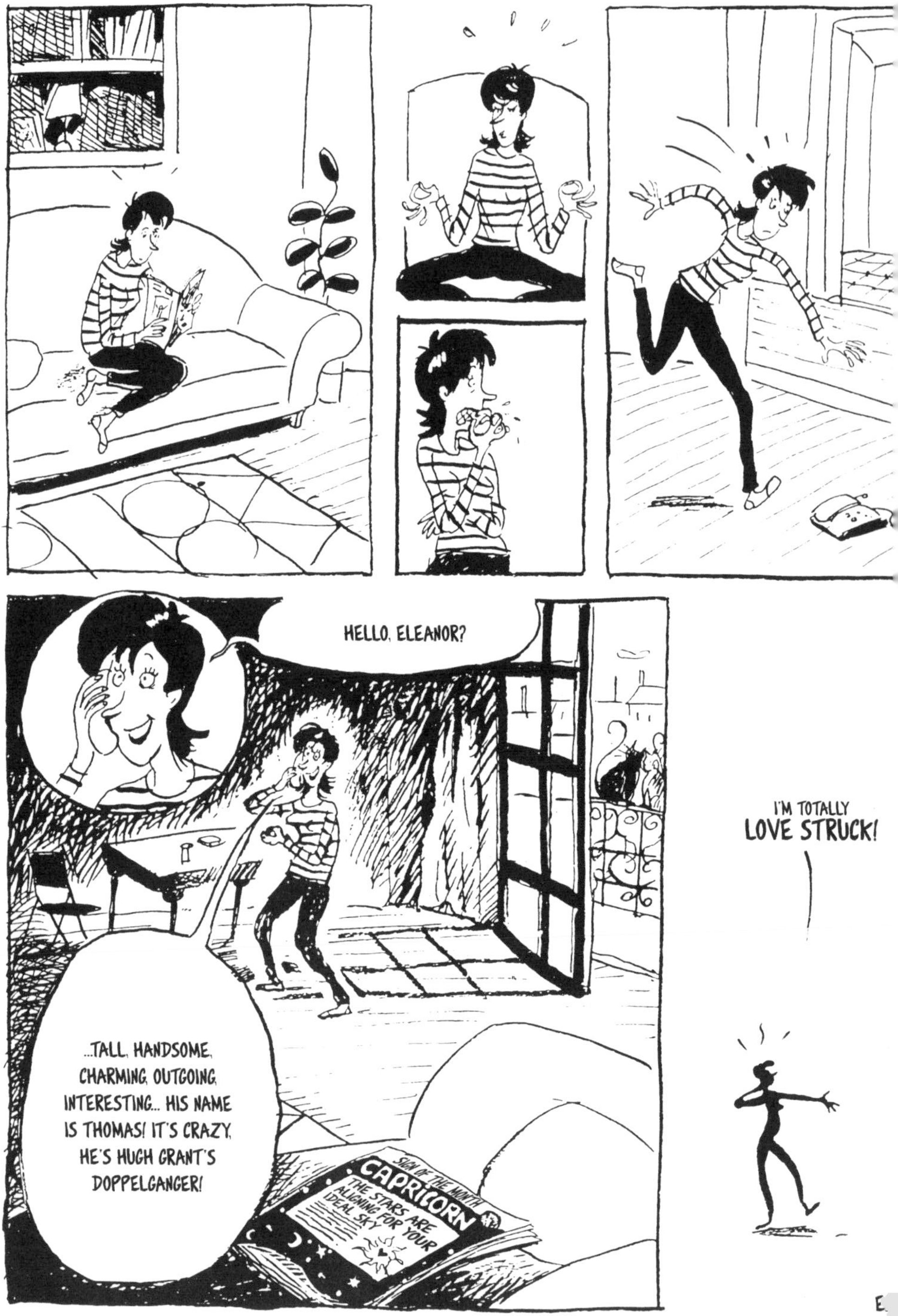
HELLO, ELEANOR?
...TALL, HANDSOME, CHARMING, OUTGOING, INTERESTING... HIS NAME IS THOMAS! IT'S CRAZY, HE'S HUGH GRANT'S DOPPELGANGER!
SIGN OF THE MONTH
CAPRICORN
THE STARS ARE ALIGNING FOR YOUR IDEAL SKY
I'M TOTALLY LOVE STRUCK!